ALSO BY LISELLE SAMBURY

Blood Like Magic
Blood Like Fate

DELICIOUS MONSTERS

LISELLE SAMBURY

MARGARET K. McELDERRY BOOKS

New York   London   Toronto   Sydney   New Delhi

MARGARET K. McELDERRY BOOKS
An imprint of Simon & Schuster Children's Publishing Division
1230 Avenue of the Americas, New York, New York 10020

MARGARET K. McELDERRY BOOKS is a trademark of Simon & Schuster, Inc.
For information about special discounts for bulk purchases, please contact Simon & Schuster Special Sales at 1-866-506-1949 or business@simonandschuster.com.
The Simon & Schuster Speakers Bureau can bring authors to your live event. For more information or to book an event, contact the Simon & Schuster Speakers Bureau at 1-866-248-3049 or visit our website at www.simonspeakers.com.
Interior design by Irene Metaxatos
The text for this book was set in Urge.
Manufactured in the United States of America
First Edition
10 9 8 7 6 5 4 3 2 1
Library of Congress Cataloging-in-Publication Data
Names: Sambury, Liselle, author.
Title: Delicious monsters / Liselle Sambury.
Description: First edition. | New York : Margaret K. McElderry Books, [2023] | Summary: Told in alternating timelines, seventeen-year-old Daisy and her mother move into her deceased uncle's mansion, only to find horrors waiting inside, and ten years later, Brittney investigates the mystery behind the Miracle Mansion that turned her mother's life around.
Identifiers: LCCN 2022006223 (print) | LCCN 2022006224 (ebook) | ISBN 9781665903493 (hardcover) | ISBN 9781665903516 (ebook)
Subjects: CYAC: Dwellings—Fiction. | Mothers and daughters—Fiction. | Dead—Fiction. | Spirit possession—Fiction. | Sexual abuse—Fiction. | Black people—Canada—Fiction. | Supernatural—Fiction. | LCGFT: Paranormal fiction. | Novels.
Classification: LCC PZ7.1.S2545 De 2023 (print) | LCC PZ7.1.S2545 (ebook) | DDC [Fic]—dc23
LC record available at https://lccn.loc.gov/2022006223
LC ebook record available at https://lccn.loc.gov/2022006224

TO MY MOM.
I AM SO PROUD AND GRATEFUL
TO BE YOUR DAUGHTER.

AUTHOR NOTE

The first time I realized what happened to me also happened to other children, I was reading a book. I had never talked about my experience with anyone. And still didn't for a while after.

The feelings that the character had were struggles I'd reckoned with for years, alone, because I was too afraid and ashamed to tell even one person in my life. I never forgot the impact of that moment.

Not all of us can speak about the things we've gone through, and that doesn't make us worth less than those who do. Everyone survives in their own way. But it's my hope that for those who need it, this novel will help show that you aren't alone. The same way that book did for me when I needed it.

That being said, this novel does include topics that may be triggering, and it's important to me to provide a list of these for readers. I have tried to be as thorough as possible here, but you can also check my website for the most up-to-date list of content warnings.

Content warnings: childhood sexual assault (off page, some details discussed), childhood physical abuse (corporal punishment, off page, described), childhood physical abuse (confinement punishment), childhood neglect, gaslighting, grooming, suicide (off page, mention), killing of a goat (off page, described), discussions of fatphobia, body horror/gore, violence, death

CHAPTER ONE

DAISY

There were two stories of how I was named. One was what Mom told people. Never casually. Only if they asked.

It was a dream of a drive long enough that you strain not to doze off, mingled with the extra-sweet tang of wild blueberries.

All of Ontario seemed to be built along rough gray roads stretching seemingly forever into the distance, where rolling down your window meant breathing in the sharp smell of burned rubber and stinging asphalt. The sort of tar-black road that scorched your feet with its heat and left the scent on your heels, smoky and stained, lingering in the air.

In this dream, Mom pulled onto the shoulder, bright emergency blinkers flashing on an empty highway. When I was little, growing up in a city, it was hard to picture a place I knew to be packed and busy, suddenly devoid. Like a ghost town. *Abandoned.* With Mom as its only inhabitant.

She stepped over the squat metal barrier between expressway

and earth, careful with the swollen bump of her belly. She walked into the wreckage of fallen trees, burnt branches crumbling to white ash that stuck to her fingers and still smelled of fire. That's where she found the blueberries. They grew in patches, short, small, and wild, alive in a field of death.

You could find the best blueberries after a burn, she'd say.

And there, in the midst of gathering the sweet fruit into the hem of her car-sweaty T-shirt, her tongue stained purple with juice, she found something else.

A daisy.

Inexplicably. In a place where only one plant seemed to grow was this other thing that shouldn't have survived.

That was where my name came from.

Now, the second story.

The one where Grandma whispered that of course a sixteen-year-old would name her kid after a flower. Which meant that the second story wasn't a story at all. Because that was the point, that there wasn't one.

That my name was nothing more than a pretty tattoo: permanent and meaningless.

CHAPTER TWO

Seeing dead people was the worst.

They shuffled from one place to another, mouths gaping wide even though most of them didn't talk. Meaning they couldn't tell me anything useful like what Noah was doing when he wasn't texting me. Mostly, they were distracting and annoying. And I seemed to be the only one cursed to notice them. I had seen them walk through people who didn't even give the tiniest shiver of subconscious recognition.

There must have been someone suffering inside the breakfast place across the street because they were clustering around it. Pressing their translucent cheeks against the window, desperate to be close to someone's tragedy. The only reason they weren't going inside was to avoid the rest of the customers, who I assumed were overjoyed to stuff homemade pancakes down their throats.

Happiness was not something the dead appreciated.

They would wait there, like the vultures they were, until the person they wanted came out, then follow them around all day while their subject was none the wiser. That was how the dead were.

They weren't even sad. They were pathetic.

And during the three hours I'd spent sitting here and scrolling through my phone to look busy, they'd been one of the few sights to look at. I had a cold coffee I didn't want and a flaky croissant I ate piece by piece to stretch out how long the server let me stay. The pastry was about half-done and now it was the early afternoon.

When I'd first gotten to the café, it was morning. The coffee aroma that had, at that time, been rich and rejuvenating now made me feel just on the edge of puking in my mouth. I was on the patio in an uncomfortable lawn-style chair, and the server had basically forgotten about me as better-paying adults made their way in. But thankfully, there weren't enough people for her to kick me out.

Which was good because I was still waiting.

The sun was on the edge of too warm—that in-between moment that at any time could switch from comfortable to an overbearing heat that left you exhausted and sweaty. And the street was flooded with weekend crowds strolling leisurely down the sidewalks. Every one of them unhindered by the translucent dead that moved among them. Eventually, those clinging leeches would fade and disappear— it was just a matter of being around long enough. Unless they were trying hard to stay. Then someone would have to make them leave.

My fingers trembled, and I curled them into fists to stop it. I didn't like to think about those resistant ones.

I shifted on the metal chair and contemplated taking a sip of cold coffee. "Daisy" was scrawled across the side so messily that it looked like "Dazy."

Noah called me "Daze." It was equal parts cute pet name and a poke at how "in the clouds" people thought I was. He knew I spent time in my head because there were thoughts there deeper than other kids my age had. "Daze" was to mock people who didn't get that.

Across the street, at the breakfast place too cool to have their name displayed, the dead remained glued to the huge glass windows—likely designed that way so *living* people could peer at you as they walked by and mentally salivate over whatever you were eating. On Instagram, the restaurant had hundreds of photos of stacked pancakes with thick blueberry sauce and house-made whipped cream. The sort of thing Noah would hate. He didn't want to go to places everyone else went.

I liked that. Always going somewhere brand-new that no one had heard of. No social media likes to tell us whether it would be good or shit. We were deciding our tastes for ourselves and sharing an unfiltered and uninfluenced account. That was his favorite part—giving the full review to his friends.

I pulled a bobby pin out of my pocket and used it to scratch my head, trying to think of the last time I washed my hair. I used to be on top of it. Notes in my phone to remind me of when to get my hair relaxed. "Creamy crack," Mom called it. Not that I needed the reminders. The instant I saw a curl peep out, I wanted to snuff the life out of it. Once every two months like clockwork. I would do it more often, but Mom didn't want me to. So I had to settle for using the flat iron to stretch out the style between relaxers.

Now I had curls growing out an inch from my head that gave way to straight ends. The straight bits were lank and lifeless in comparison. A memory of when I cared more. I'd stuffed my hair under a hat before I'd gone out. I guess that was part of being in a committed relationship for a while—you got lazy.

Noah hadn't seemed to care until now.

The door to the breakfast place swung open, and I tugged my body to attention. I went from a state of limp ivy to a snake plant, my leaves shoved up high and rigid.

The couple who walked out were so mismatched it was ridiculous. He towered over her, dressed in a faded band T-shirt, his oak-brown hair tousled in just the right way, wire-rimmed glasses perched on his nose, pale for a white guy but not pasty. The girl was small, like a kid, her head barely reaching his shoulder. She was in a patterned body-con dress that clung to her tiny frame and made her look even smaller.

She was white too. But I already knew that. I'd done my research.

All I wanted to do last weekend was check in on Noah. See if I could get him to talk to me. Then she appeared, and obviously I had to know more. I preferred not to think about the amount of effort said research had taken given Noah's stance against an online presence. But internet stalking wasn't much different from what I was doing now, so it was too late to feel ashamed.

Probably it didn't matter. That she was white. But it stuck in my head and prodded me like a toddler discovering a dead thing for the first time. Poked, and poked, and poked. I had done that too. Pushed my fingers against a cold, stiff body. A squirrel, if you want to get specific. I'd been bewildered and excited all at once. Dead things used to have more novelty. I hadn't known to be afraid early on.

How old was she?

Noah's voice, smooth and low, reverberated in my head: *Why is everyone so obsessed with age?*

She looked younger than me, anyway. Maybe sixteen to my seventeen, or younger?

I couldn't believe he went to this Instagram place with her. He hated this shit. *We* hated this shit.

He tugged her close to his side and laughed at something. They both did. That was me just the other day. That was *my* spot. He held me there while we walked, and I lay there whenever I hung out at his place. I couldn't sleep over because my mom would worry. His words. He didn't know that Mom wouldn't. The memory of being the one pulled against his body was fresh enough that I could smell the mint of his deodorant and the spicy clove scent of the gel he carefully raked through his hair.

The metal legs of my chair scraped against the ground as I pushed it aside, craning my neck, eyes following them as they walked.

Mom wouldn't have liked Noah. She thought people should date within their age zones. High schoolers with high schoolers. University-aged with university-aged. Professional working people with professional working people. And never should any mix. She was strict about the differences between girls and women, and boys and men. Girls with boys and women with men. Or girls with girls, and boys with boys, etc., she had added after a pause. How she decided when a girl was a girl and when she was a woman wasn't something she shared with me.

Noah wouldn't date a girl.

Girls were immature, no matter their age. Women were different.

But still. The idea of mentioning him to Mom in any capacity made a chill hang over my shoulders. It happened to me every so often. A shiver would work through my body, twitches and muscle spasms, without so much as a cold breeze. And after, I would feel like I was walking on the edge of something for the rest of the day.

It usually meant that one of *them* had gotten too close.

Normal people had no idea how lucky they were to never feel it.

To never hunch their shoulders and have the hair on their arms ripped to attention.

Searching.

Shaking.

And then seeing someone who shouldn't exist but did.

Staring right at you.

That was what it would be like to mention Noah to Mom.

And now after catching him like this, I was glad I hadn't said anything to her.

I scratched at my head with the bobby pin so hard that I winced. My tender scalp crying out from the metal abuse, stinging long after I stopped.

They were getting too far. I stood and shuffled away from my chair. For a moment they turned, seemingly in my direction. I curled in on myself and dropped back into my seat, ducking under the shade of the bistro table umbrella like I had delicate leaves prone to scorching in the sunlight.

I could still see them.

Watching the girl made me hyperaware of the baggy shorts and oversized sleeveless hoodie I was in. When Noah and I started dating, I was like her. Clothes that fit tight to my body, makeup done to perfection, and bone-straight hair just past my shoulders.

Noah would finger the strands and smile. He never outright said he preferred women with long hair, but I picked up on it. I was good at that with him. I noticed that the celebrities he liked had hair down to their butts. I borrowed one of Mom's wigs to get the effect.

But he didn't seem to like that much.

That girl, Stephanie—no point in acting like I didn't know her name, where she went to school, her Starbucks order, and her closest friends. Research. Besides, her Instagram was public. Her hair, blond from a professional stylist's bottle, hit right above her butt. I guess it was all hers.

They made their way to the corner and turned where I couldn't see them anymore. I should have gotten up and followed. That was the plan.

I watched the dead move out of their path. Sneering soundlessly. Translucent noses wrinkled. Pressing themselves away.

That was how fucking happy a couple they were.

I stayed sitting.

I picked at my croissant. Shoved big pieces into my mouth without wiping away the flakes that stuck to my lips, savored the way the pieces almost melted and flowed down my throat.

My bobby pin found its way to my scalp again. I fingered the curled roots of my hair. I'd let it go too long. That was comfort. That was feeling secure with Noah.

I was going to lose sight of them soon. I gnawed on my lip.

The last time Noah and I hung out, we'd gone to his place first. We always did. He liked to "spend time together" before we went anywhere. It was just code for sex. Which was fine. Before or after, it was all the same. It was good. I didn't have anything to compare it to, but I figured I could tell good from bad.

It was going to be a fun, chill night. Until we got to the party. Until I fucked up.

He was mad. I knew he was. But couples fought.

I didn't think it would end up like this.

There was no conversation. No working through it. Not even a formal breakup. Just silence.

Now he was out here with this white girl. It didn't really matter that she was white. I needed to stop thinking about that.

I shoved the last piece of croissant into my mouth and chugged my coffee. The liquid was cold, and the milk felt thick and gunky as it hit my tongue. I gagged and spat back into the cup. Over my shoulder, someone cringed, watching me.

They weren't important, I knew that. And no one else had seen. Or cared. But my face still burned as my eyes tracked the path where Noah and Stephanie had disappeared around the corner.

This had gone on too long. Me watching them, and the person who cringed watching me. Maybe that person was no one. Probably they were alive. But I didn't have the luxury of assuming.

For me, none of the dead were harmless, but some were worse than others.

Some were dangerous.

They blended in with the living, solid and opaque, and cast none of the warning cool breezes.

They did not want to fade.

And noticing what they were too late was not something you wanted to do. Especially once *they'd* noticed that you'd noticed them.

I had already learned that the hard way.

Dazy.

Dazy.

Dazy.

I stood abruptly from my chair.

My scalp stung.

I needed to wash my hair.

And my tongue tasted like stomach bile and sour milk.

CHAPTER THREE

BRITTNEY

10 years later . . .

The thing about having a name like Brittney is that it creates a certain image. An impression. People have thoughts about a name like Brittney.

Picture a Brittney. Right now. Think of who that might be.

I bet you're not imagining me.

That's the best part about my name. People never see me coming.

I stride through the office, towering over the other interns at my full 5'11" height, taking up space with a *Yeah, I'm fat, get over it* attitude, black-and-lilac-colored braids swinging above my shoulders, and my laptop tucked under my arm. The thing about confidence is that it doesn't matter if you really have it or not, so long as you pretend well enough. And at Torte, presenting anything less than what I'm bringing would get me eaten alive.

Torte used to be the sort of media company synonymous with those videos you saw on Facebook where disembodied hands showed you how to make quick meals on a hot plate as if they didn't have an entire studio kitchen. Like *you* didn't have an entire kitchen too. "Brownies 5 Ways," "Six 5-Ingredient Chicken Dinners You Won't Believe," shit like that. One day, someone had the bright idea to film interns trying some of the more outlandish recipes. Literally called "Interns Try Our Most-Hated Recipes," and it blew the lid off the internet as far as food-niche videos were concerned. That was only a few years ago, and I'm really fucking glad that I wasn't an intern then.

Today it's a company filled with talented young people making viral videos for its various affiliated YouTube channels and also people like Kevin, relics of early marketing who got their management jobs via distant uncles who themselves got to be important by being born into the right families.

From across the room, Kevin shrinks in his seat, trying to pretend like he doesn't know I'm coming for him.

That's the thing about implementing a work policy like "no closed doors" in an effort to make the workplace seem more fun and liberal than it is. It means people like Kevin, my manager and an altogether-mediocre white man who makes more than triple the basic intern wage they give my Black ass, doesn't have anywhere to hide.

We literally work in a giant warehouse that exists on a single floor where the only privacy comes from either the bathroom or the meeting and filming rooms that border the entire perimeter of the space.

Part of me knows I shouldn't bitch. Most of the other students in my film production program struggled to find internships during the summer, and of those who did, precisely all had duties that included coffee runs. A chore I have been spared from. I'm a rare case in that I not only get to make content, I also get paid in more than "experience." Except it's still barely above minimum wage. And I continue to be rejected for every government grant and loan for students because my mom's income is too high.

Once again, she's made my life more difficult than it needed to be.

I stop in front of Kevin's desk. He has three screens arranged in a semicircle around him, presumably to hide how little work he actually does. It's also completely bare. Kevin is generally uninspired. He came from a huge tech company that some family member founded and is about forty in a company where everyone is either in their early twenties, or like me, late teens, which got him a position of authority that he has yet to prove he deserves.

"Ready for our meeting?" I say, forcing my voice to adopt a chipper "Brittney" tone.

He nods and jerks to his feet, sloppily unhooking his laptop from its desk setup. "Yup, we're in the Ocean Room. . . . Did I not put that in the invite?"

"I saw, but I looked over and noticed you here and figured we could make our way there together." I grin at him, and he forces a smile back. No way am I gonna let him catch me sitting in that room twiddling my fucking thumbs while he plays his weak-ass power move and comes in late. Nah.

On our way to the Ocean Room, we pass the communal bookshelf, which I purposely look away from. It was one of those ideas proposed by a committee of people who take bonding with everyone at work too seriously. Somewhere on there is a book featuring a black dust jacket with a photo of my mom smiling proudly. Meanwhile, within the pages, she details every time she let me go hungry, every boyfriend she let shout abuse at me just for existing, and the multiple instances in which she explained what a burden *I* had put on her. All in the name of transparency so that she can say how she was "saved" and how much she's "grown." Every bit of my business now available for anyone to read. A *New York Times* bestseller for eight years alongside the four self-help books she published, the massively successful annual speaking tour, and the soon-to-be-greenlit film adaptation of her life.

People love the trauma. They adore a chance to tell a Black woman how strong she is. More than that, she represents an out. A way for people to cleanse themselves of their past and come out shiny and new. People fall over themselves chasing the same experience she claims to have had and come back with their own reports of how much they've developed.

Once the do-gooders in the office realized who I was, they set a fifteen-minute meeting to ask me if it was all right for them to have the book on the shelf because "even though we know you have a better relationship with your mom these days, it does contain painful memories." I wasn't about to say no and have them send sad-puppy-dog glances my way. What did it matter? They would read it anyway.

And how could I say a bad word about the reformed woman who I needed as cosigner for my bank loan for school *and* my rental lease? I realized pretty quickly that when you're eighteen, people don't want to give you much without a *real* adult to vouch for you. Turning nineteen didn't change anything either. I didn't want her help. But what was the alternative? Housing in Toronto is competitive. Other kids showed up with their parents, a credit check, multiple cosigners, and the cash on hand for first and last month's rent. I had spent so long suffering, it felt like this bit of freedom being away from her was worth it, even if I needed her to get it.

But it also makes it feel like I haven't left at all.

I'm still in her suffocating embrace.

Until I have the stability to carry myself, she's the only thing keeping me afloat. And she's made it very clear that my expressing to anyone that our relationship is less than ideal would mean that well running dry.

I force myself not to think of it as we enter the Ocean Room. Jayden is already inside with his laptop open, scrolling through his phone. It makes me think immediately of us in our first year at Toronto Film School. We both got the texts from our other group project teammates bailing at the same time. I was in the doorway, and he was inside our meeting room. I would have left. I'd planned to. I'd had these grand ideas of reinventing myself in college. I wouldn't be the quiet, wounded girl in the corner that I was in elementary school, too shy and scared to talk to anyone. But I also wouldn't be the completely hostile bitch that I was in high school, too furious and jaded to let anyone in. There would be a balance. I would be personable. I would make friends. And Mom wouldn't be around to ruin it just because she could.

But in that moment, staring at my first chance to reach out, I froze. My head was crowded with all the reasons I had to hate myself. The ones Mom had said outright and the ones she'd said without speaking a word. How was I supposed to ask someone to like me when *I* was only just starting to like me?

I couldn't do it.

So Jayden did it for me.

He grinned and said, "Hey, do you believe in ghosts?"

I didn't. Still don't. But I love to pick apart what people think is supernatural. We spent hours going back and forth with our theories. And *Haunted* was born. Our little YouTube show that we poured months into. Jayden's strength was the research and, despite his spiritual beliefs, a commitment to objective fact. Mine was crafting an emotional connection to the people involved and making the audience care about them.

We launched the first season and hit a million views in a month. The week after, Torte came to us with a deal. We would sell them the rights and then get to intern there in the summer after our first year of college, working on the second season. Another smash hit.

At the time, I don't think either of us had really understood what giving over our series meant beyond a check. Or even what working at Torte would actually be like. Sure, we got amazing equipment, always-accessible studio space, all the stock photos and video we could want, and an actual budget.

But we also got Kevin.

He takes a seat in a chair with an aggressively vibrant tropical-fish print. Right beside the door, as if he needs to be close to an exit. I let him settle in before I sit down. Even seated, I tower over him. This guy in his ridiculous plain black T-shirt and too-loose chinos would be the one assessing the monetary success of *Haunted*, and if it failed to outperform both its previous seasons, he would be the one to make an extra-sad face at us while he suggested bringing in some help. Which would mean having full-time producers effectively colonize what we started. Contractually they couldn't push us out, but they could make sure that none of our contributions were approved until we got frustrated enough to leave.

Back to being two ordinary college students, fighting for prospects as graduation looms. Our show, gone.

I grit my teeth, and Jayden gives me a warning look. "New laptop sticker?" he says in a friendly voice, pointing to Kevin's MacBook decorated with, I shit you not, the branding decals we get from sponsors. Most of the other managers leave their laptops clean, but of course Kevin has to "fit in" with us and somehow thought logos was the way to do it.

Kevin beams. "Yeah, just had a meeting with Airbnb. We're trying to work something out with them."

Fuck, I hate office small talk.

"For *Haunted*?"

"Not right now, but we could consider that. Speaking of," Kevin says in the world's worst transition, "I wanted to chat with you two about your proposal."

Jayden throws me a sidelong glance as if to say, *Told you.*

I purposely don't look back at him. "What about it?"

"Unfortunately, it was turned down."

"Oh?" I ask, my voice going so high-pitched that it's somehow on the edge of aggressive.

Kevin squirms. "The stakeholders feel that 'Forgotten Black Girls' as a theme is a bit isolating and niche. And they wonder if we'll have enough material by sticking to ghost stories with such specific parameters. It's a really important topic, but it feels like one part of something bigger. They would love to see you open it up wider. Everyone believes that you two can really push the limits with this season."

Push the limits? That's exactly what that theme is doing. But apparently, we have very different understandings of what that means. It's just a bunch of corporate runaround to say that no one cares about forgotten Black girls.

I think of sitting in our apartment when I was seven. Picking at the carpet. Mom had gone across the border to shop with a boyfriend. She hadn't told me, though.

No one checked in on me.

"What would you like us to do for next steps?" Jayden says without missing a beat. He adapts smoothly while I twist myself into every sort of shape to avoid being told what to do.

Kevin gives him an indulgent smile that makes me want to slap it off his face. "You'll need to redo the proposal by the end of the day. If you have trouble coming up with a concept, the stakeholders have agreed that it would be a great option to open up the floor. There are a ton of people who have let me know they have some ideas for the show, and if there's one that works, they can join you two on the project. It may be better, even. I know you guys take the summer semester off school for this. It could give you more time to better balance your work here and your schoolwork."

I bet there have been people whispering in his ear trying to get involved in our shit. What he means is, if we can't come up with something perfect by the end of the day, they'll let all the rodents have a turn picking at our meat. He couldn't care less about our coursework.

I throw Kevin the same shit-eating smile he gave us and say, "I don't think that will be necessary. We'll have something ready for the end of the day. You can forward their ideas to us to consider for future seasons if you like. We're always open to suggestions."

"Okay, well, I look forward to reading it." He gets up from his chair, itching to flee. "There's another twenty minutes on the room, so feel free to stay here and brainstorm."

"Thanks."

He leaves and speed-walks back to his desk.

"I hate him," I say with a glower.

Jayden sighs and runs a hand through his short, curled hair. It's dyed gold. He uses a bunch of temporary dyes. The product colors and styles his hair at the same time. "Obviously. But we knew they would turn it down."

"We have their highest-viewed show. Highest-viewed!"

"Yes, and what were our other seasons? First one, 'Vengeful Spirits,' and the second one was 'Love Gone Wrong.' Super-general themes. Now straight to 'Forgotten Black Girls'? Have you seen how many Black people work here? It was never going to happen."

Precisely four Black employees work at Torte. All interns. And of us, Jayden is the only openly gay person.

He's right, though I wish he wasn't. "So, what next?"

"What about that email we got?"

"No."

"Britt, come on. We'll have an inside source."

"An *anonymous* source."

"They said they would tell us who they were later. That doesn't even matter. The contacts they gave us check out."

My eyebrows climb. "Oh, so you checked them?"

Jayden has enough shame to look sheepish. "Just doing my due diligence." He continues, "But think about it. We could pump this up big. Do our usual research and stuff but even more than that. Organize interviews with the people involved. Get on location. Do a real investigation." From the way he's talking faster, I can tell that Jayden is getting excited. This isn't something he thought of on the fly—he's *been* thinking about it, even though he agreed to go with my idea of "Forgotten Black Girls."

Our usual show on *Haunted* involves us doing a huge amount of research—his always more thorough and less biased than mine—and then we both chat about the theories, pull together existing interview and podcast clips, get a liberal use of Getty images to show on-screen, and have a playful banter about what could have happened. We both agreed from the start that touring haunted locations at night was the shit we did not want to participate in, but even going during the day was out of the question because we didn't have the budget. Now the success of our last two seasons has significantly increased the amount of spending we could do. Traveling on-site isn't unrealistic anymore.

"Britt?" Jayden says, voice softer now. "Look, I would love to do this, but I know that house is personal for you. If you really don't want to, we won't. We'll think of something else. But this story embodies 'Forgotten Black Girls' without saying it."

"Personal." It's a good word.

It feels like that. Me. Her. And her house.

I swallow.

The email we got was about the mystery in a house that spawned hundreds of fan theories when the story first broke. It captivated people. Though lately all that had been overshadowed by the narrative my mom had started.

A haunted house turned Miracle Mansion. The one that she says changed her for the better. In the years since her memoir hit the bestseller lists, people have booked stays at that mansion feverishly, each of them hoping to have their problems solved by the supposed power within its walls. A cult of them forming around my mom: her, their messiah, and that fucking book, their Bible.

And the house. The house is salvation.

Except the email heavily suggested that many people missed the full story. That there was something more sinister there. And they had contacts who would tell us things they hadn't shared with others.

We could re-expose the house's dark history that had been conveniently forgotten. Relegated to true crime forums that were eventually overrun by believers who wanted to tell their stories of positive change.

If we did this right, we could bring to light the sort of pain that my mom excelled at covering up and rebranding. We could break open the walls of her house and show what it really represents.

But that would also mean digging into it. Even if it isn't my story, I would have to be reminded of that connection every step of the way. Of that house whose story, *her* story, keeps us tethered together. That house made me need her.

"Trust me on this," Jayden says as if sensing my indecision. "You know that you can, right? Trust me? We're a team. I've said that from jump. This is *our* show. No matter what rights bullshit exists. *Haunted* belongs to us."

I clench my hands into fists on my lap. We've only known each other for a couple of years, but Jayden's become a constant in my life. We talk every single day. For all intents and purposes, he's my best friend. If I can't trust him, then she's won.

"If I say no, you'll drop it?" I ask.

He nods. "Yes."

At the end of the day, we hand in our proposal for the third season of *Haunted*: "Houses That Kill." We'll go on location to a series of known haunted homes, do our own interviews with the people involved, tour the spots (during the day, thank you), and catalog our experiences. Our first stop will be the Miracle Mansion and the mystery of Grace and Daisy Odlin—including how the house racked up a body count. The very same place that my mom, in her bestselling book, claims changed her from an abusive and neglectful parent to a completely reformed woman.

Kevin basically creams his pants reading over it.

If we succeed with this, if this third season blows up even bigger, not only will we get to keep our show, but I can negotiate for the sort of pay that will let me be truly independent. A real salary during summers and a guaranteed job after graduation. No more of this intern bullshit.

I can say goodbye to my mom forever.

And I can show that her beloved house of miracles is a thin cover-up for a house of horrors.

A sham, just like her.

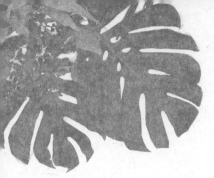

CHAPTER FOUR

DAISY

Our apartment was as open-concept as an apartment could get. In the basement of someone's Leslieville house, shaped like a rectangle, brand-new sleek fixtures and appliances, but overall, uninspired. But when you were competing against shitty run-down rentals, it was good enough. The best part being that the landlords upstairs had both a happy toddler and an unhappy marriage. Between those dead who were repelled from the home by innocent childhood glee and those that braved the child to stick themselves to the agony of long-lasting marital strife, I was ignored. I also slept to the saccharine sounds of Kidz Bop playing in my earbuds, which was surprisingly, but thankfully, effective.

Sure, it wasn't ideal.

But it was better than waking screaming to translucent eyes glowing in the dark, squatting at eye level. Better than lying under the covers night after night, forcing yourself to repeat every joyful thought you've ever had. A list you know is shorter than it should be.

Technically, unless they were corporeal, they couldn't hurt me. But it was hard to be logical in the middle of the night, shivering as a dead thing dragged its fingertip along your arm, staring into your eyes as your flesh goose-pimpled. So, Kidz Bop it was.

It was livable. A strong bare minimum. Like our apartment.

The space consisted of two twin beds squeezed into the corner with a bookcase between them, a tiny living area in the middle, and a kitchen and bathroom crowded on the opposite end. We always rented bachelor apartments. Two bedrooms, or even one, would have meant accepting something a lot more run-down for the same price, which Mom refused to do.

My plants were the only real source of inspiration in the dark space. I kept them on a shelf by the biggest window beside the door. Spiked aloe vera that I got at a farmers' market sat alongside my monstera with its thick, cut-out leaves, at least a dozen succulents, and a peace lily that Noah got me for my seventeenth birthday in a pot he bought from a friend who casually did pottery.

It was a flower, but I forgave him for not knowing that I didn't like them.

I hadn't ever said anything to him about it.

It wasn't a big deal.

Being named Daisy, I felt like everyone expected me to love the flora of the world. Mom gave me enough expectations. Not liking flowers was one of the few I could afford not to live up to.

Mom was arguing with Grandma on the phone when I walked inside.

Her voice dropped when she spied me. Not to hide the conversation, but to hide how upset Grandma had already gotten her. I could always tell when she was talking to her mom. She adopted a certain stance. Hunched shoulders, a strained neck, and twitching fingers. Grandma could be . . . a lot.

"She doesn't want the house," Mom muttered, glancing at me as I toed off my tennis shoes and yanked the hat off my head. "I don't even know if I'll take it."

I froze in the doorway.

House?

Mom's hair was done in its usual twists, long enough to fall past her shoulders, and she had on the glasses she was supposed to wear on a regular basis but that she often seemed only to wear on a whim. The huge round frames, instead of looking ridiculous, came off as effortlessly cool. Mom was like that.

I worked to look good.

She worked too but didn't look like she did, which was what mattered.

My scalp burned, but I stayed rooted to the spot, staring at her on the phone. I wanted to ask if it was *the house*. The one that everything had been leading up to. The beacon of hope that my entire life seemed to revolve around.

Once we have the house, we won't need to struggle so much.

Once we have the house, you and I will be able to do whatever we want.

Once we have the house, you'll see how much better things will be.

Mom raised her hand and twitched it away from her. Her nonverbal sign for *Go do something somewhere else.*

It was rare to see her actually bother to continue a conversation with Grandma instead of hanging up in a rage.

"What's happening?" I said. "Which house?"

She shook her head and took the phone away from her ear. "I'm dealing with this. Go do something."

"Dealing with what?"

"Go. Do. Something," she said. "We'll talk later."

I knew I couldn't stand there forever, and the tightness of her jaw showed she was only getting more agitated with me by the minute. An annoyed Mom was a silent Mom. Which meant the more I pestered her, the less she would bother to tell me later.

"I'm going to shower," I announced so that she would know I was listening to her.

Relief flooded her face, and she nodded.

Her voice stayed at a mutter level even as I closed the bathroom door behind me. The room was squished behind our kitchen without more than a foot of floor space to walk between the vanity, shower, and toilet. I glanced back at the closed door.

They could be talking about any house. I didn't know why I was getting caught up in it. In all the years that Mom ranted and raved about this house, we'd never once been to it. Why would it be any different now? Probably it was another argument about money and us buying property. Grandma, who lived in Hamilton, would badger Mom to stop wasting her money renting in the city and move away like she did. Which would inevitably lead to an argument about how Mom didn't have savings for a down payment on a house out there, and anyway, Daisy loved living in the city.

Not her. Me.

I mean, I did. I loved going to new restaurants and art galleries with Noah. I loved going to Allen Gardens and posing while he took photos of me with his DSLR. I loved hanging out with his university friends and occasionally impressing them with the odd random horticulture fact. I loved being Noah's girlfriend.

Who was I now? The girl Noah had played.

The house. The house. The house. I couldn't get it out of my head. Noah and that fucking house swirled through my thoughts. If we lived in this place, this literal and figurative symbol of financial freedom, Mom wouldn't need me anymore. She wouldn't keep falling into the emotional pits that came with a constant sense of never having enough, wouldn't keep needing me to dig her out and tend to her. And she would give me a cut. That was her promise. I could do anything with it once I was eighteen. Instead of only being able to do what she wanted. I would be free.

The house, she said, was the solution to all our problems.

As long as I didn't mess it up for us.

I stared into the mirror at my grown-out hair, makeup-less and oily face, bulky clothes, and dull eyes. With Noah, I'd known exactly who I was.

Now it was a girl I saw staring back at me. Not a woman. And I didn't recognize her.

Mom was still chattering beyond the door. I would have expected the conversation to be over by now, but it kept going. Her words were indistinguishable but forming their own sort of tone. A murmur that was obliterated when I turned on the tap and let the shower go. It spluttered at first before flaring into a steady stream.

I shrugged off my clothes and stepped in. The heat burned my already-stinging head. I didn't waste any time reaching for the shampoo and working the suds into my scalp. I tried to reserve wash days for Sundays, but I was too desperate to wait until tomorrow. My fingers scraped against the tender flesh. I dug my nails in, scratching with abandon, wild with a fever of digging up the product residue and dead skin. A sharp sting made me wince as I dug in too hard. Still, I kept going.

After rinsing it out, I went in with the conditioner. My fingers slipped through the slick curls at my scalp and tangled in the now-stringy straight ends. Again, and again, and again. I dragged them through to separate the strands, always catching on those straight ends.

Turning off the water, I stepped out and wrapped a towel

around my body, using another to try to soak up some of the water in my hair. Mom's voice filtered through the door. She was still talking. I grabbed a wide-tooth comb off the bathroom counter and attempted to drag it through my hair as I strained to hear, then winced as, again, it flowed through my newly grown curls and tangled in my straight ends. Adding leave-in conditioner barely helped. I tossed the comb. The clattering of it in the sink basin echoed through the room. I waited, but Mom didn't pause in her conversation.

I should just straighten it again.

I would look more like I did before.

More like when Noah and I started dating.

That was over now, I reminded myself.

When my fingers moved toward the vanity drawer, it was like something out-of-body. I was watching them without any connection to them. They curled around the clippers, and the cool metal felt right in my hands, the way it felt to plunge my fingers into fresh soil. Mom trimmed her wigs with these clippers. I hadn't even used them before.

I plugged the device in and listened to the rhythmic hum that filled the space. It reminded me of Noah's apartment. It was this dive at Dundas and Parliament that he shared with three other people. There was a radiator that hummed day and night. I would listen to it while we lay in bed. A constant hum like standing outside at night, grasshoppers, and cicadas, and any other insect that wanted to join in.

When I made the first cut, I jumped a bit. The wet strands of hair fell onto the countertop, and I was looking at a girl with a chunk of entirely curly hair.

My hand continued to move. From chunk to chunk, I worked, sheering off the straight ends and leaving only the grown-out curls.

The buzz sounded in my ears, growing duller, closer to that background hum I remembered.

A distant part of me was horrified. A closer part was delighted.

Why not? What did it matter? What did anything matter?

All because of one mistake. A tiny error in judgment that blew up into a big deal.

I didn't usually drink. Noah didn't like drunk girls. He liked women who sipped Merlot and got a little tipsy. But I hated the taste of wine. Especially reds. Tara pulled me into the kitchen and made "porn stars." I didn't know what was in it, but it looked like it was blue raspberry–flavored and tasted like it too. Sitting on a couch in that room with Noah, Tara, and the rest of his friends, felt like what my life should be.

Then I fucked up.

I was talking about something Megan said earlier that day in world history class. Everyone wanted to know why I was taking that when I was a biology major. Noah's grip tightened on my thigh, but it was a blip on my radar. I was lost in the haze brought on by the sweet electric-blue drink I was sipping.

Dazy Daisy.

Noah saved me. He pulled me up, and we went outside to get air. We walked around the block a few times until I sobered up enough for him to get an Uber to drop me off at home. He was going to tell everyone I was sick and had to leave.

But it was too late. Tara was suspicious and looked me up online. I made sure not to have my age anywhere when I started dating Noah, but she figured it out anyway. What sort of university student only has friends in high school, after all? And when Noah went back to the party after sending me home, she let him know what she thought about it.

She DMed me, too, on Instagram, to say what she had done. I saw the messages the next day when I woke up. Tara had the nerve to say it was "for my own good," and that she was "trying to help me."

I blocked her.

Then I sent a total of twenty-seven texts to Noah.

He never answered any.

Mom screamed.

The clipper jerked in my hand and sliced my eyebrow. Blood bloomed and pooled in the wound. I set the tool down and pressed a towel against the cut. Some of the blood slipped into my mouth, and I spat it out in the sink, crimson flowing down the drain.

Mom rushed in from where she'd been standing in the doorway and started fussing around for a bandage, though she didn't know where they were. I was the one who'd organized the cabinets. "Let me see." She pawed at my hand. I released the towel from my eye, and she squinted at it.

I nudged her aside and pulled open the right drawer. She grabbed the Polysporin and spread it over the cut before pressing a Band-Aid to the skin. I blinked and examined the damage. The patch covered up the middle of my right eyebrow. Probably I was missing some hair there too.

"You could have just used jelly from the aloe vera plant," I said. "Instead of the Polysporin."

Mom exhaled and sagged against the counter. "What the hell did you do to your hair?"

The girl in the mirror didn't have straight hair anymore. Nor did she have a mix of the two textures. All that was left was half an inch of puff around her head.

My head.

My hair.

I ran my fingers through the strands. "It's pretty short, eh?"

The deadpan look that Mom shot me was answer enough.

"Was that about the house?" I said. "*The* house?"

She frowned at me for a moment, but the slight upward twitch at the side of her lips gave her away.

Delighted. Absolutely delighted.

She breathed out, "Yes."

CHAPTER FIVE

On my knees, I gathered the last of the fallen hair on the bathroom floor with a wet piece of toilet paper. I wasn't exactly paying attention when I was buzzing it off, and most of the strands ended up on the white tiles. The humidity from the shower still hung in the air along with the lingering fruity scent of conditioner.

I couldn't stop running my fingers through my hair. Over and over, I dragged them through the curls, soft from the leave-in conditioner that Mom insisted I spread over my head.

Part of me wanted to claw at my scalp. To scream, *The house! It's the house!* Years of promises coming together in this moment.

Maybe to some people, property wasn't a big deal. But Mom had struggled through jobs our entire lives, the money she made bleeding into bachelor apartment rentals and expensive wigs with barely anything left over. For food and essentials, sure. But nothing more. "I can't be expected to live on nothing, Daisy" was the line she often used.

Besides, to me, it was a lot more than property. It was freedom in every sense of the word.

Because whenever things fell apart with her, I would have to be there, putting everything neatly back together. I owed it to Mom after everything she had done for me.

Stable Daisy.

Reliable Daisy.

And yet, at the same time, unstable Daisy. Unreliable Daisy. Crazy Daisy.

I remember the exact feel of Mom's fingers wrapping around my small shoulders, shaking me. Us tucked into a corner away from the teacher and the other girl's parents. Her voice low and sharp: "What is wrong with you?"

Tossing the piece of toilet paper into a plastic bag with the rest of my hair, I tied the ends into a knot and left the bathroom. Mom, now seated in the living room, trailed me with her eyes the whole way to the kitchen garbage.

She was on the couch with her toenails out in front of her, painting them a peach color that I hadn't seen before. Must have been new.

When I went back into the bathroom to grab my phone from the vanity, it was vibrating, lit up with "Dad." I stared at it. This was the worst time for this. Mom was going to tell me about the house. I had better things to do.

"Who is it?" Mom asked, not looking up. I was about to lie and say "No one" when she added, "Is that your dad? He usually calls today. You should get that."

With a sigh, I closed the bathroom door, grabbed my phone, and sat on the edge of the tub.

"Yeah?" I said, finally answering it.

"Your grandma called me."

Fucking Grandma. I didn't even know how she got his number in the first place. Whenever she called him, it was to complain about me or Mom. "Okay."

"Please tell your mom that I would prefer if you didn't go live in that house."

Asking why he didn't want that was a waste of time. Dad didn't live by "why." He lived by "I would prefer you" and "please respect my wishes." He was like Mom in that way. Shuttered closed like an abandoned storefront that was still trying to sell you its products.

"Who says we're going to live there?"

"Don't be contrary."

I gritted my teeth. "Why don't you tell her yourself?"

He was silent.

Dad didn't like to talk to Mom. Maybe that was just separated parents for you. But his avoidance was so polite. Less baby-mama drama, more of a deep disinterest in connecting in any way.

"Dazy?"

"Hmm?"

I could tell by his tone that I'd missed something he'd said. It was funny how I could always tell when people meant "Daisy" and when they meant "Dazy." They were the same sound objectively. But they came out different. "Daisy" made me feel nothing. "Dazy" . . . "Dazy" made me feel more than nothing—or maybe less than nothing, I didn't know.

I'm sure in Dad's head, he was saying "Daisy." But that's not how it sounded.

In my defense, he said a lot on these phone calls. If I didn't tune out some things, I wouldn't be able to make it through them. These once-a-week calls, like clockwork. But never in-person visits. He used to. When I was four, he decided that he wanted to know me after a lifetime of silence. I got about two years of infrequent visits that I could barely remember. Then, abruptly, they stopped. Work was too busy, and Vancouver was too far.

The last time I saw him, on that visit that I didn't know would be the final one, what I did remember was his hand reaching out to touch me. Then flinching back. Then forcing itself forward to stroke my head. It dropped to his side right after.

Did he feel proud about making himself do it? Like he probably felt proud of calling every week.

I never forgot. Couldn't. I tried.

"I wish you would consider what I'm saying to you," he said, followed by the sound of someone calling his name. I noticed then the background chatter, the rhythmic key strokes. Working on a weekend again. "I have to go. I love you. Bye."

I hung up.

When I came out of the bathroom, Mom was staring at me. Her face said to take a seat on the couch with her. There wasn't anywhere else to go, so I obliged.

"I didn't even realize you were transitioning your hair, and now you're all the way to a big chop." She didn't bother asking about Dad. She knew I didn't like to talk about him with her.

Her eyes raked over my little fro as surely as if she were running her sharp shellacked nails through it. Mom's relationship to her natural hair was to keep it in a constant state of protection—tied up in twists and braids or tucked under wigs and crochet hair. And here I was, sitting with mine exposed and vulnerable.

I shrugged by way of an answer. "What did Grandma say about the house?" I was shocked that I had made it even the couple of minutes I had before asking her. I didn't know what Grandma or Dad had against it, and I didn't care. I cared what Mom had to say about it.

Mom gave me side-eye, but this one was different. Not assessing my hair but something else.

I wanted to push again, to pose the question one more time. But the more you prodded Mom, the faster and harder she closed up.

Usually, I would check my phone during the space of silence when Mom decided what she did or didn't want me to know. Messaging back and forth with Noah. Gushing to Megan about him. Scrolling through whatever I felt like checking out at that moment. Now it was just the thing that sold me out—my accounts giving Tara everything she needed to expose me as the underage one of their group.

I didn't want to check anymore.

Mom fixed her eyes on the TV, where the latest episode of some reality show was playing. "She was upset with me for being given something she feels rightly belongs to my sister. She's being dramatic."

Grandma was the definition of dramatic. When I was in fifth grade, they decided to give out awards to each kid when we "graduated" so that we could feel special going into middle school. None of them mattered. Mom let me know that. "You get awards when you work hard and achieve something. You know that, right?" I didn't, but I learned.

I got an award for taking care of our class's pot of basil. Mom came to the small daytime ceremony and hung my certificate of Plant Power Warrior—I'm not making this shit up—on the fridge. Despite what she said, she still chose to display it. But when Grandma saw it and found out she hadn't been invited to the ceremony, she burst into tears.

Mom declared that she wasn't going to put up anything on the fridge anymore, and so now ours was devoid of even a single magnet. I ended up tossing my school awards in the garbage. I didn't get many anyway.

"Because you got the house? Who's giving it to us?" I asked now. I had always known about it, but the details of how we got it and from whom were not things Mom shared with me.

She swiped the polish brush over her baby toe with short and precise strokes. "Your uncle Peter died a couple years ago." She moved on to the next foot, starting with the big toe. "There was a lot of paperwork caught up in his estate, so it took this long for his lawyer to actually finalize everything and reach out."

The name "Uncle Peter" rang no bells, sparked no memory, left no impression.

"Funny," she mused. "I always thought I would have to do more to earn this. But sometimes these things just work out on their own."

Saliva slid down my throat. It made me think of rainwater slipping down thick palm leaves. Slow. Measured. Except this felt more like choking.

She took the time to finish up two more toes before speaking again. I wanted to grab the polish and throw it across the room so that she could focus solely on talking. "He decided to leave us a property up north. Your grandma feels like he should have given it to my sister, since they were married. But he hasn't. He's given it to us." Her voice drops to the barest hint of a whisper. "Just like I thought he would."

"Aunt Dione's husband?"

Mom sat still on the couch. Not just sitting. Positioned. Like a statue at the park, fixed and waiting for a pigeon to shit on her. "Ex-husband." The word rang hollow and singular.

Aunt Dione was a ghost. Not dead, just absent. My memories of her were of brief touches on my cheek, a hand slipping through mine, and the occasional glance from afar. But those were fake, of course. I had never actually met her. It was an idea of what I thought she might be like. Picturing her was like remembering someone long gone. Her image slipped through the corners of my mind and flowed away somewhere I couldn't follow.

Mom didn't speak of her. Except at the odd drunken Christmas dinner where she would make a cutting remark about "her." We were forced to spend them with Grandma because it was more trouble to avoid them than to go. But Aunt Dione never came.

Mom had no photos of her sister. No videos, either. Nothing.

Grandma was different. She had tons of memorabilia of both her children together and apart. Aunt Dione was her too-early accidental baby, and Mom came thirteen years down the line, the fixer-upper baby. The one meant to help Grandma hold on to Grandpa despite their daily arguments. It hadn't worked.

I was reminded of a wedding photo with Aunt Dione, her hair silk-pressed and tucked into a bun, secured to a flowing chiffon veil. There was a man on her arm. The only thing I could remember about him was that he was white.

That was the man who left us a house. *The* house.

"Why did he leave it to us instead of Aunt Dione?"

"We all used to be very close. Your uncle Peter was like a father to me." The words were something that should be fond, but she ground them out between her teeth. "He considered me his child, and Dione never wanted the house, and they didn't have any kids of their own, so it's mine. *Ours.*"

It was so like her. That this man—this Uncle Peter, who was her father figure—would be someone I had never even heard of. Mom was like that. Everything had to be found out. Never told. "What about his family?"

"He was estranged from them. He didn't leave them anything."

I licked my lips. "When are we going?"

Mom set the cap on the nail polish bottle and held it tightly. "I don't know. Maybe we won't."

"What?" I blurted out.

I couldn't make myself understand what she was saying. She had spent *years* obsessing over this house. Why was she suddenly hesitant now?

"You love Toronto, don't you?" she said. "Do you really want to move out of the city?"

This was the house. Freedom. There was never a thought in my mind that we might not take it, but I also hadn't imagined that it might not be in the city where I grew up. That we would have to abandon my hometown.

I would be leaving behind memories of places I'd walked with Noah, laughed with Noah, slept with Noah. If I left, what would happen to them? Would they become ghosts like Aunt Dione? Wisps of a time when life was better that called to me with sighs and gazes off into the distance, like a TV medium summoning spirits.

Though to be technical, in real life you never needed to summon them. They were always there. Flocking. Like pigeons.

"Well, do you want to go?" Mom said. She blinked at me in the ensuing silence and then let out something between a snort and a laugh. Not the sort of snorty laugh filled with mirth. Something closer to disbelief.

If this was a test, I'd already failed. Like always.

"Of course" should have flown from my lips like a furious thunderstorm, crackling and sharp. And the hesitation wasn't because of what Dad had said. I couldn't stop thinking of Noah walking with that white girl.

It was ridiculous. This was *the* house.

Mom rubbed the glass of the polish bottle still gripped in one hand, as if the friction would solve something for her.

"What's the house like?" I asked.

"It's beautiful. On a lake. Boat access only. Tons of wild blueberries to pick." She shook her head. "High-class too. Every single amenity you could want. And huge. It was a vacation home originally. Your uncle Peter was the first family member to live there full-time." The same stillness came over Mom's face. I couldn't tell what it meant because I hadn't ever seen that look from her before.

Talking about Aunt Dione made her normally pouty lips form a thin, hard line. Speaking about Grandma sent her eyes into fits of rolling everywhere possible. Chatting about work made her shoulders hunch.

This complete stillness was new.

Because however much she had talked about the house before this, she hadn't really *said* anything. I didn't know what it looked like. I definitely hadn't known where it was or who had owned it before us. And not because I never asked. This was just the most she had ever decided to share.

"Can't we rent it out?" I asked. "Use the money to pay for stuff here? Visit occasionally?" I ran my fingers through my hair again because I couldn't stop wanting to.

"No, it's in the conditions of the will. It needs to be our permanent residence for us to keep it. Otherwise it goes to Aunt Dione, who already said she doesn't want it. And so then it'll go to the government. Auctioned off." Mom stood and placed the nail polish bottle on the IKEA dark brown coffee table. "If you want to go, we'll go. You decide. We only have a few more days to accept or decline."

Sometimes Mom would do this. Let me choose. Which was less a show of her trust in me and more a show of her unwillingness to make difficult decisions.

But this was *the* house.

She walked to our small entryway area, not much more than a mat for shoes and a few hooks and baskets on the wall for keys and mail.

"Why am I deciding?" I didn't usually push back, but this felt too big. "You're the one with a job."

You're the one who wanted this. Who planned for it. Meticulously. Feverishly. Obsessively.

Except I wanted it too. Of course I did. Freedom was a single "yes" away. So why couldn't I just say it?

Mom took in a deep breath before settling back into that stillness. Her eyes met mine across the room. Perfect matches. The same too-light-to-be-black-and-too-dark-to-be-plain-brown shade. Eyes that would get lost in the night and found as it turned to day. "Because I can't be impartial. Besides, this only works if you want it to work. You need to keep everything under control."

Sometimes she acted like I was a wild animal instead of her child. A thing to be caged and monitored.

She opened the door. "You want anything from the store?"

My throat was so dry it itched. Screamed to be scratched. I wanted to tug apart the skin and rake my nails along the delicate muscle until it fell away in strips. I wouldn't have to talk then. Wouldn't have to answer.

"Dazy?"

"What?" I choked out.

"Daiii-syyy," Mom said, dragging the syllables out. "Do you want anything from the store?"

"We need milk."

"Will do." Mom stepped out of the apartment, shutting the door behind her.

There was nowhere to escape each other in the cramped space. That was why the store was ideal. It was away but not too far away, and when you went, you could focus on the task of retrieving something and bringing it back.

I ran my fingers through my hair over and over.

Away.

We could go at my word.

Up north was vague, but it would be hours out of Toronto at least. Hours along black asphalt with strip-mall views that eventually gave way to flat greenery. There would be more plants there than I could ever populate the apartment with. Maybe I could have a real garden. Not this poor excuse for one.

And once Mom was settled. Finances stable. Independent. She wouldn't need me anymore. I wouldn't have to worry about leaving her alone. She wouldn't watch me with those eyes that screamed of abandonment. I wouldn't owe her anything. And I would have the means to live my own life the way I wanted.

Probably I would never see Noah again outside of my phone screen.

I didn't know if I wanted that or not.

Besides, this only works if you want it to work.

CHAPTER SIX

Megan wanted to know everything about my hair. Why did I cut it? How was I going to style it? Would it grow back? Was I going to wear wigs all the time now? Did I hate it? Was I having a mental breakdown?

I shoved a maple syrup–soaked piece of French toast into my mouth and chewed. The day after Mom dropped the house bombshell, Megan and I were tucked into a booth against the huge glass windows of the breakfast place, which wouldn't have been my first choice. The dead crowded around it, pressing their faces up as close to mine as they could get as I worked to ignore them. Maybe I was today's sad soul that they couldn't wait to get close to. I didn't gamble. I listened to Kidz Bop the whole way here.

In movies, ghosts look like they did when they died. Bullet wounds, guts spilling out, that sort of thing. In reality, they look just like everyday people. That was why it was so easy to mistake them for the living if they were strong enough not to be translucent.

The restaurant itself was brightly lit with high ceilings and glass everywhere. Even the kitchen had glass walls so you could peer in at the staff as they fried your locally farmed bacon and cooked house-made blueberry preserves. Not jam. Not jelly. *Preserves.*

Megan loved it. Megan loved everything generally. That was the great thing about her. She was easy to be around because she delighted in all that life had to give. And she didn't care that kids who knew me from grade school insisted I was crazy. Which was important.

Her mom and dad had spent their childhoods in strict Korean households where their parents had expected their kids to become doctors or lawyers, and each of them abided. Once her doctor mom and lawyer dad had their own kids, they wanted to avoid the sort of standards imposed on them and had the money to let their children do whatever they wanted.

Megan's brother was regularly busted for tagging city walls yet praised by his family for his artistic spirit. My friend, meanwhile, spent hours every day dancing. Pliés and pirouettes came as naturally to her as her desire to try every Frappuccino that Starbucks offered. She sat across from me with her thick black hair tied meticulously into a ballet bun at the top of her head, still spouting out questions. "Okay, but like, are you gonna grow a big afro, or . . . ?"

I pulled the hat on my head down lower, as if hiding my hair would stop Megan's onslaught. "I don't know."

"You have to do *something.* You can't just wear a hat forever. I bet your hair looks cute."

Not true. I could, technically, wear a hat for the rest of my life. I shrugged instead and took another bite of French toast. Stephanie would have ordered the blueberry pancakes yesterday. No, she did. I knew she did. I saw it on Instagram. Her and Noah smushed together on the same side of the booth with the pancakes in front of her. The server must have taken the picture for them.

Noah's voice carried into my head, a vision of us sitting in a booth—across from each other, not beside—and him watching a table across the restaurant where the server was taking several shots of the group there. "Why do people always need to ruin the moment with photos? Just enjoy it. Experience it."

I agreed with Noah. We were living in the moment. He didn't want to be distracted by things like snapping pictures for clout. He wanted to focus on me. I wanted to focus on him. It was perfect.

"Hello?" Megan drew her voice out long, and I snapped back to attention.

"What?"

She grinned. "Classic Daisy." Megan never sounded like she was saying "Dazy," even when it would have been appropriate. "What are you going to do this summer? I'm off to camp, like, tomorrow for the last month before school. Wish I could have gone for more than just August, but whatever. Are you just going to hang around with Noah?"

I hadn't told her about Noah. When Megan went away for camp in the summer, it tended to swallow up bad things. If we had a fight at the end of the year, she would go to camp, and when she came back, there would be no more fighting. Something about that lapse in time when we were away from each other, her singing campfire songs while I kicked around the city, made our relationship better.

That meant, right now, she didn't need to know. Otherwise she would ask questions.

And I didn't want to answer any.

Didn't want to explain that, apparently, my boyfriend had broken up with me and was now dating this white girl. Didn't matter that she was white. Whatever.

"I might move up north." The words slipped out between bites.

Megan balked. "Wait, *what*? We've been here for a half an hour!

How are you only telling me this *now*? Like, move out of Toronto? *Why?*"

These were better questions than her other ones. "We may have a free house."

"Just rent it out, make money, and stay here."

"We're not allowed to rent it out because of how the guy who's giving it to us wrote his will. If we don't take it, it goes to the government."

Her eyes got wide. "Are you sure that's right? Do you want my dad to take a look at the will?"

Megan was always offering her parents' services for free. As if her dad didn't charge over a hundred dollars an hour, and her mom wasn't doing thousand-dollar cosmetic procedures daily. All those fees cut down to an off-the-cuff offer from their daughter. I got the intent. It was to be nice because that was how she was. But I didn't want it. "No, it's okay."

"It's not okay! You're seriously just going to go? I'm not even going to get to hang out with you a bunch before you leave because of camp."

Maybe it shouldn't have been shocking that Megan was upset. But she was *my* only friend. Not the other way around. She had more than enough other people to hang out with. I guess I didn't think losing me would make an impact.

I didn't know if I could include Noah in the count of people that would miss me, but at least Megan would.

"But you'll be back after school finishes, won't you?" she asked.

I blinked at her. "What do you mean?"

"Aren't you going to apply to universities back here?" Megan tucked her hands under her chin and frowned at me. "You're not going to stay there forever, right?"

Everyone at school was obsessed with these huge dreams that

only 1 percent of them would ever achieve. Megan would probably spend years training as a dancer and competing against people only to land somewhere in the middle as far as professional dancers went. Eventually, her parents would pick up that slack, and she would do whatever sustained their wealth long enough for her to make use of it. She could do nothing and still end up with that future. Which wasn't me hating on her. She was literally my only friend. It was just reality.

Going to university thinking you can work your way into a dream was a waste of time. It was an expensive exercise that, in the end, came down to whatever you'd had since you were born, according to Noah. I agreed. He went to university because he loved learning about new things, not because he thought it would help him achieve anything. It wasn't his fault that his parents had money. At least he was upfront about his privilege.

Mom worked hard for years to get us our shoebox apartment, only to be offered a huge house for free. She could have done nothing. Could have avoided struggling at all, and this still would have come her way.

That was how life was. Nothing you did really mattered. You couldn't actually control most of your future.

We were like plants that way. Each of us working hard to grow and survive. But it was all about the soil you were planted in from the beginning and whether someone chose to water you or not water you. To offer you new pots when you grew out of the old ones or release you from water as it pooled around your roots and threatened to drown you. You could only get so far on your own.

My pot was just there. Existing.

Moving wouldn't change any of my plans because I didn't have any.

Not before Noah anyway.

After meeting Noah, I had thoughts of going to university. Of learning biology and specializing in something to do with plants. Probably I would just end up working minimum wage at a garden store, but it didn't matter. I liked being around him and his friends. It felt like I had something to contribute. Something to say. And people wanted to listen.

Now I had Mom with her stillness and Megan with her questions. And our friends who were really her friends. More kids with long-shot dreams and rich parents. I wasn't like them. I could go somewhere new. Maybe kids in small towns would have less suffocating ambitions.

Unless I fixed things with Noah. Then I could have everything back.

"I don't really care about school," I said.

Megan raised an eyebrow. "Isn't your mom really strict about you studying? Doesn't that mean you kind of have to care about it?"

I almost laughed. Right. Mom's study sessions. Evenings where I couldn't hang out with Megan or her friends and instead had to spend a night with Mom. Learning. Her trying to form me into that picture of perfection that I could never fit. Shoving square-pegged me into a round hole. It was just as painful as it sounded.

It was easier to lie and call them "study sessions" than to say what really happened on those nights.

"I don't care about her, either," I said, lying again.

Megan caught on to the insincerity without any effort. "You pretend that you don't care about anything, but really I think you spend so much time caring about other people that you don't have room for what you want. Like, you *do* care but feel like you can't, you know? Do you actually want to move?"

I pushed another syrup-soaked bit of bread past my lips and forced myself to chew.

"What did your dad say?"

"He said that he would prefer I not go."

"Because it would interrupt school?"

I shrugged. "He didn't give a reason."

Megan pressed her lips into a line.

I wanted to shrug again, but it felt too much like acting as if I didn't care instead of me really not caring. Which I didn't. It was a lot better than what Dad did, which was pretend to care when he didn't.

Silence stretched between us until finally she pouted and said, "You'll miss our prom next year."

I laughed. The sound was so sharp from my chest that it was almost painful.

"I'm serious! You can't go to a prom with a bunch of country kids. It'll be so shitty."

That was why I liked Megan. Everything was so simple. Easy. That was what life should be. Struggling didn't get you anywhere anyway, so why bother?

Megan put down her mug of coffee. "Are you really going to go?"

I wasn't sure what to say. Because what should have been a "yes" had first become an "I don't know" and now felt a lot like a "maybe."

I couldn't control much, but maybe I could control this.

Maybe I could leave the city.

Maybe I could leave Noah.

Maybe it would be better to chase the freedom I always wanted even if that meant being without him.

I didn't know. Not until I spoke to Noah.

And we *would* speak, whether he wanted to or not.

Noah's apartment low-key looked like a drug den. Partly because it was on Parliament Street just off Dundas, and if you walked a block without seeing someone high, then gentrification had gotten too wild. Or the city had finally started giving a shit about the people who lived in it that didn't have money. The former was a lot more likely. The building towered up by several floors and always had a group of people hanging around in front.

I stood off to the side and ignored one of the guys on the stoop calling to me. Things like that barely clocked on my radar. There were more pressing matters. Like the translucent bodies that dragged themselves down sidewalks or lay in the grass twitching. Some of them liked to do that, especially if they were fresh—reenact their deaths. They'd lie on their backs and scream soundlessly, mime being stabbed or foam at the mouth. Chills crawled over my neck.

Fuck them.

All of them.

I left Megan after brunch with a tight hug that was uncomfortably comforting and a promise to text lots if I ended up going. I expected her to ask about what would happen with Noah if I moved, but she didn't. Part of me felt like maybe she understood that was a question I wouldn't want to answer. Sometimes I felt like she could see every layer of me, stripped bare, but chose not to mention it.

I peered down the street. Noah had no social media, but today he was hanging out with Dave, who absolutely did. Dave had a photography studio space that his parents paid for, where he invited girls for photo shoots in neon-colored string bikinis with their eyebrows drawn three times thicker than necessary. He was the sort of guy who documented his entire life on the internet and thrived on the court of public opinion.

It was how I knew Noah was planning to visit his studio today. He usually only spent an hour there because, apparently, Dave was "insufferable," even though they were supposed to be friends. He should be getting home about now. I hoped, anyway.

I scuffed the toe of my tennis shoe against the sidewalk and pressed myself farther into the shadows. I didn't want him to see me until I wanted him to see me. It wasn't like he would run away. Probably.

Noah hopped off the streetcar at Dundas just as I was considering checking Dave's Instagram again. He was wearing my favorite jeans. Not *my* jeans, obviously. His. But my favorite pair of his. They had that light-wash look that screamed vintage, and he'd rolled up the hems just enough to show his ankles. He looked like he was fresh off a shoot for a band's album cover.

My face flushed. I was wearing *sweat*pants. Paired with a ratty crop top, a zip-up sleeveless hoodie, and this shitty hat.

Fuck.

Why didn't I dress up more?

I could have done something.

I shifted on the spot as Noah walked closer.

Closer and closer.

Then gone.

Straight past me.

Instinctively I grabbed on to his arm. He reeled back with wide eyes, and I dropped my hand like it burned to touch him.

Noah blinked at me, then his eyes flared wide. "Daisy?"

He hadn't recognized me. Of course he hadn't. I looked terrible. I had a knit hat on my head in summer, and besides that, when had I ever worn hats? I swallowed. "Hey."

I wanted to say so much more. *How could you do this to me? What's up with you and Stephanie? How old is she? Do you not love me anymore? What did I do?*

I'm sorry.

It felt wrong for me to apologize, but I wanted to do it anyway. I wanted to fix this.

But my mouth wouldn't move beyond "Hey."

Noah looked around and dug his hands into his pockets. "What are you doing here?"

"Schnitzel," I said as an explanation, pointing my finger down the street. Schnitzel Queen was only a few blocks away. It was one of the first places we'd gone together. He'd talked about how people were afraid to hang out in his neighborhood, so that's what we'd done. Hung out there.

"Right," he said, like he knew it was an excuse. "Look, I gotta go—"

"I'm sorry that Tara freaked out or whatever. Over my age. And that we fought." The words flowed free and loosened the painful tightness in my stomach a bit. "Did it bug people? I'm not even that young. Like, soon I'll be eight—"

"Look, Daisy . . ." Noah ran his hands through his hair and exhaled. "We really just shouldn't have hung out. Tara was pissed at me about you being so young, and she was right."

What?

Tara was right?

We shouldn't have *hung out*?

What did "hung out" mean?

We were *dating*.

"But you always said that age didn't matter." The words ran out of my mouth. Timid. Meek. Like a soft piece of shit. I hated myself for saying them.

Noah shrugged. "It's just like, it's a big chore. I know you're mature for your age. I really do, Daze, but other people don't get it."

I felt the exact way his nickname for me sounded. Like I was floating. Aloft. Untethered. Drifting in the breeze, up and up into the frigid air, my head popping from the pressure. Raining blood and carnage onto the streets.

"How old is Stephanie?" I asked because I couldn't stop myself from saying it. "I saw you with her."

Noah's eyes narrowed. "How—never mind, she's eighteen."

"*Actually* eighteen?" Or eighteen like how I used to say I was eighteen?

"Of course actually eighteen. Age of consent is sixteen, by the way, which I know you know." Noah shook his head at me. "So what, did you follow me out here to ask how old Stephanie is? Social-media stalking us or something since you know her name?" His eyes flitted to my hat, then back to my face. "You need to get over yourself and grow up."

He turned away from me, still shaking his head, and started walking toward his apartment.

"I'm moving!" I shouted to him. "Out of the city! Up north!"

Noah shouted back at me without turning around. "Good for you!" The sentiment was kind, but his tone turned it into something ugly and sarcastic.

The people on the stoop of Noah's apartment were staring at me.

I jerked my eyes away from them.

And then, for no reason other than carrying out my lie, I went to Schnitzel Queen and ordered a meal.

I tucked myself into the tiny space inside and shoved breaded-and-flattened pork cutlet slathered in ketchup into my mouth. My eyes burned, and my throat hurt twice as bad from holding tears in, but I did it.

The last thing I needed was to cry and have some dead piece of shit come over to try and lick the tears. That was their favorite. The salty agony called to them. That was why I could never let tears cool on my face. Another mistake, made only once. I had run away from the playground, left out again by the other kids, hated and feared. Tears streaming down my face, I'd collapsed underneath a tree and lain down—limbs spread like a starfish, eyes shut. Pretended I was somewhere else. I had thought it was the wind blowing on my cheeks.

A breeze wafting over my skin. When I'd opened my eyes, a woman was crouching over me, her translucent tongue pressed against my face, feverishly lapping up my pain.

It was not an experience that needed a repeat.

After finishing my food, I shoved my earbuds in and blasted a "kid-friendly" version of a song that was, if you actually paid attention to the lyrics, not all that happy. It would still work. The tone was enough.

I was tired of wanting Noah.

I was tired of being here.

I wanted to get out. To get away from other kids and their useless university dreams. Away from Noah and Stephanie, who was apparently eighteen but looked even younger than me. I wanted to go someplace where no one would ever know that I'd had long hair, or wore makeup, or thought that I meant something to a guy.

I would just be a girl with a little fro.

I wanted to be free.

And for that, I would need the house.

CHAPTER SEVEN

BRITTNEY

Noah Durand is the sort of guy who wants to look poor despite the fact that I've seen his couch in the window of a high-end furniture store on King Street. It looks shabby and mismatched. But a quick Google lets me know that it's worth nearly double what we got for selling the rights to *Haunted*. That being said, Torte ripped us off.

Jayden and I were in our first year and hadn't made any sort of media connections that could tell us we were being offered scraps. Both of us were just happy to be able to pay our tuition for the semester. Everything felt so shiny. Torte made it clear that this was also an investment in our future at the company. More money to come.

That promise hadn't exactly been fulfilled, but if this season went well, maybe it would be. And that meant talking to Noah, unfortunately. Or fortunately, I guess, if you consider that we got our proposal approved. Barely a month later and we have a corporate credit card, a tight filming schedule, and a full set of interviews lined up for half the season. Thank you, life-sucking media corporation that I need. Thank you, creepy anonymous contact.

We can't officially do "Forgotten Black Girls" as a theme, but starting with the mansion is at least close.

Noah walks around his condo and makes a show of preparing tea for Jayden and me. Like everything else in his place, it has a long, involved story. This particular oolong he collected when backpacking through China, which he feels is the better place to travel—Southeast Asia is suffering over tourism and doesn't need any more white people going there. His words, not mine.

He reminds me of Mom. Always posturing. Pretending to be better to hide how ugly his insides are. Except he's an amateur in comparison. A lot of people could spend ten minutes with this guy and figure him out. Mom has been fooling everyone for years. Eight years, if I wanted to be exact about it. But if I'm even more honest, it's been longer than that. She's just gotten especially good at it since she became famous.

I adjust myself in one of his dining room chairs—there are four and they're all different—and share a look with Jayden. He avoids my gaze, probably because he knows he would laugh, and thanks Noah for the tea he sets in front of us.

I would note that Noah didn't bother to ask if we actually wanted tea.

I clasp my hands together tightly on top of the table. I made the mistake of finally listening to one of Mom's voicemails. I can usually get away with ignoring five messages in a row before she starts threatening to remove herself as cosigner on my lease. It says in bold font on the contract that losing my cosigner means breaking the contract. Meaning I get kicked out.

Eventually, I have to pay attention to her. But I still had a couple of times left. I could have ignored the message, but I didn't. Maybe it's because of this investigation, like poring over a shitty mother-daughter relationship is ma king me crave my own. Not to mention getting involved with this house. I can't help but wonder how she would feel if she knew that I stood to ruin her precious brick-and-mortar salvation. To show its hideous insides. As close as I can get to exposing hers.

Even if it gives me a thrill, it's too much mental energy devoted to her. And it's beyond what I should be thinking about. First and foremost, this is about forgotten Black girls.

Though a part of me whispers that I might belong to that group more than I think I do.

Now I'm distracted when I don't want to be and more irritated than I already suspected I would be, dealing with this trust-fund asshole. Not to mention, the incense he lit—also from the backpacking trip—is making me light-headed with its heavy patchouli scent.

Finally, Noah sits in one of the chairs across from us. We get everyone mic'd up and test the sound. Jayden then slides over the release form and starts to explain it, but Noah waves him off and signs it.

"I support the arts," he says by way of explanation. "I love what you two are doing with your channel. I'm so tired of seeing video series full of white people."

I smile at Noah as Jayden rises to turn on the cameras we set up when we came in. One facing Noah and one facing us. The brand-new light illuminates all our faces. "We aim to please," I say.

I have a thing about white people who constantly complain about other white people. It feels like they're waiting for me to pat them on the head and congratulate them for being allies. "Ally," a.k.a. being a decent fucking person.

And Noah, yeah, I'm not giving this guy any brownie points.

Jayden slumps back down in the chair. "For the purposes of

this show, please speak of everyone in the past tense, regardless of whether they remain living or not."

Anyone embroiled in the supernatural or true crime already knows what happened, but according to Torte focus groups, most viewers rely on us to introduce them to cases. And those ones don't want to know who's dead or alive until the end. If you think about it too hard, sure, it's kind of fucked-up. These aren't just stories, they're real people. Maybe that makes me just as bad as Mom's audience. We're all trauma seekers in the end, aren't we? But we're not all doing it for the same reasons. If you're a murderino, you're going to be constantly performing a moral balancing act. You can take it up with your god in the end because I don't have time to judge.

Jayden continues, "To help us set the stage, who was Noah Durand ten years ago? And what was his connection to Daisy Odlin?"

We decided it would be best to let Jayden lead because people find me "intimidating." It's bullshit on their part, but it's a good strategy. Unlike me, he knows how to make people feel comfortable, so they'll relax more if he starts.

Noah nods, pulling himself up and looking into the camera lens with a smile. Like we aren't talking about a case with multiple dead girls. "I was in my final year at the University of Toronto, majoring in philosophy. Though I didn't like to put limits on myself. I could be a philosopher one day, artist the next day, performer after that."

I hate this guy.

"My connection to Daisy was . . . complicated."

"How so?" I interject.

Noah rolls the words around in his mouth. "We met through a program at my alma mater. It paired up university upperclassmen and high school kids so you could help coach them. I signed up for people who didn't know what they wanted to major in because, honestly, you get more interesting mentees that way."

More interesting mentees. I bet you also get a lot of young girls who don't know what they want to do with their lives. Lost girls. I tilt my head to the side. "You were her mentor?"

"Yeah. She just had some issues, you know? She had problems in school when she was younger that made it hard for her to connect with people her age. Her dad was living in Vancouver and would just send her and her mom a check every month. He talked to her, sure, but it was very business-like. Perfunctory. He worked in corporate." Noah gives us both a significant look as if that should tell us everything we need to know about Jordan Hill, Daisy's father. Like Noah's own dad isn't the CEO of a corporation. He says, "Her mom was really obsessed with goals and trying to get places. Unnecessarily intense about it. Had her doing all these study sessions."

"Ambitious," I supply.

Noah doesn't like that. "Hmm, I guess that's the word people like to use. She was restraining is what I would say. She wanted Daisy to have this perfect plan where she gets straight As, goes to a top university, gets a degree, gets a job, marriage and 2.5 kids, same old."

"Did Daisy not like that?" Jayden asks.

"Daisy was a smart girl, but she wasn't a *smart* girl, you know what I mean?"

I hold my tongue and pull it into something polite. "She wasn't *book* smart."

"Exactly. Which, honestly, is better. Most creative people are the sort who fail in school. Besides, like I said, she had a hard time connecting with her peers, so she didn't like it. She was more mature than them."

I can picture Noah telling her that: *You're mature for your age.* We know about Daisy's school issues too. Though they seem specific to her elementary school days. In high school, her MO was more of a loner than someone ostracized.

Jayden jumps in for me. "Okay, you were Daisy's mentor. Did you maintain that relationship up until she left for Timmins?"

"Not really." He shrugs. "To tell you the truth, I was glad she was going."

My brow rises. "You were glad?"

Noah shifts in his seat and takes a sip of the tea that none of us have touched. "She was getting . . . She was just too much. She was obsessed with me."

"Obsessed?" Jayden echoes. His gaze slips sideways to me. "Like . . . what was she doing?"

"I started seeing this woman, and Daisy was crawling all over her social media. I don't even know how she found her. I hesitate to say 'stalking,' but it felt a lot like stalking. She always knew where we were, and I didn't use social media. I still find it's not worth the effort. But this woman did. And Daisy knew her name and all this stuff about her already. It was fucked-up." He pauses. "Is this censored?"

I catch Jayden forcing down a laugh. "You can swear. We bleep it."

"Okay, cool."

"She was jealous of the girl?" I ask.

"Woman. Yeah."

Jayden eases into the next question. "Do you know any reason why Daisy would have been so possessive of you? Why she would think she had a claim?"

Noah shakes his head and looks away from us out his window—a perfect Toronto skyline. A literal million-dollar view. It's a far cry from the place near Parliament he had when he knew Daisy. Background research revealed that his current condo was under construction at the time, and while his parents had paid for the highest-class dorm room possible on campus his other years, he insisted on living in "the real Toronto" for his final year of university. His ex-friend Tara, who'd clued us in, had rolled her eyes as she explained.

I can picture it. Him taking up a housing spot in an affordable neighborhood for clout when he had the means to live anywhere he wanted.

I press my lips into an easy smile. "According to Daisy's best friend at the time, Megan, you and Daisy were dating."

He laughs. I don't know him well enough to tell if it's fake. "Daisy *would* say that to her friend. Like I said, she was obsessed."

"You never dated?"

"No!" He shakes his head. "Anyway, I was twenty-one, and like I said, she was in high school. She was seventeen."

"Age of consent in Ontario was sixteen. Still is."

"That doesn't mean you have to do it." His voice has a hard edge to it, and his fingers tap on his teacup. "She needed a lot more mentorship than I could give. Professionals." He raises his hands. "Which, I think, is positive. I wish more people considered therapy. I go once a week." He's backtracking on the judging tone he'd let slip when he said "professionals."

I don't even want to talk more with him about Daisy. To expose her to him in any form. Megan turned us on to this guy, but clearly she didn't have a good grasp of his character.

Or maybe she did, and that's why she sent us his way.

"Thank you so much for your time," I say, which is the subtle signal for "We're done with this shit."

We take Noah's mic, he gathers the teacups, and Jayden and I stop the recording and pack up the equipment. Noah rambles on about something I don't pay attention to while Jayden humors him.

My phone vibrates, and I pause before taking it out of my pocket.

The same familiar number.

Mom doesn't call every day. She spaces it out. This time, it's two in a row. There are three voicemails from previous calls. I only bothered listening to the first one. It's like she can sense that I've had a win and is swooping in to drag me back down.

"Ready?" Jayden chimes, slinging the lighting pack over his shoulder.

"Yup." I toss my hand behind me, which is as much of a goodbye as I can be bothered to give Noah.

Outside, I stretch my arms over my head and adjust the camera bag on my shoulder. Jayden pulls out the vlogging camera and starts recording again, pointing straight at me. "What do you think?" I forgot about the new angle of showing our opinions live as it happens. That's the style of this season. Record as much as possible and get rid of what we don't want in the final cut. The hope being that it'll feel more organic and that the audience is investigating with us instead of just watching a summary after.

"What a catch," I say, trying to shove Mom from my thoughts.

Jayden rolls his eyes. "He wasn't that bad."

"I hate guys like that."

"Rich white dudes? Yeah, welcome to the club." Jayden moves beside me, holding out the camera in a selfie style to capture us both. "I think his was a necessary interview. People say the house forced Daisy into a psychotic break. But he's part of the point of view that she wasn't that stable to begin with. And he's not the only one with that opinion. She might have needed early intervention that her mom couldn't get for her."

"I thought you were on the side of believing it was ghosts?"

He grins. "Oh, I'm open to the spiritual theories. But I also think that existing mental health conditions could have contributed to everything that went down. I'm not going to rule out facts and say everything was supernatural. If anything, Noah's account supports your theories more."

"Yeah, my theory that gross dudes always love to say the girl is the crazy one to cover up their own shit." I scowl. "You think he's telling the truth? That they weren't actually dating?"

"I don't know."

"Come on! Did you meet the same guy that I did?" My braids fly around my head as I shake it. "He became a mentor so he could prey on easy targets. Sure, they were within the age of consent, but he knew it wasn't super socially acceptable for a twenty-one-year-old guy to be dating a seventeen-year-old, so now he pretends like it never happened. It's classic gaslighting."

Jayden shrugs. "*Or* you think that because he's clearly an asshole. It could be that, yeah, he's a creep, but maybe they truly never dated. Maybe he was kind of interested, but she got too intense and he backed off, but she kept up with that fantasy." He widens his eyes. "Remember what the people who went to grade school with her said?"

"She was eight when that happened. And she wasn't like that in high school."

"Or maybe she just learned to hide it better."

"You love to play devil's advocate," I say with a scowl.

He grins at me. "It's good content. If I never challenge you, people will get bored."

I know he's right, though I don't care to say it. Half of our comments are people who love our banter, which wouldn't exist if Jayden just agreed with me. Which usually he does. But on camera, he has to push the envelope. And he's good at it.

He sighs. "I know you care about the girls. That's your thing. You get into the emotions of the people involved and can't help but sympathize with their side of the story. But that's not my thing. I'm here to find out the truth. We *both* are."

Jayden and I both produce documentary content—except I've always wanted to tell a story. When you tell a story, you choose a main character, get close to them, and make people connect to who they are on an intimate level. Jayden, on the other hand, likes to state the facts, no matter how ugly they are. It's why we work great together. There's a balance.

I don't want to tell the story of a Daisy who obsessed over some rich asshole, who lashed out and hurt people when she shouldn't have. In my mind, she was the victim. But Jayden will always be there to show the other side. Because if she wasn't who I think she was, he won't shy away from it like I would.

"Did Megan know who the contact was?" I ask.

Jayden smiles. "Stop trying to figure it out. The contact is gonna tell us who they are at some point."

"But *did* she?" I press.

"Nope. She thought we got her number through Tara."

"How does Megan know Tara?"

"She runs in the same Toronto art circles as Megan's older brother. Tara was talking crap about Noah one day, and Megan's brother knew he had been involved somehow with Daisy."

I press my fingers to my temples. "That's so fucking complicated. And Tara?"

"Thought we got her number from Megan." Jayden shakes his head. "You know we're trying to solve the mansion case, right? Not the case of our mysterious contact."

"They know enough that it seems like it would be better to inter-view *them*."

"Maybe we will once they reveal themselves." He wiggles his fin-gers when he says "reveal," and I can't help but laugh.

"Speaking of interviews, can we get anyone who knew Peter Belanger?"

"Why are you acting like you haven't seen the list of people we booked?"

"I know. But we should still try and find someone close to him. He lived in a mansion by himself. Wife left him over some mysterious conflict. Estranged family. Taught kids piano. Piano! The number one creepy instrument. The gothic writes itself."

"I think the violin is a lot more haunting."

"Jayden!"

He laughs. "Guy was like a pariah. No one has anything to say about him. Kevin even got interns to call around town to his former students. Every single one is tight-lipped. No comment. No interviews. His family wants even less to do with him. We could ask Grace—she's always said he was like a father to her. Seems to be the only one who actually liked the guy."

"Suspicious."

"It's not a crime to be unlikable."

"Fine. This is also assuming we can actually land that interview with Grace. That's a promise our contact has yet to deliver on."

"They said they'd give us more details when we get to Timmins."

"And what if we're just chasing a ghost?"

Jayden's smile practically cracks his face in half. "God, I hope so."

I roll my eyes. "You're so cheesy. You know that's not what I meant."

"Look, they know a lot about this house. Maybe they haven't told us everything, but they got us the contacts we needed and the info to make them talk to us. If we'd called Megan and Tara cold, we would have just asked them about Daisy. Which is the thing *everyone* asks them about. They probably would have said no, just like they said no to every other outlet. *But* the contact told us to ask them about Noah, who wasn't on anyone's radar, and they were overjoyed to vent about him. Bro is desperate to gossip about his teenage maybe–maybe not girlfriend. It's gold. This person is onto something."

I can't disagree there. Noah probably never came forward because of the scrutiny of his involvement with a young girl. But now that the case has cooled and someone is paying attention to him, it's a different story. "They'd better come clean eventually," I grumble.

Jayden stops recording and packs the camera away. Fuck, this is going to be a nightmare to edit later. But we both agreed that we would rather have too much footage than not enough. I pull out my phone and get an Uber set up to take us to the airport.

"Time for Timmins," Jayden says, propping his hands on his hips. Clearly excited about this adventure.

I am too. But it would be nice if we didn't have our own mystery of this cryptic contact added to the investigation. I echo back his words with less enthusiasm, "Time for Timmins."

CHAPTER EIGHT

DAISY

Traveling back from Noah's was quiet. I stood on the streetcar, gripping the warm silver pole and staring out the windows, though there was enough room for me to sit if I wanted. There were dead here, too. Sniffing the backs of people's necks or peering aimlessly out the windows just like I was doing. They blended in with the city. More endless faces in the crowd that only I could see. Their number never getting noticeably bigger or smaller. After a while, one would disappear, and another would replace them. At the very least, I had learned to stop reacting. That brought me nothing but trouble.

Somehow I managed to stumble off at my stop and make my way home. The street cracks tripped me up more than I wanted, and the familiar smell of cheese and meat that wafted from the nearby Pizza Pizza was nauseating.

I watched a translucent dog trot across the street. It was rare to see animal ghosts. They didn't tend to stay behind for whatever reason. I didn't mind them. Unlike people, they kept to themselves.

Still, I stayed away. They were cold to the touch. Like most things, I'd learned that the hard way.

I walked down the narrow staircase toward our basement apartment, sucking in and pushing out a harsh breath just before opening the door.

Mom was closing the fridge as she turned to me, two slices of bread held loosely in her fingers.

"Let's go." I didn't need to say where.

A stiffness settled into her bones, that same strange stillness that made her seem less real. Not a person but a thing. An object that looked like my mom. Her twists were pulled into a high ponytail, and her glasses were perched on her nose, but behind them, her eyes were as stony as her body.

I stood in front of her, my fingers twitching, unable to keep the same level of stillness that she could. My hands kept smoothing my clothing when it didn't need it. In a lot of ways, this decision felt inevitable. But then, I could have said no. She made it my choice, after all.

And if it failed, it would be my fault too.

"Okay," she said, dropping the bread on the counter. "I'll send work my two weeks." She pulled out her phone, presumably to type the email.

She worked at a marketing agency as one of their many website designers. She was a junior, had been for years, which meant she was generally underpaid and underappreciated. Her words.

She never got promoted anywhere. She just hopped. Every two years she switched to a new company that would pay her just a bit more. But she never stayed long enough to shrug off the "junior" title. She said she changed jobs so often because it was the only way to get more money in the industry. I thought it was to avoid setting up anywhere long-term.

Mom was like an air plant. She could be moved from pot to pot and still survive. When her companies held employee parties, she stayed home. When coworkers invited her out, she turned them down. By the second year, they learned that she avoided being social with them, and the next year she would be gone.

I knew why *I* kept to myself. It was hard enough to hide what I could see from Megan. It only worked with her group of friends because they couldn't care less about me.

But Mom didn't seem to have any reason to distance herself.

I guess the positive was that it probably made leaving easier. That was how she could just pick up her phone and send off her resignation email like nothing. She was used to it. The temporary nature of everything. Staying in the city was something she said that *I* loved.

I think she always knew the house was in her future, even though it was technically my choice.

But the stillness, the way her body changed, made it seem like something about moving was hard, and I didn't know what.

And Mom didn't want me to know either.

"I need to make some calls," she mumbled, pulling on her shoes. Going outside because I guess that she didn't want me to hear.

I looked at her abandoned pieces of bread and saw deep finger indents where she had been holding them.

Our entire apartment—our home for the past two years, filled with its IKEA furniture and many plants—all fit into a standard-size U-Haul. I didn't even realize Mom had her driver's license before today. It never came up. There were a lot of things about Mom's life that she just didn't volunteer. It didn't seem to matter either whether it was something actually important or a mundane detail. Like knowing how to drive.

Soon we would be hours away. Away from Toronto. Away from Noah.

It was only then that I realized I didn't even know where we were going beyond the vague "up north" description. That hadn't been part of my decision that was solely wrapped up in getting away from Noah. "Where is the house? Like, specifically."

"Timmins is the closest major city. The house is about an hour's drive from there."

I Googled as she drove. Timmins had 41,000 people and three major mines with more on the way. Shania Twain had grown up there—Mom explained that she was a country singer who'd been popular in the '90s. Being that my mom almost exclusively listened to hip-hop, R&B, and rap from that decade, she wasn't surprised that I didn't know her.

"What's it like?" I asked.

"I haven't been there in years, but it's probably mostly the same. Some places closed and others opened, I'm sure."

"When was the last time you were there?"

I could tell she was fighting the stillness, forcing her body to jerk with the wheel. It made me think of a tomato plant, caged with wire, trying to find room to move. "I was sixteen the last summer I spent out there."

It was the first time I was hearing about it. "Did you go a lot?"

"Every summer since I was ten."

Six years. For *six years* Mom went to a place and spent an entire summer there. And she never mentioned it. I knew she and Aunt Dione had issues, but it seemed unreal that she hated her sister enough to cut out an entire time period from her life. "You have literally never talked about this before."

Mom shifted in her seat. "It was a long time ago."

"You were sixteen when you stopped going." I rested my chin

on my fist. "Did you stop because you had me?"

"Something like that."

That was the end of the conversation, I knew. There were so many Mom shutdowns that I'd learned to recognize over the years. Different ways she made it clear that a topic was off-limits. I slumped in my seat and stared out the window.

She was watching me out of the corner of her eye. But she didn't change her mind. Didn't open the conversation again.

Instead, she got a playlist of '90s and '00s hip-hop going and started singing along. Quiet at first, muttering under her breath. But within the next half hour, she was loudly belting Mariah Carey, though she didn't have the voice for it.

A smile cracked on my face, and I started singing along to the ones that I knew. And Mom didn't mind if I swore, so long as it was in the context of a rap song that came out before I was born. After a while, I even managed to convince her to put on my music—not the Kidz Bop for once, since inside the U-Haul, I was safe from the dead. She sang along with it all, happily stumbling through the ones she didn't know well.

Times like this, I didn't care as much that I didn't have a mom who cooked for me or told me every detail of her childhood. We connected in different ways. Not every mother-daughter relationship was going to be like a holiday movie.

It was these moments when I thought that freedom could mean coming back sometimes. That I wouldn't leave her forever. I could return for these compact moments that shone bright spots into a dim ditch.

I would have to go back sometimes to help anyway. That was an added bit of our bargain.

The rumble of the van sunk into my skin, penetrated my muscles, dug into my bones. It seemed to sing *away, away, away* with every highway bump. I loved driving. Adored that the dead could never keep up. They became blurs, shiny bits of the scenery.

The roads were familiar. Last year, I was on this northern highway twice. Once with Mom, when we went to Wonderland. We loved the roller coasters and made a point to get out there at least once every summer. And a second time also headed to Wonderland, but with Megan and her friends for Halloween. The whole theme park was turned into a haunted fairground, and actors ran around trying to scare you. I liked the fakeness of it. The manufactured horror. It made me feel like the dead in the crowds were a part of it. I could pretend that they weren't real either.

"What's there to do in Timmins?" I asked, taking a break from singing.

Mom tapped her fingers on the steering wheel. "A few local businesses. Bakeries. People are nice." She shrugged. "You find things to do."

In Toronto, you didn't need to find things to do. They were always happening. You just needed to go outside. Still, Noah would have loved Timmins, from the sound of it. He liked going to towns no one had heard of and finding local shops.

But Noah wouldn't be coming.

I kept thinking of him walking away, throwing words over his shoulder like I was nothing.

He didn't want to be in my life anymore. And I shouldn't want to be in his, either.

Suddenly determined, I found an app that would lock me out of my socials and grabbed a random string of numbers and letters online to set as the password. It was the sort of thing that I couldn't remember without saving it in a Notes app.

I didn't.

I navigated away from the page.

No more looking up pictures of Noah, Stephanie, or his friends. No more location markers to follow. No more videos to examine.

Now I couldn't see Noah through a screen unless I tried really hard. Reset my entire phone or used Mom's or something.

I liked to think I wasn't that pathetic.

Highway scenery drifted past: road stops mostly containing Tim Hortons and filled with half-exhausted people on their way somewhere; endless swaths of needled trees and rock formations; the odd car pulled onto the shoulder with flashing blinkers. If I rolled down the windows, I would have smelled a mix of fresh, untainted air spiked with the occasional tang of manure from nearby farms while hot wind whipped against my face.

I'd forgotten what it was like when it was just me and Mom. When it wasn't her and me wrapped up in Noah, or me and her wrapped up in her job or the house or our lessons.

But now I remembered.

Eight hours of driving had passed, and the most painful thing I'd had to endure was stiff legs. Otherwise, Mom and I had spent it singing along to music, listening to and commenting on podcasts, or chatting about whatever topic happened to come up.

It was sad, but it was the closest I'd felt to her in years.

"We're here." Mom pointed at the sign that proclaimed we were entering Timmins.

I watched for her to be overcome by that same stillness, but it didn't come. Around us, the foliage-lined highway didn't change much except for the sudden increase in local signs pointing us to restaurants and making suggestions for paralegals.

The last time Mom was here, she was sixteen. A year younger than I was now. "Did you meet Dad here? In Timmins?" The idea of it hit me suddenly. She must have.

"At Kenogamissi, technically. Where the house is." Her voice was easy. Casual.

I stared at her. "You didn't mention it before now."

She shrugged. "It's not as if you ever asked. I know you don't like to talk about your dad."

My fingers twitched, and I fixated on the signs we passed by.

It wasn't that I didn't like to talk about Dad.

I didn't like to talk about Dad with *her*.

He had texted me several times during the drive. Asking why I hadn't listened to him. Pleading for us to not move. But, of course, when I'd asked him why, he'd had nothing to say. He and Mom were so fucking alike.

Driving through Timmins wasn't as foreign as I thought it might be. It was a lot like traveling through a Toronto suburb except the houses were a little bigger and the roads were a little clearer. There were fewer people out on the streets. Fewer dead, too.

You didn't need a large population to have a lot of dead people. You just needed sadness. Small towns with enough tragedy could be as populated with the translucent pests as a big city. Thankfully, that didn't seem to be the case here.

Eventually, we stopped in the driveway of a house that I knew wasn't ours because Mom had talked about lakes and boat access. This was in a neighborhood that screamed planned development. Every house was new and giant.

She parked in the driveway and, before she got out, said, "Please call your dad. I know he's been texting you because you make that sour face when he does. I'm sure he would appreciate a conversation."

I held in a sigh and nodded.

Satisfied, she left and went to the front door of the house. Knocked and waited. She seemed so small standing on that stoop under a single porch light in front of a three-story home.

As ordered, I called Dad.

He picked up instantly. "Are you there?"

"Not yet. Mom is stopping at someone's house. She said to call you." It was important to let him know that this non-Saturday communication was not my idea and not something I wanted to do.

"Look, Daisy, just . . . please tell me if anything strange happens while you're there."

It was hard to know what "anything strange" was when you literally saw dead people. "Strange, as in . . . ?"

"Your mom, she might have a hard time living there."

"It was her idea."

He laughed. "I know. I just think she's a little out of her depth. If anything happens, let me know, and I can get you a plane ticket."

"To where?"

"Well, to Hamilton. You can stay with your grandma until we figure something out."

So if something strange happened and I was so afraid that I needed to leave, he would pay to ship me off to *Grandma*. I would have laughed if it weren't so predictable.

"What's my favorite color?" I asked.

"What?"

"Favorite plant? What music do I listen to the most?"

"Dazy."

"Do you know? Do you know *any* of those things? We've talked on the phone every Saturday for more than ten years."

He was silent on the other end. His breathing was too fast. Agitated. Nervous. I couldn't tell.

A door closed, and I jerked my head to the house. Mom was walking back out. A single look at her face told me she was pissed. Her right fist was clenched at her side. "Mom is coming back. I have to go."

"Please be careful."

I hung up.

Mom had barely gotten into the car when I said, "What's my favorite color? And plant? What music do I listen to the most?" Maybe this would make her random bad mood worse, but I had to ask.

She stared at me, the fury melting from her face into something blank and neutral. A rush of tears pricked my eyes.

Finally, she said, "Green. Monsteras. Kidz Bop."

I sucked back the tears in a gasp and turned away, hiding the smile that tugged on my lips.

She started the engine and pulled away from the curb.

That was the difference between Mom and Dad. One of them pretended to know me, to care about me, and one of them actually did.

CHAPTER NINE

Something had happened inside that person's house.

The thing Mom had fisted in her hand was a set of keys that she tossed into the tray under the dash. I figured that she got them from the lawyer if they were for our house. And whatever they had talked about inside had inspired the anger that I knew she was suppressing.

By the time we pulled onto a gravel road I hadn't even seen, it was dark enough that Mom had to flick on the headlights. The U-Haul groaned as we bumped along the rocky roads whose pebbles flew at the windows and clinked intermittently like sharp nails rapping on the glass.

Mom parked near the water and hopped out of the van. "Grab your essentials. We'll come back for the rest tomorrow."

"We're just going to leave our stuff out in the open overnight?"

"Daisy." Mom put her hands on her hips. "It's a small cottage community. No one is going to steal our things." She dug out her purse, and I grabbed my backpack.

The campground was marked by lights twinkling over the space—from small lamps to RV lights to cell phones being used as flashlights. There were roaring campfires with people who, as we walked to the boats, glanced over at us and didn't look away when we spotted them, the way people would have in the city. Mom smiled and waved at them, and only after returning the gesture did they go back to their fires.

"When people look at you, you gotta wave to them," Mom said. "That's how people know you're friendly."

In Toronto, it was the opposite. Strangers who waved at you were uncomfortable people you wanted to avoid.

I followed Mom to the dock, where she used the light of her phone to peer at the different boats before stopping at one. It was hard to see the details in the dark, but it was larger than any of the others around it. There were two main seats up front that were plush and looked leather, and another set of three seats in the back.

"Jump in," Mom said, tossing her purse into our new ride.

I grasped onto the side of the boat and climbed in. She put the key in the ignition. It roared to life, then dimmed to a gentle purr. Driving boats was another unknown Mom skill to add to the list.

As she untied us from the dock, she took a look at me. "There should be jackets stashed somewhere. It's warm now, but it'll get cold once we get going." She gritted her teeth and sighed, looking around us. "I didn't want to do this at night."

"Should we go back into town? Get a hotel?"

She shook her head. "No. It's a quick boat ride versus an hour back into town, and I'm exhausted. We already have to go back for groceries, which I also wanted to avoid, but it's too late now. I'll fig-ure it out."

Really, we should have stayed in town for the night. I wasn't sure if it was impatience about seeing the house, or if what happened at the lawyer's place rattled her so much that she didn't think of it. But I wasn't about to suggest what we should have done. It would just annoy her.

I found the jackets, one for her and one for me, and then we were off.

I had been on precisely one boat before. It was the ferry from Toronto to the Toronto Islands. It was so giant that you could barely feel the movement.

This wasn't like that. The breeze whipped and rippled the jackets so much that it sounded like the flapping of birds descending on us.

After the initial burst of speed, Mom slowed down significantly, squinting at the shore.

Everything was dark. The water was a shadowed silhouette moving alongside us, and we were long past the lit-up cottages along the water. Only the dark shapes of trees swept by on the banks.

After a while, we reached a point where Mom slowed down so much it almost felt like we stopped. Her exhale was loud enough to hear over the engine. The smoothness that we had during the ride turned unbalanced as the boat adjusted to the change in speed. Mom carefully brought us in next to the dock and started to tie up the boat.

Meanwhile, I stared. "Holy shit."

Mom didn't bother telling me not to swear.

From the dock, a set of sleek concrete stairs, lit by hanging lights in the trees, led up a hill to the sort of house that seemed like it belonged on TV. I counted four separate floors climbing into the sky, and I needed to turn my head and scan to see the whole house. That was when I spotted another roof, though significantly smaller.

"There's *multiple* houses?" I asked.

Mom's laugh rained down like shattered glass, fractured and

sharp. "Two. The main house and the bunkie, where we'll stay."

"We're not staying in the main house?" I watched her face as she swung her purse onto her shoulder, but she turned away before I could examine her expression too much.

"No, I've got plans for the main house. Remember?"

Right. The house was supposed to be a hotel or a bed and breakfast. Something like that. She was always fuzzy on the details. But other people would stay there. I'd just assumed we would too.

She started up the stairs. "Come on."

I followed Mom as we climbed the concrete steps that gave way to gravel crunching under my shoes, the mismatched rocks leading up the driveway to the imposing and massive house that would now be our home.

Swinging lamps snaked along the trunks of nearby trees. They illuminated the path but also created shadows along the bricks of the mansion that didn't exactly highlight it in an appealing way. It was a pattern of two shapes: part of the house was made up of flat walls, but in between were walls that jutted out in semicircle formations and likely had window seats inside. Each floor was marked by long and narrow windows with white trim and soft billowing curtains whose color I couldn't make out in the half-light. The brick walls and triangular boxy roofing reminded me of old Toronto homes, though it seemed to have its own unique charm. It was well maintained but had the vibe of a place that had existed for a long time.

"It looks haunted," I said, sliding my eyes to Mom, a half smile on my lips. A self-indulgent joke. Though I suddenly realized that I couldn't see any dead. No cold hanging in the air, either, beyond the coolness of summer at night. Usually they would enjoy something like this old, unoccupied house.

I noticed Mom hadn't responded and turned to her.

She was staring at the house.

It almost looked like she had the beginnings of tears in her eyes.

But it was too dark to see, and by the time she turned to look at me, I felt like I had imagined it. "We're going to make it work," she said. "We are, aren't we?"

I nodded, not sure what else to do.

Mom abruptly turned and walked toward the right side of the grounds.

I looked back at the house.

Something curled in the pit of my stomach, and I refused to acknowledge it as fear. I couldn't mess this up. Not after everything. I let my eyes crawl over the brick and mortar.

The house didn't actually look haunted. Really, it just looked old, not only in time but old money. The sort of house with a history of privilege passed down. Of easy living. People with these houses had a legacy that stuck to the original hardwood floors, and there was a lingering scent of dust that spoke of horseback-riding lessons and fully paid private education. Mom and I carried with us a history of cheap four-ingredient dinners, homey artificial scents, and a sort of middle-class poverty. Meaning you aren't really poor, so you can't bitch about it, but you'll probably never own property in your lifetime.

Except now we did.

"Bunkie" wasn't a word I was familiar with, but I had an idea in my head of what it would look like. A small-scale house, maybe big enough for a couple of bunk beds. Hence, bunkie. I imagined something tiny and cramped that didn't make any sense to live in considering that we had inherited a giant mansion.

The bunkie, in reality, was bigger than any apartment we had ever lived in, and I suspected the size of many normal houses. It was propped up away from the ground with stairs leading to a front deck and another porch in the back.

"Who has a mansion and then builds another house beside it?" I asked.

Mom pushed her way inside the place, dropping her purse on a side table and flicking on the lights. "Your uncle Peter said it was built because not everyone likes to stay in the main house. It gets noisy with a lot of people, I guess. I think sometimes staff stayed here too."

"Peak rich-people behavior," I muttered. Mom didn't respond.

It was spotless inside and smelled like it was freshly clean—Pine-Sol and lemon Pledge—and the ceiling was covered with exposed wood rafters. The bunkie was built with the same sort of modern open floor plan that I was used to in the city, but it clearly had two separate bedrooms while I was used to living in places without any. I expected one or two dead people to be hanging out inside. Empty spaces were usually sad by nature, which they enjoyed. But there were none, just like the rest of the property. I crossed my arms over my chest and forced myself to believe that I wasn't doing it for comfort.

This place wasn't exactly a beacon of joy. So why weren't they around?

I wandered into one of the rooms, where a queen bed filled the space along with a vanity. My feet carried me forward, and I dropped onto the vanity seat.

I stared at the girl looking back at me.

A girl with a little fro who had no idea how she'd gotten where she was.

"Do you want this as your room?" Mom popped her head in the doorway.

I blinked at her. "My room?"

"Yup. There are two, so you get one."

"Yeah," I said, the words falling out of my mouth, slack. "This room is good."

I had never had my own space. Everything was always open and exposed. I should be happier. I knew that. But I could only wonder what would happen if my earbuds died. Or if I had a particularly bad nightmare. I imagined a dead body lying on top of me, desperate to cling to the inherent sadness in my fear. I would be so cold. Shaking. Trembling. And when I screamed, would Mom be able to hear me through the door? Or worse, would I stay asleep? Getting colder and colder. And she would find me in the morning.

Dead. Frozen. And no one would be able to explain why.

I cut off the thoughts and shook my head. I needed to stop.

Dazy.

Dazy.

"Dazy?" Mom said, and I jerked my head toward her. I hadn't even realized that I was staring at the bed. Imagining it. "Are you okay?"

"Yeah. I'm fine."

I was fine. Everything was fine. I only had one of the dead lie on me once. *One time.* And I woke up. Besides, it hadn't happened again since I'd discovered Kidz Bop. I didn't even have any knowledge to prove one could kill me like that. Translucents were basically harmless. I was *fine.*

"It's going to be all right, you know," Mom said. "We're here now. This house is going to save us, you'll see." She smiled at me. It wasn't still or stiff the way I thought it might be now that we were here. It was the sort of smile I tried to hold in my head when I thought of her. Soft and beautiful, like it was feathered at the edges, more like a dandelion blowing in the wind than a twitch of lips.

I didn't ask her what we needed saving from. From her perspective, probably just from being lower middle class.

"Yeah," I repeated.

"Good. Now, I feel sweaty and gross, so I'm going to jump in the shower."

"Study session tonight?" I asked. She'd said she was exhausted earlier, but it was Wednesday. That meant it was time for Mom to unsuccessfully drill perfection into my head. At the very least, I hadn't cried after one in years, which was nice. That was how it was the first few times. Now I was numb to it all.

She let out a soft sigh. "At some point, you need to stand on your own two feet." She planted a hand on her hip. "There's only one uncontrollable factor in this equation. You and I both know it. Now you just have to show that you can manage."

I couldn't form a sentence.

Mom left me alone in the room for her shower.

Show that you can manage. Meaning don't screw up. Don't ruin this.

A muscle in my jaw twitched and flexed without my permission.

I watched my reflection as I ran my fingers through my hair for the millionth time. Already I had been with this version of me for a couple of weeks, and it still didn't quite fit. It was like staring at someone else making my movements.

I paused and ran my finger back over one spot. Instead of smooth scalp, there was something hard and cracked. I scraped my nail over it. The feeling of the ridge was like when I pushed Mom to leave the relaxer on longer than we should have. The chemical would burn into my scalp, so slowly that I didn't notice until the skin felt scorched. A scab would grow over the burn, and I would peel it off days later.

By the time I was with Noah, Mom and I had perfected the timing around how long to leave the relaxer on. I didn't want to imagine the face he would have made if he'd run his fingers through my hair and pulled off a scab.

But this was different. It felt the same, but when I tried to lift it from my scalp, the pain was sharp and stinging. I dug my nail in harder around the perimeter to loosen it, pushing myself off the vanity chair to get closer to the mirror.

I must have nicked myself with the clippers, maybe when Mom surprised me. I couldn't think of any other way I could have gotten a scab on my head.

I speed-walked into the living room and searched in Mom's purse for the travel-size beauty kit I knew would be there. I took out a pair of tweezers and went back to the mirror.

Probably I should have just left the scab alone. But I couldn't. It was there, and I knew it. And I wanted it gone. I had made a fresh start with this hair and didn't need a scab making it something scarred.

I tugged on the edge of the skin with the tweezer, trying to ignore the way the pain made my teeth clamp together and my eyes water. In the mirror, it was lifting the tiniest bit.

Just a little more.

I paused when a flash of white peeked out from under the scab instead of the crimson of blood I expected. Leaning closer to the mirror, I squinted.

And there, from under the scab on my scalp, a tiny white worm about the size of a vine leaf stem wiggled out. Bone pale, with deep grooves marking each millimeter of its body, writhing on my head.

I screamed.

The tweezers flew out of my hand, and it seemed like one scream wasn't enough. Two, then three, burst out from between my lips. I sprinted from the room and ran around the bunkie until I found the bathroom.

The shower curtain was closed and the water was running, but there wasn't a single peep. *"Mom?!"* I screeched.

Her hand reached around the barrier between us, shaking the slightest bit, and she poked her head out. Her features were jittery. Scattered. Somehow she seemed more shaken than I was.

"There's a maggot on my head." The screams were gone from me. My voice came out in a flat tone.

It broke whatever had rattled her. "What?" She turned off the shower and wrapped herself in a towel.

"There's a scab on my head, and there was a worm coming out of it."

"A worm or a maggot?"

"I don't know! It was white and fucking gross."

"Don't swear."

"*Mom!*"

She dug around on my scalp with her nails, searching through my curls for the grub. "I can't see anything."

I moved away from her and leaned close to the mirror, looking for the spot. I ran my fingers along my scalp in the same way that I had before.

But I couldn't find it again. "I don't get it. It was there. I lifted up the corner of the skin."

Mom tugged the shower cap off her head, and her twists tumbled out of it. "It was a long drive, Dazy. Maybe you just need some sleep?"

I wasn't caught in a fucking daydream. "I saw it."

"Why don't you shower next, then? Kill it with some good scrubbing."

"Does that work for lice?"

"Was it lice?"

"I don't know! It looked like a worm." I crossed my arms. "Where would I even get lice?"

"The TTC."

If I was ever going to get lice, the Toronto public transit system was probably the best bet. "Do you think just washing my hair will work?"

"I don't know, Black people don't get lice."

"I highly doubt that there isn't a single Black person in this world who hasn't gotten lice."

Mom sighed. "You know what I mean. We can see the doctor when we go back into town."

"Okay."

She pointed at the shower. "For now, may as well see what scrubbing does."

I stood in the bathtub under a spray more scalding than I would usually endure in the hope that it would kill whatever was there. My fingers probed along my scalp—half expecting something alive to wriggle against my fingers—but nothing happened.

After the shower, I methodically parted my hair and checked for both the scab and the creature, but I couldn't find either.

Whatever I saw, it was gone now.

CHAPTER TEN

t was a mistake to think up north wouldn't be as hot during the summer. I was hit with a thick waft of heat so humid that it was like I could feel my curls unraveling and losing their fine gelled definition from what I slathered on earlier. Mom insisted it was surprisingly hot for the area, which usually cooled off closer to September. It was already past mid-August now, and still scorching.

It smelled like the country. Even through the blazing heat, the air was crisp in a way you could only manufacture back home by mowing your lawn. There was a tickle in my nose from the spice of it that could also be allergies. Pollen sneaking into my sinuses, ready to swell them. The constant ringing of nature was imposing. Crickets or some other bug. They were loud and never-ending. One sound stood out, an insect making a sharp clicking noise. Predatory in its distinctiveness.

As Mom predicted, no one had victimized our U-Haul, which sat untouched exactly where we left it. The campsites at the boat launch were even more populated and busy now that it was daytime. The night after the "porn star" incident, I'd woken up bleary-eyed and sick to my stomach. The way that everything had looked then—clear, stark, in the light of day—felt so much different from how it had been in the darkness.

In the light, everything was illuminated.

I could see the dead properly. The campers were clearly too jolly, so no ghosts were near them. There were only three bobbing in the water. Probably reenacting drowning deaths.

In the darkness, everything was hidden.

Maybe that was scary for some people. But I knew what lay in the dark, and it was better not to see it at all.

I turned away and stuck a single earbud in my ear, letting Kidz Bop create a safety zone of happiness.

I wiped sweat off the back of my neck and adjusted the thin straps of my tank top. Mom handed me another box, and I walked, legs spread out and braced for balance, waddling down to the boat to dump it in.

Last night I fell asleep sprawled out like palm leaves—large and taking up as much space as possible—with my fingers still moving through my hair. And yet I hadn't found the scab or the worm. Now my hair was crusty with the gel I had run through it. I didn't think it was supposed to be crunchy, but I wasn't sure, and Mom always put her hair in twists, braids, or wigs—whatever would help her avoid styling it directly—so she didn't know either.

"Good morning!" A white man hopped out of a truck and walked toward us, waving with a beaming smile. His hair was gelled into a stiff hairstyle that I could sympathize with, and he wore his T-shirt tucked into his shorts. The woman who followed him, also white, had short teak-colored hair and wore a matching pair of shorts, but mercifully, hadn't tucked her loose blouse into them.

I looked at Mom to see if she knew why this man was talking to us.

She widened her eyes at me and mouthed, "Wave."

I jerked my hand up in something like a greeting, though I suspected I was already too late.

"Good morning! You really didn't have to come all the way out here." Mom brushed her hands off on her jean shorts as if we had gotten dirty moving cardboard boxes. "This is my daughter, Daisy. Daisy, this is Mr. Helms. He's the lawyer who wrote your uncle Peter's will. He has some papers I need to sign."

So this was the guy who had somehow pissed Mom off the other night. He seemed so aggressively friendly that I couldn't imagine what he'd said that had been so offensive. But then again, how many times had I said something seemingly innocent that annoyed Mom? It was hard to avoid sensitive topics when she would never tell you what half of those topics were.

"Daisy! I love that name," the woman chimed. She reached out her hand to Mom and then to me to shake. "I'm Paulie, that's P-A-U-L-I-E. I'm Perry's better half."

Why did this woman think I cared how her name was spelled?

Mom forced out a laugh and nudged me.

"Thanks," I said. "I like your name too. It's . . . unique."

"Thank you!"

Mr. Helms and Mom signed the documents using the side of the U-Haul as a surface, and Paulie signed as a witness.

"That's it!" Mr. Helms made a show of jerking out his hands. "Sorry again that I couldn't have this ready for you last night. But the house and land are yours now. You must maintain a permanent residence on the property to keep ownership. This can be bequeathed to your daughter or an immediate family member if you pass. I can write that up for you if you drop by the office."

"And the renting . . . ," Mom said, her voice trailing off.

He clapped his hands. "One hundred percent within the grounds of the will. Let me know how business goes—I would love to hear. Estate will cover the property taxes for a couple of years, but that income will help, so I hope you reel a bunch in. The Okekes seem to be doing well with clients out on their end, so that's a good sign." He paused and looked between me and Mom. "Do you know them?"

Paulie's eyes went wide. "Why would they know them? They're new to town."

"I spent a few summers out here when I was younger. I might know them." Mom turned her head from Paulie to Mr. Helms.

Paulie waved her hand. "Ignore him."

Mr. Helms said, "Well, they live right out your back door anyway. Just go through the bush, and you'll find them on the other side if you ever want to say hello."

"They're *psychics*." Paulie made a low "woo" sound and wiggled her fingers.

I blinked. We were going to be neighbors with the local weirdos. Also, Mr. Helms had casually said the word "bush," and no one but me seemed to care.

Paulie clapped her hands. "Here, let us help with your things."

"Oh no." Mom blanched. "I couldn't ask you to—"

"Nonsense! We'll help out, won't we, Perry?"

And so Mr. Helms and Paulie helped us load the boxes onto the boat. It seemed impossible that everything in the U-Haul would fit on it, but it was a big boat and a small van, so somehow it worked.

Then we were off down the lake, water spraying lightly onto the boxes while I kept an eye on the fragile planters that were encased in layers of bubble wrap, their plant inhabitants sequestered in boxes.

Something would die.

Most of my plants didn't like to be moved multiple times during a short period. Even after I bought new ones, I let them sit in their purchased plastic planters before I moved them to nicer ceramics. They had been shut away from light for a day and night too.

I may have carried nothing but leafy corpses up north.

Now that I wasn't exhausted from eight hours of driving, I could properly take in the bunkie. The huge main living area consisted of not one but two separate couches, both leather. The kitchen, like our old one, used the island to function as the dining and eating space, but the island itself was several times larger than any we had and included a sink built into it. The bathroom even had a double vanity.

I took a moment to check on my monstera. There were slices along the leaves in the distinctive way the plant was known for. People liked to describe it as "Swiss cheese." I disagreed. To me, it looked like a clean rot. As if something had eaten away at them with sharp, angular teeth.

I ran my fingers along the edges, remembering that Mom knew it was my favorite, even though I only had one. I never bought more or propagated it. She understood why. We had a history together that Dad and I didn't. Just like my connection to the dead. Rotten things called to me, whether I wanted them to or not.

After moving the plants out from their boxes, I made a mental list of to-dos. Some needed less water in general, so their dry soils didn't bother me, but others needed more regular nourishment. I also had to decide where to put them. Some needed to be by the windows in direct sunlight, and others I had to place on the kitchen island so they would be *out* of direct sunlight.

Mom's eyes followed me as I did all this. She had already abandoned the stack of her boxes filled with clothes and wigs in a corner of the bunkie and instead sat on one of the shiny leather couches typing away at her computer. The only thing she had bothered to set up was the TV, since the bunkie didn't have one.

"What are you doing?" I asked.

She hummed under her breath before answering, "A little research. Thankfully, your uncle Peter spared no expense on the mansion and bunkie's satellite Wi-Fi. You're very lucky. Some kids out here have to survive without."

I fought not to roll my eyes. Clearly, she was also benefitting from the internet, but sure, make it all about me. "Researching what?"

"Airbnb."

"Airbnb," I parroted. It made sense. "Will it take long to set up?"

"Not long. The estate's been paying for regular maintenance and cleaning thus far, so the property is in good shape." She leaned back into the couch. "All it needs is a little extra oomph. A couple of fruit baskets, greeting the guests at the door, and we're off."

Mom's voice had that edge to it. She got that way sometimes. There would be a plan, and she would figure out the steps she needed to take to get there, and explain how it would take off.

Every idea was the next best thing.

Except the next best thing never happened.

It was always just enough to keep us floating in that lower-middle-class bubble.

It was mind-blowing, really. I knew what hard work really amounted to—more of the same. But Mom didn't. No matter how much she tried to break out, she always ended up in the same place. Switching jobs to get basically the same salary and the same career level. Starting businesses that were supposed to make more money but just broke even.

All of it was so . . . fruitless.

But this was definitely the longest she had ever committed to something.

I was reminded again of how much planning had gone into her ideas for the house—years before we even had the house.

I was starting to wonder if I had even made the choice myself or if the whole act of letting me choose was an indulgence. What would have happened if I'd said no?

I knew she thought this Airbnb would catapult us into something new and big. Something that brought in a lot of money. But really, it would probably make just enough to equal what we would have had in Toronto. There, we lost money on rent. Here, we would lose it on starting a business. It would be the same. But somehow she thought it would be different.

This time it *had* to be. Because if this didn't succeed, she wouldn't get what she wanted, and neither would I.

"Should we go into the house today?" I asked.

"No," Mom said, her voice sharp. "They're cleaning. We don't want to get in their way."

Didn't she just get done saying the property was well maintained? And I hadn't seen anyone around the house besides us. I opened my mouth to say as much, then shut it. Mom's brow was furrowed as she stared at the screen instead of me in a way that felt purposeful.

Fine, whatever. What was one more day waiting to check out the house compared to the years leading up to now?

"There's a forest behind the mansion, right?" I had spied a gathering of trees back there as we brought boxes into the bunkie. If I couldn't explore inside the house, I could at least take a look at some of the local plants.

Mom's brow smoothed, and she finally looked at me. "Yeah, it's back there. There's blueberries and stuff if you want to pick them. Just be careful. They grow in bushes low to the ground. Don't eat those blue-black berries that grow higher up—they taste like crap, and they'll give you the runs."

She had an obsession with blueberries. Refused to get any in the grocery store, but any time there was a farmers' market, she would go through the routine of asking for a sample, pop it into her mouth, and always find it lacking. That would then give way to a story about the wild blueberries up north in which she'd consistently manage to avoid mentioning how she lived here during six summers of her life.

I pushed my face into something like a pleasant expression. "Will do."

"Actually"—she put down the laptop—"maybe I'll just come and show you. I need to introduce myself to the neighbors anyway."

"Why?"

"You don't want me to come?"

I shook my head. "No, not that. Why do you have to introduce yourself?"

Mom sighed. "Because it's what you do up here. Plus, what if someone decides to attack us or something? Don't you want to be running off to someone you know?"

If someone went through the trouble of taking a fifteen-minute boat ride out here to murder us, they deserved the kill. "Yeah, sure."

"Good! Let's go."

As we passed the imposing mansion to get to the forest, Mom reached out and ran her fingers over the bricks. Gently, like a caress, a small smile coming onto her face. Then it was gone, her face neutral again as she turned away and walked toward the trees.

I slowed my steps and stared at the building. Trying to see whatever it was that brought her so much joy. Maybe it was the idea of it more than anything. But I thought that studying it might reveal something more. In the light, the bricked walls were clearly in shades of gray. The huge double doors to enter were marked by brass knockers, and if not for the swinging ivory curtains, I would have been able to see into each of the rooms.

One of the curtains flapped as though someone were playing with it from the inside. Then it stopped. Abruptly. The fabric pulled tight and still.

"The garden is over there," Mom said, standing between the forest and the mansion, pointing to a path leading away from us through a hedge filled with dead flowers. Their dusty brown and black petals littered the ground around the archway and, with just a glance, I could see more leading inside a glass building. "Not a lot of gardeners in the area, apparently. Perry said that the woman your uncle Peter hired to organize the maintenance of the property couldn't find one. That'll be a good project for you, getting the garden up and ready for guests to see, and later prepping it for the winter."

"The plants will all be dead in winter."

"They won't. The greenhouse has heating."

How much money did Uncle Peter have? His powers seemed limitless when it came to this property. Excluding finding a gardener. My fingers itched to explore the greenhouse and discover what sort of plants were out there and what the conditions were like. I had looked forward to growing outdoors for once, but the greenhouse was a better deal. It was more like what I was used to: plants in controlled environments.

I decided to spend tomorrow in the greenhouse as I followed Mom up the steep path into the forest, where the thick tall trees blocked out sunlight and swallowed us whole.

CHAPTER ELEVEN

The property seemed to expand exponentially without any plans to slow down. What started as a clear path through a few trees became rugged, and stray branches grew wild. Light above turned into something patchy, and the area filled with shadows. There were ditches that dropped sharply into deep gorges, and a heady scent that might have been grass but had a depth of humidity to it. Like a steam shower in a meadow that I could inhale like smoke. And everything was overlaid with that same predatory-insect hum that stung my ears as I stumbled along behind Mom.

"Do you know where you're going?" I asked, skirting over a fallen branch. Lots of the trees were spiky pines whose needles littered the earth.

Mom bobbed her head. "I used to come this way sometimes. Your uncle Peter had it cut in back then, but I guess he let it grow out in the last few years."

It was always "your uncle Peter" as if I had a special claim to this man I had never met. He was more hers than he would ever be mine.

But maybe she didn't like that.

And I had no idea why.

Light broke through the trees after about five minutes of walking, and we came out into the bright summer sun. Power lines towered over a flat field of grass. It stretched out in front of us for a few feet before coming to a stop in front of yet another copse of trees and forest. Purple bunches of flowers and my namesake grew in patches. I stared at the skeletal towers. Now I didn't know if the humming was truly from the insects or if it was these lines.

Mom crouched, searching through the greenery until she made a satisfied grunt.

"What?" I said.

She held up a tiny berry. "Wild blueberries. I told you."

I knelt beside her and stared at the short bush with tiny blueberries clinging to it. They were minuscule when compared to the giants packed in plastic pints at the grocery store. I hadn't ever actually seen the fruit out in nature, growing. Megan went berry picking with her family on a regular basis. They called it their "Canadian" activity, like when they went to sugar shacks in the winter.

Mom pushed a few into my palm. "Try them."

I popped one into my mouth and squeezed the juice out with my tongue. I expected that same sharp, bitter taste we got from the ones in the city, but instead it was sweet without a hint of sour. "Oh," I breathed.

Mom grinned at me. "Northern Ontario wild blueberries. Best in the world. And free!" She looked around the field. "You find a lot more if you go to an old burn. Maybe we'll drive out to one eventually. I was thinking of buying a used Jeep for errands and things." She popped a couple of berries into her mouth and hummed.

Satisfied, finally.

Beside the patch of blueberries, small single daisies bloomed. I trailed my fingers against the soft white petals of one.

I thought of Mom's story of my name. That road trip and the stop alongside the highway.

Was it just a version of this place that only existed in her mind?

Sanitized and stripped of anything that might hint at her past.

Plucked like a daisy and put into a manufactured dream where she could make it her own. And then told as a story.

As a lie.

"Should I get my license?" I asked, instead of questioning the origin of my name aloud. "To drive the Jeep?"

Mom scowled, got up, and shoved a few more berries into her mouth. "Let's go see these neighbors."

Rain check on the driving, I guess. Too much independence with a license.

It took only a couple of minutes through yet another bundle of trees before we hit a gravel road leading up to a house. It was nothing like the mansion. The home was built like the sort of log cabin you would make out of clay as a kid. Stacked-up cylinders. It even had a chimney.

The one thing they had over us was their garden. It was utilitarian in a way. I spied heads of lettuce and tomatoes, and leafy shoots that hinted at carrots and other root vegetables, laid out in neat rows.

A couple of people my age were there too.

A boy sat on the ground tugging the odd ripe vegetable from the soil. The knees in his jeans looked torn by actual wear, not by a worker in a factory expertly slicing and ripping. His shirt had matching gaping holes along with what looked like a mustard stain. His midnight skin was ashy too. I was used to Black boys carefully moisturizing their elbows and hands. This one didn't seem to care much. His lips had probably never been in contact with ChapStick.

Meanwhile, a girl stood beside him, saying something to the boy though I was too far to hear. Either way, he didn't seem interested in talking to her and gave her a less-than-friendly look. She wore box braids in her hair so long they almost touched her feet. Her top was cropped above her belly button, exposing the light brown of her skin, and her jeans were ripped so much she may as well have done without pants. The shades perched on her nose glinted in the sunlight.

"Jesus, that hair." Mom eyed the springy twists on the boy's head. They were the only thing he seemed to have spent time on. His curls looked more moisturized than mine, to be honest. "Your dad was on it with his hair too. He would do a wash day and be holed up in the bathroom individually twisting each curl. High-maintenance country boys."

This was why I didn't like to bring up Dad with her.

Mom spoke about Dad in two ways. The first was all business. *Call your dad. Your dad sent this for you. Answer the phone, your dad is calling.* The second was worse. Because otherwise, she talked about Dad as if he were dead: wistfully and in the past tense.

Like he went off to war to defend our white-and-red maple leaf flag, to honor us with his sacrifice, and came home in a box. Buried with shining medals of gold pinned to his chest while we stood in sinking mud.

When really, teen pregnancy was a little too much for him. Mom always said they met "at a cottage." Dad spoke of his summers without place names when I still bothered to ask. His memories were of an experience colored pink with jumping into frigid lake waters and screaming from the cold, and of course, pretty girls who visited for the summer and provided story fodder for when you got back home. Or a tale for you to spin to your child about the girls you hung out with as if that weren't inappropriate. It was the most he ever gave to me of himself.

They were his fun memories. Ones that I guess were probably tainted by the responsibility of having a child. Now he suffered through the duty with weekly phone calls and a check every month. Maybe that was why Mom had the room to romanticize him. Maybe it would be better if she were the sort of baby momma who talked shit.

Mom squinted at the boy, though she had her glasses on and shouldn't need to. The frames cost $250, paid for by her old job's health-care benefits. No benefits now. "He looks your age."

I hated boys my age. "Maybe."

Mom called out, "Hello!"

The boy whipped his head up and blinked at her. Automatically he raised his hand and waved at us. Mom waved back. I didn't. Neither did the girl. "You're the people who inherited Peter's place?" he asked.

"How does he know?" I whispered to Mom.

She muttered back, "Cottage communities are small. Get used to your neighbors knowing everything about you and your business." She smiled at him. "Yup! Is your family home?"

Perhaps bored of the conversation or maybe just not wanting to meet us, the girl gave me and Mom a brief glance before she walked away into the forest.

"Is this why the lawyer thought we would know them? 'Cause they're Black?" I asked. It would explain why Paulie was so adamant in grilling her husband about "Why would they know them?" and all that.

Mom pursed her lips. "I'm sure that's not why."

"I'll get my mom out." The boy glanced at me for a beat longer than seemed necessary, and I stared over his head. He didn't react either way, only turned around and headed into the house.

"You have so much attitude." Mom shook her head at me.

I scowled. "I don't! People always say I'm quiet and spacey. You can't have your head in the clouds *and* have attitude."

"And yet somehow you thrive."

"Whatever."

"Mm-hmm, there it is."

We both ignored that there were other ways people liked to describe me. But I suspected we were trying to forget about that. I was, anyway. Mom seemed to find it necessary to remind me every once in a while, as if she were afraid that I had been too thorough in my forgetting.

I looked away, back the way we came. There was no sign of where the girl went. The boy seemed annoyed with her. Maybe a girlfriend or some ex he was fighting with? Something about the way they interacted didn't feel like siblings.

"Hello!" a voice shouted.

I whipped around as three women came out of the house, the boy trailing behind them. The woman who called to us had a thick wrap around her head. It looked distinctly African—though I didn't know enough to guess at what specific region of the continent the style might be from. I pulled my shoulders up. Somehow I've always felt like I needed to prove myself to people who were born in the place our ancestors came from. There was this feeling like they were the way we were supposed to be. They were Black people. Me and Mom, we were something else. I knew that wasn't true. Obviously we're all Black, but I felt removed in some ways.

Grandma was a kid when her parents immigrated to Canada from Trinidad and Tobago. She used to talk about how their accents embarrassed her. I guess that's what happens when you're plopped in a majority white suburb. Grandma had a relaxer on her head before she turned six and very firmly insisted that she was Canadian, period. If that made my great-grandma upset, she never showed it.

I remembered the plantain she used to fry for me—her wrinkled fingers dropping the yellow slices into hot oil and the sweet caramelized bits that stuck to my teeth. I didn't know her for long. But I knew that after she was gone, Grandma was not going to make that for us.

I didn't eat fried plantain again until this year, when Noah brought me to a Jamaican restaurant on Gerrard. He insisted that he knew my family wasn't Jamaican like most people would assume. He knew my background, properly. The plantain was good, but it wasn't how my great-grandma had made it. Though I didn't tell him that.

The woman adjusted the wrap on her head and beamed at Mom. She looked a few years older. Mom-age. Because Mom herself wasn't really mom-age, she was younger. "I see that you've met my son, Kingsley." She waved at the boy.

"King is fine," he corrected.

The woman clicked her tongue. "I'm sorry, did you name you or did I name you?" He kicked at the dirt and said nothing. She looked around for a moment. "Your little friend take off?"

"Not my friend," he said.

"Just as well."

The girl. They must be talking about her. I looked at Mom, who shrugged at me.

"I'm Tambara Okeke." King's mom motioned to the other women. They were both built thick and didn't wear the same head wrap; instead they had their hair styled into mini twists. From their face shapes I could tell they were twins, younger than Tambara, though still older than Mom. "My sisters, Corinne and Yolanda."

Mom smiled at them. "I'm Grace, and this is my daughter, Daisy."

"Beautiful name," Tambara cooed at me.

I could never tell if people were being genuine or not about my name. If they actually liked it or if they were just startled that I, with my resting bitch face, could be called something so delicate and sweet.

"I remember you," Tambara said, staring at Mom. "When you were a girl. Not that I was much older. I visited once to offer Peter a cleansing for the house. I invited you over a few times too, just for tea and a chat. But you never ended up taking me up on it."

Mom's lips flattened into a stiff smile. "I'm so sorry, I don't recall."

"That's all right. It was a long time ago. I wished I could have come by more to get to know you all better, but Peter was strict about his property line and didn't much like unexpected visitors."

"He and my sister were very private."

I looked back and forth between the two of them. It made sense that they would have crossed paths at some point during the six summers Mom spent here, but it was hard to tell if Mom really didn't know her or if she just didn't want to talk about knowing her.

"You're all psychics?" I asked, remembering what Paulie had said. Besides, Tambara had casually mentioned a "cleansing," whatever that was. I had the decency to not wiggle my fingers when I said it like Paulie did, but Mom still gave me a pointed look. I was curious, though. They didn't have dead on their property either. The entire area seemed to be devoid of them. Which would be great if it weren't so strange. For that reason only, it was suspicious and concerning.

Tambara didn't seem bothered by my question. "Of course, we do palm reading, tarot, the works." She nodded at her sisters. "They do reiki too."

I looked at King, whose gaze was firmly on the ground.

His mom caught my eye. "Kingsley is our shining star. For the last little bit, he's had the most accurate predictions of any of us." She scowled. "Though he seems to prefer spending his time digging in dirt or cruising around with his friends."

I didn't know how to respond to that, so I didn't. None of them, frankly, looked like people who had psychic abilities. But to be fair, I had no idea what someone I actually believed had those abilities might look like.

It felt like a performance, their entire presence. Making light of the whole thing. Like it was a game. Fun, even.

Probably they had never woken up to someone dead hovering over them or lying on top of them. They had never met a corporeal. Hadn't had their face pressed into the ground, trying to breathe, and breathe, and breathe, but all you can do is inhale dirt, and you're suffocating, and you're dying, and—

Stop. I needed to stop. I let out a short breath. Forced myself to calm down.

The adults kept talking, something about palm reading, but I could feel King's eyes rise from the ground to land not on them but on me.

I ignored him.

Fucking fakes.

Tambara said, "Actually, it's great you're here. We heard about Peter. So sorry for your loss. We would love to come by the house and do a spiritual cleansing to help give you a fresh start. Very similar to what I offered him when you were younger. I hope you'll be more open to it." She paused for a moment, and her gaze became heavy. "Are you planning on living in the house?"

Who asked something like that when you inherited a mansion? I guess maybe they could have assumed we would use it as a cottage or rent it out. But it felt like more than that.

Mom's lips tightened the slightest bit. "No, we're living in the bunkie. I think the house is a bit too much space for us."

Tambara and her sisters visibly relaxed, their shoulders dropping. King went back to looking at the ground. "I can definitely see that. It's a lot of house."

She laughed along with my mom, though neither of them seemed to be in high spirits.

One of the sisters, Yolanda or Corinne, I couldn't tell which, said, "If you're free now, we would be happy to come do that cleansing."

"Oh shoot," Mom said, her voice making a surprised sound that rang hollow. "We have a lot going on today, plus quite a few workers in the house. Can't have anyone in right now, but maybe another time?"

The skin at the edges of Tambara's eyes creased. "Of course. Another time."

As far as I knew, we had absolutely no plans for the day. And I had still yet to see any sign of these workers Mom kept talking about that were, apparently, inside the house right now.

Even though she said to get used to our neighbors being in our business, she hated for other people to be mixed up in her life. The local psychics coming over to the house to poke around and do their weird ritual definitely counted as being too close for comfort. Uncle Peter must've thought the same if he'd turned it down before too.

"Maintenance, eh? I hope it's not too bad," Tambara said, then tilted her head to the side. "What do you think you'll do with it?"

Mom smiled. "Nothing a little elbow grease can't fix. The greenhouse will need a bit of work too." She pointedly ignored the last question.

The sister, Yolanda maybe, jerked her head at King. "Let us know if you need him. He's off for the summer, and he's a green thumb." She waved at the garden. "He does all of this for us. We don't even go into town for vegetables anymore. He wants to look after some pigs next year, right?"

King shrugged.

Tambara didn't seem to appreciate the encouragement of her son's gardening and made a grumbling sound under her breath. "You know Kingsley doesn't like to get involved. He observes."

I wasn't sure what she meant by that, but it made her son seem like a creepy stalker. Though I guess I wasn't in a position to judge.

She shrugged, unconsciously mirroring her son. "But if you need help in the greenhouse, I can get him over there."

"I'm sure I'll be fine," I told her. "But thank you." I leveled a look at Mom that said I could be polite when I wanted to.

Mom said, "We just wanted to come say hi. If you ever need anything, feel free to stop by. I hope to be a lot more neighborly than my late brother-in-law."

"We just might have to do that," Tambara replied with a big smile.

We said our final goodbyes to the Okeke family and trudged back through the forest. As I was assaulted with the musk of damp wood and buzzing sounds of insects hidden in the trees, I looked around for the girl, without any luck.

A shudder fell across the back of my shoulders like a limp branch trailing across the skin. I hiked them up to my ears and stopped, searching the trees. It took a moment to find the source, but then a translucent man stumbled out, wearing camouflage. He didn't have a lot of pep to him. Maybe that was why I wasn't seeing many dead— they were all too old. But that didn't make sense either. Usually when one left, another appeared to take their place. It wasn't exactly one for one, but there was more of a balance.

Either way, he wasn't looking at me. Clearly there was someone or something sadder and therefore more appealing that he was focused on.

"Dazy?" Mom called from ahead.

I turned and caught up with her.

Finally, we made it back to the house. Not the bunkie. The mansion, proper. Mom went around to the huge double doors and settled into her stillness. We stood there for a while. Silent. Unmoving.

"Can we go in now?" I asked.

Mom jerked as if she had forgotten I was there, forgotten she was there too. She became another piece of decor like the trellis with dead roses and ivy that led to the greenhouse. She pegged me with a look, irritated. "No. If you need to go in for any reason, I'll let you know, and we can go together."

"But—"

"Do not go into the house," she snapped.

I recoiled.

Now I needed supervision to enter a house? How did that make any sense? And I knew she would never tell me if I asked.

What was up with this house?

She caught herself and leveled a playful grin at me that was stretched so tight it looked like plastic wrap was pressed over her lips. "How about dinner? I'm starving after being given the third degree by those neighbors."

They'd barely asked anything, but I guess to Mom, even the simplest question was torture. "Why not just let the Okekes do their cleansing?" I asked. "After they do it, they'll move on." It wasn't like their ritual would actually do anything.

She frowned at me. "Listen here. People love to be in your business. That doesn't mean you have to let them." Done with the conversation, Mom pivoted and headed back to the bunkie.

I stayed in place, still staring at the mansion.

Mom walked ahead of me without noticing. Though she must have known when the bunkie door swung shut behind her and I wasn't there.

Maybe she didn't care.

As I left to follow her, tearing my eyes away from the building, I caught sight of the man in camo gear walking out of the woods with shuffling steps, still in his near-transparent state. He dragged himself to the house, pressed his body against the bricks, and groaned, low and throaty.

My lips curled and I jerked away, my footsteps loud in my ears as I rushed home.

CHAPTER TWELVE

BRITTNEY

At the Timmins airport, you walk right from the plane onto the asphalt tarmac. That's how small the place is. Thick heat blasts our faces as we follow the crowd to the entrance of an airport whose building makes up maybe one-sixteenth of a terminal at Toronto Pearson. But it does have a cute local restaurant inside, diner style, with eggs cooked on a flat top. And somehow the amount of people waiting to collect loved ones is as much as any major airport. People rush to greet their friends and family as we file into the space and wait to grab our equipment from baggage claim.

I'm just happy they don't have a bookstore so that I'm not forced to stare at a cover of Mom's face superimposed onto an image of the mansion. The last thing I need is to watch someone pick it up and for me to know that, soon enough, they'll be aware of all the lows of my childhood and somehow come away from it seeing my mother as the hero.

Once we have our stuff, we call a cab. No Ubers here. And neither of us is old enough to rent a car. The guy that pulls up has a French accent, and I let Jayden handle the small talk as we both get into the back seat. The first topic of conversation being the unseasonably hot weather. Can't say I'm sad to not be participating in the chat.

We drive down a long stretch aptly named "Airport Road." I stick the camera out the window and capture B-roll of the trees passing by. It must be a main street, but there are only two lanes, and it seems to go on forever. Mostly foliage and the odd gigantic house with a bunch of shit in the yard—tractors, kids' play sets, trailers in desperate need of repair.

"Why is it that the more space you have, the more you fill it with crap?" I say.

"People like having stuff," Jayden replies with a shrug. "And in a small town, you probably get bored. Gotta have things to entertain you."

"That's right," the cab driver chimes in. "Wish some people would clean it up a bit, though. It's a little *broche à foin*, you know?"

I have no idea what that means with my limited French, but I nod along anyway.

We finally turn off Airport Road and begin to pull into civilization. Houses appear on the sides of the streets along with smatterings of teenagers on bikes. The real mark of life is the Tim Hortons coffee shop that greets us. There's a drive-thru with a lineup infringing on the grocery store parking.

Jayden points. "They have a Starbucks!"

"God bless American capitalism," I mutter.

Finally, we stop in front of the law office—Helms & Associates. It's on top of a walk-in clinic that sits conveniently next to a Shoppers Drug Mart. The sign on the window is a muted olive green with slightly off-white lettering. It's modern. Chic in a way that doesn't seem to belong to the small-town vibe.

I grab one of the cameras while Jayden grabs the other, and we split the lighting between us. After thanking and paying the cabbie, we take a micro-size elevator up to the third floor. The office itself is even nicer than the sign. The waiting area boasts sleek cream armchairs with olive-green accent pillows, there's a full-service espresso machine, and the walls are decorated in tasteful black-and-white shots of the town.

The receptionist pops out. She's white and about our age in dress pants and a cardigan. Her hair is cut in a trim style that frames her face and is sheared neatly at the nape of her neck. "You're here for Mr. Helms?"

"Yup," I say, bringing out my limited amount of Brittney charm.

"I'm Carolyn." She grins and takes in our equipment. "He said you would have cameras."

"That we do," Jayden says, raising his.

She lights up and claps her hands. "I have watched all of the episodes of your show. I loved that one you did about that couple in Alabama. That was unreal."

Jayden responds with a grimace. "Yeah, that one was wild."

In the second season, we looked into a case where a couple had been luring in young girls to kill and eventually each got jealous of the other one's "relationship" with a captive and decided to have a knife fight that left them both dead. People claimed their ghosts still stuck around their old house to terrorize women.

Carolyn lets out a tiny sound that I guess is a contained squeal as she ushers us down the hall. "This is so exciting!" We stop in front of a room with a blank plaque on the door. Our guide waves us inside. "You'll film here. I cleaned it up for you."

The room is bare in a way that speaks of disuse but is still impeccably furnished and decorated like the rest of the office. It's set up with an armchair behind a desk and two chairs out in front of it.

Even the window coverings, slim pull-down shades, are up so that natural light floods into the room.

Carolyn smiles. "Does it work?"

"It works." At least we won't have to worry about not being taken seriously.

"Perfect. Can I get you anything to drink? We can make lattes, and—"

"Earl Grey latte?" Jayden asks.

"Absolutely!" She turns her gaze to me. "And you?"

"I'm good."

She bobs her head in a nod. "I'll make the latte and let you get set up. Mr. Helms will be in soon."

We get the cameras and lighting into position as she leaves.

"Gotta love that small-town charm, eh?" Jayden nudges me.

I sigh as I get my mic into place. "It's hit-and-miss. They weren't very nice to all our girls."

The mansion had a body count in that year Grace started the Airbnb—some dead, some injured. All girls. And the way the Black ones were talked about was very different from how the white victims were. In YouTube videos about the case, the thumbnails were either the white girls or the mansion, or a combo of the two. Sometimes it feels like it has to be intentional. But it isn't. It's subconscious. It's natural for people to forget or ignore Black girls. Effortless. And when they do pay attention, they don't often have nice things to say.

"We don't know that," Jayden replies. "That's why we're doing these interviews. We've only seen the worst of what people thought of Daisy and Grace. And if people in the community weren't very friendly, maybe it was because they didn't know them yet. That's the thing about a small town. People need to know you to care."

"What are you, the small-town expert?"

"I spent like two years living in Barrie when I was little. To most people in Toronto, it's basically small-town living."

I snort. "We'll be sure to add 'lived in Barrie once, small-town expert' under your name in post."

"Hello, hello!" Behind me, Mr. Helms walks into the room. I recognize him from the news coverage of the case. He's got a full head of salt-and-pepper hair and looks like he's in his fifties or sixties. Carolyn squeezes in behind him and delivers Jayden's Earl Grey latte. "Oh! Good idea," Mr. Helms exclaims. "Do you mind—"

"Black coffee, I'm on it."

He grins at us. "She's on the ball, that one." He takes a seat behind the desk as though he sits there all the time, not like it's an extra room set up specifically for us. I help him get mic'd up since Jayden is still in the process of setting up his own mic.

Once that's done, Jayden slides the release form across the table to Mr. Helms. "Just to get this done before we start."

He takes the form and, like any good lawyer, actually reads it. He puts his signature on the bottom line just as Carolyn drops off his coffee.

She closes the door to the office with a grin. "Break a leg!"

Gotta love our fans.

I press record on both cameras and collect the form.

Jayden says. "Thank you for meeting with us, Mr. Helms."

"Oh God, Perry is fine."

"Perry," he repeats with a smile. "I'm Jayden. This is my cohost, Brittney."

"I know you!" His own smile reaches up to his eyes and crinkles them. "My daughter watches your show. She was the one who said I should do the interview, though I don't like to get too involved in the media." He shakes his head and presses his mouth into a frown. "When those people came and talked to me, they just twisted everything around and made a big mess of it."

I fight a wince. Tower didn't exactly do us any favors with their exposé. They were a more "serious" media company than Torte and prided themselves on being "real" journalists and telling "real" stories. Hyperliberal, which I liked. But still predominantly white video producers, which I found predictably hypocritical. Toronto-based like us with a name that honored the famous CN Tower. Their story on Daisy and Grace was messy as hell. "We really aren't anything like them," I say.

Perry gives me a small smile. "Yes, that's what she said."

"Does your daughter live in town?" Jayden interjects.

"Oh no. She's gone down to the city like everyone else her age. She's an interior decorator." He says the words "interior decorator" with an inflection on them like the phrase is French—foreign and fancy. He waves around us. "She did the whole office."

That explains why it's so modern in a place where shabby chic seems like the more prominent style. "Do most young people from here go to Toronto?"

"Everyone always wants to go down south. Then they realize how damn expensive it is, and they start coming back up here to make their money so they can go back down again." He lets out a loud exhale. "That's why I was happy to see those girls start a business up here, you know? Everyone wanted to stay at that house for a weekend. Even people in town! And it got featured in the Porter magazine and everything."

Porter was the airline we'd flown, and their in-flight magazine is actually a legit publication. I'm not surprised that the Airbnb got featured.

"While we're on that topic, we may as well formally get started." Jayden gives him the past-tense spiel, then asks, "Who was Perry Helms ten years ago and what was his connection to Daisy Odlin?"

"He was a guy with a lot less gray hair," he laughs, and Jayden chuckles along. Despite myself, I smile too. I never had a dad, so I wasn't exposed to the "dad humor" thing. It's kind of endearing.

"Sorry, sorry, I'll be serious. I was a lawyer in Timmins at Helms and Associates and responsible for Peter Belanger's will as his lawyer and executor. I knew Daisy because her mom Grace had inherited the property. I also represented Daisy on the criminal charges that were brought against her."

They hadn't let cameras into the courtroom, but I remembered an article that had described Perry Helms as tired but passionate. The media had blown up the case completely, and there was outcry from angry people on the internet demanding that she be tried as an adult and sent to jail. Which wasn't even being seriously considered by the Crown.

His biggest hurdle, I imagined, was the people coming forward to claim that she'd previously had violent tendencies. Nearly killing a girl when you were eight would do that.

I ask, "Did Daisy and Grace seem happy about the success of the Airbnb?"

"Well, yes, until . . . until later." He fumbles over his words and pauses to take a sip of his coffee.

Jayden shifts in his seat. "Until someone died."

"Yes."

People who follow my mom's teachings like to say that the good of the house outweighs the bad. That the unfortunate happenings there are outliers and exceptions to the rules of the Miracle Mansion. But they've never had the whole story the way we could get it. The truth is that the house already had a body count before Grace and Daisy got there, and after, it had two more.

I jump in. "You consulted with Grace about that incident, correct?"

"Yes, well, she didn't know who else to call." He leans his head heavily on his hand. "Grace was a mess, even though she was usually so put together. She was like her sister in that way."

I choke on my spit and exchange a look with Jayden. As I'm dying on saliva, he comes in for the save.

"You knew Dione?" he asks.

The information that we found only noted Perry being Peter's, Grace's, and Daisy's lawyer without any recorded contact with Dione. Peter and Dione had never bought property together, a lawyer in Toronto had handled their marriage license and her side of the divorce, and he hadn't left her anything in his will, so Perry didn't have his hands in that, either. As far as paper trails went, he'd had zero interaction with Dione.

We had strongly considered skipping him because so much of the court proceedings was public record. But our contact insisted that he had more to give when it came to Grace's past. And here it was. Not a lot of people had known Dione when she was a Belanger.

"Sure, I knew her," Perry says with a shrug. "Town like this, you tend to know a lot of people. And she was Peter's wife. I would see her sometimes in the grocery store or something. Real quiet. Real private."

He says that, but even the sort of people who love giving their two cents on everything have almost no material on Dione. "Did you and Grace ever speak about her?"

"God, no. I mentioned her sister when Grace came to pick up the keys from me on the first night they got in, and she shut it down."

"What did you say to her?"

"Just asked how Dione was making out. It was her ex-husband that had died, after all. And Grace and Dione used to be thick as thieves. Back when Peter and Dione were still in school in Toronto, they used to bring Grace here for visits. Cottaging, you know. Grace didn't have a good relationship with her mom, as far as I knew, and Peter and Dione were basically like her parents. That's really how I first got in contact with Peter, family court things I can't get into, but there was intent to make their little family official. You know what I mean? They were all so close." He takes a slow gulp of coffee. I want to throw it across the room and tell him to just talk.

I assume that he means Peter and Dione wanted to legally adopt Grace as their own. Though that never happened.

Perry continues, "Grace just said she and Dione didn't speak anymore and grabbed the keys. The next day she was fine. I guess she just didn't want to talk about her. I don't know what happened between them. My wife is always saying that I can't read a room and I'm too nosy, so I don't know."

I force myself to pause and give him time to breathe. "Were you surprised that Peter left the house to Grace instead of Dione?"

Perry takes another sip of coffee and has a moment to let it languish before it goes down his throat. "Not at all. Like I said, Peter and Dione acted like they were her parents. And those two never had kids of their own. As far as anyone was concerned, that was his daughter." Perry gives a satisfied nod. "He showed me pictures of Grace and Daisy on Facebook when we were working on the divorce, and you could just tell he was so proud of her. Honestly, I was surprised by the divorce until Peter mentioned that since Grace stopped coming, Dione spent all her time in Iroquois Falls getting her practice set up. He never actually saw her. She didn't want to be in the house, it sounded like. Shame to see a family fall apart like that. And she had no interest in the property during the divorce settlement, of course."

I nod along with him. What he said lined up with interviews that Grace had given in the past about her relationship with Peter. That he was like a father to her. Grace didn't have a Facebook account anymore. She'd apparently deleted it a few years ago. According to some friends, it didn't have much on it to begin with. Just a couple pictures of her and Daisy.

The Dione bit is new and juicy, though. I didn't realize that she basically hadn't even lived in the house after Grace left. Clearly, something had changed among the three of them, going from tight-knit family to each of them living in a different place.

"Why do you think Grace took the house?" I ask. "She had been away from Timmins for nearly sixteen years by then. Why make the switch?"

Perry grins. "Same as everyone else who comes back up here from the city, I would guess. Helluva lot more affordable. Plus, a free house on Kenogamissi and an estate with a good chunk of money? It would be a hard offer to pass up. And she was having a time, seemed like. Single mom and all that, not making a lot of money. Besides, apparently Daisy wasn't an easy kid to raise alone down there."

Sure, maybe Daisy was a handful. But Grace didn't seem to be having as difficult a time financially as she wanted people to believe. "You know what they say about something that seems too good to be true," I say.

He frowns. "Yes, well. The house had its fumbles. But people love it now. 'Miracle Mansion,' they call it."

I press my lips into a thin line.

"Thank you so much for talking with us," Jayden cuts in, chipper and ready to save the mood I soured. He knows people. Whether they're angels or assholes, he can make them feel comfortable and understood in a way I never can. Maybe because seeking the truth makes him objective. And how I approach things makes me any-thing but.

Perry meets his eyes. "Well, you know, I feel terrible about how everything went down. Grace just had such a tough go of it. It seems selfish to hold back. And I trust you two to tell things right a lot more than those other guys."

It's nice to see some people still have integrity.

But now I'm wondering how much Grace has.

We end the recording and say goodbye to Perry. Once we're outside, Jayden gets the vlogging camera and hits record as we lean against the building. "Thoughts?"

"Yes." I scowl. "Everyone seems to have a mistaken impression that Grace Odlin was in the struggle living in Toronto when we know she wasn't."

"Look at you, getting in objective facts."

"Shut up."

We checked in about the different marketing jobs she'd had over the years, and while we couldn't find her salary, we knew what the going rate was. When she left Toronto, she should have been making close to $80,000 a year. She was a senior website designer, after all. Her baby daddy, also in marketing and based on his position in Vancouver, was likely making about $120,000. We consulted a family lawyer who guessed that he would have been sending her at least $1,000 a month in child support. She had spent two years at a design college and should have had no problem paying off that student loan fast.

So Grace Odlin would have been doing fine for money. And unless she had a secret drug habit, had more than enough to live in Toronto. And definitely enough to afford more than the tiny bachelor apartments where she and Daisy stayed.

Jayden shrugs. "It's easy for people to believe a Black single mother isn't financially stable."

"She played off that. She wanted people to think they had nothing but scraps." I shake my head and cross my arms.

"Did she? Or did people make assumptions, and she was annoyed enough to not bother correcting them?"

"Daisy didn't think they were well off either."

"And how do you know that?"

I grin at him and pull up notes on my phone, scrolling back through transcripts. "Here! On our call with Megan, when she put us on to interviewing Noah, she said that when she suggested to Daisy that she come to her camp for the summer, Daisy said that it was too expensive."

Jayden rolls his eyes. "That doesn't mean anything. It could be that Daisy didn't want to go and made up an excuse. Or that maybe it was affordable, but she knew Grace wouldn't let her go."

"Urg!" I groan, and flop my head back onto the wall with a thunk.

It's a control thing, plain and simple. Mom could have left money when she took off without telling me, but she didn't. Having access to any kind of cash gives you freedom, just like the conditional type I'm enjoying now. Grace didn't want Daisy to have that. She wanted a daughter who needed to rely on her. Who was desperate to help with her business because she assumed they would be out in the cold if it failed.

I say, "Grace Odlin didn't need the money. She could have easily afforded a nicer apartment in Toronto. Financially, there was no reason for her to come out to Timmins and uproot her and her daughter's lives."

"Maybe she wanted a fresh start. Or just wanted to launch her own business instead of working for ad agencies?"

"Is there anything you agree with me on?" I snap.

Jayden sighs. "I just don't think we have any evidence right now to definitively say why Grace would pretend to have less money than she did. And if you spend this entire case thinking of her as the villain, you're going to have some serious confirmation bias." He reaches over and turns off the camera. "Look, I know you want to tell this story. I do too. But you're also cool with chilling at Torte and doing *Haunted* forever. You know that's not my deal. This is my springboard into the documentary world. I want to be taken seriously. It's why I do the objective bit of this. But it's starting to feel more like I'm just a sidekick here to bitch at you."

I chew on the inside of my cheek and look away from Jayden.

"What's going on with you?" he adds. "You're not usually this biased when it comes to investigations. It doesn't feel like we're playing off each other. It's feeling a lot more like arguing. And we just got some great new info about Dione, and you want to talk about Grace? What is that?"

He's right. Usually, I can play both sides more. Yeah, sometimes I get caught up and he has to play devil's advocate, but never this much. And even I was excited about the Dione stuff, but this Grace shit . . . It hits hard.

I flop onto the ground. "My mom has been calling me."

"Okay . . ." Jayden joins me there, still confused.

Jayden and I only worked together for the last two years, but somehow he knew more about me than people I had known a lot longer. We worked for days on filming and then countless hours editing the footage. We spent more time together than we spent with anyone else. He's not only my best friend—he's my only friend.

But I've never told him the truth about my mom. He thinks we get along, like everyone else believes, but that we're still healing our relationship more than we say publicly. That the house is difficult for me to face because it reminds me of how she used to be before it supposedly reformed her.

Not because I know it's the place that powers her lies.

"And things are . . . all right?" he asks.

"I don't know. I let them go to voicemail." Somehow I still can't make myself tell him. Can't force myself to share this truth with the one person I feel closest to.

I think of Mom standing over me, cigarette ashes falling, and me, hunched over, eyes on the ground. Braced, not against an expectation of physical blows but the mental assault. Preparing to be reminded of why I was nothing. Her saying, "You behave now. And don't go shooting off your mouth. I'm the only one taking care of you, you know? There's nowhere else to go. No one else wants you."

Even now, she's still taking care of me.

"Yeah," I say. "I think it's just throwing me off a little. Because we're looking into the house."

"I'm sorry. I knew this would be hard for you."

I shake my head. "No. You were right. This was the right move."

Our cab arrives shortly after, and we head to our hotel.

This is more than the mystery of Daisy and Grace.

This is more than forgotten Black girls and dead bodies.

This is about the place where my mom's life changed forever on a last-minute getaway she took with a boyfriend ten years ago when Grace first opened the place. It doesn't matter if she actually transformed the way she said she did. She became a different person. But not a better one. Just different.

Her lies aren't only masking *my* pain. They're concealing the pain that's in that house. The things that we need to bring to light. I can't talk about the bits of our relationship behind her shiny new veneer, but I can talk about Daisy and discover what really happened in that house.

I will crack every single bit of this puzzle wide open and expose whatever and whoever's hiding within the pieces.

"Holy shit!" Jayden gasps beside me.

"What?" I ask, leaning toward him.

He shows me his phone, set to our email. Not the Torte one,

but our personal *Haunted* one that we'd set up to run the YouTube channel. The contact said they would prefer to communicate with us there.

At first, I don't realize what I'm looking at. Then I'm grabbing the phone and gaping at the screen.

Our contact hasn't revealed who they are yet. But they've shared something juicy enough to distract from it.

CHAPTER THIRTEEN

DAISY

Everything in the greenhouse was either dead or dying. The arch that marked the entrance to the space was riddled with gnarled branches naked of any blossoms and filled with shriveled green and brown bits. From there, you walked along an outdoor hallway with trellis walls that should have been packed with thriving roses and ivy, but even it was limp and yellowing like walking through a tunnel with a pale sickly glow.

The end of the hallway was marked with glass doors that were pristine. I expected them to be browned and so grimy that it would be impossible to see through, but they were shiny and sparkling. Clearly, the cleaning staff had felt that much was appropriate. Inside, the greenhouse was less than tidy.

Pots lay in various states. Some were upright with dead branches poking out of them. Others were tipped over onto the ground. Even the plants that looked like they were cacti were dead in their potted graves.

The greenhouse itself was about the size of the bunkie. It stretched out in a huge rectangle with high arched ceilings as if it were a church instead of a place where plants came to die.

The lack of hum in the air suggested that the heater Mom said was in here wasn't currently running. Which made sense since it was summer. I had no idea what she was doing for the day while I checked out the greenhouse.

But she had made sure to reiterate that I wasn't allowed in the house without her and should spend my time working in the plant graveyard.

Through the glass windows of the greenhouse, the giant manor loomed in the distance, the same way it did from my bedroom. I found myself checking it before I went out now. Just in case the dead man was there again.

The dead loved abandoned buildings. There hadn't been any in the bunkie, but the way that man latched himself to the house . . . It wasn't like he'd just stumbled upon it. It was like he was stumbling *to* it. I needed to check inside. I needed to see if there were more. If there were corporeals, there was no way I could just live beside the house without doing something. I would need to take care of them.

I refused to let anything or anyone ruin this. Not when I was this close to getting everything I had ever wanted. But how was I supposed to know what I was dealing with if I didn't go in?

Mom thought she was the expert on everything, but she didn't know what I did.

We'd come all the way out here for this house. This beautiful, amazing house where Mom had spent those elusive summers she'd never thought to mention. But I couldn't go in by myself.

'Cause that made sense.

I bit the inside of my cheek.

There was something in there that she didn't want me to see. A secret. Something she wanted to keep hidden like everything else in her life. That was the only reason that tracked.

My phone rang, and "Dad" lit up on-screen. Right. Saturday.

"I'm busy," I said when I picked up.

I answered the same way once when I was out with Megan. She asked why I didn't give him more of a chance.

What did that mean, exactly? That I should act happy because he called me once a week and pretend like it didn't matter that he either lectured me about what he thought I should be doing or talked about himself? That I should be more grateful and act like it didn't matter that he sent gift cards for places I didn't like on Christmas instead of just spending the holidays with me?

I was the kid, so shouldn't *he* be the one trying? Shouldn't *he* be asking *me* questions about *my* life? Shouldn't he have to try to figure out what topics made me happy or upset?

Why wasn't he giving *me* more of a chance?

I wanted to say that to her but couldn't make myself do it.

How much they kept inside and left unsaid was the thing that upset me the most about my parents. But apparently, I wasn't any different.

Dad cleared his throat and said, "What are you busy with?"

It always started out like this. As if there were a real interest in what I was doing. "I'm working on the greenhouse. It's a mess, so I have to clean it up."

I willed him to ask what I was planting. What did I want to do with it? Was I excited to work with a bigger space? How had my plants survived the move?

"Hmm . . . and how is the house? Nothing strange? You're doing okay? Your mom is fine?"

A waste of time, like always.

A knock sounded against the glass panes, rattling me, and I

whipped around. At the entrance to the greenhouse, King stood with a wheelbarrow filled with big bags of soil. He didn't wait for an invitation before giving the doors a nudge open and carting them inside. He mouthed "Sorry" when he realized I was on the phone.

"I have to go," I told Dad, and hung up.

King set down the wheelbarrow with a less-than-gentle clatter. His hair was in its usual style, curls popping and juicy. I forced myself not to touch my own hair, which I knew was dry as hell with the curls matted together. Currently I was hiding that mess under a silk-lined hat that Mom had bought for herself and never ended up using.

"Sorry for interrupting." King gestured to the cart. "Your mom asked me to bring these over for you. Said you might need some help, too."

"I don't."

"Wow, okay." He let out a surprised laugh and shoved his hands into his pockets. They were the same ripped jeans he'd worn yesterday, and his palms were marked with dirt as he tucked them in. "You're just going to do this by yourself?"

"Why are you so desperate to help?" I didn't want to be prickly. Not really. But I didn't have patience for boys my age. They had ulterior motives and were shit at hiding them. Noah was always upfront.

Except when it came to dumping me. I guess he missed the boat on that one.

King rolled his eyes. "I'm not desperate to help. I'm being a nice person. I don't know if you have those in Toronto?"

He was saying "Toronto" wrong. The way he pronounced the *T*s was distinctive—hard and sharp. Everyone who lived there softened it. Made it bend. The whole word became loose and carefree. Like it didn't even matter. Though how you said it *did* matter.

"Were you born here?" I asked.

"Yeah."

It explained a lot. "Was it all right?" I said, curiosity getting the better of me. I couldn't imagine growing up here.

"Like was it all right 'cause it's a small town? Or 'cause I'm a Black man?"

I snorted. "Oh, you're a man?"

"Is this how you make friends?"

"I'm not trying to make friends." I shrugged. "And both, I guess."

He pulled his hands out of his pockets. "It's good, I like it. I like being outside. Fishing and riding Ski-Doos and shit. Also, contrary to popular belief, people in small towns aren't always raging fascists. No one's throwing around the N-word."

What the fuck was a Ski-Doo?

Instead of asking, I muttered, "Good to know."

"There's some ignorance, but that's everywhere." He gestured to my hat. "People will ask about your hair. They just will. You don't usually get touchers, but if you do, just tell them not to. Same old shit, I guess." He looked around the space. "You really don't want help?"

"Send your friend over—she can help."

"Who?" His whole face jerked with the expression.

I wanted to pull the words back into my mouth. Suddenly I felt unsure about the girl I'd seen talking to him. I continued anyway, "There was a girl with you when we came by on Thursday. She went into the forest—"

"—the what?"

"The forest between our houses?"

He laughed. "Oh shit. You mean the bush?"

"Same thing!"

"I mean, yeah, but like, you can't be out here calling it a forest like it's from a Stephen King book."

Was I seriously being made fun of for *not* calling something a bush? Did no one in this place see the connection? "Fine! The bush. The girl had long braids and sunglasses."

All the mirth drained from his expression. "That's Ivy. She lives a lot farther out, but sometimes she hangs around here. I wouldn't mess with her."

"Do I seem like I run around fucking girls up?" My body gave an involuntary tremble as I said it. Like I was daring him. Pushing him. Testing to see if he could read it off me. If somehow he could tell that I had pressed my hands to a tender throat and squeezed as hard as I could.

He shook his head slowly. Treating me like Mom did. Like I was a dangerous, wild thing. "Do what you want. I wouldn't hang out with her is all I'm saying."

Something about the words made my fingers twitch. I knew he was trying to tell me what to do without telling me what to do. It made me think of blue liquid sloshing in a red cup and Noah's voice in my head telling me not to get sloppy.

My lips curled. "Maybe I want to hang out with her. You were. Maybe she'll be my best friend."

"I wasn't hanging out with her. She was bothering me, and I was ignoring her. But like I said, do what you want. I'm trying to save you a headache."

I rolled my eyes, but my shoulders dropped a bit. "I thought we were the only families out here."

"Basically. But if you go farther out and don't mind some rough terrain, you can get into town from here."

"It's not actually boat access only?"

"No. I mean, you can't get through with a regular car. You would need a truck or Jeep." King sank down onto the edge of a flower bed. "You can get through with a four-wheeler, too, if you don't mind being on it for an hour and getting pussy-whipped by tree branches."

I guess that explained why Mom wanted a Jeep. In winter, we probably wouldn't be able to use the boat anymore. "What's a four-wheeler?"

King openly laughed at me. Like my question was the most hilarious thing he had been asked in a while. I was suddenly glad that I hadn't also asked what a Ski-Doo was. Once he'd composed himself, he smiled. Bright and shiny. Like a magazine cover. "You're really like born and bred Toronto, eh?"

"Yeah, well."

"It's like . . . It's hard to describe. Google it."

I would. If only to avoid getting laughed at by anyone else.

"You'll get used to the northern terms and stuff fast at school," he said.

Suddenly I was bored with King. I went to the nearest pot and yanked the dead plant out of the soil. Chucks of dirt rained down on the denim of my overalls, the legs left long but rolled up at the ankles. I was going to need yard waste bags.

For now, I just dropped them on the ground.

King didn't do anything but watch me as I walked silently from pot to pot, tugging out roots and tossing them aside. His eyes were so heavy-lidded that he looked half-asleep sitting there. "I hear you guys are looking to run a business out of the house. Hotel or something? I wouldn't recommend it."

I didn't even bother asking how he found out. "Is this the small-town shakedown? You and your psychic family don't want us setting up something on your turf? You'll probably get more customers."

"That house is dangerous."

I was so tired of people telling me things about this house without any explanation to back up their bullshit. "Is that why you want to do your cleansing thing?"

"It could do you a lot of good to let us do it." He paused and whispered so low I barely caught it, "Probably."

"Probably?"

"If it's not too late. My mom thinks it isn't. It can't hurt."

Even if these people somehow knew about the dead, I highly doubted that their cleansing would be effective. I'd tried so many things over the years to keep them away from me. I couldn't conjure up constant happiness, so Kidz Bop it was, but there was always a point where things went too far. That was when you needed people like me. Or maybe just me, since I had yet to meet any others. What you didn't need was the Okekes and their band of fakes. I was for entertaining their delusion to get rid of them, but Mom never would be.

I stood and walked closer to King. "And if we don't? If we say no, and we run our business, what are you going to do about it?" My heart jack-hammered in my chest. This house, this Airbnb, was my route to escape. The instant that Mom was financially stable, I could leave. I could be done with the shit I had dealt with my entire life.

I moved eight hours away. I let go of Noah. I left Megan—literally my only friend. I gave up *everything* for this.

King didn't say anything, just shook his head and started unloading the hefty bags of soil from the wheelbarrow and making a neat crisscross pile with them off to the side. Maybe he was exasperated with me or maybe he didn't like confrontation.

When he was done, he hiked up the wheelbarrow, muttered "Bye," and left.

I had implied that I wanted him to go, but somehow part of me hadn't expected him to do it.

It was kind of ridiculous but also a revelation that I could make him do something. That he would listen and follow what I said. Even when I hadn't said it explicitly.

Noah was immovable. He wanted people to be open-minded to

his opinions, but he didn't like to change his own. It was the same with directions. If you asked him to do something, he would come back with points about why he shouldn't. Like once when his roommate asked if he could throw the trash in the bin on our way out, there was a lengthy explanation about why it would be better if someone else did it. Or if he did it some other time.

Maybe he was just lazy, yeah. But it never felt like that. It felt like opposition for the sake of it. Seeing how far he could go.

I hadn't thought about it much before now. I just never told him what to do, so I didn't end up having to deal with it.

Almost an hour later, I had a giant pile of gnarled roots like tiny fingers peeking out of the dirt with pale flesh, soft and soggy. I hadn't even managed to clear out half of the pots sitting on their shelves, and there was still everything in the flower beds.

The door creaked open, and I turned around. King stood with a pile of brown yard bags. "Just came back to drop these off." He laid the bags down and turned to leave.

If I wanted to, I could let him. Or I could make him stay.

"Can you help clear out the other side?" I asked. My voice came out like I wanted it to. Smooth. Aloof.

He paused and surveyed the greenhouse, taking in what I had done already and what was yet to be done. "Yeah, sure." He waved his hand at the mess. "You want to get rid of them all? You may be able to salvage some."

"I don't want to salvage any. There are too many flowers. I don't plant flowers."

"What do you plant?"

"Shades of green."

He pressed his thick lips into something like a tight smile, but it had more levity in it than any I had pulled in the last few weeks. "You're the boss."

I *was* the boss.

King pulled out his phone and waved it at me. "Can I put on music?"

"Do what you want."

We worked, gutting the dead plants and shoving them into brown paper bags, while King's music floated out, compact and tinny, from his phone. It sounded like a mix he had made himself. Nothing went with anything. One moment it was thumping rap beats, and the next it was crooning folk music.

Every time I caught sight of the house beyond the greenhouse glass, I wanted to sprint to the doors, tug them open, and run inside. Just to see. We came for this house, and I had never been in it and was never supposed to be. Not unless Mom chaperoned.

I nodded to it over King's shoulder. "You ever been in the house?"

"No. Don't want to."

"'Cause it's dangerous?"

"So you do listen?"

"Is this a psychic thing? You think it's something to be worried about?" I asked, ignoring him. I doubted that he and his family were what they claimed. Reading palms and doing reiki for cash. I didn't know what the real deal looked like, but somehow I didn't think it was them. They were too happy about it. You shouldn't be that full of joy if you dealt with death and beyond. Death wasn't a fun occasion, as far as I had experienced.

King scowled. "Something like that."

I clicked my tongue against the roof of my mouth, where it made a sound that snapped like the branches I broke in two to better shove into the yard waste bag. "What do you do, then, to become a psychic? High school diploma plus a four-year at psychic university?"

He sighed heavily and narrowed his eyes. "When you grow up with a family of psychics, you just kind of do it. Some parents teach their kids to play baseball or do crafts. Mine taught me how to read tarot." He met my eyes. "I know you think it's a joke or whatever. But way back in the day, like literally a hundred years ago, my aunt came for work out here and my family came over with her. It was hard to meet new people. Especially as a Black family. Telling fortunes and stuff was how they integrated into the community."

Great. Now I looked like an asshole. "Sorry," I mumbled. "They came from somewhere in Africa?"

King snorted. "Like way back. But more directly, they came from a settlement in Nova Scotia. My mom and aunties wear traditional things because they think it helps the psychic vibe and makes them feel connected to our culture. Or, assumed culture, anyway." He yanked out a wilted flower by its roots. "Our family didn't want to keep the enslaver name passed down to them, and one of them supposedly thought this was our original tribe or something like that. So Okeke it was. A Nigerian name, apparently, but we could never find out anything more."

He rattled off the information like it wasn't much of anything, but even without a clear resolution, it was still a history. I didn't know anything about our family name or any more details beyond my great-grandma being from Trinidad. Maybe Grandma knew, but I wasn't going to suffer through talking to her. And Mom was never one to share information even if she did know.

I brushed dirt off my overalls. "Does that mean you'll do psychic stuff as a career? Teach your kids when you're older? Family business and all."

"I would rather not."

"Isn't that what your mom wants?"

"Do *you* always do what your mom wants?"

I bit down on my tongue to keep it still. The standard retort would have been to deny it. But the truth was that I couldn't think of a single insistence where I hadn't done something Mom asked. I didn't always do a good job. Actually, most of the time what I managed was subpar. But I did it.

I let the silence swallow any need to respond. The gentle notes of King's music stretched the time between us. It was some sort of instrumental that had been playing for the last five minutes and didn't seem close to stopping. I broke into it. "I don't want to do anything, really."

My answer had been delayed, but King responded without missing a beat, "Except garden."

"Maybe."

He parked his butt on the ledge of one of the flower beds where his phone rested and changed the song to some sort of R&B slow jam.

"Is that what you want to do? Just plant things?" I asked as I sat on the ledge opposite from where he was, thinking about his vegetable garden that his mom seemed irritated about.

He said, "Plants will always do their best to grow. People, not so much. The wasted potential is annoying."

"What makes you think they aren't? Maybe their best efforts are just shit?"

"Maybe. I just don't think most people are like that. They self-sabotage." He shrugged. "Not everyone. But a lot. It's hard not to get along with a plant."

I shook my head. "Plants can be frustrating. They grow or don't when they want. You do your best to take care of them, and half the time it doesn't matter. If you want something from them—herbs to eat, aloe to use for sunburns—they can screw you over."

"Why do you even like taking care of them, then?" he asked, eyebrows pinched together.

"I'm used to it." It was the only answer that made sense. Taking care of plants was something I had always done.

When I was nine, I wanted a dog. I had seen a dachshund running around and begged Mom to get me one. She came home with a monstera and said that if I took care of it, then I could have a dog. I was enchanted by it. The giant shiny leaves with their seemingly rotted edges. I was determined to care for it and get my puppy.

The plant died, of course.

Those delicate leaves wilted and browned. The green was infected by yellow spots.

The deal was off, but I kept trying. I was determined to make it survive. I asked Mom to take me to a nursery and get a replacement. I researched how to take care of it on the internet and made diligent schedules. It wasn't a starter plant. It wasn't easy to care for.

But after months of trying, it still lived. And kept living.

So I kept asking for more.

Never another monstera. That one was special. And I wanted it to be the only one. It had survived. I had helped it do that. It was the rotted thing that I made live, and it never hurt me so long as I cared for it.

Eventually, I had four plants I was watching over, each of them thriving. Mom brought up the dog again.

"But dogs are a lot of hard work," she said. "You might be too busy for the plants. They may die, and that's okay. Things die sometimes."

But it wasn't okay. Not to me. I was invested in the greenery in a way I had never truly been in whatever furry thing I had seen on the street.

So I rejected it.

Maybe I shouldn't have. The dog would have loved me back.

CHAPTER FOURTEEN

King and I managed to clear the entire greenhouse in time for dinner. The space was sparse but clean. A giant room with rows upon rows of raised stone flower beds filled with fresh soil and empty of anything else. These were punctuated by sleek lacquered freestanding wooden shelves where the potted plants would sit. And along the far wall, facing the mansion, were the tables where plants could be snipped, potted, and repotted, with a bunch of shears and tools hanging.

As King and I walked out of the greenhouse and through the rotten trellis and archway, I knew that would be the next project. I reached up and trailed my fingers along the arch. They came away dusted with crumbling brown leaves.

"You're going to pull those down too?" he asked.

"Yeah." I looked at him sideways. "Why? You want to help?" King wasn't bad, but that was the thing about boys my age. There was always this feeling of them trying to weasel their way into your life.

To set up the next meeting, and the next thing, and the next thing. That insidious structure of "get to know you" that was really "try to fuck you."

"Nah." He shoved his hands in his pockets. "My family is doing a séance, and my mom wants me to be there to observe."

Even that sort of casual, *can't hang out with you 'cause I have plans* reply felt like a move. "Cool."

"Cool," he echoed, and gazed out over my shoulder. "Hello again."

I turned around and watched Mom making her way up the steps from the boat launch. Her hands were filled with grocery bags.

"You want any help?" King offered.

Were small-town people really this helpful constantly?

Mom shook her head. "I've got it. Were you two clearing out the greenhouse?" She had this little smile on her face.

I hated it.

"Bye." I waved at King over my shoulder and grabbed the bags from Mom. Without waiting for her, I marched into the bunkie.

The groceries were desperately needed since we'd been surviving off the very limited amount of food we'd brought with us from Toronto, though I didn't even realize that's what she planned to do today. I picked through them. A couple cans of beans, some instant noodles, a few frozen pizzas, a bag of chips. It didn't seem like enough for what would've been an hour-long trip into town.

Mom walked through the door. "Why are you always so rude?"

"Are we college students now? You didn't get fruit or anything?" I wasn't going to turn down pizza pops, but I wouldn't mind the odd vegetable. "Also, shouldn't we be stocking up? So you don't have to keep going into town?"

I could imagine Noah staring down at the offerings that Mom had brought home. He had a lot of thoughts about the things you should put into your body. And how much at any one time. He'd notice the way I would break out if I indulged too much. It was for the best, I'd figured. Him noticing helped me notice.

"I have to keep going into town anyway to get things set up and make contacts." Mom pulled up a stool at the island and ripped open a bag of All Dressed chips. "Besides, in town, I met a woman I used to know from my summers here. Her family owned a farm. Now she runs it. All organic stuff, and they deliver boxes on a monthly basis. We're too far out of the delivery zone, but because we knew each other and this order is larger, she said she would bring the first round. I'll grab future ones when I'm in town. We'll get fresh in-season veggies and fruits. I also got us a half cow and a full goat. Plus milk, of course." She grinned at me. "We'll have lots. Don't worry."

"It sounds expensive." The Airbnb wasn't making cash yet. Why was she spending so much?

"It's good for you and it supports local business. Plus, we got a bit of money in the inheritance deal."

I shoved my hand into the bag and popped a couple of the sweet-and-salty chips into my mouth. "How much?"

"Don't worry about it. Enough to get this Airbnb started. A photographer is coming around tomorrow to take photos of the house so we can get it up online."

I raised my eyebrows and paused with a chip halfway to my lips. "Inside the house."

"Yes."

"They can go inside? Alone? But I—"

"Don't even start," she snapped. "I want to get guests in as soon as next week. Let me know what plants you need, and I'll order them."

"I'll make a list." I flicked my fingers against the counter. "Why are we here?" I looked Mom in the eyes, and she narrowed hers at me.

"You wanted to come here."

"We're really not going to go inside the house?"

"If necessary, we will. And it's not currently necessary." Mom let out an exasperated breath and leaned back on her stool, balancing on the back legs. "I'm not going to have this conversation with you over and over."

"I just don't understand how we're going to run this whole operation like this."

"You don't have to, Daisy!" she cried. Her voice was strained. "I'm the adult. Let me worry about it. All you have to do is manage the garden, go to school, and . . . you know. That's it. Just be a kid."

This was not how this was supposed to go.

There were the plans Mom and I made, and now, apparently, there were alternative plans that she made on her own. Ones where I was less of a helper and more of a bystander. Leaving her the sole responsibility of making this business work.

What should I do now? Make university plans? Ride around on a four-wheeler through the bush? What a fucking joke.

As if she could sense my confusion, Mom sighed. "You'll figure it out." She put her hands on mine. "This isn't like Toronto. I don't need you to support me. I'm going to handle this."

Mom handling things didn't usually go well. She would "handle" the bills, but then work would overwhelm her or she would get too caught up in something else and suddenly we had overdue fees because she had forgotten to pay. Or couldn't. It was hard to tell. She wasn't a good handler. She was more of a worker. If you set her at a task, she would put her head down and do it.

She gripped my hands tighter. "Have some faith in me."

I didn't think faith was something that I had to give.

"Okay," I said. Because most of the time, it was just easier to lie. "So everything leading up to this was useless, then, since you don't seem to need my help?"

"That's not what I said. I said, *as necessary.*" She released my hands and leaned back. "And if I do need you, I expect you to put into practice everything we worked on together. I didn't do all that with you because it's fun. Just . . ."

Don't fuck up? Do as you're told? Instead I said, "Everything is different now."

"No," she countered. "Everything is as planned. Just stop trying to do it all. Just do what *you* need to do."

"Can you clarify that more?" I pressed. Not because I didn't know but because I wanted her to say it.

"Don't play games with me," she snapped. Grabbing a bowl, she dumped nearly half the bag of chips into it and retreated to her room.

I woke up the next morning with the distinct feeling of an itch on my scalp, and when I reached up, something moved under the probing of my fingers. Goose pimples danced over my skin. I should get up. Needed to get up. I had to check. But at the same time, I couldn't, wouldn't, didn't want to.

A knock sounded at my door before it creaked open. "Knock knock," Mom said as if she hadn't literally knocked. Her twists were pulled into a bun on the top of her head, and hoop earrings glinted from her ears. No glasses today. She was wearing a soft burnt-orange T-shirt and dark-wash jean shorts.

Something was on my head.

I wanted to shout and scream it. No, I wanted to shave my head. To part with the small bit of hair that I had left and hopefully shred the maggot in the process.

Mom didn't seem to notice the cogs turning viciously in my head. "I'm going to visit the Okekes. I feel like they were prickly over me not letting them do their cleansing or whatever, so I'm going to smooth things over. I'll be gone for a bit, but if the photographer or the food delivery comes, can you please take care of it? I left the front door to the house unlocked for photos; you just need to point them there. I'm sure I don't have to repeat it, but you will not be going inside, just the photographer. Delivery you can bring straight into the bunkie."

"Sure," I croaked. Too distracted to be annoyed at her for once again harping on me staying out of the house.

She frowned. "What's wrong? You didn't even go to sleep that late."

Now she noticed. "Is there anything on my head?" I whispered.

"Stop it!" she shouted. The sound was too loud in the small space, echoing through the high ceilings. "We are not going to do this again. Get it together. You know what's real and what's not, don't you? Because if you don't, then we can leave right now and skip over you imploding."

My shoulders curled in. "I know what's real," I mumbled.

"Good." She exhaled so heavily that her chest seemed to go concave with it. "There's nothing there. You know that, and I know that. If you keep thinking about it, you'll keep thinking that it's happening. Just forget it."

I didn't say anything in response. She was right, I knew. I saw what I saw, but then it disappeared. I was overthinking it. Letting it get to me.

I lifted myself up and swung my legs off the side of the bed.

Mom was practically vibrating looking at me. She couldn't wait to leave. She didn't like to stand still. She always wanted to be moving. Still on the outside but twitchy on the inside. That was why she jumped through so many jobs, I figured. The idea of idleness must terrify her. And probably she didn't want to be around me when I was like this.

I, on the other hand, liked doing nothing. Being nothing. Wandering through life doing whatever I wanted without any set plan. Wasn't that better anyway?

What was the point in deciding on anything? Until I was free of her, it didn't matter.

And now all that was so up in the air. Plans had changed. I felt like a leaf, torn away and thrown into the wind, tumbling without any destination. Once again, Mom tossed me adrift, and now I would have to figure out how to reach the ground and start over.

"What are your plans for the day?" Mom asked. It sounded innocent but probably wasn't.

All I wanted to do was wash my hair and scrub off any trace of the feeling of maggots wiggling through the strands.

"Gardening?" Mom suggested.

"Sure."

She clicked her tongue. "Do whatever you want to do, Daisy. Just do *something*. Your aunt was like that, you know? Would stay inside all day in that house and wanted me to do the same. It drove me up the wall. I will literally die if I come back here later and you're in the same spot."

For fuck's sake. "Will do."

Mom had gone nearly my entire life barely mentioning Aunt Dione, but now here she was, talking about her. Maybe a side effect of being back at the house where they all used to live.

Her eyes lingered on me for a moment before she came forward and pressed a kiss to the top of my head. I imagined a maggot wiggling free and sneaking between her lips. An infection that only I could pass on.

Mom left, and I forced myself into the bathroom. I washed my hair as thoroughly as possible and applied a ton of deep conditioner. Turning off the shower, I tied a plastic bag on my head and looked up tutorials for styling short curly hair on YouTube. I had to dig through a few of the drawers in the bathroom cabinet to find Mom's stash of products. Most of them were nearly full and some even brand-new.

Eventually, I found a wash-and-go tutorial using the creams and gels that Mom owned. I tore the bag off my head and jumped back into the shower to wash away the deep conditioner. I probed along my scalp for moving bits but of course couldn't find any.

Mom was right. I needed to stop thinking about it.

Once I was out of the shower, I leaned my phone against the point where the bathroom countertop and wall met and followed along with the woman on the small screen. I didn't have any idea what I was doing. It felt like I was just slathering random stuff on my hair in the hopes that it would somehow be decent.

In the end, I was left with curls that looked good but were covered in a white cast of product that the YouTuber assured me would dry clear.

I dressed warmer than Mom had. It was technically summer, but the sweltering heat that was here only days ago had become a chilled sweater-weather temperature. The pullover I grabbed was a forest green and warm enough to make me sweat. Which I preferred. I grabbed a couple of cheese sticks from the fridge and stuck them in my pocket before heading out.

The air was crisp on my hands and ears when I stepped outside. I made my way toward the greenhouse but couldn't help taking a look at the mansion. It was the same as ever. Vast and unyielding.

It was strange to imagine Mom here as a kid. That she would have run up those steps and into that massive house summer after summer. She would eat her meals there, play there, sleep there. Now she wouldn't step foot in it "unless necessary."

A woman pushed through the trees, and I froze. Then the sheen of her skin caught the light. She was dead.

I gripped my hands into fists in my pockets and realized that I didn't have my earbuds on me. It was easier to forget here because, besides this woman and the man, I hadn't seen any other ghosts.

Only she didn't even look at me. She was making a beeline for the house.

I swallowed.

In that moment, it was like the discarded leaf that was me grew a root into the ground.

I rushed forward, heading directly toward her, telling myself to keep going. To not stop.

I could do this.

I *needed* to do this.

If I couldn't go inside the house, then at least I could try and learn something about it through someone determined to enter.

The woman didn't even turn her head as I thrust my hand through her chest, grabbed at where her heart would be, and held firm. Cold lashed at my arm, and every instinct told me to pull away. To run. To never do this again, but I ignored them.

I closed my eyes and tried to sort through the flashing images.

Thomas. He's two today. Child bouncing. Stairs. Flashing lights. Thomas is okay. I'm not. Green leaves. Rustling. Wind. I have to go. It's calling me.

When I opened my eyes, she was staring at me.

I let go of her and stumbled back, trembling, tripping over my feet.

Fuck. Fuck. Fuck.

Then she turned and walked through the wall. Into the house.

Apparently, there was something better inside.

From the corner of my eye, orange flashed. I jerked my head toward it, expecting Mom in her burnt-orange shirt. Instead it was a girl. She was wearing a tank top in the sort of fluorescent shade I had only ever seen on construction workers. Braids draped down her back, and a faint whistle on the wind sounded as she turned and walked into the trees.

Ivy.

Had she seen me?

I knew what I would have looked like. Some girl sticking her hand into the air, then freaking out over nothing. I remembered what those eyes on me looked like. They stared at me from child faces, wide and terrified, while I lay there on top of her body, and she was still.

But Ivy hadn't looked at me like that.

King had recommended avoiding her.

But then again, King could kiss my ass.

He would probably enjoy it too.

CHAPTER FIFTEEN

The ground was wet, but the leaves on top of it were dry. They crunched underfoot before giving way to mud that squished against the soles of my shoes. At least I'd worn black ones today. The trees surrounding me were a mix of the pines I'd seen before and another tree I was less used to seeing, with bark that was peeling off in neat sheets. The predatory clicking was still in the air. Mom had solved the mystery by letting me know that it was probably spruce bugs—giant insects about the size of a bottlecap with antennae twice as long as its body, whose bites were, apparently, excruciating. Unsurprisingly, knowing what was making the sound hadn't made me feel any better.

Overhead, it looked darker than it was because of how the branches reaching to the sky overlapped each other. The dampness in the leaves picked up into the air and made scents feel moist. I walked faster and kept my head swiveling, looking for that pop of orange.

There were chirps in the trees. When I stared up, packs of birds sat there. They were little things, the sort you could cup in your hand. White-breasted with a gray head and a patch of black over its eyes like a raccoon. All of them circled around each other, chirping like I was in a Disney movie.

"They're butcherbirds." The voice was so close that it felt like she was whispering into my ear. The heat of her breath warmed the back of my neck and smelled as damp as the forest. Or bush, as King and everyone else around here would say.

I forced myself to turn slowly. When I rotated my head the appropriate amount, I let my body follow at a leisurely pace.

Though her voice had sounded like she was right behind me, Ivy was several feet away. She stood with her hands loose at her sides, dangling and aloft like her namesake. Her sunglasses were huge with frames the same fluorescent orange as her jacket. She flipped her braids over one shoulder.

"Butcherbirds?" I repeated.

She smiled. It made her lips look wider than they originally seemed. Comical almost. I couldn't tell if she was pretty or not. "They're carnivorous." She held out her hand, and I half-expected one to perch on her finger. But none did. Instead, I followed her gaze to the group of birds gathered.

"What do they eat?"

"Lizards, bugs, frogs, even other birds—small ones usually." She lowered her arm. "Their talons are quite weak."

"That's why they only attack weak prey?"

Ivy's smile got wider. "No. Sometimes they can hunt birds bigger than they are. They just don't rely on their talons." She laced her fingers together, tight, as if in prayer. "They strike as fast as possible. Precisely. At the neck or head. Then they shake their prey until it dies. Afterward, they impale them on thorns. Food storage." Her expression evened out to something more neutral. "Shrikes make the most of what they have."

Unbidden, a vision came to me of the maggot from my hair. Of it undulating, impaled, on a thorn in the bush, and a butcherbird pecking away at it as it twitched. Bit after bit of doughy white flesh disappearing into that small black beak.

I swallowed.

Ivy noticed, and her gaze locked on my throat. "You should wear orange in the bush. People hunt here. You don't want to get shot by accident."

"I don't have anything that orange."

She barked out a laugh. It was too loud and abrupt. "It is fucking ugly, isn't it? I don't blame you."

"It just wasn't a thing I needed," I said with a shrug.

She smiled again, wide, too wide. Everything she did was too much of something. "No, I bet you didn't. Not a big thing in Toronto. But it's a big deal here. People love a good hunt."

"How do you know I'm from Toronto?"

"Look at yourself." Her voice was level, but there was something sharp in it. "Do you like it here?"

"It's all right."

Ivy walked forward until she was standing beside me, shoulder to shoulder. I had to turn to the side to meet her eyes. It was a strange way to talk to someone. Up close like this, I could see the color through the darkness of her sunglasses. Warm brown.

She tugged the orange hat off her head and pulled it onto mine. "There. Now you won't get murdered. Not by accident, anyway." I expected her to smile, but she didn't.

Ivy was strange. Maybe this was what King meant. He didn't seem like the sort of guy who would enjoy talking to her. I guess that he liked people who were straightforward and easy to understand. That wasn't her.

And I wasn't him.

I liked complicated. I enjoyed different. Noah would say, "We hate boring." People who were like everyone else were never going to change the world. That was what he thought. I never wanted to change the world, but I agreed. I didn't care about people who wanted to talk about the mundane. *What are your hobbies? What university are you going to apply to? What do you want to be when you grow up?*

Ivy seemed like the sort of girl who would have gone inside the house.

I pointed back toward it. "We inherited that mansion back there. Have you ever been inside?"

"No," she said, and licked her lips. "But I want to. I'm sure you've explored every inch by now."

My chest tightened. "Not quite."

"Do you want to?"

"Yes." There was no hesitation. I did. I wanted to go inside. I couldn't leave the dead to themselves. That was a bridge that would burn me if I let it go unattended. Even a single corporeal could destroy everything, and it would be my fault.

Beyond that, I couldn't pretend that I wasn't curious. About this property, this house, and what Mom had kept secret for years. It all came back to the mansion. If I could go inside, maybe I would finally understand why Mom was the sort of person she was. And I couldn't know any of that if I didn't go in.

"King said it was dangerous." I didn't know why I said it. Maybe I wanted her to know that I wasn't going to listen to him. "He doesn't seem to be your biggest fan either."

She shrugged. "Sometimes the feeling is mutual."

"Is that why you left like that the other day? When me and my mom came to say hi, you walked off."

Ivy stared at me for a few seconds, like she was thinking of how much she wanted to let me in on whatever private drama her and our neighbor had going. "I was kind of trying not to be noticed at that moment. King's family doesn't like me much either . . . but I guess I failed at keeping a low profile."

It was hard to think of Ivy, with her bright shades, ever successfully going unnoticed.

Rationally, it made no sense to go into the house with this girl I barely knew.

But somehow it felt right.

Maybe because I was intimately familiar with the experience of being the girl no one liked.

This one time, I couldn't listen to Mom.

"Should we go?" I asked.

Ivy grinned. It was then that I thought, yes, she is pretty. "Let's." She held out her hand to me.

It was a pact. Agreeing to this thing that both of us wanted to do but felt sure that we shouldn't.

I hadn't come this far up north to do nothing.

I reached out my hand and shook hers.

CHAPTER SIXTEEN

We decided to enter the house through the front door. Maybe there was a sneakier way to do it, but I didn't want to waste time, and Mom had already left it unlocked for when the photographer came. The wood finish of the door was smooth underneath my fingers. There was a small balcony over the top of the entrance, which meant standing in shadow when we were in front of the door.

I pushed the door open, and we slipped inside. As I pressed it shut behind us, I struggled not to get lost in the scene of it. Saying that Uncle Peter had money didn't quite capture what I was seeing.

He was really fucking rich.

The entryway was enormous and full of daylight from the many windows whose curtains were thin enough to let light in. Two grand staircases embraced the space, one from the left and the other from the right, both meeting in the middle for a moment and then veering off to their respective sides. It was the sort of setup where you would expect a couple to come out, each from their own wing, and meet in the middle for photos. Not prom ones either. Something better. Dignitary photo shoots or something. The banisters were casted with gold and decorated with gleaming metal filigree designs, the vines of a plant twirling with gold leaves. The steps themselves were enrobed in a lush midnight-blue running carpet that matched the accents in the shiny flooring. Everything was centered around a crystal chandelier that must have cost as much as a full university education.

But none of this was what first caught my attention.

I forced down the shiver that pushed its way inside me. Vomit clung to the back of my throat.

The dead were everywhere.

I'd expected three, maybe four, of them. With the possibility of one troublemaker. But this . . . Already I counted ten. Translucent bodies dragged their feet as they passed through the walls and slunk down the stairs. One woman lay draped over a chaise, staring up at the chandelier without pause. None of them even looked at us. Which was the most unsettling part.

I stepped back and knocked into Ivy. I turned around to apologize and stopped at her expression. She was beaming unrestrained. The person she'd been in the bush had melted away. She'd seemed older then. Now she looked like a child. Her cheeks strained from the force of the grin on her face. Still too wide but not weird anymore. Outside, Ivy had looked my age, but now that struck me as so wrong that I felt kind of ridiculous for even thinking it.

"How old are you?" I asked.

The smile dimmed but didn't disappear. "Fifteen." She entwined her fingers in mine and pulled me forward. "Come on, let's go upstairs. That's where the best stuff is."

"How do you know that?"

She faltered for a moment, her grip on my fingers going slack before firming. "I don't. But bedrooms just tend to be juicy and personal, don't you think?" She looked at me over her shoulder as we climbed the stairs. "You don't hide your secrets in the kitchen."

Probably I should have tried to read one of the dead already inside. I hadn't gotten much from the woman except that she seemed to be drawn to the house somehow. But I couldn't do it in front of Ivy. And if I were being honest, I wasn't exactly itching to do it again.

Ivy walked through a dead man crouched on the steps, and I fought not to flinch. But of course, she was completely unaffected by the experience. I was the only one trying to casually dodge them. It was an art in and of itself. If I avoided them too obviously, she would notice. But walking through them made me so cold that I would shiver for at least fifteen minutes, and that was a hard no. I was still cold from what I'd done to that dead woman earlier.

I watched Ivy's back as she moved. I understood why *I* was looking for secrets. Why *I* wanted to understand what sort of history my mom had here with family I had never met. But I didn't quite understand what secrets would be here for Ivy.

Suspicion crawled up my throat. It made me think of the maggot, inching its way up my esophagus and crowning at my teeth. Ivy was the bird. The delicate shrike, waiting for it. Or waiting for me, tangled up in thorns.

I physically clamped my teeth together to shut out the image.

No.

I needed to stop.

I had been wrong before. So, so wrong. The soft grass of the playground under my knees while I squeezed at her throat. The other kids screaming at us.

Fight! Fight! Fight!

And my own voice so loud in my ears that I thought blood might gush from them. Screaming in her face as it turned violet.

Spit foaming in my mouth and slapping against her cheeks.

"You're not real! You're not real! You're not real!"

The way their faces changed when she stopped moving.

"You coming?" Ivy stopped to look back at me.

I hadn't even realized that I wasn't walking anymore. "Yeah."

We made our way up the right-hand side of the staircase. The hallways were bright, lit by smaller versions of the grand chandelier, with huge mirrors between the doors that made the space appear larger than it was.

The first turn we came to wasn't a closed door but an open archway. I turned into it and was met with a sunroom. Every wall was made of glass including the ceiling. Stepping into the space brought a chill to the back of my neck.

There were a dozen or so ghosts populating the space. It was like all the ones that should have been milling around outside had squished themselves into the house. It was one thing for the dead to gather. But to specifically focus their attention on one spot, in these sorts of numbers . . . It flew in the face of everything I knew about them.

What was it that was drawing them here? The house itself? Or something inside it?

"Boring," Ivy droned from behind me. She stood in the doorway with her head resting on the opening. "Let's go somewhere with a closed door." She disappeared around the corner, the sharp footfalls from her boots echoing.

I pressed my fingers to the cool glass and peered out. From here, I could see the lake through the trees. It was still and quiet. Our property was much farther out from the run of cottagers around us. If I were in a room at the back of the house instead of the side, maybe I would even be able to see the chimney of the Okekes' log cabin.

As I stared into the glass, a reflection shone in it.

I flung my body around and jerked away from the man lingering behind me. My heart struck my chest with measured blows, and I forced my breathing to regulate.

This was why I fucking hated ghosts.

I shook myself and entered the first room with a closed door. It was an ordinary sort of bedroom—or as ordinary as a rich-person bedroom can be, anyway. It had a giant bed in the middle of the room with one of those cushioned benches right in front of it. A huge window rested off to the side with midnight-blue curtains that matched the accent sheets on the bed. The other side of the curtains must have been white, since that was what was visible from outside the house. There was a private bathroom in the corner featuring both a bathtub and shower. And a vanity was pushed against a wall with a small, cushioned stool behind it.

No wonder Mom planned to run a hotel out of here. If every single room in this place had giant bedrooms this fancy, it would make a killing. I wandered over to the vanity, and only then did I remember the ridiculous hat on my head. Tugging off the orange beanie, I stuck it in my jeans pocket and examined my hair.

The beauty guru hadn't lied. The white cast from the product had gone and left in its wake curls with a juiciness that could rival King's hair, though they were somewhat smushed from the hat. I twirled a piece around my finger and let it spring back into place.

Not that long ago, my hair used to be just under my shoulders. It took no effort to imagine Noah sliding his fingers through the strands.

Noah. My phone lay in my pocket, still social-media dead.

I couldn't check even if I wanted to.

But that didn't stop me from wondering.

Was he thinking about me? Did he miss having me around?

Or was he preoccupied with Stephanie?

Maybe she liked it when he pressed his fingers to her throat.

Maybe it excited her the way it should have for me. Maybe Noah didn't have to sigh and grab lube halfway through and look into her eyes and say with a laugh, "I've literally never had to use this before," like it was funny. But it didn't seem like it was supposed to be.

A flicker in my hair broke me out of my thoughts. I pressed myself closer to the mirror. The vanity dug into my stomach, but I pushed anyway. I moved my curls aside, and there it was.

Out of a tiny hole in my head, a tip of white was wriggling.

I pulled my eyes away and searched on the vanity table. In the corner was a small nail kit with a pair of tweezers. I lifted them into my hand and raised my eyes back to the glass.

I half expected it to be gone. But it was still there, undulating in the hole. I reached up and used the tweezers to grasp it. Immediately it tugged, as if it wanted to recede back into my scalp, but I wasn't going to let it. I pulled upward and slowly began to drag the body out.

A quarter of an inch. Half an inch. An inch and a half.

The body wasn't ending. I had never seen a worm this long. It kept stretching, and my eyes watered from the sting of yanking it from my body. It was like it was wrapped around something vital, and each pull made it curl tighter.

The white of its body was wriggling, and my stomach churned, and saliva gathered in my mouth.

"Fuck, fuck, fuck," I cried, spit flying from between my lips as my arm stretched almost a foot away from my head, still tugging until finally it pulled free. I screamed and tossed it away from my body along with the tweezers. It flopped onto the ground and shrunk in on itself, squirming pale white on the blue accented floor.

I kept touching my head, worried about more coming out.

The maggot paused. No undulating. No wriggling. Still.

Then it moved.

It seemed to home in on where I was and went straight for me. I imagined it crawling across my body, wet and slimy, trying to make its way back into my head. I screamed and scrambled backward. I hit a wall, and it kept moving toward me. It touched the toe of my shoe, and my mind went blank.

I smashed my foot against its body, and a cry vibrated in my brain and made my vision tunnel. I was a one-girl marching band. Stomping and stomping on its pale body. And it was bleeding. Was it my blood? Or its blood?

I didn't know, but the more I crushed it with my foot, the more blood spurted from it, and the more the screams pressed against my skull until there was only the screaming and stomping, and a pale maggot becoming flatter and flatter.

"What are you doing?"

I froze.

Ivy had her hand on the door and was regarding me with her eyebrows pressed down, and her sunglasses perched on her head.

The maggot was dead. My black tennis shoes felt soaked even if I couldn't see the red of blood through the canvas. My chest was heaving. "It—it was in my head."

"Gross."

"I—" I stared at her and wiped spit from my mouth. "It came from my head." I couldn't stop saying it. Because she could see it. It was real. This was *real*.

Ivy retrieved a towel from the bathroom and cleaned up my mess on the floor. She bundled the whole thing together and shoved it into a wicker basket that I thought was decoration, but upon closer inspection, I saw it was lined with a clear plastic bag. A garbage.

She shrugged. "Cleaning people probably won't ask questions about it."

"You've been here before." It felt right coming out of my mouth.

Ivy walked through the house with a familiarity that I didn't think was just her being comfortable with breaking rules.

She grinned. Too wide. "A few times."

"Why did you tell me you hadn't?"

She sighed. "If I told you, then you would have just asked me a bunch of questions about it. I wanted someone to come with me."

"You could have just asked me to come with you." Sweat ran down the back of my neck. My breathing was hitched and rough.

"What would have been in it for you? Why just come hang out with me? You don't even know me."

"Isn't that what we're doing now?" I threw my hands out. "Hanging out."

"You wanted to know what it was like. You didn't come to me because you wanted to hang out. You came to me to see if you could avoid it. Or better, maybe you could get me to come find what you wanted." Her face was grinning, but her tone and words didn't match up. "When I said I had never been, that plan went out the window. It made sense at that point to come together. Strength in numbers and all that."

I let out a shaky laugh. "Why would I need 'strength in numbers' to walk into a house? It's just a bunch of wood and bricks."

"Then why are you afraid?"

I swallowed back the immediate retort to deny. Goose pimples rose on my skin from the sweat cooling on my neck. I wiped it away hastily. King had said the house was dangerous. It was seeming like Ivy knew that too.

When I came in here, it was because I thought the dead were the issue. The threat. The thing that I needed to make sure wouldn't mess up Mom's operation. But it was more than that. It was this house. Something about it was wrong. And it was drawing the dead inside it for some reason.

Ivy's smile dropped from her face. "I let the photographer in, by the way. We should go."

"Is there a back way out?"

"Follow me."

I trailed Ivy out of the room. We left the house via a smaller staircase at the back of a hallway that led into another, more cramped hallway. "This is the servant entrance." She grinned back at me. "Not slaves, though, isn't that nice?"

"It's something," I muttered.

Ivy paused with her hand on the door. "Hey," she said suddenly. "What's your name?"

"Daisy." The word was out of my mouth before I had a chance to wonder if I should have said it. Probably she would have found out anyway. Small town and all that.

"Pretty," she murmured before pushing the door open. It clicked shut behind us.

Chirps in the air drew my gaze up where a handful of shrikes were sitting in the trees.

Ivy stretched out with a big yawn as if we had been on a leisurely stroll. Like I hadn't just been screaming and stomping on a massive maggot that bled crimson. "I'm going to go home," she declared.

"Cool." I didn't know what else to say.

She disappeared into the trees, and I kept standing there.

Shaking. Listening to the butcherbirds call to one another.

CHAPTER SEVENTEEN

Somehow I managed to shuffle from the back of the house where Ivy left me to the front. Grass compressed underfoot until the ground gave way to the gravel that was our path. I didn't look back as I headed for the bunkie. My body was empty. Light and used. Almost as if the worm had added a vital weight, and now that it was gone, I was a listless husk.

A white couple walked up the driveway toward me. The woman looked like an Instagram model for a tattoo shop. She was all soft pale curves and ink. Blond hair cropped short around her round face, and everywhere that her black skull-decorated sundress didn't touch was marked—bright pink blossoms, dark gray stormy skies, mermaids with bejeweled tails, and more. The man with her was half her size and not nearly as impressive. He was out of place next to her glam. He wore a plain T-shirt and jeans and had a short ginger beard. These must be the farm people who Mom knew and met in town.

I glanced down at my sweater. It was like we were living in two different seasons.

The woman smiled as she made her way over with a crate. The man was carrying one too, along with a rope that held a goat at the end of it. A literal live goat. It bleated as he tugged it behind him.

"Hey there," the woman said. Her voice was higher than expected, and friendly. "You must be Daisy. I'm Helga. This is Joe."

She couldn't have looked less like a Helga, and he couldn't have looked more like a Joe. "That's me," I said. My voice sounded harsh and strained. Like I was a fifty-year-old smoker instead of a shaken seventeen-year-old.

Joe nodded at me and jerked his head at the mansion. "Food going in there?"

"No." The word snapped out of my mouth, sharp, slicing. Joe blinked. "It's just—it goes in the bunkie. There's a photographer in the house right now."

"Ah." He pivoted to the smaller home. "Fine if I drop it inside?"

"Yes, please," I mumbled.

Joe and Helga exchanged loads—her grabbing the goat's lead while he took the crate from her and headed to the bunkie.

Helga tilted her head and examined me. "You all right, hon?"

I could have burst into tears. I wanted to throw myself at this woman's feet and blubber about what had happened. Nothing would have made me happier than to cling to her dress and cry into the skull pattern. "I'm fine. Thanks."

She gave me a slow nod. I stood in place saying nothing because I honestly had no idea what else to do with myself.

Joe came back out and pointed to the goat. "Where do you want her?"

"What?"

"The goat. Where should I tie her up?"

I stared at the animal with its beady eyes. Goat. Mom said that she'd gotten a full goat. Here I was thinking she had suddenly developed an interest in making curried Trinidadian dishes, and instead there was a live one.

"I honestly . . . don't know." I kicked at the gravel on the ground.

"All right." He looked around the property and spotted the greenhouse. "How about I just put her in there for now?"

"Sounds good."

Joe took the lead from Helga and took off with a goat that was, apparently, now our property.

Helga's smile dimmed as she followed Joe with her eyes. She forced the smile back as she turned to me. "The goat, that's just for the milk, eh?"

I didn't know, but I doubted Mom would be slaughtering it for meat. "Yeah."

Her lips were twitching, trying to keep the smile going. "Right. Of course." She looked around the property. "Is your mom here?"

"She went to see the Okekes."

"Aha. I'll catch her another time, then." Helga pivoted to leave, and I had to stop myself from tugging her back.

I stepped toward her. "You knew her when you were younger?"

Helga turned back, her smile more natural now that we weren't having an awkward conversation about the goat. "I did. We used to hang out in the summers. Your dad, too." She pointed across the lake to the bank on the other side. "We had a cottage right over there. Just beyond the tree line."

She knew a version of Mom that I never had. It seemed strange, that Mom had lived a whole life before I came along, with friends and experiences that I knew nothing about. Meanwhile, that was the only part of Dad that he seemed to like talking about. But even his version was sanitized. It never mentioned Mom. "What was she like back then?"

Helga tilted her head to the side. "Hmm, quiet at first when you met her. But then she would open right up. I always felt like she took a lot of care in choosing her friends." She grinned. "It made me feel special to be picked. I think she hated most people."

I couldn't imagine Mom, who seemed to hold a spare smile in her pocket for everyone, hating most people. She was a generally friendly person and extended the same amount of friendliness to everyone. A small portion: packaged, pretty, and pleasant. Hate was so intimate. You had to know people properly. To care about them. And I struggled to imagine Mom extending that much of herself.

I didn't have that problem.

Joe came around the corner. "Goat is secured. I put some feed inside for her too."

"Thank you," I said.

Helga doubled back to press a hand against my shoulder. "Give your mom my best."

"I will."

As soon as they left down the path to the boat launch, I made my way to the greenhouse. The goat stood there in the center looking as lost as I was.

A goat.

She really got a live fucking goat.

My fingers twitched. I reached into my jeans pocket and pulled Ivy's hat onto my head. The thing was probably going to ruin my curls.

I had gone from wanting nothing more than to collapse onto my bed to vibrating with energy in one go. The mansion sat innocently beside me. The photographer was inside there, snapping photos, maybe even of the room where only a few minutes ago I was smashing a maggot to death.

I needed to see King.

Mom didn't want that cleansing, and I didn't think it would work anyway, but he knew something more about the house than I did. He might talk. Mom wasn't going to give me any details. She wanted to avoid it. She was running around making plans and buying goats.

I peered into the forest with its shedding pine trees and shrikes.

Then I made my way toward it.

Now that I had seen the butcherbirds, I couldn't unsee them. They filled the trees with their small gray, black, and white bodies. I picked my way through the bush, hopefully in the right direction. None of the trees or foliage seemed particularly familiar, but there was only one path, as far as I could tell, so it stood to reason that if I continued on it, I would eventually get to where I wanted to be. My shoes were still bloody. I could feel it even if I couldn't see it through the black canvas.

The spruce-bug sound was gone. Now it was more of a deep hum like cicadas. I didn't know if there were actually any in this area or if it was something else. Meanwhile, the dampness of the leaves threw the same scent into the air. Wet earth.

I tucked my hands into my pockets and kicked at the mud.

Megan would probably love this. Right now, she was running around in nature at camp. Not even upset about the complete lack of data service out there. Playing some sort of game with the kids or lounging on the sidelines with the other counselors. When she tried to get me to come along, part of her selling point was all the hot guys she worked with. It was times like that when I wasn't sure she actually understood the sort of person I was. Or maybe she did. She acted like she liked Noah, but sometimes I got this feeling that she might secretly hate him.

Not to mention, how would I even get a job as a counselor without any experience? That made her bring up the "youth" section of the camp, where ages went up to seventeen. Because that was what I wanted. To be a camper while my friend was a counselor. Not to mention the cool $1,000 a week the camp charged to attend.

Sometimes, I thought Megan forgot that only one of us was rich. Or maybe she was just that optimistic.

Noah once said that he didn't even speak to his high school friends. That his real friends were at university. I'd wondered if, when he was done with school and a full-time adult, he would be saying he didn't even speak to his university friends and that his real friends were at work. Though I never said it to his face.

He, like Megan to him, seemed to secretly hate her. It was a dynamic that I didn't understand, so I kept them away from each other.

It didn't matter now, anyway.

Mom was too singularly focused for friends. But I guess she hadn't always been that way.

A branch snapped behind me, and I turned. Nothing. No Ivy popping out. No King or Mom. Not even any dead. Just trees and the path winding behind me. I tugged my hat more firmly on my head. Hunters maybe.

I needed more orange things to wear. I didn't exactly like the idea of being shot. In Toronto, I didn't even know someone with a friend of a friend who owned a gun. It wasn't a thing.

I knew people hunted out in the country or in places like this, but it was one thing to abstractly know that something happened and another to hear a gunshot ring out beside you. I continued down the path and tried to avoid imagining being shot.

When the sound of a thicker branch breaking came again, I stopped without turning.

No other sounds came. Nothing but the chirping of shrikes in the trees. The dampness in the air seemed to get heavier. Like someone had slapped a wet towel against my face. I struggled to breathe through it.

It was three more steps forward before another crack came.

I bit down on my lip, and my fingers twitched.

I listened, waiting for another crack, but it was silent. "Very funny, Ivy," I shouted, just in case it was her. "Real cute." My teeth clenched and unclenched.

Without thinking, I stepped backward off the path into bushes.

It took only a second for me to realize there wasn't anything under my shoe.

A sharp cry flew from my mouth as I tumbled head over foot. Branches and rocks scraped against my body and face as I rolled down the sharp hill. I reached my hands out to try and grab hold of something but failed to do anything more than scrape my fingers and palms.

I fell farther and farther down until I hit something that made me scream. And only then did everything come to a stop. My chest was heaving from my harsh breathing. My whole body throbbed like a giant wound, and my eyes were squeezed shut.

I forced myself to open them.

Thorns.

I was surrounded by dry vines armed with short spikes. My back stung from having landed in the thorns, and I suspected the similar stinging on my face was from the same culprit. I had rolled into what seemed like the middle of the bush. My earth and sky were thorns.

To my right was the hole where I'd broken through, all the way up to the trees pressed so close together that there was no way I could tell there was a drop without knowing the area. Which I didn't.

I needed to move.

But the pain forced me to be still.

A chirp sounded next to my head. I turned and came face-to-face with a butcherbird. It stared at me with its black, beady eyes. Another chirp rung out to my right. In the space where I'd crashed through, another shrike was there, hopping forward until it was almost resting on my palm.

A bead of sweat slid down the back of my neck.

The shrike near my hand moved closer to my finger.

My breathing quickened.

The bird, so swift I barely saw it, leaned down and pecked at the underside of my pinkie. The beak immediately drew blood, and I yanked my hand back. I swore that the bird looked pissed about it too.

A sharp pain bloomed on my temple, and I whipped my head around to where the other shrike sat. Crimson shone on its beak.

I tried to inch away from them, but all it did was scrape my body against the thorns. The shrike by my hand chirped louder and faster. It took only moments for more shrikes to pool in through the hole I'd come through.

My chest heaved. Oxygen seemed impossible to get. I kept breathing and breathing, but nothing was coming in.

There were at least fifteen shrikes waiting at the mouth of the thornbush.

Butcherbirds gathering around their prey.

The one by my finger chirped once.

It was the only warning I got before they descended.

A scream ripped from my throat. And it kept going on and on. I jerked and writhed as what felt like dozens of beaks snapped at my fingers and face, and the more I tried to throw them off me, the more I scraped myself on the thorns.

Everything was stinging slices and agony.

And suddenly I was freezing. Teeth chattering even as I sweat from fear.

Then the dragging started.

Something yanked on the collar of my sweater and started to pull me back. I screamed more and started grasping at the thorns with my fingers. Trying to get purchase wherever I could and kicking my legs out to stop it. My hands were so covered in blood from my efforts that the vines were slipping from my grasp.

"Daisy! Stop!"

I could hardly hear my name over my own screaming and fighting.

Despite my best efforts, they managed to drag me out of the thornbush, and only once I was out did I realize who was doing the dragging.

"Mom?!" I sobbed.

She was panting heavily on the ground next to me. I threw myself at her, burying my bloody face in her chest and crying so hard that I was shaking. Words were coming from my mouth, but I didn't know what they were. Couldn't decipher them.

I could only feel the soft cotton of my mom's shirt as my tears and blood soaked through it.

When I chanced a look up into her face, she was staring back at me, pale, trembling lips, and sweat beading on her forehead.

She was just as afraid as I was.

CHAPTER EIGHTEEN

BRITTNEY

The thing about farms is that they smell like shit. That's hyperbole. More specifically, every farm with *animals* smells like crap. It's just the way of the world. You have a bunch of living things wandering around and using your entire property as a combination eating-and-shitting playground. If that playground was the sort that gave you a few good years before you're murdered and eaten.

I'm not preaching. I eat and love meat. But fuck, it stinks.

The cab pulls up the gravel driveway past a sign that declares SOUTH PORCUPINE FARMS in hand-painted acrylic, smoothed over with a thin shine of varnish. The car windows are open to the rancid smell because it's shockingly hot for a northern town, and apparently, the cab's AC is acting up.

I'm tempted to fiddle with my phone again, to look at the contact's message. Jayden and I spent all night poring over it. Wondering how we could confirm what we were being told and if we could trust them.

Grace and Dione are hiding something. They have been for years. If you want to know the truth, you'll need to push harder on them and their past. Without them, you'll never understand the full scope of why she's dead.

That message is why we're at this farm. Why we have a brand-new list of questions. And why our interview will likely be twice as long as originally expected.

I step out and stretch my arms above my head while Jayden works on pulling out the equipment from the trunk, the navy blue color he worked into his curls shining in the sunlight. In front of us is the Bouchards' house. Honestly, it's beautiful. One of those perfect two-story family homes with a porch out front, windows with bright red shutters that match the color of the door, charcoal paneling over the whole thing, and even a little welcome mat.

The farm itself is behind the main home. There's a huge barn with the same charcoal paneling and red accents as the house and large fenced-in pens where horses, pigs, cows, and goats, of all things, roam. Each in their own separated area. Even the chicken coop has the same colors. Someone loves a theme.

The front door of the house opens, and three kids flood out from behind a woman. They've got heads of shiny white-blond hair, which should make them look like creepy children-of-the-corn kids, but they've got friendly smiles on. The woman beams at us. The kids must have gotten it from their mom. She has periwinkle-colored hair with blond roots coming through the top. Her arms and legs are covered in more tattoos than I would expect of someone who so meticulously color-coded their property.

Colorful, friendly, and fat. I love her already.

"Brittney and Jayden?" she calls out.

I smile. "That's us. Helga?"

"That's me!"

Jayden starts rolling, though we haven't signed forms yet. He can't resist an establishing shot.

Helga steps aside for us to walk in, and when I glance down at the welcome mat, underneath "Welcome" in print so fine it makes sense that I couldn't see it from over by the car, it says ". . . to your worst nightmare."

It's definitely mom-chic.

We walk into a mudroom littered with children's jackets, sneakers, bikes, and other outdoor toys. Jayden and I kick off our shoes and follow her into a combination living and dining room plus kitchen.

The couches are giant leather monsters that you get at places like Bad Boy and the Brick with seven seats and individual cup holders. The TV is so massive it nearly takes up the whole back wall. The kitchen in comparison has sleek high-end finishes. I've seen those exact drawer pulls in a furniture shop in Toronto for sixteen dollars apiece.

"What can I grab you? Tea? Coffee? We have a Keurig, too." Helga is already pulling mugs out of the cupboards.

"I would love an Earl Grey latte if you can make it," Jayden says.

"How do I make that?"

"Steamed foamy milk added to Earl Grey tea." Jayden takes out the tripod and looks around. "Should we set this up in the dining room?"

"Absolutely, go ahead." She points a mug at me. "For you?"

"Tea is great. Just black. Anything fruity is nice."

Helga beams again and sets at it.

I hate this idea that fat people should be jolly. That somehow we owe the world smiles even when just walking around in our skin makes people judge us. Everyone else is encouraged to love themselves, but we do it and suddenly we're promoting obesity. To force the idea that you should be the happiest motherfucker in the room at all times despite it is bullshit.

But Helga isn't like that. She's not "jolly" for the world. She honestly just seems happy.

"Have you lived here long?" I ask her, leaning against the breakfast bar separating the beautiful kitchen from the living room monstrosities.

Helga pulls out a full box of tea and sorts through the options. "My whole life. This used to be my parents' farm. My dad got sick when he was only about forty—I was twenty then. It was hard for him to do the farm alone, and it was their only income, so I came back from school."

"That must have been hard. Only one year left, I would guess?"

"Yeah. I was sad about it, of course, but family comes first, and it worked out in the end. I basically took over, started implementing some greener, more ethical practices. Met Joe on a dating app, and he had just gotten laid off from the mines, so he started helping out too." She picks up two steaming mugs and heads over to the dining room table, where Jayden has finished the camera and lighting setup.

I follow behind her, and Jayden and I take another few minutes to get everyone mic'd up. After, he slides over the release form. Helga takes a quick look at it and signs. "My dad ended up making an amazing recovery in the end. He's sixty-three now. But my parents still retired when they were forty-five because we had everything under control. They gave us the house and shipped off to Florida. We renovated the entire property. They're in town now, actually. They just stepped out for a bit. Come back every summer to see the kids that they're still upset I didn't have sooner."

I laugh, and it's not forced. "Didn't want to pop them out at twenty like your parents?"

"Nah. A few girls got pregnant when I was a teenager, a lot more right after high school. It's not uncommon. I kind of just wanted to wait for a while longer. Until after school at least. But then we were so busy with the farm that we really didn't have time. But then we got three in a row, more than enough for me."

"Not at all a smooth transition, but while we're on the topic of girls who got pregnant early, we may as well start." I hope the lighter tone makes things less grim, but the fall of Helga's face tells me that it hasn't much. I give her our usual opening spiel and point out what camera she should look at.

"Ten years ago," Helga begins, "I was already more than a decade into running South Porcupine Farms with my husband, Joe. I grew up with Grace Odlin, Daisy's mom, which was really my only connection to Daisy herself."

"And you knew Grace when she was pregnant. You all were sixteen then."

She nods. "Yeah. Even though her mom carted her off to Toronto permanently after that, she seemed overjoyed about being pregnant."

It was hard to tell with Grace whether she'd loved it up north or wanted to escape. Sometimes it seemed like both at once. "How did you two meet?"

"Grace was always walking around. She would get up early and walk outside for hours and hours. Picking blueberries in the bush was her favorite. We were on the property just across the way. My parents had a cottage there before they retired and would invite the whole extended family down. Grace took a boat out to walk on our side, and we ran into each other."

She pauses and smiles. "Or not really. It was more purposeful than that. Grace has always been beautiful. My guy cousins had seen her walking and poked me to go say hi and make nice. I went over because I was curious too. I got there, and she snaps out, 'Who are you?' and I said, 'Helga, who are you?' and she said, 'Grace. You don't seem like a Helga,' and I said, 'Well, you don't seem like you're going with grace.'"

"She was kind of rough," Jayden says after a sip of his latte.

"I liked it, though. I'd always wanted to change my name when I turned eighteen. But after meeting Grace . . . I don't know, being friends with her, I wanted to own everything that I was. Even this name."

I straighten in my seat. "So you were close?"

"I wouldn't say so."

The shock must show on my face.

Helga shrugs. "Grace was the sort of girl you couldn't quite belong to, you know what I mean? You have friends where you just orbit around each other. You belong to the same universe. But Grace always hovered beyond ours."

"She kept herself at a distance."

"Yeah. When she came back to town to open that Airbnb, she was different. Friendly. Open. Approachable. I would have never called her that stuff before, but suddenly she was."

Jayden tilts his head. "Did it seem fake? Like she was pretending to be someone else?"

She leans back in her chair and ponders over the question while staring at a collage of kids' art stuck to the wall behind us. "Honestly? No. I think she was just happy for once. It was only when she came back that it hit me how miserable she'd been as a kid. I thought it was just her personality. But seeing her as an adult, it didn't seem that way anymore. Like, this was the person she could have been."

"Do you know why she might have been unhappy?" I press.

Helga fingers her wedding ring. "She lived in a nice house, but she seemed to hate her sister. They used to be really close when she was younger. It changed at some point. I don't know why. I knew she didn't get along with her mom, either, and that her dad took off when she was little."

We had called Dione so many times that I had the woman's phone number memorized. Over and over to grab an interview with her. We always wanted her, but now we need her. Except she has no desire to talk to anyone. "Grace never contacted you after she left?"

"Nope. I emailed her our wedding invite, baby shower invites, invites to the kids' birthdays. Nothing until she showed up out of the blue at the farm and asked if we would sell her a goat."

"A goat?"

Helga lets out a nervous laugh that's too high-pitched. "Yeah . . . She said Daisy liked the milk. I even asked her, Daisy, when we brought the goat by, if it was for the milk. She said it was. . . . Anyway, they signed up for weekly fruit and veg and also quarterly meat pickups." Helga spins her ring slowly. "I told her we could just get her the goat milk, avoid the upkeep of the animal, but she wanted it. She apologized for missing events too."

"She was getting every email, then?"

"Every single one." She sighs. "She said Daisy was a hard girl to raise. Especially in Toronto. Especially on her own."

"She was strapped for cash, then?" Jayden asks.

"I guess that was the impression. But I don't know. I grew up with Jordan, too. Bit of a flake, yeah, but he wasn't a deadbeat. He would have paid on time."

He did. Grace's baby daddy didn't want to meet with us and lawyered up so fast to get us off his back that Kevin immediately forbade additional contact. Nevertheless, Jordan sent receipts. He'd paid out Grace on the first of every month since Daisy's birth without fail. He also had phone records to show that he'd regularly called his daughter during that time. Which wasn't what we asked for. We weren't investigating whether he was a good dad, but I guess he's self-conscious about it.

Helga continues, "Now . . . after everything, I think she just meant the emotional labor. Daisy . . . I mean, you know what happened. I could see her being hard to raise."

I almost scoff. Grace Odlin is a master at playing the victim. But Jayden is right—I need to separate her from my mom. Give her the benefit of the doubt and look at it from all sides. Maybe it wasn't a manipulation. Grace could have legitimately struggled as a single mother even if she had money.

Jayden asks, "What did you think of Grace and Jordan's relationship? They split up when she left, right?"

"They did." Helga plays with her ring some more. "He worshipped her—we all did. But then . . . something changed at some point. He got weird after going in the house. He didn't like it."

"Had you been inside?"

She shakes her head. "No. Grace never wanted us to come over. Only Jordan went because, well, you know how teenagers can be. His parents were always around. But with Grace, the mansion was huge, and if Peter had a piano lesson, he couldn't also keep an eye on her, so it was more ideal if you wanted privacy."

"For sex," I say bluntly.

She nods and blushes. "He only went once, though."

"Did he say what upset him about it?" Jayden asks, leaning forward. I fight not to roll my eyes. I bet anything that he's hoping she'll say that Jordan saw a ghost.

Helga shrugs. "Not with me. Maybe with Katie?"

Jayden deflates, and I stifle a laugh. "We'll be chatting with Katie later. We'll ask," I say. "Speaking of Grace's home life, what was her relationship with Peter like?" I don't care much about Peter, but it would be good to balance what Perry said about him with thoughts from someone Grace's age.

Helga grimaces. It's fast. She smooths it over quickly. But it's there. And it's unexpected.

I feel Jayden's head tilt toward me and know he noticed too.

"Not a big fan?" I ask.

"I . . . It's not really . . ." She sighs and fluffs her hair. "I don't want to get hit with anything about defamation. I just didn't like him much."

"Was there a reason for that?"

She swallows. "It's just . . . He was supposed to be like her dad. But like, my dad hugs me, and it stops. But with him, it was like he hugged her for so long, it felt weird, and—" She cuts herself off with a laugh. "I'm sorry, this is so not even anything, right? Would you mind cutting it? I feel bad talking about him like that. Grace has never said a negative thing, and she lived with him. I really didn't know him. And his family are kind of big in town. I don't want to seem like I'm spreading rumors. Those Tower people really dug into them after everything. I don't want to add to it. They're a nice family."

Kevin would have absolutely refused. Helga had signed the form. The footage was ours now. But with one look at Jayden, I nod. If Kevin doesn't see it, he won't know it exists. "We'll cut it, don't worry."

She sighs and smiles. "Thank you. I really appreciate that."

I wish I didn't, but I know what she means about Peter. Mom has a brother. He visited us once. Hugged me for too long too. Maybe it didn't mean anything. But I always remembered it. He wanted to stay over for the night. Said he didn't have anywhere else to go. Mom didn't let him. I never told anyone. I could picture myself happening to tell the story to someone who enjoys long hugs with their uncle. How upset they would be. How mad the implication would make them. It's not worth it. Besides, what is there to tell? Nothing happened, right? I was fine.

And yet, it's always stood out in my mind as the one time that my mom protected me.

"What did you think of Daisy when you met her?" Jayden asks, deftly switching topics.

Helga's fingers pause around her wedding ring. "She reminded me of how Grace was when we were younger."

"Miserable?" I ask.

"Yes. I couldn't understand why, either. Grace was so happy, and her daughter wasn't. But Daisy was the one who asked to move up here. She should have been happy." Helga pauses as if she has more to say but can't quite find a way to say it.

"And?"

"She didn't know anything about Grace. That was the impression I got. She seemed to want to know so badly what sort of person her mom was growing up. But it was like she was afraid to ask Grace herself. I met up with Katie—she teaches at Timmins High now—and she would talk about the questions Daisy would ask her. What was Grace like when she was younger? Were they friends? Did Katie know her dad? What things did Grace like to do? She was honestly a lot like you two. She was investigating, except the subject was her own mom."

The sound of kids screaming reaches our ears, and Helga shoots up. "They're back. Is that all you need? They're gonna bug the hell out of me."

One of the boys shouts, "We want to ride horses!"

Helga rolls her eyes. "Of course. See, now I gotta saddle them up and watch to make sure the things don't trample them. The joys."

"Sounds like a good time for everyone," Jayden says with a laugh. He pulls the camera onto his shoulder. Still rolling.

"Do you mind if I ask you one more thing?" I smile and hope that she says yes.

"Sure."

"What happened with the goat? When you were kids." I hadn't missed Helga stumbling over that bit about the goat earlier.

Helga's face twists, and she licks her lips. "That wasn't my idea."

"I know."

"Grace was . . . She could convince you of things, you know? I didn't . . . I don't know. She . . . It just, it happened. My parents were really upset. I wasn't allowed to be around her anymore, but then it didn't matter because she left." Helga glances over at her kids, then back at us. "It was hard. We had become this tight-knit group. Even if we all weren't necessarily 'close,' we felt bound to each other. And Grace was our leader. There's always a leader, even when you don't pick one. So we did what she wanted."

I swallow and give Helga a short nod. "Thank you for your time."

"Of course." Her shoulders sag, and she looks at the mudroom where her kids are loudly debating who will ride which horse. "I feel awful about what happened. Just thinking about her in that house all alone. No one should die like that."

"No," I say. "They shouldn't."

"I always hated it. The way they talked online was just terrible. I'll never forget everyone obsessing about what Daisy did to those girls, even though she was little when the first incident happened. It was like that was all she was. Some violent criminal. Ridiculous." Helga shakes her head. "I'm preaching to the choir, aren't I?"

I smile. "I like knowing the choir isn't just us."

She laughs. "Very fair. Oh, I'll get Joe to drive you back."

"That's fine, we'll get a cab."

"Please let him drive you. I feel bad sending you kids away when he can take you—and I know you're not 'kids,' but still. Better than waiting around for a car."

I look at Jayden, who shrugs. I don't feel like unpacking being called a "kid," and it seems like she isn't going to let us say no, so we nod and collect the mic from her.

"We'll just be out front," Jayden says. "Gonna get a bit more footage."

"Perfect—I'll send him out when I go in the barn," Helga says as she helps us weave around excited children and make our way out with the cameras and gear.

Only once we're in the driveway and out of earshot does either of us speak.

"Guess we can't talk about what she said about Peter," I start.

Jayden shrugs. "Not on-camera, but I'm wondering if anyone else will have something like that to say." We let the words settle for a moment before Jayden hits record. "Okay, about Helga's accounts of Grace. Do you think she knew Grace? Like, really?"

"I don't think anyone really did. Not then. Maybe that was why Daisy was so obsessed with asking. Because what she knew wasn't matching with what other people did. Maybe she was searching for someone who *really* knew her mom."

It's too close to home. I know exactly what that's like. There are two versions of my mom: the abusive parent and the reformed parent. But I'm the only one who knows that's a lie. A half lie, anyway. She did change. After the mansion, when she left the house without telling me, there was food in the fridge. When she kicked me out for privacy with boyfriends, I had a hotel booked. She would even come to drop me off so that no one questioned a twelve-year-old alone in a Super 8. That's the thing about abuse. It can shift and adapt. But what never changes is the control she keeps over me. Every facet of my life was ruled by fear. That's who my mom has always been.

And no one else knows.

I grit my teeth. I can't project my experience onto Daisy and Grace. Not until we know more.

"I don't think Daisy found anyone who knew the Grace that she did," Jayden says.

"No," I mutter. "But Katie Kurukulasuriya is pretty damn close."

Out of all of Grace's friends, Katie is the only one who was in the mansion multiple times. She refuses to go inside to this day.

I want to know exactly what she knows.

Jayden crosses his fingers. "I really hope she saw ghosts."

I roll my eyes even as a smile creeps onto my face.

CHAPTER NINETEEN

DAISY

Morning was a combination of things. It was the shade to my window being open when I swore I'd closed it, bright sunlight streaming across my face along with the shadow of the mansion. It was Mom moving around the bunkie, going through her morning routine before leaving to do things she never bothered to tell me. It was seeing myself lying in bed in the reflection of the round vanity mirror as soon as I opened my eyes.

About a week separated the incident and the first day of school. The days passed in a way that was both instantaneous and grueling. As much as I wanted to put distance between myself and what had happened in the bush, I was equally unexcited about going to school. Especially knowing that King had seen. It was only after I calmed down and Mom and I got up that I noticed him. Apparently, after Mom's visit to his house, he had come along with her to check on how I was doing with the garden, when they heard me screaming.

After they'd found me, he wouldn't meet my eyes.

Now I lay in bed in my usual sprawled starfish form while my phone played a gentle dinging tune that was supposed to be less jarring than the usual alarm.

I used to have it set to birdsong.

Thankfully, I'd had the foresight to change it. This would have been a very different morning otherwise.

I dragged myself out of bed and shuffled to the bathroom in the underwear I fell asleep in. Mom was rushing around the bunkie with a wicker basket. She shoved snacks and water bottles into its cloth-lined interior and hastily tied a bow around the bottom.

She had been like this since the incident. Jittery. On the edge of frantic. Covering it all up by throwing herself into doing things for the house. But I could tell that something had changed. The confidence she had going into this had waned.

And it was probably my fault.

"What are you doing?" I paused in the middle of the living room to watch her.

She stopped, though her body still twitched like it desperately wanted to move. "We have our first guests! They wanted to check in early, which honestly is better anyway because I can drop you off when I grab them."

Guests. The Airbnb. Somehow, despite the fact that I had spent the last few days with my hands in soil, repotting the new snake and spider plants, pothoses, cacti, et cetera in preparation for guests, I had forgotten that people would actually be staying in the house.

First day of school and the first day of Mom's business.

"Who are they?" Who would come out here for a chilled September getaway on a Tuesday?

Mom said, "A couple who live a town over. They said this is the first year all their kids are away at university, so they wanted to relax for back-to-school season for once. They'll be here for a couple of weeks."

What was more relaxing than tearing a maggot out of your scalp and smashing it to pieces? "Is this . . . a good idea?" It wasn't a smart question given everything, but I couldn't not ask it.

"What?"

"Everything."

Mom paused and stared at me. "You haven't gone in the house, have you?"

"No," I lied.

"I need you to listen to me, Daisy. Really listen to me. We can't have any more unpredictable things like what went down the other day. That shouldn't have happened at all. That wasn't in the plan."

Get your shit together, you're screwing it up, was what she meant. "I didn't go in."

Her eyes seared into mine. "I can't help you if you don't listen to me."

"I didn't!" My shout echoed in the room, slapping against the walls and flying back at us.

Mom sighed. "I know you're nervous. But we didn't spend all those hours working on this together so you could get flustered on the first day."

"Yeah, okay," I said.

I went to the bathroom to get ready, and the shuffling sounds from outside signaled that Mom was back to frantically running around. After washing up, I found myself staring at my face. The cut over my eyebrow had healed, but no hair was growing over it. Most of the scratches had already scabbed over and were in the process of falling off. It didn't look normal, but thankfully, it did look like I'd just fallen somewhere. Not like a dozen birds had attacked me. Though my hands still itched from the scratches across my palms.

Mom hadn't seen them. The butcherbirds.

She said she saw me thrashing around in a thornbush, screaming.

I assumed that King saw the same thing.

The words I was apparently mumbling that I couldn't remember were "the birds." *The birds. The birds. The birds.* Over and over and over again.

I returned to my room and got dressed in one of Mom's college sweatshirts and a pair of black jeans. I even managed to douse my hair with a spray bottle and use a couple of products to semi-successfully refresh the curls on my head.

Maybe I should care more. But that had been the point of coming here. That I shouldn't have to care as much about what didn't matter. What was important was that this business worked. That Mom was thriving so that I could finally leave and see who I was without her in a world that didn't feel as suffocating as it was now.

I walked out of my bedroom with my backpack and searched the fridge for something I could combine into a halfway-decent lunch. Usually I was better about putting it together before I left. Mom had stopped making me lunches when I was nine. She was working for a start-up at the time, and the hours and influx of projects made it impossible for her. It was easier to just take over.

"I made you a lunch." Mom reached around me in the fridge and pulled out a small series of containers. Some sort of sandwich, sliced-up apples that were browning, and two cheese sticks.

I blinked at the offering. "Thanks. I could have made it."

"It's fine. I had the time. That's what parents do, you know, make their kids lunch." She pressed the containers into my hands. "Your job is to be a teenager, remember? The garden is the only other job, and that's basically done."

"What about—"

"If I need you for anything else, I'll let you know."

I shoved the lunch into my backpack. "Okay."

"Let's get down to the boat."

Mom led the way to the dock with the basket in her arms, which I guess she wanted to immediately present to the guests. I stumbled after with my backpack.

"Are you going to show them around inside?" I asked as Mom started up the boat and untied us from the dock. It was still eerie how so few dead wandered outside. Especially now that I knew where they were gathering.

"I'm not, actually. I had plaques put on the room doors. Theirs is labeled, and they booked that specific room. I included a map for them," she said.

"They're going to think it's weird that you won't just show them." I wondered now if she had experienced anything like I had inside the house. If that's why she was avoiding it.

Mom pressed her lips into a line. "I'll figure it out."

"Mm-hmm." I wrapped my arms around myself against the chill of the wind whipping past us. Mom had, apparently, thought of everything because there were several blankets set up in the back of the boat instead of the brightly colored jackets. "Wait, did you get the Jeep? Are you driving me to school and then picking the people up?"

"Yes, I got the Jeep, but no, I'm not dropping you off. I'm going to be too busy for that, and the guests are already here. I've arranged a ride for you."

"Like a school bus?"

"Buses don't come out here."

A ride, she said. I was too tired to poke her more about it. Mom wanted to keep everything close to her chest. Even shit you wouldn't think would be secret, she would make into one. Everything was a mystery you never ended up solving.

We reached the dock, and Mom tied up the boat. I hopped off and slung my bag onto my back.

"There they are." Mom beamed at a couple who were standing next to a pickup truck with their suitcases. "You must be Ted and Mary. Welcome!"

The couple were white, middle-aged, and friendly-looking.

After I finished taking them in, I noticed King sticking his head out of the smallest truck I had ever seen. It was bright red and somehow wasn't much bigger than a minivan. The front grille of it proclaimed "Mazda," and I was confident that it hadn't been built in the last two decades.

"Mom . . . ," I said, turning toward her.

She waved at me. "That's my daughter, Daisy. She's going off to school."

"Nice to meet you," Mary said, and her husband gave me a smile.

I shuffled closer to Mom and whispered, "King is my ride?"

Please no. Not after he saw me like that.

"Yes, he's being very nice to do this. And if you don't get in that truck, you can't go to school, and you're sure as hell going to school." The quiet sharpness of her voice didn't leave room to argue. "As a bonus, see if you can get his family off our back. I know his mom is poking around about if we can run an Airbnb, which we can. I don't know what's up with them. But if you can say anything to persuade him to get them to knock it off, I would appreciate it."

She pressed a quick kiss to my head and directed the couple to the boat. I listened to Mary's squeal of awe over the basket as I reluctantly climbed into the passenger side of the truck.

King was silent on the drive. Not in a way where it seemed like he didn't have anything to talk about. Or even in a way where he was trying to distance himself from the weird new girl. It was forced.

Frosty. A purposeful shutting out. His profile was ramrod still as he cruised. I doubted he was actually this attentive of a driver. This was punishing.

Maybe he, like his mom and aunts, was annoyed with us for running the Airbnb out of the house that he himself proclaimed was dangerous. Despite Mom's words, I couldn't bring myself to broach the subject.

The road was populated but not packed the way it would have been during rush hour in the city. There were cars and trucks alongside us that added to the scenery that was otherwise just trees and billboards. The dead had returned too, ambling along on the grassy shoulder.

It wasn't like this had never happened to me. I could count on several fingers the times when Noah had cut off contact because he was upset with me. I guess considering how he had shut me out, I shouldn't have been shocked about the Stephanie thing.

I curled in my seat.

It was like being a kid. Except, Mom wasn't the type to do the silent treatment. She wanted results. And the silent treatment didn't do anything for anyone.

And to add on to everything, there was this . . . discomfort. The more we drove, the more my stomach tied itself in knots, like I was doing something wrong. Probably just first-day-of-school anxiety.

He exhaled. "I'm feeling upset that you blatantly ignored what I tried to tell you about that house and Ivy."

"Are we in a therapy session? What is this 'I'm feeling' stuff?"

"My mom says that it's important to express your feelings directly because we aren't the sort of psychics who can read minds."

I snorted. I couldn't help it. It was compulsive. And I just kept on laughing. For some reason it was the most hilarious thing I had ever heard. When I tried to respond, all that came out was a wheeze and more laughing.

"I'll wait for you to be done." Shockingly, he didn't sound mad. In some ways he sounded as entertained as I was.

I took a deep breath, and the laughs fizzled out. "You can't control me."

"I'm not trying to control you. I'm trying to give you advice. If you wanted to go skating, and I told you the ice was too thin for that this time of year, would you go just because you thought I was controlling you? Or would you figure that, living here all my life, maybe I know a thing or two about ice thickness and was trying to help?"

I squished down farther in the seat. When he put it like that, it made me look like some impulsive and reckless person who did the opposite of what people said for the sake of it.

Besides, how did he know I went in? He wasn't guessing, I could tell. He *knew*. Had Ivy told him? "I wanted to go in the house. Ivy was the only person who was willing to go with me."

"Why?"

"I don't know, she's weird."

He pressed a hand to his temple. "I mean, why would you want to go inside?"

Probably there was a simple answer. But there wasn't really. There wasn't one way to explain it, because to do that, I would need to explain several other things. "I just needed to."

King looked over at me for longer than he probably should have, considering that he was driving. "I've decided that I'm going to help you with the house."

I blinked. "Who said I need your help?"

"My mom and aunts want your mom's business to fail because of how dangerous that place is. The only way they'll stop trying to do that is if you let me help you. Which one would you prefer?"

"Is neither an option?"

"No."

"Then fine, you, I guess."

Fuck me.

I didn't know what King had in mind as far as assisting with the house, but at least this fulfilled Mom's interest in not having the Okekes interfering with the business. I didn't want that either. And if it meant having to deal with the psychic neighbor boy for a while, so be it.

We pulled into the driveway of the school. It had a huge sign, this blue thing that was structured like a grid with silver letters over the top that proclaimed TH&VS—which, the wording underneath explained, stood for "Timmins High and Vocational School."

There was a new parking lot in the front that I guess was just for teachers because King pulled around on a gravel road that broke into a woefully uneven back parking lot. No one drove at my high school. It was in the middle of the city. If you made the decision to drive, you just looked like you weren't actually from Toronto, because who the hell would choose to sit in hours of traffic just to roll up in a car?

We got out of the vehicle. Like at every high school, there were at least a dozen ghosts loitering around. The drama in a school building could easily produce the amount of sadness needed to attract the dead. Thankfully, people tended to be happier on the first day of school. A feeling I couldn't sympathize with. But there it was. My usual strategy was to find the happiest-looking person and sit as close to them as possible. It's how I'd ended up meeting Megan.

King said, "I have a free period at the end of the day on Tuesdays, but I go over to the Sportsplex to do swimming lessons for kids. I'll be back here by the time you finish."

"You're a psychic moonlighting as a swimming instructor?"

He scowled. "Some of us need part-time jobs if we want spend-ing money."

Mom refused any request I made to have a part-time job. She said it was because she wanted me to focus on studying. I thought it was because taking care of her was already my part-time job, and if I had another one, I wouldn't have time for the former.

"Whatever," I muttered. The school loomed beside us. I almost preferred the mansion. The administrator had sent me my schedule online. I barely remembered choosing the classes. Mom had insisted that I get a good base of operations. Math and science. I was shit at them all. It didn't really matter.

King stared at me. "Was it worth it, going inside the house?"

"I don't know yet." I knew that I wasn't quite prepared for what was inside, for the amount of dead there and for the way the house itself felt, but I hadn't really learned anything besides that. Mostly, I wondered what Mom knew. What made her so desperate for me to not go in? And why was the house drawing the dead to it?

"Are you going to keep going?"

"Yes." Despite what happened there, despite what happened in the bush, I couldn't keep away from it. Something in there was wrong, and I needed to know that it wouldn't affect the business. "Are you going to suggest I stay away from Ivy again? Or warn me off the house?"

"I don't warn people twice. It's a waste of my time. I do it once, they don't listen, always, and then I stop." There was a cut to his voice. "People don't like to hear certain predictions."

I raised my brow. "So you predicted everything that would hap-pen to me up until now?"

"I didn't, actually," he said with a frown. "You're one of the few people I couldn't get a read on. Not until that instant when we found you in the bush. And now I can't again."

I couldn't believe this guy was really trying to act like he was psychic. "Well, what's my warning based on what you learned in that instant?"

His stare was as dark as his eyes. "The warning is the same. And like I said, I'm done telling you how to stay out of danger. But if you want my help instead of my mom's and aunts' interfering, don't go inside without me." He walked into the building, and all I could do was scramble after him.

There wasn't anything standout or special about Timmins High. The walls were the same off-white as most schools, with those ceilings that are a series of squares that you can push out of place if you jump high enough. The hallways teemed with long and thin lockers that had this strange faux marble finish. At my old school, they were painted a constantly chipping blue. This school was loud the way most high schools were, with kids talking over each other, lockers banging, teachers telling students to be quiet or not to run. And it was punctuated by the scent of something that could be either body spray or lingering vape smoke.

Walking through the halls with King was not the experience I expected. Almost every person we passed stopped to say hello to him. To give him a fist-bump greeting or just ask him how his summer had been. Even the teachers did it. Each time he introduced me, and I mumbled something that could count as polite without inviting people to think we were going to be friends.

As we left yet another greeting behind, I tugged on King's hoodie. "Holy shit, are you popular? You?"

"Wow."

"I just . . . I mean . . ." I threw my arms around like that would explain what I meant.

"Because I'm the only Black guy you've seen so far, so they must be wildly racist and bully me?"

Well, shit, when he put it like that . . .

"I get it. In a lot of small towns, it's rough for Black people. I'm not pretending like racist shit never happens here. But my family's been a part of this community for a long time, and that means something to people. So if someone does mess with you, tell me, and I'll take care of it."

"What are you, the psychic mafia?"

"I'm serious, Daisy. Maybe it's not common to have each other's backs like that in Toronto, but it is here."

I hunched my shoulders. I didn't know how to react to someone who barely knew me saying they would watch out for me. And it didn't feel like a come-on, which made it even harder to understand.

"And in case you actually care, the popularity thing only happened in the last couple years." He shrugged, though it seemed forced. "I dunno, maybe everyone suddenly realized that I'm tall and good-looking."

"Is that so?"

"I do own mirrors. There is nothing wrong with being aware of what you look like. I'm a good-looking guy, you're a good-looking girl. It's pretty obvious even though it's technically subjective."

My eyebrows climbed near my hairline. "Is that you shooting your shot?"

"No. You honestly seem like a lot of work, and I'm trying to live a reasonably lazy life."

At least he's direct. "Good. Because despite your 'obvious attractiveness,' I'm not interested."

"Glad we could agree on that." He stopped in front of a door and pointed to it. It was mostly wooden, with a small window of frosted glass and a gold label that read MAIN OFFICE. "This is your stop."

"Thanks," I muttered. "For the ride."

He tucked his hands into his pockets and regarded me. "Remember, if you're going in that house again, tell me. Otherwise I'll let my mom and aunts be as annoying as they want."

"I thought you weren't going to warn me anymore?"

He gave me a scathing look. "That wasn't a warning—that was a promise." And with that, he took off down the hall.

I turned away from him toward the office door.

New school. New town. New start.

I traced my fingers across the scratches on my face. I was doing a bang-up job already.

CHAPTER TWENTY

ew people liked school. I knew that. It was a fact. But sometimes it felt like I was the only one who could understand how truly depraved it was. I slid into my last class of the day and made my way to the middle of the room. It wasn't a big space, though it also wasn't the capsule size I expected for a small town. The desks were in neat rows of four across, with chairs that were attached to the desks themselves. At the front of the room, there was both a blackboard and a mounted TV screen along with the teacher's desk, which was empty.

The walls were covered with posters of different internal biological processes, including one for photosynthesis, which was just about the only one I could remember.

I took my seat next to a girl named Mackenzie who had been a reliable person to sit near for most of the day. She was white with strawberry-blond hair that fell to the middle of her back and warm honey eyes, and she hummed everywhere she went. The dead couldn't stand her. It was perfect.

The downside was having to make small talk with her so as to not look like a creepy stalker. Thankfully, she had friends in every class, so it didn't last long.

More students trickled in. Even though a good chunk of them had seen me throughout the day, their gazes still lingered when they passed by. I opened a notebook and stared at it, pretending there was something important written there.

The problem with school was that people were so desperate. They wanted to be liked. They wanted good grades even if they didn't actually know what they would do with them. They wanted to make an impact they thought would last. Everyone wanted something. And school just encouraged you to want everything that much more until you were a sensitive ball of need with your entire life's worth pinned on an institution that didn't give a shit.

I thought that in a small town, it would be easier. Maybe somehow people would want less, which seemed ridiculous now. Everywhere I turned in the halls, there were flyers up for different clubs and activities. At lunch, in a sunken area in the center of the school, they had this giant fair about the extracurriculars you could do.

It was the same.

The teacher walked into the room. She wore yoga pants with flared bottoms and a matching sports jacket. She looked South Asian with her dark hair cut into a bob that didn't quite work for her face, but the hairstyle was cute enough. Somehow every time I saw a non-white person, it was like a revelation, even though there were a decent amount of people of color. Not as many as my old school but way more than I had expected.

The teacher's eyes roamed over the room and stuck on me for a moment. I guess she wasn't new since she picked me out so easily. But she was one of the younger ones, maybe around Mom's age.

"I hope everyone had a good summer," she said, standing at the front of the classroom. "I'm Ms. Kurukulasuriya. I do accept Ms. Kuru conversationally but that does not mean you can avoid ever learning to say or spell my name." She turned to the blackboard and wrote out "Kurukulasuriya." "I expect assignments to be made out to the full thing, and I *will* dock you points if you get it wrong, so be sure to write it down now."

I scribbled her name in the corner of my notebook. Not because I cared about the points, I just didn't want to be the asshole who messed it up. Grades were the last thing on my mind.

I should have started a countdown until graduation. It would have given me something to look forward to. Before, that thing would have been university with Noah. I would have spent my senior year like most kids, wanting to do better than my usual "just getting by" mediocre grades. I would have wanted to get into the right school and program. Maybe I would have even wanted Noah to come to my graduation.

I would have wanted more and more until I became like everyone else in here. In the end, I would have been as desperate as Mom. It never ended with her. She wanted a better job, and she got it, and then she wanted an even better one.

I almost felt free without Noah. I could go back to not wanting anything.

Almost.

Because there was still real freedom to run after.

Ms. Kuru scanned the room. "I see we have a couple of students who are new to the area."

I ducked my head.

"Josie, who is joining us from New Liskeard." She pointed out the white girl with her dyed black hair and hoodie. "And Daisy, coming all the way from Toronto." Her eyes landed on me. I looked up at her and forced something like a smile on my face.

I didn't even want to smile. It just started happening.

She had introduced two new students, but people only wanted to look at me. Ms. Kuru was no exception. Her eyes lingered on me for a moment before she got on with the lesson.

Mom had strongly suggested I take biology because of my interest in plants and because it was, apparently, good for university. Altogether, in my three years of high school, we had maybe talked about plants once, though I did consistently manage to do the topic for all my projects and assignments.

As class went on, I noticed Ms. Kuru's eyes more and more. She had looked at Josie maybe once, as much as any other student, but her eyes kept landing on me over and over. It made me think of touch-me-nots—small plants with tiny leaves that fanned out to look larger. When you stroked them, they couldn't help but fold inward.

It was like existing in this seat meant that Ms. Kuru couldn't help but stare at me.

Touch-me-nots responded to protect themselves from harm.

What threat could I be to my biology teacher?

When class finally ended, I was one of the first to jump up with my bag.

"Daisy, do you mind staying back a moment?"

I was almost out the door and would have liked nothing better than to just go through it. Instead, I stopped and went toward Ms. Kuru. She smiled, bright and shining.

Josie's eyes lingered on us, possibly unsure as to whether this was a new kid pull-aside, but Ms. Kuru didn't say anything to her, so she moved on.

"Yes?" I prompted.

She sat on top of her desk. "Let's just wait for everyone to make their way out."

Oh God. It was a "private" conversation. A few teachers had had these with me over the years. Discussions about how they'd felt I wasn't applying myself the way that I could. Where they'd tried to counsel me to do better. Where, objectively, they'd tried to be good teachers.

The last person made his way out the door, and Ms. Kuru clapped her hands. "There we are." She pivoted on the desk toward me. "How was your first day?"

"Fine."

"Wow, big talker, eh?"

I shrugged in response.

"Is your mom Grace Odlin?"

That was ... not what I expected. I pulled myself straighter. "Did you know her?"

"In a way, I used to take piano lessons with her late brother-in-law, Peter." She treaded on the words lightly, as if she expected them to spark something.

I nodded. "We're living in his house."

"In the *mansion*?!"

I stepped back from the force of her voice. It was panicked. High-pitched. Sharp.

"Sorry." She held up her hands. "I'm sorry, I was just surprised . . . Your mom . . . Well, I just didn't think that's where you would be living."

"We're actually living in the bunkie. My mom turned the house into an Airbnb." I took a step forward. "Did you know my mom well? Were you friends?" I almost asked another question but clamped my mouth shut. I didn't need to ask a million at once.

"Grace wasn't really a 'friends' person. But we hung around each other during the summers. Your dad, too. There was a little group of us." She kept lacing her fingers together and then unlacing them. "Have people already stayed in the house?"

"The first guests came today."

She bobbed her head in a nod. "I see. Has Grace—are you close with your aunt at all?"

"Aunt Dione? No."

"Because . . . of . . . I mean, right, yes. That makes sense."

I furrowed my eyebrows. "Because Mom doesn't like her." I drew the words out long until they sounded like a question.

"They didn't get along, I remember." Ms. Kuru leaned closer to me. "Are you doing okay there? I know your mom had a hard time during her summers here."

I thought of pulling the maggot from my head. Of fighting off the shrikes in the thornbush. "We're fine."

"I'm glad. I would love if you could tell your mom to give me a call." She reached into her desk to produce a sticky note and wrote her number on it before handing it to me. "I would really appreciate if she did. My wife and I would love to have her over for dinner. Both of you."

Mom wasn't a "come over for dinner" person. Maybe she was when Ms. Kuru knew her. She was capable of being many different versions of herself. Had been my entire life.

"Okay, I'll tell her." I started inching toward the door.

"She's a good mom." She said it like a statement, but the way she stared at me seemed to make it into a question.

I smiled and lifted up the sticky note. "I'll tell her to call you."

The commute from school back to the property was long, but at least I only had to do it for a year. Mom picked me up right on time at the boat launch where King dropped me off. Apparently, the Okekes had gone through the process of cutting in a sort of road for themselves so King could drive around to get there. Uncle Peter, according to Mom, had valued the privacy of making it difficult to take a direct path to the property. Though she was working on changing that, since during the winter we wouldn't have use of the boat and would need some way to get guests to the house.

I wrapped myself in the blankets while Mom drove.

A dead man tripped off the dock into the lake and thrashed dramatically in the water before sinking below its depths. He waited a few moments before resurfacing and trudging back to the dock to do it all over again.

"You'll be happy to know that everything is going fine at the Airbnb," she said, talking loudly over the sounds of the engine. "I told them to text me if they needed anything, and I put whatever they want just over the threshold."

"So you technically went inside?"

"Opening the door and putting something in is very different from entering it. So if I'm ever not around, I'll text you to grab them things, and you can drop it off just like that."

"When would you ever not be around?"

Mom shrugged. "I don't know, just in case." She waved her hand at me. "How did things go with King?"

"He said that he'll get his mom and aunts to stop poking around about the house stuff." I didn't tell her that he only agreed to that if he had the exclusive right to be involved himself. She didn't need to know what she didn't need to know.

"That's my girl!" she chimed, sounding genuinely delighted. "How are your teachers?"

"Fine . . . Why?"

"Just making sure. Not everyone who works with children should. And I want you to get appropriate attention, get your grades up. You should call your dad too, tell him about your first day."

"He called on the weekend. He'll call this weekend too. I'll tell him then." I wasn't going to spend extra time on him. During our last conversation, I had to neatly skirt over what happened with the shrikes, then listen to a lecture about how I should "start the school year off right," because I "had a tendency to not take my education seriously." I let the silence sit for a moment before I said, "Actually, one of my teachers is an old friend of yours."

She turned back in her seat and squinted at me. "Who?"

"Ms. Kurukulasuriya."

"Oh. Katie." Mom spun back around as if the mention had bored her.

"She asked you to call her."

"Don't have her number."

"She gave it to me."

Mom didn't say anything for so long that I thought she'd just decided the conversation was over. Finally, she said, "I really don't think it's appropriate for her to pull you aside for personal favors like that."

"I was fine with it. She wants to have you over for dinner with her and her wife."

"Right. Forgot that she was married." She muttered it to herself, and I strained to hear over the sounds of the boat. Mom reached back with her hand. I dug the Post-it out of my pocket and handed it to her. She tucked it into her own pocket without looking.

"The woman who dropped off the vegetables, Helga, you were friends with her, too? All of you and Dad?" I didn't like talking about him with her, but I was trying to see the full picture.

"You can't be friends with people you only see in the summer, Daisy."

False. Megan had what seemed like hundreds of friends from camp who she kept in constant contact with and insisted were her best friends. At which point she would pause and assure me that I was her *best* best friend. Which I already knew, but okay.

I wasn't like those friends, and I'd always thought that was exactly why Megan and I worked. People had different groups for a reason. They were the ones she snuck sips of beer with around a campfire. I was the one who she could tell that she felt like a failure, and I wouldn't brush it away. I felt like that all the time. I understood. And Megan was the one who, no matter what I held back from her, knew me anyway.

I wondered now what sort of friend Katie Kuru had been to Mom. And how she knew to be afraid of the house.

CHAPTER TWENTY-ONE

I woke to the sound of the goat bleating so loud that it felt like it was standing in my room with its furry mouth beside my head, screaming its grievances into my ear. The flapping of wings joined that chorus. The sound was so intimately familiar that I knew it was them. Butcherbirds. I curled onto my side and squeezed my already-closed eyes tighter together like that might block out the noises somehow. Even covered with my blanket, I was cold, and the chill stuck to my skin in a way a duvet couldn't warm.

Another alarmed bleat forced my eyes open. The first thing I saw was the mansion. My shade was open again. The house sat as it always had right outside my window. None of the lights were on, only the dim ones strung through the trees. At this time of night, the guests would have been asleep either way.

I got out of bed, and just as I reached to tug the shade closed, a bird slammed against it. I slapped my hands to my mouth to stop a scream from coming out. Leaning close to the glass, I searched for a corpse on the ground, but it was unfazed. It hopped back up and flew away. With a quick flick of my wrist, I tugged the shade down, not wanting to look at the house or its birds anymore. They made my scalp itch.

Something was missing . . .

I touched my ears and immediately noticed a lack of earbuds. When I searched for them, they were sitting innocently on my vanity. But I swore that I'd put them on to sleep. Then again, I guess it didn't matter. The dead weren't going to come to me when the mansion was there.

Not having Kidz Bop on explained why I could hear the goat so clearly. The whole night I was in and out of sleep with the sound of it bleating incessantly and so loudly that I kept expecting Mom to run out to the greenhouse and shut it up. I couldn't hear the birds anymore, but the sounds still played on a mental loop in my head.

I shuffled out of my room. Mom wasn't running around the bunkie like yesterday. I guess she didn't need to since the guests were already here. I knocked on her door. "Are you going to drop me off?"

She was rolled up in the sheets like a periwinkle cocoon, with a silk bonnet over her hair. She opened a bleary eye. "Can you go meet him at his house? I'll text him to wait there."

"Through the bush?" I would have to go back in there. That place that reminded me of shrieking shrikes and thorns digging into my skin.

She rubbed at her face. "You got lost. You freaked out. It's okay. I sprayed some trees neon so it'll be easier to follow the path. You'll be fine."

I wondered if she was thinking of that girl. Of the bruises on her neck in the photos her parents threw across the desk while they screamed at Mom. Of her pulling me into that corner and shaking me and saying, "What is wrong with you?"

My hands trembled.

She sighed. "You can't live your life afraid, Dazy."

I laughed. It was a shock when it came out. Harsh.

Dazy.

Dazy.

Dazy.

I would never forget the sound of those children chanting. The crushing sense of despair that rushed into my little body as they forced my head to the ground.

How could I live like that and not be scared? How could I when the dead roamed free?

Mom said, "You're either a victim or a fighter. And I know which one I raised. Do you?" She pulled the covers over her head and curled up further.

I slammed her door shut and rushed to get ready. There was no premade lunch waiting in the fridge, which wasn't surprising. It was always like this. There would be promises to make life different, and then something would shift, something I couldn't see that she could, and suddenly it would be over.

Usually, I got two versions of my mom.

The hopeful one. The one that made plans for businesses and got us into new apartments, made school lunches, sang with me in the car.

And the other one. The one who would lie in bed not doing much of anything while I planned life around her, who wouldn't tell me jack shit, the one who insisted on those fucking study sessions, who—

I didn't even want to get into it.

I tugged on my coat, grabbed my backpack, and made my way out the door. I was a foot from the bush when the glass of the greenhouse caught my eye. It was frosted over from the cold, and the goat was nowhere to be found.

Shit. I hadn't turned the heat on in there yet, and it was already freezing.

I turned back and made a quick detour to the greenhouse. I pressed open the doors and entered the space. It was frigid to the point where I was lucky nothing had died already. Just needed to find the heater and set it to something moderate. It would warm up while I was at school.

My shoulders relaxed as I stared at the greenery surrounding me. The plants should be acclimatized enough for me to move them out of their original plastic containers straight into the soil soon.

I weaved through the aisles trying to locate the heater.

Instead, I found the goat.

There wasn't much else to do but stare. It was quiet. No more bleating. I pulled my phone out of my pocket and texted Mom to not let the guests into the greenhouse.

At the same time, a text from Megan came in: Oh my God, I am having the worst morning.

You and me both, I replied.

Jaime used up all the hot water, and my new bangs won't sit right. What happened to you?

I didn't know how to answer. What could I even say?

I located the heater, turned it on, and left.

The second I walked out, King was standing there. "Your mom told me you needed a ride."

"Yeah," I said, and made my way past him before he could say anything else.

I had zero desire to discuss the goat.

The same cold of the greenhouse persisted outside. I came out from the bush onto the Okeke property with stiff fingers shoved into my pockets. The Mazda truck sat alongside their garden that was not much more than dirt now. Already harvested.

King got in the driver's side while I made my way to the passenger's. I slammed the truck door shut a little too hard. If King noticed, he didn't see any reason to comment on it. Just glanced at me and then away as his mom pulled up beside my window. I rolled it down, and she leaned in. She was wearing another head wrap, this one filled with bright oranges and smooth topaz shades.

I was already hiking up my shoulders, getting ready for her to push her cleansing or question the Airbnb.

"You're welcome to come by anytime, you know. Even for a quick palm reading." She rested her hand on the windowsill. "We're neighbors, after all. Glad to see you getting along well with Kingsley."

I hated to give him any credit, but King had stuck by his word. His family seemed to be backing off. "Sure, thanks." I didn't have any intention of visiting for any sort of consult.

"And don't forget to pick up groceries on your way back," she said to King.

He bobbed his head in a nod. "I won't."

Tambara backed away from the vehicle, and I put the window up.

Driving on the road that the Okekes had put in was like riding on a wooden roller coaster. Uneven and shaky. The truck trembled as it drove over the grass and rocks.

"Fuck, this road is rough," I muttered.

King seemed unaffected. "It is what it is." He turned an eye to me. Assessing. Calculating. "Are you okay?"

"I'm fine."

"Did something happen?"

"No."

"I can tell you're lying, you know."

"How?" I snapped. "Because you're psychic?"

He pressed his lips together. The cool weather had forced him to use some sort of ChapStick, and his lips glistened when the light hit them the right way.

I turned and stared out the window as we finally pulled onto level ground. We passed the boat launch and turned straight onto the highway.

"Are you going to leave next year?" King asked. He kept his eyes on the road.

I shrugged. "I don't know."

"You won't go back to Toronto for university or something?"

"Maybe."

"Or you'll just stay here?"

"No." I wasn't going to stay with Mom, not if I succeeded. But what else would I do? University in Toronto wasn't what I wanted, but where else could I go? I didn't want to think about it. "Are you my guidance counselor?" My knuckles cracked, and I clasped my fingers together to stop the compulsion to crack them more. That feeling was back. The unease, getting worse as we went. I was already having a shit day, and it wasn't helping.

"Just making conversation," he mumbled. And didn't bother trying again for the rest of the drive.

When we got to school, I left the truck without saying anything to King and booked it into the building. Classes felt like a blur. I seemed to jump from one to the next. In my third period, I even forgot I had gone to the other two and had lunch already. I didn't have a class with Ms. Kuru today either, so I couldn't even try to bleed her for information.

Then the school day was over, and King was cruising to the local grocery store to do the shopping for his family that I had to come along for. Which was good, actually, because I needed things to make my lunches.

"I'll meet you at the entrance after." King pointed to a bench behind the checkout line, and I nodded.

It was an ordinary Metro grocery store. There were neat displays of fruits and vegetables. Right at the entrance was a cooler filled with a mix of drinks, from Coke to kombucha. The floors were sparkling, and there was an aroma of the pizza they were cooking fresh in the back, which you would think would be disgusting but actually looked pretty decent. Better than Pizza Pizza anyway.

Metro was higher-end than the budget grocery store that Mom and I would usually go to back in the city. But now that we were getting local organic stuff, I figured we were spending a little more.

Our joint bank account had its usual couple hundred bucks in it, but we must have had more somewhere now. Mom was bulk buying those plants and farm goods, and that required a lot more than a couple hundred bucks.

I couldn't even conceptualize how rich my late uncle was. Ms. Kuru said he'd taught her piano. Was that his whole job? I imagined you didn't make the kind of money he seemed to have by being a music teacher. He must have been born with a bunch stocked up already.

"Oh, hey!" Mackenzie came up the aisle in a loose sweatshirt and tights. She was dressed as casually as I was, but somehow on her it looked like athleisurewear and on me it looked like giving up.

I forced myself not to glance around. She was clearly talking to me. "Hey." I really hoped she hadn't assumed we were friends because I had to cling to her happy energy in classes.

"Did you come here with King?"

Ah. I got it. She wasn't actually here to talk to me. It was a round-about way to talk to Mr. Popular. "He's my ride, so . . ."

"That's so nice that he gives you a ride. He's such a nice guy."

I flicked my eyes to the side like an excuse to exit to this conversation would appear and save me. "Yup."

"I wanted to let you know that our dance tryouts are happening Thursday at lunch if you want to come. I saw you here and thought I would say something. I only just found out like, ten minutes ago. The coach texted me."

"Cool."

"Cool!" She pointed around the aisle. "I'm gonna go back to my mom. If she loses me in the store for like five minutes, she has the cashier do an announcement."

I was probably supposed to laugh, but I didn't. Megan said that my problem with socializing was that I entered every conversation like I immediately wanted to leave it. When I noted that *was* the case most of the time, she sighed.

"Bye," I said.

"Bye!" She flounced off, and I was left standing in the middle of the aisle with a bag of frozen vegetables in my hand.

"Are you friends with Mackenzie now?" King walked up from behind me pushing a grocery cart stacked with an assortment of food. Actual things you could make meals from. Not the pile of junk that Mom had brought home.

I scowled. "No. I just happen to sit near her sometimes. She wants me to try out for the dance team because I guess she assumes I have rhythm?"

He frowned. "Weird. And you didn't say anything to her about being interested?"

"No. One, why would I want to do dance? Two, I'm not here to make friends."

"Is this a reality show?"

I ignored him and finished my shopping. I was about to pass the next aisle when I noticed Ms. Kuru standing there idly with a red basket dangling at her side. There was a woman beside her pointing out the different items. She was white and her dark hair was significantly shorter than Ms. Kuru's, basically sticking to her scalp, and she wore leather pants and a jean jacket. She looked, honestly, too cool for my teacher. But she also looked too cool for this town in general.

Ms. Kuru had basically grown up with Mom, and yet here she was, shopping like a normal person. Meanwhile, my mom was at home doing God knows what. Sleeping still. Or cruising around in the Jeep that I hadn't even seen yet, doing her mysterious errands.

Maybe browsing through Airbnb listings to compare ours to the others in town. Using that marketing brain to find a way to make more sales or get into the local paper. It was never enough to just do her own thing. She needed acknowledgment and acclaim.

Ms. Kuru, on the other hand, was teaching biology in the same town she grew up in. Maybe even the same school she used to go to. Happily married and happy to stay here. I mean, I'd never planned to leave Toronto, but the city was constantly under construction—it was basically like living in a new place every few years.

I couldn't tell who I would rather be. Maybe Katie Kurukulasuriya was the easy answer, the right answer. Stability. And yet it felt like shoving myself into a mold. Pressing my insides against the blades of a cookie cutter until it fit the way I wanted it to. Losing bits of me that couldn't make it into the shape and being left with something that was pretty and uniform and just like everyone else. Except for the bleeding from the missing parts.

It was exactly what it felt like to be my mom's daughter.

Noah always said that he liked me because I was different.

It was the same reason I liked him.

But how different was Stephanie? What was special about her?

I met King at the checkout. "Can I see your phone?"

"Okay . . ." He unlocked it and handed it to me. Which in and of itself felt small-town. I could do anything to it. Or maybe it was just that he knew I wouldn't mess with his shit when he was my ride.

I pulled up Instagram and found Stephanie. Noah was every-where on her feed. It was like every single picture was of the two of them. I showed the screen to King. "What do you think of her?"

"She looks like she's twelve." He squinted at the photos. "Oh, it's Noah."

I froze. "What?"

He looked at me, nonchalant. "Your ex. Noah Durand."

"Why do you know that?" I breathed.

"Because you do."

We stood there, each of us holding our groceries, not moving. Other shoppers had to weave around us.

King moved out of the way and headed to the door. "We should go."

Inside the truck, I still had his phone, still on Stephanie's Insta-gram page. I navigated away from it and set the phone down in the cup holder, then waited for King to speak.

He sighed. "I know things about people. Past, present, and future. Not like infinitely. Just a couple months back or forward," King said, staring out at the road. "I didn't always. My mom did before me, then it went away, and now I have the ability and she doesn't. I've been like this for a couple of years. It's weird, though—you and your mom are some of the few people I've met who have these blocks that stop me. Don't know why."

"Then why do you—"

"It was in the bush. That moment when you were lying in the thorns. I was at the top of the hill and spotted you. It was just before you started thrashing. Just one moment for everything to flood in. Then it was blocked again."

I wasn't going to entertain this. I couldn't. There was no way he was actually psychic. "You can find out a lot of things on the internet."

"I know you can see the dead."

"No!" I snapped, shocking myself with the force of my voice. "No, you don't. You don't know *anything* about me."

I felt like shit. I wanted to go home. I was trembling.

This couldn't be real. It couldn't.

Because if there were other people with abilities, why had I been alone like this for so long? Why had I suffered through feeling like the only fucking cursed girl on the planet? He couldn't just come out of nowhere like he was the solution.

That wasn't how life worked.

That wasn't how *my* life worked.

"It's not about you not being good enough for him." King's voice was low and careful. Like I needed handling with kid gloves. "Just so you know."

"Fuck off."

He let out a long exhale but didn't say anything else.

I wished that I had Megan's version of a bad day. A colder-than-usual shower and messy hair. That would be nice.

Instead, I had to go home and figure out why we had a goat with its throat slashed in our greenhouse.

CHAPTER TWENTY-TWO

Something was wrong with my left ear. There was a sort of clogged rustling sound in it, like listening to dried leaves shake in a plastic bag. I couldn't get rid of it. I thought about bringing it up with Mom but didn't. It would just go down like mentioning the worm had. Instead, I made a mental note to find some Q-tips. Maybe I had a wax blockage or something.

I tossed the frozen pieces of goat into the slow cooker along with some potatoes, onions, soup stock, and a very generous helping of curry powder. I'd found the recipe online since it wasn't like anyone in my family could or would teach me how to make Caribbean food. The bunkie was quiet for now, save for the sounds of my chopping and slicing. Light poured through the open windows and added warmth to the space, though I'd already jacked up the heat.

Helga and Joe were able to come and salvage the goat. They laid it out on the kitchen island, stripped off the skin as easily as peeling off your winter coat, and butchered it. It actually wasn't a hard job given that the animal had only a single clean slice across its neck.

That was the bit no one would talk about. That it was clearly not another animal who had attacked the thing. Someone had opened the door to the greenhouse, gone inside, and slaughtered it.

Mom watched Helga and Joe chop up the goat from across the room. Her arms limp by her sides. Still wrapped up in her blanket. Eyes blank.

I was the one who had the sense to freeze the meat since I figured she wouldn't be ready to eat it right away.

I got the distinct feeling that little by little, day by day, Mom's plan was falling apart. The house was supposed to mean smooth sailing for us. But it had yet to prove it.

Her eyes had cut to me for a moment then, and I felt the blame there.

My fault.

It was hard to tell why. If it was my fault for making the decision to come here or for what happened in the thornbush, or if it was just a general feeling that I was a failure and it was reflecting on her. Even though I wanted to help and she, for some reason, wouldn't let me.

Either way, it had already been over a week since the goat was killed, and she hadn't bothered to broach the topic with me. But I could feel her eyes following my every move. It had made me worried enough that I'd avoided going into the mansion again, just in case. Because despite what had happened in there, I still hadn't figured the place out, and I needed to make sure whatever was wrong with it wouldn't ruin this business.

I rested my hands around the lip of the slow cooker. We only had two neighbors. I couldn't see what Ivy's family could get out of murdering a goat on our property.

A good scare, maybe.

The Okekes had more motive if they wanted to ward us away, but King had said that he was helping and that his family would back off.

And despite my best efforts, I believed him.

Even if we hadn't talked any more about what he'd said. Nothing about his "knowing," or me seeing the dead. I shut it down. And of course now I kept thinking about it. But how was I supposed to bring it up again after everything?

Sorry, I freaked out because I had an existential crisis about not being the only person with a supernatural power even though that's what I've wanted my entire life, let's chat?

What a joke.

Mom slammed open her bedroom door, and I jumped.

"Oops, sorry, didn't mean to scare you," she laughed. She'd swapped out her twists for a body wave wig that fell to her mid-back and was wearing a form-fitting sweater dress with black tights. It reminded me of the girl that Noah replaced me with. "Guess what?" she asked.

I put the lid on the slow cooker and set it to eight hours. "What?"

"We're booked up! We've got someone coming every weekend from now until the end of the year." She beamed. "Even a good chunk of people during the weekdays. I'm trying to get those filled up too."

"Remind me why they want to come here?"

Mom narrowed her eyes. "It's about marketing. It's a perfect place for autumnal vibes or a winter wonderland getaway. Ideal for couples wanting some isolation, or people wanting to unplug for a while, scholars or academics or artists who need a retreat." She gesticulated with her hands as she listed our future clients. "And I managed to get a partnership with one of the local taxi services. Guests get picked up right from the airport and brought to the campground, and get a discounted rate too. I just have to grab them at the boat launch."

Maybe I was wrong. Things seemed to be going according to plan after all.

"Why did we buy a goat?" I asked.

Mom's expression deflated. "Can you just stay on topic and celebrate with me?"

I pressed my lips into a line.

"Goat's milk is good for you."

Mom got her information from a variety of sources, none of which she could accurately cite. My shoulders slumped. "I'm glad we're booked up."

"Thank you! That's the attitude I want. Now, I need to go into town. I've got some flyers to get printed, and a few businesses have agreed to put them up in the windows." She tilted her head to the side. "What are you up to today? Fun Saturday plans?"

The question on paper was more casual than how it came out of her mouth. "I thought I would go on a walk," I said.

"Where? In the bush?" She lifted her eyebrows at me.

I got it. Last week I was insisting that I couldn't go in there, though I had anyway because I needed King as my ride to school. Now I was going for fun? "I'm fine. I've been going through there this whole week." I crossed my arms over my chest. "I won't be alone, either. I was going to find Ivy."

"Ivy?"

"She lives farther out than the Okekes, but she walks around in the bush a lot."

Mom bobbed her head and flipped her hair over her shoulder. "Maybe you should bring her over for dinner later."

"I'll ask." I wouldn't.

"Good, I would love to meet your friend." She came over and pressed a kiss to the top of my head. She smelled like a mix of orange, guava, and cloves. It was from one of her favorite body sprays that she preferred over perfume, which was "too much." "I'll see you later. Enjoy your walk."

Against my desires, I texted King to come by.

This was the first time Mom would be gone for long enough to do something. Last weekend, the goat incident had made her into a homebody, attached to the TV and moping around the bunkie. Now that she was back in action, we needed to take advantage of it. And I'd promised him that I would let him know the next time I went into the house.

I refused to feel useless. There was no way the dead in that house wouldn't eventually create problems. Not to mention, the house must be drawing them in for a reason, and I didn't think I was wrong to assume that it wasn't something innocent. Mom acted like she knew what she was dealing with, but she was in over her head.

After Mom left, I played on my phone while I waited for King to get here. Megan had been manually sending me her photos in batches since I wasn't using social media. I sent her some shots of the greenhouse that she responded to with a wall of heart-eyed emojis. She was like that. I appreciated it, though.

King's text came through saying he was outside.

I tossed on my jacket, shoved Ivy's hat on my head, and left the bunkie. The frost on the ground mingled with the fallen leaves and created a mix of the seasons. Dry cracks and brittle flakes.

I rounded the mansion and paused for a moment. There were shrikes perched on the ledges. Up until now, they seemed determined to stay in the bush, waiting in the trees. Sticking my pinkie nail into my still-noisy ear, I stared at them.

"Digging for gold?" King said.

I jumped and yanked my finger out. Tugging a tissue from my pocket, I cleaned my finger off and hoped he was giving me the courtesy of looking away. I had stayed under the cover of the house to probe around in my ear for a reason. He wasn't supposed to just walk over.

"Seriously," he said. "Something wrong with your ear?"

"It's fine."

He didn't seem convinced but didn't push it. King had a bright orange vest over his light jacket, and a hat in the same color pulled onto his head. Great, now we were matching.

"You don't usually wear orange out here," I said.

"It's bird season." He caught me looking at the shrikes and laughed. "Not those. Partridge. Bush chickens. People will be hunting. Better to be safe than sorry."

I tugged my hat farther down on my head and nodded. "You came."

"I said I would."

"Right." My voice snapped more than I wanted it to. It was meant to be cool and measured. Instead, it sounded petulant. I could picture Noah glancing at me and muttering, "Don't act like a little kid, Dazy." I'd forgotten that sometimes he'd called me that. I didn't know. Maybe I'd thought he'd really meant "Daisy." But when I played it back in my head, it didn't seem right. It felt like "Dazy."

King let out a breath. "So we're going into the house?"

I nodded. "Yeah, I was just going to get Ivy."

"Here I am." As if she were summoned by the conversation, Ivy slid out from behind one of the trees where shrikes were nesting in the branches. The bird population on this property was starting to feel like a problem.

Ivy was fitted in a camo-print sweatshirt and bright orange jeans. I couldn't even conceive of where she found pants that bright or why anyone would make them. They hurt to stare at directly.

"Do you like my pants?" she asked with a grin, fully aware, I was sure, that they were the ugliest things I had ever seen.

"I was just going to come get you," I said to her.

She smiled, bright teeth, and eyes covered by her usual shades. "Great minds think alike."

"Fucking A," King muttered. "Now it's a field trip."

"I've never been on one," Ivy said, her voice eager, excited.

I strode toward the house. "Don't worry. They're not that fun."

It took about seven tries to get into the back door. I had the foresight to grab the ring of mansion keys that Mom kept in her room. She put them in the same place she had our extra keys in our old apartments—buried in the back of her top dresser drawer. For someone who kept so many things close to her chest, it was almost laughable how obvious she could be in other ways.

I pushed open the servants' entrance, and we filed in. King had his hands shoved deep into his pockets and kept soundlessly scuffing his sneaker against the floor. Ivy, as usual, looked overjoyed to be where she wasn't supposed to and practically skipped ahead of me and King.

A ghost strolled by, and a shiver ran across my skin. When I looked away, King was staring at me. "See something?"

I could deny it, but why? If I wanted to bring it back up, this was my chance. "No one important."

He nodded. "Don't know if you remember me saying, but my great-aunt used to work here. Kind of looks like my mom. Died nearby too."

"It's not really relevant unless she died either unhappy or unsatisfied." I kept my voice low so Ivy wouldn't hear. "Besides, she would probably be gone by now."

"The dead don't leave here unless they're forced. She passed that down. But you're right, she was pretty satisfied with her life, so I guess she would be gone."

I blinked at him. "Wait, the dead in the house don't naturally pass on over time?"

"Apparently not. According to my great-aunt, when the house works the way it's supposed to, it actually *makes* the dead pass on. Until then, they can't. As soon as they come inside, they're stuck."

What kind of place was this? I hadn't ever been in a building that could affect the dead like that. "What else do you know about the house?"

"Unfortunately, not much more than you do now that I've told you everything. All I know is that it draws them in somehow and then makes them pass on. But if I have this knowing ability, it means that something's gone wrong. My great-aunt always had a sort of . . . affinity. It's what drew her out here. To the house. She got a job here and the knowing came to her, seemingly out of nowhere. My mom says the mansion is almost like a living organism, and it's part of an ecosystem. Its function is to make the dead pass on. She thinks my great-aunt developed the ability because when the mansion, for whatever reason, stops pushing ghosts into the 'great beyond' or whatever, it needs someone to help bring it back to its true nature."

I raised my brow. "So, your ability is the result of . . . what? Some supernatural equilibrium or something?"

"I don't know." He shrugged. "None of us can say actually why she developed it. Only that it was clearly in response to the house not doing what it was supposed to. My great-aunt found a ritual to attach her blood to the house, and with it, our bloodline. It's why her ability cycles through us. She also learned about the cleansing and how it can help reset the mansion, force it back to factory settings, I guess. The catch is that you need the homeowner's permission to do it or it won't work. When I got the knowing a couple of years ago, we asked Peter about doing one, and he told us no. He said no to my mom back when she had the knowing ability too. Then he died, so we were kind of stuck. But now you're here."

"Are you coming or not?" Ivy shouted down the hall at us as if this weren't a covert operation.

I sighed. Even if King and the whole thing with his great-aunt was real, I still didn't believe in this cleansing, but at this point, it would be worth convincing Mom to do it just in case. "Let's go before Ivy comes back here."

"Why is she here again at all?"

"Because she knows something about this house. Wait, can't you know what she does?"

"No . . ." King threw me a strange look, his brow furrowed. He opened his mouth like he planned to add more, then shut it.

"What?" I thought it was a normal question considering that I didn't know anything about his weird psychic abilities, but apparently not.

"Nothing. I just . . . She's like you and your mom, blocked."

We reached Ivy, who was standing with her hands on her hips. I said, "I just want to check on the guests who are staying here." Make sure there wasn't an unaccounted-for corporeal who could be messing with them. If they were okay, then it would make me feel a lot better about the Airbnb. The house weirdness could be investigated after. "I don't know what room they're in, so maybe we can split up and look?"

"That is some white-people bullshit," King said.

"Okay, wow."

He threw his hands up. "I've also never been in here, so I don't even know where to start looking. And may I remind you, I've been told that this house is dangerous my entire life. I don't think splitting up is the best idea."

"You can't just know that you'll be okay?" I pushed.

Ivy's eyes got wide. "Ohhhh, going to use your psychic powers?"

I wondered exactly how much Ivy knew about what King could

do. I assumed she didn't know about me, and I liked keeping it that way. It was one thing to have King know because, apparently, I couldn't hide it from him. But I didn't want it getting around town that the new girl saw dead people. Mom would freak.

King said, "The house is an object, not a person. Besides, it's a huge block too. I can never know about anything that happens inside here. I see people come in and go out—that's it."

Maybe that was the reason for the shifting and the discomfort. For the lack of desire to split up. King had been living his life "knowing" for the last two years. But in this house, he didn't.

He couldn't be cool and calm like he usually was.

For once, he was scared.

"You'll see a lot more in the house by yourself than you will with a group," Ivy said.

King pointed at her. "You see that shit. That sort of creepy shit is what I do not need. I don't want to see *anything*."

I sighed. "Fine, let's stay together." I turned to Ivy. "Does that work for you?"

She shrugged. "It's nice to be in a group sometimes."

I forced myself not to think too deeply about anything that came out of Ivy's mouth. In the back of my mind, I hadn't forgotten that she'd lied to me about being in this house before. That she'd known something was wrong with it and let me come inside.

But she was also the only person who seemed to actually know about the mansion. King, by his own admission, didn't know much more than me. And if Mom knew something, she wasn't going to share. Ivy, however, might be convinced.

"Lead the way." I threw my hand out with a flourish as I addressed her.

She pushed her sunglasses onto the top of her head. "Here we go."

CHAPTER TWENTY-THREE

We followed Ivy and her fluorescent pants through the hallways in a similar direction as when the two of us were last in the house. My eyes tracked the dead we passed. Maybe I was being paranoid, but it felt like there were more now. I ground my teeth together and tried to focus on any potential active threats as we followed Ivy.

As she walked, she touched everything. The banisters, the walls, the frames of the hanging paintings, everything. It was like she was lacking stimulation and needed to feel. King, on the other hand, *avoided* touching anything. He walked in the middle of the hallways, squishing in on himself as if that would put more distance between the house and his skin.

"You still feeling good about that decision to help me?" I asked him.

He scowled. "If I can make a difference? Yes." There was something to the furrow of his brow that had me examining his face more.

"You know something, don't you?"

"I told you, I don't know more about this house than you do."

"Not that. Something else. Something is going to happen, isn't it?"

He swallowed.

"Tell me."

"I can't. I know these things . . . but if I say exactly what's going to happen, there's no changing it anymore. It gets locked in. Warnings are all I have, and you've already ignored the biggest one."

"Because I went inside the house."

He nodded. And in that instant I knew that this ability he had was not one he wanted.

I imagined having all the answers at my fingertips and wanting to throw it away. I could know exactly why Mom was the way she was. I would know about her childhood, her friends, her past, what made her so . . .

I would know everything that I had been struggling to learn even a piece of.

Mom would cease to be a mystery.

"You don't like knowing things, do you?" I said. "Even when it could be useful?"

"Do you like doing what you can do, even when it's useful?"

I didn't.

I knew very intimately what it was like to have an ability you didn't want.

It wasn't just dealing with it. It was the isolation of being the only one.

I couldn't imagine someone like King, who was so surrounded by friends and family, being anything like me. But in this one way, we were the same.

"The problem isn't knowing. It's that when I try to help people avoid the worst, they don't listen." He stared pointedly into my eyes.

"They run into the same mistakes over and over, and I watch it happen. My best efforts fail time and time again."

I swallowed. "I'm sure not everyone—"

"No, Daisy. *Everyone.*" He shook his head. "No one wants to be advised. They don't want to make better choices. That's why it doesn't matter if psychics are real or fake. Everyone just wants to do whatever the fuck they want to do." His gaze seemed to penetrate my skin, slipping underneath the soft epidermis and slicing its way inside with careful cuts. "No exceptions."

"Then why come? Why try to help me anyway?"

He smiled then. It was tight and strained. "Apparently, I'm a glutton for punishment."

We were interrupted by Ivy waving her hands from down the hall and pointing at another door. Just outside of it was a bag of garbage waiting for pickup.

That was where the guests were.

King started over, but I stopped after only a few steps. There was a moan creeping out from underneath a door. Quiet and low at first, then louder. Croaking and pained. I pressed my hand to the door. It was cold.

"Daisy!" Ivy whispered. And "whispered" was a generous description of her near shout.

I forced my eyes away from the moaning door. I needed to concentrate on the guests right now. This was something I could look into later.

When I reached the two of them, Ivy pressed her ear to the dark-washed wood. Polished to perfection like everything else. I made my way closer, but King kept his distance.

Ivy and I faced each other with our ears on the door. Brown eyes staring into brown eyes.

For a moment, there was nothing, just this light buzzing sound, so faint I probably wouldn't have noticed if I weren't listening intently. I thought it was the same sort of rustling already in my ear, but it was completely different. Like an insect.

"There's a bee in here," a woman said.

Steps sounded as the man presumably walked around. "It's too cold for bees. Maybe there's a nest in the house somewhere?"

"Just get rid of it!" Her voice trembled. "There's another one."

"Yes, I see it, I've got it." His voice was more impatient than hers. His stride sounded heavy as he moved around the room.

I stared into Ivy's face for a hint of a reaction to what was going on, but her expression was carefully neutral.

The buzzing got louder. It didn't sound like one or two bees. It was like a handful. The sort of amount you might expect from a bee-keeper, stretching out their clothed arm with dozens of them dancing over the fabric.

"Ted!" the woman screamed. "Do something!"

Ted and Mary. The couple that I met on the first day of school. Unless we were booking multiple Teds in.

"I'm gonna go get the host." Ted's footsteps marched over to the door.

I jumped to my feet and stumbled back, ready to sprint somewhere where he wouldn't see us, but Ivy stayed in the same spot.

The doorknob jiggled, over and over again.

I didn't need to be up against the door to hear their voices anymore.

"Ted!" she screamed. Her voice high and alarmed.

The door shook as Ted rammed against it. "It won't open!"

"Ted!"

"I'm trying!"

Mary stopped speaking. And started screaming. The cries were shrill and high-pitched. I couldn't picture them coming out of the smiling older woman I had met at the boat launch.

I was frozen. Suctioned against the far wall.

King wasn't. He lurched forward and tried to open the door from our side. Twisting the knob to no avail. Even when he resorted to slamming his own shoulder against the wood, nothing happened.

And the whole time, Ivy stayed in the same spot, with her ear pressed against the door. "It won't open until they give something up," she said.

"Give *what* up?!" King yelled at her.

Ivy tilted her head. "I don't know. Whatever the house wants from them."

Ted joined in the screaming. I had never heard a grown man scream like that. The terror was all-consuming. Their cries pressed against my body and pushed me into a space that was small and cramped.

I couldn't breathe.

I needed to get out.

I turned away from King and Ivy.

And I ran.

"Daisy!" Ivy's voice was loud as she called after me, but it wasn't urgent or scared. Her tone was almost lazy. Chiding.

The walls echoed her voice.

I passed the room with the groaning. The moans had gotten louder. They joined in with Ted and Mary's screams. A symphony of suffering.

Dazy.

Dazy.

Dazy.

I pressed my hands over my ears, and nearly kicking open the back door, I stumbled into the cold autumn air. My breath huffed in front of me in a fog that I kept breathing back in, making myself dizzy.

I fell to my knees with my hands shoved against my ears. The screams and moans mingled with the chanting of children. It was like I was back in that playground with its rusted paint that stuck to my tiny fingers, and their bodies pressed against me, screaming in my ears.

Dazy.

Dazy.

"Daisy!" King burst out the back door, and Ivy trailed behind him.

The shock cut through the roar in my mind, and I was left trembling on the ground.

Ivy walked casually with her hands in her pockets and her sunglasses slipped back on.

"What the fuck is wrong with you?!" I screamed at her. I could picture it. Me diving at her, threading my fingers around her throat, screaming, *Are you real?!*

But I couldn't. I couldn't do that again. I gripped my hands into fists at my sides.

She narrowed her eyes at me. "There's nothing we could have done. King tried. It didn't work."

"How did you know what it wanted from them?"

"Because I listen," she snapped.

"You *listen*?" I laughed. "Do you get off on that? *Listening* to people scream and cry?" My ears exploded with the sounds of chirping shrikes. It was like I was back in the thornbush, thrashing and being pecked over and over again.

Ivy frowned. "Isn't that why you wanted to go in? To see what might happen to them?"

"No! I wanted to make sure that they were okay. That something like this *wasn't* happening. But you knew. You knew before we even went in." I shook my head so wildly that my brain felt like it was rattling, and stumbled to my feet. "There's something wrong with you."

What is wrong with you?

The shrikes were digging into my skull. The sounds kept repeating and repeating there. Mingling with the fucking rustling sound in my ear that wouldn't go away.

"Daisy . . . ," King started.

I whipped my head toward him. "She's like you. Both of you just know things. But no one can tell me, right? Fix it, then. Do your fucking cleansing. I'll make my mom say yes." I was panicking—I knew that. I couldn't make Mom do anything.

King shook his head. "I think . . . I think it's too late. We're supposed to do the cleansing at the first sign of something being wrong when the ability appears. It's been such a long gap since Peter died, so we weren't sure. If everything was fine inside, maybe. But this . . . I don't know what that was. But it's not something my family can fix with some herbs and smoke."

"Of course," I laughed. So we were doomed. And King knew it.

"Daisy—"

"Don't come near me anymore. Either of you."

Ivy's face twisted, and she stepped toward me. "You don't mean th—"

"I do mean it!" I screamed. "Get away from me, you fucking freak!"

Her flinch was like thousands of branches cracking at once. It was sharp and splintered. The butcherbirds went quiet.

"Daisy, please," King said, walking closer.

I stumbled back away from both of them and ran around to the front of the house.

"There she is," Mom said.

I froze on the spot.

Mom was standing near the bunkie with her jacket on, and beside her were Ted and Mary. They each had on matching grins, and their suitcases were packed and ready.

What the actual fuck?

"Ted and Mary are just checking out. I'm going to ferry them over to the boat launch," Mom said.

Mary winked at me. "Your mom showed us that beautiful greenhouse earlier today. I can't believe you did that all by yourself."

"Very impressive," Ted said. "We have to pay our kids just to get them to mow the lawn."

This was wrong. This couldn't be happening.

Mom frowned at me. "Daisy?"

"I have to . . . I have to go." I turned and ran back behind the mansion.

King was gone, but Ivy was still standing there by the back door. I ignored her and fumbled with the keys. Once I got the door open, I ran up the stairs, taking them two at a time until I reached their room and threw the door open.

The knob gave way easily.

I stood in the doorway, panting. There were rumpled sheets with a few towels thrown on top of them. Otherwise, it was a plain room. Ordinary. No evidence of the torture that had just happened to the couple.

A soft pressure leaned on my shoulder. I knew it was Ivy. It should have felt upsetting, overbearing, disgusting, to have her this close to me. But it wasn't. It was almost like I wanted her there.

She sighed. "They don't remember after they give something up. This is my first time actually seeing it happen."

My body trembled.

"You have to be special to remember. Like me or you." She snuggled closer to me. "That's why we have to stick together."

"Why is it like this?" I croaked, throat swollen from nothing. A feeling only. Ridged pink muscle, wide open, and still constricting. Suffocating.

Ivy trailed her fingers against the wall. "Why are you the way you are? Or me? Or the birds? We don't know, and yet here we are." She turned to me, her eyes hidden behind her sunglasses. "But once we exist, for the most part, we want to live. The house is no different."

I shook my head. "No. It's not normal. Other houses aren't like this one."

"And not all humans are monsters, but some are, aren't they?" She grinned. "You're searching for something profound. Something to tug at your heartstrings. A Disney villain origin story, but there is none. The house is an animal. And it wants to feed. Just like those birds on the roof with their kills trapped on thorns."

". . . And what does the house eat?"

She tilted her head. "I think it's supposed to eat the dead. That's why they come when it calls. But it must prefer the living. Maybe it's like the difference between vegetables and steak?"

"The dead." I hadn't heard wrong. That was exactly what she said.

"Oh. Right." Her grin got wider. "I can see them too."

This wasn't happening. It wasn't. It couldn't be.

She was like me. Had been, this whole time.

I couldn't make myself believe it.

"Ivy . . . ," I whispered. "Are you real?"

"Of course." She brushed it aside like it was ridiculous, and my chest compressed. Ivy draped her arms around my shoulders. They tightened around my neck for just a moment. It was enough to throw me back into memories on a bed, his fingers pressing against my throat so hard that a tear leaked from the corner of my eye. Him panting on top of me while I waited for it to be over.

I had become that girl again. Gasping under fingers.

I needed to stop thinking about that.

I needed to *focus*.

Even if Ivy was just fucking with me about seeing ghosts, it didn't change the fact that they existed. King had said that somehow the house could make the dead pass on. What if it was doing that by eating them? The thing that, according to Ivy, it was supposed to do. Except there were so many dead walking in the halls and lounging on furniture. Was the mansion seriously skipping over them as meals in favor of the living?

I asked, "Why has the house stopped eating the dead? Wouldn't that be like dessert or something after the human meal?"

"Animals don't eat dessert," Ivy said, her voice deadpan.

"You know what I mean."

"I think it's full. And it would rather fill up on the living." She smiled, a slight quirk of the mouth. "But its stomach is growing."

I shivered, and Ivy noticed.

She leaned her head against mine. "Don't worry. It likes you." Her voice was a whisper. "No one likes me at all."

Tears were in my eyes. I couldn't tell if it was from the memory or from the stinging, hollow loneliness in Ivy's voice. "That can't be true."

Ivy paused in consideration. "You're right, it likes me too. I can tell."

I swallowed. "Why should I not worry just because it likes me?"

She laughed. "That's easy." She brought her mouth close to my ear. "Because that means it might resist how very delicious it would be to make you scream."

CHAPTER TWENTY-FOUR

BRITTNEY

L et the record state that it is not easy to haul heavy camera equipment through a campground park. People look at us curiously from their tents and RVs as we march down a dirt road, staring at the different signs marking the campsites. It's hot enough that I'm very aware of the dampness under my arms and tits, and I've gotten at least four mosquito bites since we got out of the cab. There's a distinct buzz in the air from all the bugs, and where it doesn't smell like an evergreen car air freshener, the scent of BBQ permeates.

Big Water Campground is where Katie Kurukulasuriya and her family have come for the last few years at least once during the summer. And our visit happened to fall on one of those times, so it's the place where she could speak with us.

A truck rumbles past, and I glare at Jayden. "We should have gotten the cab to drive us down here."

"Why are you mad at me? You didn't say anything either," he shoots back.

He is technically correct.

We had the taxi drop us in the paved parking lot several blocks behind, not realizing we could have had him drive much farther in.

And Jayden, of course, is filming the whole struggle. "Is that necessary?" I ask, staring into the lens.

"It's a part of the journey. Sharing every aspect of the process is an integral building block of the documented truth. And our viewers are interested in the whole thing. Not just the interviews and semi-animated background history."

Tariq, who's our newly appointed assistant video editor, promised that he could do some animations for us while we did voice-overs of the background history. Last season, it was just me and Jayden putting together rudimentary text on-screen with some timelines. Because of Torte, we had access to way better equipment, technology, and stock images that didn't come from free sites. They gave us resources but expected us to do all the work ourselves. Now things are different.

This is going to be the season that breaks us out. That puts *Haunted* into a category of its own. Maybe even good enough for a streaming service to buy it from Torte. That would be better than just having them promote us. The streaming company would have to hire us too. And maybe the move would tempt Jayden to stay on board just a little longer before leaving me for his dreams of hard-hitting serious documentary stardom.

As long as this season goes well.

My phone vibrates, and both Jayden and I look at it. I reject the call.

After our conversation in the car, I told him that I wouldn't be listening to any more voicemails. Even without fully understanding my relationship with my mom, he agreed that was for the best. That was the plan. And yet I couldn't stop.

She knew how to reel me in. What I wanted to hear. The countless apologies I knew I deserved that she never gave to me. Typed out in a manuscript but never said aloud in my presence.

Until now.

Now I had voicemails saying things like, *"I'm sorry that I never watched any of the videos you did in school."*

"I'm sorry that I didn't spend more time with you."

"I'm sorry that I let Robert hit you."

That was the one that hooked me. Truly reeled me in. Robert, a man my mom dated from when I was six to ten. He was a guy who believed in corporal punishment. Not just for being bad. For anything.

For forgetting to say "please." For not washing the dishes right. For breathing too loud.

And she let him. She would sit on the couch and say, "If you behaved, then he wouldn't have to do this."

They broke up when she saw another woman's number in his phone.

In my mind, I know it's all fake. She's probably using the transcripts of her voicemails in another book. If she really wants my attention, all she has to do is threaten to stop cosigning my lease again. But she seems to prefer this method.

"There it is!" Jayden points to site #34.

There's a massive RV set up, complete with an awning that has an arrangement of lawn chairs underneath it. The family themselves are in a separate netted structure with a picnic table inside, where they're sitting with cans of pop and burgers.

Katie spots us and waves. She has shoulder-length brunette hair and wears a loose pink tank top with matching shorts. Her entire family peers at us curiously. There are at least six of them, all adults, though there are some kids' toys scattered nearby that hint at children somewhere.

She gets up from the bench, but not before squeezing the hand of a woman with a black pixie cut. Her wife, Anna Rossi. I recognize her from Katie's socials.

"Hi! I'm Katie," she says as she reaches us. "Brittney and Jayden?"

"That's us," I say. "Where can we set up?"

"You can come into the RV." She walks over to the massive structure and pulls the door open for us.

Inside, it's a spacious layout. We walk into the kitchen and lounge area. It's not particularly modern, covered in dark wood finishes and nearly matching dark brown suede. There's a dinette that Jayden makes a beeline for, and off to the side of it, a big love seat and two armchairs. On the other side of the RV are two doors; one I assume goes to a bedroom and the other the toilet. In the hallway between them are two sets of bunk beds with curtains. More than enough for a family to be comfortable together.

"Did you want anything to drink? We have Coke, ginger ale, all of that. I can boil water for tea or coffee, too, if you like?" Katie hovers around the kitchen area.

"I'm okay," I say.

Jayden turns around and does a quick examination of the options. Without a Keurig or equivalent machine in sight, he's unlikely to get his famed Earl Grey latte. "Coke?"

"You got it," she says, and goes to dig in the fridge.

This is the most interesting part of the routine to me. The constant repetition of hospitality. Sometimes I want them to offer nothing, just to see the pattern break. This busy-making dance that everyone wants to do to prolong the inevitable of sitting down with us and talking about unpleasant things.

Even people who seem desperate to talk about those things like our dear friend Noah.

Katie sets the Coke down on the table and holds her own can of iced tea. I wave her into the booth so she stops hovering around it. She complies.

This time, I'm the one to slide the release form over while I examine her face. She looks younger than she is. Her face is moisturized like she takes special care, even when out here camping.

"Do you come here every summer?" I ask. She already let us know in her email that she's a fan of the show. I don't need the Jayden warm-up.

Katie finishes with the form and slides it over. "Just about. I have the whole summer, Anna and my parents have a lot of vacation time banked, and my sister has been on maternity leave basically for the last two years, so we've been coming for about a month between end of July and beginning of August."

"How many kids does your sister have?"

"Two. Both boys." She pauses and smiles. "We don't have any plans for our own, so it's nice to have them around."

"Better to be fun aunts anyway."

She laughs. "I don't know if I'm that. Anna is, though. She's always got some game invented to play with them."

"I'm sure you have your charms too."

"Rolling," Jayden announces, and slides into the booth beside me. It's not really big enough for both of us. He's twisted a bit off the side, but we manage. I'm not overjoyed about being squished in, but I suck it up since there isn't a better spot, considering the lighting.

I give Katie the full spiel.

She straightens in her seat. "Ten years ago, I was teaching biology for grades nine to twelve at a high school in Timmins. Daisy was one of my students, and I knew her mother, Grace, when I was a kid."

"So you came to Big Water for part of the summer. Were you in town for the rest of it when you were younger?" I don't have to say "when you were sixteen" because she already knows.

Katie gives a brief nod. "Yes."

"And you went to piano lessons at the mansion year-round, including the summer?" Jayden and I both agreed that it would be best to stick to her experiences in the mansion and see where it went organically from there.

I couldn't shake the unease about what Helga said about Peter. But it was still better to start with the house.

Katie fiddles with her iced tea can. "Yes. My parents were insistent that I learn to play properly. There were teachers in town, of course. I begged to learn with them. But Peter had played in orchestras and big theater productions in Toronto. He studied at the Royal Conservatory too. He was the best. And that's what they wanted for me."

"Teachers in town would have been closer," Jayden supplies.

Katie nods, scratching at the can.

I tilt my head. "Is that why you wanted to go with the teachers in town?"

"It would have been easier to get to."

"Not what I asked."

Katie snaps her head up from staring at her can.

Even Jayden's head turns a bit. It's a push, yeah. Maybe too hard. But I want to give her an opportunity to open up about what being in that house was like for her. She'd been in the mansion every other week for years since she was ten. Even Grace had only been there in the summers. Aside from Grace, Katie had had the most exposure to whatever went on inside.

Everyone says that house drove Daisy out of her mind. Grace certainly isn't normal, but Katie is. And yet she seems plagued by something, if the twitch of her fingers is any indication. Either way, it's up to her to decide to tell us.

Katie swallows and takes a sip of her iced tea. "I didn't like being in the house very much."

"Was there a specific reason for that?"

She goes quiet.

We sit there as she stares at the top of her iced tea can. Thinking isn't good. Thinking means your interviewee is deciding what facts to share or omit from their story.

"Were you afraid of being there?" Jayden prods, his voice several times more gentle than mine. "Did something scare you?"

Katie plays with the tab of the can. "I was always afraid there," she whispers. "I was scared when my parents drove me. I was terrified on the boat. I wanted to crawl out of my skin in that house."

I wait for the "why," but it never comes.

Jayden clears his throat. "Was Grace afraid too?"

I lean back a bit. That's his way of telling me to back down. Let her talk about someone else and take off the spotlight.

"I couldn't tell." Katie's shoulders relax as the conversation turns away from her. "Grace was unshakeable." Her lips quirk up a bit. "I would have breaks during lessons, and there would be snacks waiting for us. Dione usually put them together. Grace liked to eat outside; I did too. But she would want to run around through the bush. Once, we weren't wearing hunting oranges, I don't know why, and this shot fired. I was so scared, I crouched down into a ball. Grace just stood there. Still and quiet, listening to the shots. From the sounds she figured out how far away they were, reassured me, and we left."

"You felt like she wasn't afraid of anything?" Jayden asks.

"Yeah. And in the mansion . . . she just seemed so unaffected. Besides, she loved that house. I caught her more than once leaning her head against the wall, her eyes closed, this gentle smile on her face. When she was pregnant, she said her baby would be special because she and Jordan made it in that house."

"Special how?"

Katie shrugs. "No idea. Pregnant people say weird things some-times, right?"

"Was she? Was Daisy special?"

"You know—and maybe this will sound bad, and I don't mean it that way—but she wasn't."

Damn, girl.

My eyebrows must go straight into my hairline, because she laughs.

"I've seen kids like Daisy while teaching: kids who had private struggles, kids where you could see the weight on their shoulders, but they wouldn't or couldn't share it with you. Grace was the same way." She pulls the tab off her can and puts it on the table. "Struggle with school. Struggle with family. Struggle with authority. And depending, either people would act like you were born to be that way or something was wrong and you needed help."

"Depending on . . . ?"

"Race is a big one. I'm sure you know that. Gender too."

Jayden and I nod. We do know. "Forgotten Black Girls" wasn't just about the media preferring to highlight a "nice white girl" instead. It was also the girls who everyone expected to fail from the start. Expected that they wouldn't have a dad. Expected that their moms were struggling alone. Expected that they get poor grades and not achieve because that's just how it went. And if you lashed out, that was what they expected of your ghetto ass too. Left alone to slip through the cracks. And when you failed, they would say it was your fault. If you succeeded, you were a special case. Not like those other girls.

And that's just covering what I know. Jayden has his own expe-riences too. Being a gay Black boy. Having a better home life than me didn't spare him his own set of expectations. His own ways to be forgotten.

Jayden adds, "You said Grace was like that too. What about when she came back to town? Did she seem different?"

"I wouldn't know," Katie responds with a laugh. It has an edge to it. Like a coating in your mouth. Bitter. "She didn't want to talk to me. At all."

I frown. "Do you know why?"

Katie releases a long sigh. "I tried to talk to her about something. When we were sixteen. She was caught up in some weird ideas, stuff she wanted to do that . . . I didn't want to. By that time, Jordan had gotten kind of strange with her, but he wouldn't say no when she asked for something. And Helga worshipped Grace—I did too—so we would do anything she said. But I just felt like maybe she was motivated by something else. That something had actually scared her and that this was the way the fear was manifesting."

"Is this about the goat?"

"That fucking goat," she mumbles, and flicks the discarded tab of her iced tea can.

The goat was the thing that was shared and spread online when Tower came for Daisy and Grace. After the incident in the mansion, Tower returned to town with a goal to launch a full-blown smear campaign—digging up dirt and interviewing people, including Mr. Helms. The goat, which was previously in all the Timmins newspapers, resurfaced with their insistence. The original headline was: TEENAGE CULT SACRIFICES GOAT.

Jayden leans forward. "What happened?"

"Grace came to us: me, Helga, and Jordan. We usually hung out in the summer, so it wasn't abnormal. But she was wired. I remember thinking she was high."

"Did she do drugs?" I interject.

"No," she laughs. "It was just so out of character that that was where my head went. She was saying we needed to help her. That she needed a goat's stomach fresh out of it."

My mouth drops open some, and I immediately snap my lips closed.

"I know," Katie says, shaking her head. "She wanted our help finding one. It was a huge mess. We went to Helga's parents' farm. They were at the cottage—her whole family was—so we had to sneak over there at night. The plan was to blame it on bears or something."

"You were all just cool with killing this goat?" Jayden doesn't bother to keep the skepticism out of his voice.

"Grace could convince you to sell your soul to please her. She knew how to make you love her even when you weren't sure that she loved you back. And at the same time, she made herself seem vulnerable even though you knew she wasn't afraid. Like she needed you to protect her. It's hard to explain."

I think of my mom breaking down via voicemail about Robert. She was afraid of him too. What was she supposed to do?

But I don't have memories of her afraid. I can only remember her sitting there, saying it was my fault that he had to discipline me.

I know exactly what Katie means. "Would you say she was manipulative?"

She flinches. "No, that . . . that makes it seem like she used people. She wasn't the way she was on purpose. It wasn't calculated."

That's the question. Was she or wasn't she? Isn't that the mark of a master manipulator, if no one feels like they're being played with? My phone burns in my pocket.

Jayden gives me a warning look that I know means he thinks I'm pressing the Grace thing too hard.

I move on. "So you went to the farm?"

"Yeah. Helga got a knife from the kitchen. Jordan was like . . .

scared to let Grace have the knife. He kept insisting that he could do it. But it wasn't like he wanted to. He only went into the house that one time, but he was so freaked out after. The things he said . . ."

"What did he say?" Jayden asks, and I can hear the fever in his voice.

Katie shakes her head. "You're going to think this is so unhinged. He said Grace could talk to the house. Like . . . through the walls. By then we knew she was pregnant, and he thought the baby was going to be wrong because they made it in the mansion."

Jayden is practically vibrating. "Like something about conceiving Daisy in the house was going to affect her?"

"Yeah. Which is so strange because I'm sure lots of babies were conceived there and were fine."

"Not necessarily. It was a summer home. The Belangers didn't live there full-time until Peter took ownership. Weekend visits with kids can be busy. Not a lot of extracurricular time."

"Circling back to the goat," I cut in, trying to keep Jayden on track this time. He deflates a bit but doesn't stop me. "You decided to kill it. Jordan wanted to do it; Grace didn't want him to. What happened?"

Katie says, "Grace agreed to let Jordan do it but under her direction."

"What was that like for you? Watching them?" I ask. Listening to her tell the story, it seems unreal, though I know it isn't.

Katie shakes her head again. "I didn't like it. The goat kept crying. I ended up crying. I—"

We let the pause stand to give her a moment.

"I held its mouth shut. Grace asked me to, so it wouldn't make so much noise. And I was happy to do it because I didn't want to listen. But then it moved so much once Jordan cut it. And I could feel . . .

I could feel when it died. Because it went slack." She takes a deep breath. "Grace pulled out its stomach, washed it off, and put it in this cooler bag filled with ice."

Maybe this was just a messed-up bunch of sixteen-year-olds, or maybe this was proof that Grace Odlin had the ability to convince others to kill for her. Is that what she was hiding? And what about Dione? How did she get involved?

"But you got caught." Jayden slides his Coke to the side. Turned off by it, probably.

"Yeah. Helga's parents had just put in surveillance cameras. They didn't tell her, so she didn't know. Brand-new 'cause of the bears." She snorts. "Exactly who we planned to blame, but then it was us on the cameras. Their farmhand was the one who monitored them. Saw us and blabbed. Religious guy—it upset him. Though it would have upset anyone, and it did."

"How did that end up connecting to you and Grace falling out?"

Katie takes a huge gulp of her iced tea. "She was growing maggots in the goat stomach. Huge, disgusting things." She shudders. "She wanted to put one in my ear."

"She wanted to do *what*?" Jayden blurts out.

I can't say I disagree. "She wanted to put a *maggot* in your *ear*?"

"Yes. She said it would protect me."

"From what?"

Katie twists her hands in her lap. "She was scared. That was when I really understood how scared Grace was. I thought she was fearless, but she wasn't. She just hid it better."

"Scared of the house the way Jordan was?"

"I think Jordan was more scared of Grace than the house, to be honest. But Grace and I, we had our own monster inside that mansion. I tried to talk to her about it, about the thing I *knew* we were both afraid of, but she didn't want to. She got mad at me. She denied everything." Her eyes well up. "It made me feel crazy. Just . . . crazy that she was pretending like what was happening wasn't happening. Because I *knew* it was happening to both of us, and she . . ." Katie breaks off then.

"What were you both afraid of?" My voice is so quiet, I'm low-key shocked that I said anything.

Katie bites her lip and shakes her head. "I'm sorry. I can't. I thought about telling you ever since you booked me. But I just can't do that to her. My truth is hers, too. And if I tell it, everyone will know, and she won't have had a say in it. Grace Odlin was not a good friend to me, but I can't help being one to her. She had the capacity for it. She did. I know she loved me in her own way. But she had to focus on surviving. There are no friends in survival. Everyone else is just a raft to keep you afloat."

I'm exhaling before I realize it. Sinking back into the dinette cushions.

Either Katie is right, and she and Grace were scared of the same thing. Something she won't talk about. Or she's wrong, and Grace was terrified of something completely different. Or maybe a bit of each because now we had whatever freaked out Jordan in the mix.

Fuck me, now I really wish he hadn't lawyered up like that. I'm sure Jayden wishes that even more. That's his only obvious super-natural lead thus far.

"Thank you," Jayden says. "Are you okay?"

"Fine. I've got a good therapist." She smiles and wipes her eyes.

Maybe I should leave it, but I can't stop myself from asking, "How did you feel about Dione and Grace's relationship? You weren't all friends until after it fell apart, right? But you were studying piano there for much longer."

"I don't mind talking about what it was like to know Daisy or

Grace, but if it's all the same to you, I would rather not comment about Peter or Dione. For the same reasons as before. Those two feel very much like Grace's business."

I want to point out that Peter was Katie's teacher too, not only Grace's stand-in dad, but I can see the way her face is shutting down. We're losing her. And we still need one more thing.

"Of course. Thank you." I hesitate for a moment, and only continue when Jayden nods in the corner of my eye. "Hopefully we'll get to chat with Grace. She's a hard one to pin down, though."

Katie blinks as she scoots out of the dinette. "She won't give you an interview?"

"Nope."

"Maybe if you offer not to talk about the goat? Hates that conversation. She did it again when she came back, you know?"

So now Katie wanted to be chatty? Not that I was going to walk away from any content she wanted to give. She shut down Peter and Dione, but she seems like she could talk about Grace for days. "Did what?"

Katie sets her can on the counter. "Helga called me. She said that Daisy found a dead goat on their property. One that Grace bought from them, supposedly for the milk. Its throat had been slit, and Grace had the gall to pretend she was shocked. She had to call Helga to butcher it. Didn't let them throw out any of the pieces, including the stomach. Some BS about using extras for soup stock."

"Did Helga ask Grace about it?"

"No. She managed to stay on Grace's good side by knowing what topics to leave alone."

"Had Grace asked her or Jordan to put a maggot in their ears?"

"No," Katie says with a little laugh. "They were never in the house. Jordan refused to be after that first time, and Helga didn't have cause to be. They didn't need protecting."

"Who did need protecting?" Jayden interjects. "Why would Grace do that again?"

"I honestly don't know. Grace looked rosy on the outside, but I don't think she had dealt with anything on the inside. That was why . . ." Katie stops and presses her fist to her mouth. It takes her a moment before she can remove it. "I was sorry that I didn't talk more about what happened in that house. I'm still sorry. And I know that it's not my job to speak up for everyone, but I wish I could."

Jayden puts a reassuring hand on her arm. "It's all right, we understand. We appreciate you doing this much."

"Thank you, and I admire you two so much." She meets my eyes. "Not just because of *Haunted*, either. Those things you let your mom share in her book. Those are intimate and painful moments. I can't imagine how hard that must have been. Especially when you don't owe anyone that level of detail about your life. And you're so young. To have unpacked that much at your age, it's amazing. I didn't see any miracles in that house when I was there, but what you've done for yourself feels like one, except it's all your hard work."

I force my face to stay neutral. As far as anyone knows, I consented to let Mom share everything about our lives in that book—as much as an eleven-year-old can, anyway. And I keep cosigning it every year. I know Katie isn't like the average reader or fan. This isn't about calling a Black woman strong. She's sincere, and that makes it worse.

She can't see that house as a place of good, but she can't see the truth of my mom, either.

No one can. No one but me.

"Thank you," I say, grabbing the rest of the equipment. "And thank you for your time, too."

Katie steps toward me. "How are you going to do this if Grace won't talk to you?"

"We think she will, actually."

"Really?"

I grin at Katie. "We've managed to reach Dione. I think that once her sister gets to say her piece in the story, Grace will be eager to do the same."

Katie looks very impressed. "Guess you don't get millions of views without having some skill in the game."

"No, you don't."

Katie heads back over to her family, embracing her wife when she gets there, while Jayden and I make the trudge back to the parking lot to call a cab—they normally don't come out here, so we had to prearrange our pickup.

Jayden waits until we're out of shouting distance of the camp to say, "Look at you. Smooth as ex-lax. I got worried when she started talking about the goat again. Though that was also prime content."

"I'm a professional," I reply, sticking my nose into the air.

Jayden laughs.

The truth is, we don't have an interview with Dione. But our contact assured us that we could get one. Tell Katie we have Dione, and she'll tell Helga, and Helga will tell Grace. At which point, Grace will contact us to be interviewed. And then we'll call Dione and tell her that her sister has agreed to chat with us. Making sure we have email proof of Grace agreeing, of course. Then, we get them both in the room for the interview of the goddamned year.

This time, I'm the one who pulls out the vlogging camera and points it at the two of us. "Do you actually think this is going to work?" I ask Jayden.

He shrugs. "Contact hasn't steered us wrong thus far."

"Please tell me I'm not the only one trying to guess who this mysterious contact is."

Jayden wiggles his eyebrows. "I think it's our dead girl. Reaching out to us from beyond the grave."

"You *cannot* be serious."

"Why not? They know a lot of stuff. Besides, did you hear what Katie said about Jordan? The house was *talking* to Grace. What if it was spirits? What if it's the same supernatural force that affected Daisy?"

I look dead at the camera. "Do you hear this? This is the guy who's supposed to stick to objective fact. *I'm* the emotional one."

He laughs. "Speculation is fun, but we do have a truth coming. Both of those women are allegedly hiding something big. If we get them in a room . . ."

"We can learn the truth."

And I'm ready to make them tell it.

CHAPTER TWENTY-FIVE

DAISY

Already almost a month had passed since we moved, and while October in Toronto was a slightly chilled version of September, in Timmins, it was the signal to begin winter. Snow fell intermittently in soft flakes that coated the ground in a thin dusting, and melted shortly after. Some people continued to stubbornly wear short sleeves as if it weren't happening.

I stepped on damp leaves as I made my way through the bush to King's place. The air was empty of predatory insects and instead developed a silence that was so crisp I could almost taste it. Like a fresh spray of ice-cold water onto your tongue. Chilled but refreshing.

Despite my declaration that he and Ivy stay away from me, I needed King for rides, and he was either gracious or pitying enough to continue offering them. Our drives were quiet and awkward. But his family never restarted their campaign against us running the Airbnb. I guess that despite everything, he wasn't mad enough at me to go back on his promise to keep them away.

Ivy, I had successfully avoided. Since the Ted-and-Mary incident, we'd had four more weekends of guests, each of them awarding
Mom with five stars. One woman, a Black lady who came up from
the city with her boyfriend, even claimed that she felt like an entirely
new person after staying. That she was going to write a book about
it. Toronto people could be so dramatic.

But it delighted Mom all the same. She was thriving—her own
words.

Meanwhile, I kept finding myself awake in the middle of the
night. Up suddenly and shifting, restless. And Mom would be just
outside my door, shuffling and then stopping. One night I called out
to her, but she didn't say anything. The next day I asked her about it,
and she denied it.

I knew that I should be going into the house. Trying to do something about a situation that was clearly wrong. But I dealt with the
dead, not with houses who fed on the living. King had basically told
me it was too late. It was probably going to get worse.

Based on what King and Ivy said, the normal function of the
house was that it called in the dead and forced them to pass on
by consuming them. Now, for some reason, it was ignoring them
and going after the living, leaving the house to fill with ghosts who
couldn't leave. And I had no idea how to fix it.

There were more butcherbirds than ever now. They coated the
trees in dashes of salt and pepper, but the mansion had become their
true home. The guests loved them, taking photos and videos. One of
them, some sort of bird-watcher guy, insisted that they should have
already moved on from the area by now. It was too cold for them.
Besides, they weren't even native to this region.

And yet they stayed.

I pulled my coat tighter around my body and walked faster.

It was darker in the mornings now, and the shadows that bounced off the trees and bushes made me uneasy. Like something was crouching, building momentum, and getting ready to pounce. Every crunch of leaves and snap of a branch made me twitch.

King was in the already-heated truck when I got there. We made our way to school in the same tense silence that we had existed in for the last few weeks. Which meant I usually spent our drives scrolling through my phone.

That feeling I got every time we left the property hadn't gotten any better. I was starting to worry that it was the house somehow. That it was pulling on me. But that felt paranoid. So I used the distraction of my phone to drown the thoughts out.

Finding things to do with my time that didn't involve social media was mind-numbing. I texted Megan a lot, though she wasn't attached to her phone. She had dance practices, studying, and hanging out with all those friends that I hadn't liked very much. So mostly I spent my free time watching long, exhaustive vlogs of people caring for their plants—doing hauls, showing off their collections, etc. I hoped that Noah or Stephanie didn't feel compelled to start a YouTube channel so that I wouldn't be forced off it, too.

I pressed my head against the window for the rest of the drive and got out promptly without looking at King when we arrived.

It took until the end of the school day for me to realize something was wrong.

I sat in Ms. Kuru's class while she handed back our first test. She had only given it out last Friday. I kept comparing her and Mom in my head. Over and over. They'd both spent so much time in the house when they were younger and yet were so different.

Ms. Kuru was, as far as I could tell, boring. She took only a weekend to grade tests for at least two classes of thirty because she probably had that much time on her hands. Mom, meanwhile, was on a high of business success and somehow still managed to go into town every week for some sort of social appointment.

But maybe that didn't make Mom more exciting than Ms. Kuru—just busier.

My test package landed on my desk with a soft flutter. Ms. Kuru gave me a wide smile that I didn't return. That wasn't the expression that teachers made at me when they handed out tests. A slight frown, yes. A pitying glance, frequently. An encouraging yet strained "Better luck next time," definitely. Never an outright smile. I couldn't even remember studying for it. I didn't care to. And sure, it was biology, but it wasn't about plants.

I stared down at my paper and kept staring.

Staring and staring.

The white of the pages were crisp and sharp. It was like Ms. Kuru hadn't even taken them home. They were pristine.

My tests didn't look like this.

There were usually a bunch of circles, handwritten notes, slashes, and crosses. Disappointment in crimson ink.

That was not this test.

The number in the corner proclaimed 96%.

My fingers shook, and I started flipping through. Page after page after page. Nothing, then—

There it was.

Question twenty-three. I hadn't gotten full points on my answer.

My gut flared, and I ground my teeth. I found myself checking over the question to figure out what I had done wrong. My face was so close to the paper that I could see where the ink bled slightly darker in some spots.

"Daisy?" Ms. Kuru asked.

I jumped in my seat. "What?" I blurted out.

The class filled with the sound of snickers.

She gave me an indulgent smile. Patient. Like I was her perfect little student. As if I weren't used to maintaining an unremarkable C average that regularly infuriated my mom. "Are you even trying?" was a familiar snapped phrase.

I wasn't. Though I didn't tell her that.

"We're going through the questions," Ms. Kuru said. "Do you want to share your answer for number one?"

I flipped to the beginning of the test and read out what I had written. What I had put down that I didn't remember studying.

That I didn't even remember putting down in the first place on a test that I didn't remember taking.

It was correct, of course.

When it came to question twenty-three, some guy in the class, Kurt, said his full answer.

I didn't care. I knew I didn't care. But I still diligently flipped to question twenty-three in my packet and wrote in the part of the answer that I had missed.

And I fucking hated Kurt. Just a bit. And I didn't know why.

I shook my head and forced a steadying breath out.

When class ended, Ms. Kuru waved me over. I would have given anything to leave, but I stayed. "Yes?" I said.

"You did a great job. You've really turned things around." She was beaming at me.

My jaw ached. "What?"

"All the other teachers have been saying how strong your performance in class is. Honestly, you were marked down as a student who might need extra help with your transition here, but you've been doing amazing. Your mom must be so proud."

What the actual fuck? What were they even talking about? I

could barely remember my classes, let alone think of something I did in any that would be remotely impressive.

Ms. Kuru leaned against her desk. "I would suggest that now you take the time to work on your participation more. That's five to ten percent of your grade in all of your classes. I think if you focus on that, then you can pull a high average. Your grade twelve results can have a lot of sway with universities."

I stopped paying attention then. The rest of her speech was a mash-up of droning about my grades and my future that became a soft whispering in my ear, right along with the rustling that had yet to stop. If anything, it felt like it had gotten louder. Distinct, even. Less like leaves and more like the sound of wind whipping through trees, a hint of a whistle.

And it was familiar . . . like I had heard it before, but I couldn't remember where.

When it was over, I gave a more decisive nod to seem like I had been listening.

"Daisy?" she asked. "Are you okay?"

"Fine. My ride is waiting. I need to go." I sped out of the classroom. Past students milling in the halls, their loud voices bouncing off the metal lockers and slapping me in the face. I gritted my teeth and kept on until I made it outside and hopped into King's truck, shivering, slamming the door shut behind me.

"What are you doing?" he asked, making a face.

"What?"

"You have no coat. No hat. No backpack."

I looked down at myself. He was right. I missed grabbing my bag from the classroom and hadn't stopped on the way to my locker. "Something is wrong with me."

King didn't look confused or startled. He pressed his thick lips into a line and met my eyes straight on.

"Well?" I said.

"Well?" he echoed.

"You know things!"

He let out a slow, languished breath before putting the car in reverse. "Sometimes I know things and shouldn't say them."

I laughed, sharp and disbelieving. "Really? That's all you've got? Some vague bullshit?"

"You already know. You don't need me to confirm it."

I didn't respond, and he didn't say anything back.

We drove home in our usual silence. I got out of the truck and started to head into the bush when something hit me on the head. It was heavy but soft.

I turned around and pulled it off. I was looking at King's thick coat.

"Hat too," he said, pointing at the ground where it must have fallen when he threw it. "You can give them back to me tomorrow."

I tugged both on, glad for the warmth now that I was outside the car and the chill was pulling on my skin, digging into my bones, and working the sting of ice through my insides.

King stood and watched me for a moment. "I figured it out, what's blocking me with you now. It's not the same as what was stopping me before. I still don't know what that was. But it's different."

"Thanks for more vague bullshit."

He tilted his head up to the sky and said, "I thought it would be better. Not knowing. Honestly, it's what I've been wishing for ever since it started."

"And it's not?" I tucked my hands into the deep pockets. His jacket was better than mine. I could barely feel the cold. I was near drowning in delicious heat.

"I saw a lot about you in that one instant. Then I got blocked again. The things I still know are just what I can remember. And it's not like I have some perfect memory. It's easy to forget stuff. For some memories to bleed away the more time passes. I worry that I've missed something important. All the time. It's like this constant dread." His breath misted in the air. "I'm afraid for you."

I wasn't used to people telling me their feelings. Not things like this anyway. Megan wasn't shy, but even she held back. I knew she worried more about her ballet technique than she ever expressed aloud to anyone. Mom was locked up like a high-security prison, and Noah's sharing of feelings was exclusive to things that he was passionate about—what upset him or what he loved. It wasn't ever anything that might make him look unsure about himself.

No one had ever told me something like this.

I didn't need King to be worried about me. I had taken care of myself for so long. I was used to it. "Then stay away from me."

He laughed. I blinked at him.

He kept on laughing and laughing. Tears sprang to his eyes from the force of it.

"What?" I barked.

"No . . . I just . . . It's good advice."

I glowered at him. "Can you at least set up a ride for me, then?"

King smiled. It was different than his others. I hadn't even realized how in tune I was to them. There was his smile for other students in the classroom hallways, this wide, carefree sort of grin. His smile for teachers and other adults, big but polite somehow, restrained.

This was different. It was open. His eyes moved with it. Crinkled in a way I hadn't seen before, and it came with a chuckle.

"It's good advice," he said again. "But I'm not going to follow it. Not unless you want me to stay away. So don't worry." He walked to the door of his house.

I shook my head. "You don't even know me."

He paused there. I knew that he'd heard me. The corner of his mouth quirked the slightest bit before he walked into the house.

The door shut behind him, and I stood there with his coat. Shivering, even though it was warm.

CHAPTER TWENTY-SIX

stared at the door to the Okeke house for longer than I wanted to. For once, I felt properly insulated against the cold with his hat and coat. Nice guys were a weird concept for me. Maybe that was sad, but maybe it was just realistic. Either way, I was starting to feel less than great about constantly going off on him. But at least that was something I felt capable of fixing.

I turned to leave when I saw her—one of King's aunts. The twins whose names I had already forgotten. There was a sort of glazed look in her eyes as she walked toward me. She must have been behind the house because King and I hadn't seen her earlier.

Her coat wasn't zipped up, and the shoes on her feet were slippers.

I waved at her awkwardly, but she didn't wave back.

She kept walking right past me with shuffling steps, slippers soaking through.

"Ms. Okeke?" I said.

My voice seemed to snap something. She jerked, and her gaze

concentrated on mine. Eyes suddenly clear. "Daisy?"

"Are you . . . okay? I can get King."

"I thought I heard . . ." Her face morphed quickly from confusion to terror. It was so naked and plain that I stepped back from her, looking around as if expecting to see what had shaken her. She lurched forward and grasped onto my arm. "You need to leave that house. Now."

Not more of this bullshit. King was supposed to have put a stop to this. "We can't leave."

"You *must*. Can't you hear it? It's never been this loud. *Never.*"

She shook her head at me and rushed back to their house. Probably I should have gone after her. But I didn't want to. I didn't want to talk about what we might both be hearing.

The warmth of the coat felt like it was sucked away with her words.

And finally, I remembered.

The woman. The dead woman whose memories I read. There had been a rustling sound with wind. That's when I'd first heard it. It was the house, drawing her in . . . but now living people were hearing it. The way Ms. Okeke was stumbling forward was exactly the same as the dead I had seen.

I think it's supposed to eat the dead. That's why they come when it calls. But it must prefer the living.

The bookings. I thought it was because of Mom's marketing skills, but when had that ever worked for any of her other businesses? If Ivy was right, the house was supposed to call to the dead. To *eat* the dead. But it wasn't eating them anymore. There *were* more of them in the house. Everyone was being drawn in, but the house was only feeding on the living.

I swallowed. It wasn't affecting me the same, though. Not like Ms. Okeke. But then again, I wasn't exactly normal.

I turned and entered the bush. Walking to the house with nothing but the shrikes to keep me company. This was so wrong. Everything was wrong. This place was supposed to be an escape, but it was starting to feel more like a trap.

"Hey," Ivy breathed on the back of my neck, and I whipped around.

"What the hell?!"

She poked me and pointed forward.

I was already at the edge of the bush that broke out alongside the mansion. Usually I saw the flashes of lights that came from our bunkie, because whatever Mom did during the day, somehow she always made sure she was home when I came back.

That wasn't what was happening now.

Tonight, there were at least five different people standing in front of the house with black uniforms covered by thick black vests that declared POLICE over the top in big white brick letters. Red and blue lights flashed bright from the direction of the dock, presumably how they had gotten onto the property in the first place.

An invisible hand seized my chest and squeezed.

My eyes darted around, searching for Mom. My lip trembled.

I saw a body bag, zipped up.

No.

I wanted to escape from her, yes, but I didn't want her gone.

I kept looking, desperate, and finally, I found her. Mom sat on the front steps of the house.

I exhaled so sharply that it whistled on the wind. Caught in the air and tossed away. I took two more quick breaths in.

Mom was fine. No. She was alive. That was more accurate. Her gaze looked empty. Vacant. Beside her sat a guy with his head in his hands. He didn't seem that much older than me. His shoulders were shaking. He wasn't small, but in that moment, he looked it. Tiny. Minuscule.

"What's going on?" I whispered finally.

Ivy rested her chin on my shoulder and leaned close to my ear. "Somebody died."

"*What?*" I croaked.

"They were in the house, and something must have happened. I think the mansion is starting to get greedy." She grabbed my right arm—her fingers digging into the puff of the coat.

It was unnerving. This discussion of the house like it was a living and breathing thing. Feeding. Eating. It brought to life the image of a slick tongue, wet with saliva, and pearly whites ripping into flesh. "The house killed them?" I asked, trying to control my breathing.

Ivy said nothing.

"Did it or didn't it?!"

She shoved me away from her, and I stumbled forward onto the frigid ground. When I looked back, she was running through the trees. "Fuck," I muttered, and picked myself up.

When I looked at the house again, Mom was staring at me.

Mom sat on the couch wrapped up in a blanket with a warm cup of hot chocolate in her hands that she wasn't drinking. Every light in the living room was on, and the police were long gone, thankfully. They'd taken the black bag with them. The husband had caught a ride into town with the cops to stay at a hotel there. "Husband" was shocking. Married teenagers weren't a common thing in the city. But those guests were.

Not anymore, though.

Understandably, he didn't want to stay in the place where his wife had died.

Where she had stopped being a person and started being a body.

I made my way around the kitchen gathering supplies. Oats, brown sugar, flour, and the apples that Mom picked up from Helga last week. The oven was preheated to 375 degrees. I washed the apples carefully and brought them over to the island, where a chopping block rested.

I found a paring knife and began the process of peeling and coring the apples. They were bright red with small patches of green on them. Mom liked apple crumble. It was easy to make too. I always baked it for her birthday paired with huge scoops of vanilla bean ice cream.

There was a show playing on the TV, but I knew Mom wasn't watching it.

Or she was. Staring at it. But not taking it in.

"Drink your hot chocolate," I said.

She immediately raised the mug to her mouth. When she took it away from her lips, she swiped a tongue over her top one, catching the bits of sweetness left there.

I finished peeling both apples and grabbed a bigger knife to cut them down to size. "Should we do something about the birds?" I asked. "There are a lot of them."

"We shouldn't have come here," Mom said. Her voice was its usual volume, even its usual tone, but there was something else in it that seemed to be missing.

I shook my head. "What are you talking about? We were always going to come here."

"I asked you if you wanted to."

The knife slammed on the chopping board as it tore through the apple. I cut it in half again before picking up the paring knife and slicing out the core. "But we were going to. Even if I said no, we were going to come. Weren't we?"

Silence filled the room. The truth of the words sat heavily in the space.

And they *were* true.

Even if Noah hadn't happened. If I had begged to stay in Toronto. We would have come. Of course we would have. Who said no to a free house? Who said no to no mortgage or rent? Who said no to piles of money sitting in an estate for you to use? Who would turn that down?

And if they were me, who said no to the freedom to live your own life? To the cash to be able to go where you wanted when you wanted? That was everything Mom promised me.

More than anything, she had always wanted this house. Known about this house. Made sure I knew about it.

It was always going to be a part of our lives.

King was right. Knowing was useless. Because even when people knew that something bad could happen, they still went through the motions of whatever they planned to do. I knew it didn't matter if I wanted to go or not, and I still walked around like it did.

It didn't matter what I wanted.

It had *never* mattered what I wanted.

That was why it was better to not want anything at all.

Mom said, "The birds are new. They weren't around when I was younger. They're usually farther north, but I guess they've migrated."

The knife slammed back down on the cutting board, and I forced a breath out of my mouth.

"I'm sorry," Mom muttered.

"No, you're not," I said.

She took a gulp of the hot chocolate and curled in on herself. "Where do you go at night?"

"I don't go anywhere," I snapped. "I'm asleep. You're the one walking around in the middle of the night, skulking around my door like a creep."

"I'm checking to make sure you're there."

I set aside the diced apples and looked around the kitchen for a shallow Pyrex baking dish. I found one in the warming tray underneath the oven and dumped the apples inside along with some dashes of cinnamon and nutmeg. Now I needed a bowl to combine the other ingredients.

"Daisy?" Mom called.

"What?" I gathered the flour, brown sugar, and oats into my arms and transferred them to the island.

"Where do you go at—"

"I'm not going anywhere!" I screamed. "I go to school, and I come home. I garden. I stare at the TV. I watch videos on my phone. I don't do anything else."

"Watch your tone." Her voice this time was familiar. Sharp and flat at once.

I swallowed and tossed some flour into the bowl. "Sorry."

"You've been different lately."

Each new ingredient went in with no measurement other than me eyeballing it. "How so?" I thought of the rustling in my ears. Of my lost memories.

"Did you go in the house?"

"No." I kept my eyes on the mixture and dragged my fingers through it, working it into a dough that crumbled between them. "You've already told me not to a million times. We go when you need me. Which is, apparently, never."

Mom set her mug down on the coffee table and buried her head in her hands. I thought she might cry, but she was silent. "Nothing is happening the way it was supposed to happen. That girl shouldn't have died. I don't understand what's going on."

"Something is wrong with that house."

Mom laughed, high-pitched, hysterical. "The house is not the issue. Why don't you understand? That house is *saving* us." There was a fever to her voice. She desperately wanted me to believe it. To buy into what she was saying.

"Then why are you so afraid of going inside?"

"I never said that."

But she was. She acted like it was only a rule for me, and yet she followed it better. Mom knew something was wrong with the mansion. How could she keep denying that it was playing a role? Keep acting like she knew *nothing* when she must have known *something*.

She lifted her head. Her eyes were wide and darting, her mouth open the tiniest bit to let out small staccato exhales. "No one was supposed to die," Mom said quietly, looking away from me.

Whatever it was that she thought she knew about this house when we came here, things had changed. She was losing control, if she ever had it in the first place. Her grand plan, her life's work, was crumbling just like the dead rose petals in the greenhouse trellis.

"Obviously," I replied. "No one starts an Airbnb with the hope that people will die in it." Butter. I was missing butter. Of course I was. I washed my hands in the sink and dug out a stick from the fridge.

"What are we going to do?" Mom said. "Daisy?"

"I don't know." I paused and stared at her. "What happened? Inside the house? With the girl?"

"I haven't gone in."

For fuck's sake. "I know. But do you know what happened?"

"No."

"What did the husband say?" Did he remember what had happened in there? Or was he like Mary and Ted, screams one minute and big smiles and five-star reviews the next? This whole thing was a mess.

Mom leaned her head on her knees. "He said that he was hanging out in the room and assumed she was exploring the house. Made them some lunch and went to find her once it was done, and then . . . he did."

"Maybe he killed her?"

She shot me a sharp look, and I held it. Mom knew. I would bet my right arm that she knew what had happened in that house. And now it seemed more obvious than ever that she was aware that I knew more than I was meant to.

And yet she insisted that it was normal. But if not the house, who was to blame? Immediately I thought of Ivy shoving me to the ground and running into the bush. She was untrustworthy, definitely, but a murderer?

I took the butter and tossed it into the mixing bowl. It coated my fingers, and the dry ingredients began to stick into distinct crumble-size pieces.

"Do you think they'll shut the Airbnb down?" Mom said, her gaze imploring.

Someone was dead, and she wanted to know if her business would be safe. She was still trying to make this work.

Her and this fucking house.

I dumped out the topping from the mixing bowl onto the apples and shoved the whole thing into the oven—its door closed with a clatter that echoed through the space.

"I'm sure it'll be fine," I said, because as usual, it was easier to lie.

Mom put her hot chocolate on the coffee table, curled into the blankets, and lay down on the couch. Exhausted.

I was too.

Tired. Drained.

But I never got to rest like she did.

And now I would have to abandon figuring out whatever was going on with me.

There wasn't any urgency in why I was scoring A's on tests I hadn't studied for.

But there was a lot of urgency in stopping the house from killing people.

I couldn't give up.

Not now. Not ever.

CHAPTER TWENTY-SEVEN

wanted to stay home with Mom the next day, but she pushed me off to school muttering about me "being a teenager."

When I stepped outside to walk to King's house, I was faced with the mansion wrapped in yellow caution tape. The wind whipped the tape in the air, where it slapped against the bricks with a snap that felt louder than it was. The shrikes had already started using pieces of it in their nests—spindly little things made of moss, feathers, and thorns. One over the top of the entryway had a brown mouse speared on one of the spikes, half-frozen and half-eaten.

I cast my gaze away and continued forward. When I got into the truck at King's place, I handed him back his coat and hat, along with the last thing that I had hidden away.

"Is that . . . for me?" he asked, but reached out and took the small terra-cotta pot before I answered.

It was a basil plant. I'd grown the herbs inside the bunkie and trimmed off a bit for him before I'd left. "I figured it would go well with your vegetables. I noticed you didn't seem to have any herbs," I mumbled.

King blinked at me. "A present?"

"It's to thank you. You kept your mom and aunts from trying to ruin the Airbnb. And even in the house, I know you were trying to help. So . . . thanks, I guess . . . and sorry, for being a bitch or whatever."

I remembered how excited Megan had been when I'd brought her a pot of mint. We hadn't been friends yet. But she had chattered my ear off about some sort of drink her dad made with the crushed leaves. The next day, I'd just given it to her. I'd had a lot.

It hadn't seemed like much, but we'd become friends after that.

King stuck his neck out for me time and time again. I didn't get why he was doing it. But after yesterday, after he said he was worried for me . . . he'd offered me something that no one else ever had. I needed him. It was only fair to offer something back.

There was still yesterday's incident with his aunt to discuss, but I hadn't figured out how I was going to bring that up yet.

He grinned down at the plant, and I could feel my face heating and puckering. "I thought you weren't here to make friends?" he asked.

"I'm making an exception. Now drive."

"Yes, ma'am," he laughed. "Just let me put this inside."

After King put away his basil, we made our way to school. He talked about anything and everything during the ride *but* the dead body found on our property. I started to think maybe he didn't know. But about two seconds of walking the school halls with people whispering at every turn clued me in to the fact that he was just being polite.

I hauled ass to Ms. Kuru's class to grab my backpack before my first period while barely saying hi and bye to her.

Now I was more aware of how I was at school. I would find myself sitting in a desk that I remembered walking to, but the whole class would be over, and I couldn't recall what had happened during the lesson. I would search though my bag and find completed homework and assignments that I didn't remember working on.

It wasn't supposed to be like this when we came to live here. Moving to Timmins was supposed to be easier.

In some ways, it was. Noah faded more every day. Or not faded, but changed. Like I had been looking at him from across a field of sunflowers. Small and beautiful. And the longer I was away, the closer I got, and for the first time, I could see him properly.

And I would remember that I didn't even like flowers. So why was I in this field with him?

In other ways, it wasn't. Like the death that Mom would likely be questioned for. Like my missing memories. Like the house torturing people who then forgot what had happened to them. Who were giving something up to escape it.

The mansion was calling people to feed on, and they were listening.

How long would that go on? The feeding? The killing? If the house was never stopped . . . would we keep having dead bodies? I couldn't let that happen.

I needed to fix it. Mom couldn't. Her specialty was starting things and ending them later when they inevitably went belly-up. She wouldn't even let me go inside the house, for fuck's sake.

If I could learn more about her and the history of this house, about how it functioned, how that girl died, all of that, I could stop it.

At the end of the school day, I got into the truck with King.

"Glad you were able to get your jacket today," he said as he turned on the ignition. It had gotten cold in the vehicle over the school day, and I could see my breath fogging in the air.

I twisted my hands into my jeans and swallowed. "I need your help." My voice was small in a way that I didn't want it to be.

King didn't ask me to repeat myself. He just stared for a moment. I was taken back to only a month ago when we'd stood in the greenhouse together and I'd asked the same thing. Asking for help wasn't a thing that I did. But here I was, asking him for the second time.

He could have questioned me. Checked what was in it for him. Instead, he said, "What do you need?"

Mackenzie opened the door to her house with a flourish and beamed at us. Unsurprisingly, I hadn't gone to her dance tryout, but she didn't seem to have any hard feelings about it. She lived in a two-story that from the outside was a marvel of perfect, meticulous architecture. It wasn't special. But it did seem brand-new. All the houses on Bonaventure Drive did. Everyone had a top-of-the-line truck or SUV sitting in their driveway. It was the same street that Mom's lawyer lived on.

"Come on in," Mackenzie chirped. "My mom will be home in a couple of hours. She'll probably know more stuff."

"Thanks," King said when I didn't respond.

We both kicked off our shoes in the foyer and stepped into the entrance with socked feet. The ceilings in the house were high, not as much as in the mansion, but pretty far up there. A grand piano rested in the entranceway, which split in one direction to a living room with a massive U-shaped couch surrounding an equally massive TV, and on the other side was a kitchen with a fridge about double the size of a normal one.

Mackenzie waved us over to the couch. "I'm gonna find that box my grandpa has around with the pictures and stuff. I'll be back."

She disappeared up a carpeted set of stairs as King and I sat down.

"Big house," I said.

King shrugged. "She's got, like, five siblings. They're at university now, though. She's the youngest."

Looking around the place, I didn't doubt that they had the money to pay for six kids to go to university. It was probably a drop in the bucket. Timmins didn't have private schools to suck up rich-kid education funds. Likely, Mackenzie's parents had everyone's tuition saved well before they needed the money.

Mom had a college fund, too, which she insisted was small but would help. I guess I should have been glad we had savings at all. It didn't matter anyway. No point in having cash if you get slapped with murder charges.

If it was deemed a homicide at all. I still didn't know. Mom hadn't given me any more details.

Mackenzie came back down the stairs with a stack of two boxes. They were the sort that you could buy in Home Sense. Cute things with flower print all over them and a magnetic clasp.

"My grandma picked the boxes," she said with a laugh, and dumped them both on the coffee table before sinking to her knees in front of it.

King and I both slid to the carpeted ground beside her to get a better look.

She riffled around in the box and pulled out a worn sheet of paper folded over. She pushed the box aside and unfolded it, spreading it out and pressing it down. "Here we go, Belanger family tree. This is just the copy. We have a fancy painted one that's at my grandpa's house with tiny portraits of us. It's super cute. Len MacDonald did it." She paused and looked at King. "Do you know him?"

"Yeah, he did the murals at school, right?"

"Yup! He's pretty good."

It took me only a quick scan of the scrawled names on the family tree to find Peter. The uncle that I never knew. Aunt Dione's ex-husband.

There were a lot of Belangers in town, but according to King, Mackenzie's family were the only ones who were directly related to Peter. Though her last name was Gagnon, Belanger was her mother's maiden name. It was why I hadn't made the connection.

According to the family tree, Mackenzie's mom was Peter's first cousin. Their dads were brothers. Peter's dad was the younger of the two.

"Do you know how Peter's dad died?" I asked. The only thing I knew about my uncle was that he was estranged from his family, according to Mom, but still seemed to benefit from their wealth. King had filled me in on Peter inheriting the mansion when his dad died.

Mackenzie bobbed her head in a nod, strawberry-blond curls bouncing. She frequently alternated between a slick-straight look and these perfect loose ringlets. "Ice-fishing accident. He went out on the lake when it was too thin and fell through. That was ages ago, though. My mom was like twenty when that happened. I wasn't born yet, so I didn't know him."

Jesus. "What about Peter?" I asked.

"You don't know how he died?!"

"My mom didn't say."

Mackenzie looked scandalized. I should have just asked King in private. "Brain aneurysm."

"Oh," I said.

"Completely random! He had gone out to the gas station between the house and the town. The attendant remembered. Just picking up milk, totally normal. And then he went home and had that aneurysm. Just dropped dead. Your aunt was never in town, and they were divorced by then anyway, so he was by himself." She shook her head. "He had a lesson he was supposed to do the next day, so that's when they found him. My uncle—he's in the police—said that he was slumped in his armchair, like he fell asleep." She seemed to catch herself at my expression. "Sorry . . ."

"It's fine." I didn't really care about Peter. I hadn't known him to mourn him. I guess I could see why Mom wouldn't want to chitchat about a death like that. It was sad. Dying alone. "You have photos of the house?"

"Yes!" Mackenzie dug around in the box, which seemed like a disjointed array of photos wrapped in different rubber bands, pulled out a stack, and laid the pictures out. "My, like, five-times-great-grandpa built it in the 1900s during the gold rush here. It was a summer home. You should see the thing he built on Dalton Road for their everyday house! Gold money got you a lot back then, still does. Peter had his dad's stocks in it. We have some too."

That explained where my uncle got all his money.

I looked at the photos. It was the house for sure. There were some of the mansion alone, lots of others with family members standing in front of it, and some where they were inside. I didn't know what I could find out from them, but it was better than nothing. I raised my phone and took pictures of everything lying there. "Have you ever been in the house?"

"No, Mom hated Peter. And he's owned it the whole time I've been alive. So she won't go."

I blinked at her. "Really?"

She nodded meaningfully with wide eyes. "Yeah, it was really weird. Everyone else in the family seemed all right with him. But he never used to come to stuff. Like we have a reunion every five years, and he never came once."

"My mom said he was estranged from the family."

Mackenzie crossed her arms. "That's not our fault. We always invited him to things. Unless it was, like, just our immediate family because Mom didn't want to have him over." She flicked her hand over at the grand piano. "I wanted him to teach me piano since he's like an actual concert pianist, and she said no. I don't know. Sometimes you have cousins that you don't like. She's the only one who was bothered by him, though."

It was the first time I had heard of anyone not liking Peter. Mom insisted that he was like another parent to her. Aunt Dione was the one she had a big hate-on for. "I guess you never met my aunt, then?"

"No. Maybe my mom did, though? You can ask her when she gets in."

I asked, "Wait . . . So your mom's dad, he's older than Peter, isn't he? Why didn't he or his kids get the house?"

Mackenzie eyes lit up. "Okay, so this is the spooky thing. It's a nice summer home, but apparently, way back when, weird things happened, so the family kept going less and less."

"Weird things?" Like people being tortured in bedrooms?

She shrugged. "No idea—everyone was really tight-lipped about it. The small-town rumor mill is strong, and I guess they didn't want it going off on them. Anyway, and don't mention this to my mom 'cause she hates this stuff, but my grandpa told me that when they stayed the odd weekend, there would be whispers in the night. Like someone's voice, but no one was ever there. He used to put up huge tantrums to avoid going."

I resisted the urge to dig a fingernail into my ear. The rustling wouldn't stop. But that wasn't like what Mackenzie was describing. It didn't sound anything like someone's voice.

"Does your mom not believe him?" I asked.

"No," she said. "She says that his brother, Peter's dad, used to bully him a lot. Pretty badly, apparently. Even though his brother was the younger one. It's why we're not super close with them in the first place. Either way, she thinks that he was probably teasing Grandpa and doing the whispering himself. Whatever it was, the house would have gone to Grandpa, but he didn't want it and didn't want any of his kids to have it either. Peter was an only child, so he got it. He's the only one who has ever actually lived there full-time." She raised her eyebrows at me and said with a laugh, "You haven't noticed any whispering, have you?"

I shook my head and stuck a plastic smile on my face.

I sat quietly staring at the pictures while King and Mackenzie talked about school, people they knew, and town stuff.

There were only a couple of pictures with Peter in them, I guess because he avoided family functions. He was cute enough. I could see why Aunt Dione would have liked him. He seemed pretty tall, side-parted blond hair with a bit of light brown mixed in, easy smile. A nice guy. Or someone who looked like one, anyway.

"Too bad you never made it to dance tryouts," Mackenzie said.

I tore my eyes away from the pictures and shrugged. "Not really my thing."

She frowned. "You said that you did dance at your last high school."

"What?"

"On like the first day of school. Remember? When we sat together in English. I was talking about being on the dance team, and you said you used to do ballet and contemporary at your old school."

My face went slack. I searched rapidly through my memories for something, but I couldn't grasp anything. School was like this blank slate of me walking through halls, and the day beginning and ending without much in between.

The door cracked open, and Mackenzie jumped up. "My mom is home. Hold on, I'll grab her. You can ask her about the house but not about Peter 'cause she'll freak. She haaates him." She walked out of the living room into the entryway, and I kept staring after her.

"Hey," King said. "You okay?"

"Yeah," I mumbled. This missing time had been happening since the first day of school.

My skin crawled. It was like the worm was back, but instead of being in my head, it was crawling beneath my skin. Writhing in the slick warmth of muscle and blood. As if I could press my finger against my neck and feel it squirm under the gentle thud of my pulse.

Mackenzie steered her mom into the living room. "This is King, you know King, and Daisy. She's new. Her mom moved into the mansion, you know . . ." The rest of the sentence trailed off in French. I caught something that sounded like "Kenogamissi" and "pépère." All I knew from French class was how to conjugate verbs poorly, how to ask to use the bathroom very well, and not much else.

Ms. Gagnon was like an older copy of Mackenzie. The same strawberry-blond hair and petite frame, but with wrinkles around the eyes that didn't go away when she stopped smiling. She wore a pantsuit with her hair tucked back in a neat bun.

She moved forward and reached out her hand. "Nice to meet you, Daisy."

"Nice to meet you, too," I echoed back.

King rose, and she pulled him into a hug. "King, always nice to see you. How is your mom doing?"

"Good, as usual," he said with a grin.

Ms. Gagnon released King and made her way over to the couch across from us and sat down, her legs neatly crossed at the ankles. "Mackenzie said you needed to do a bit of research for an independent assignment?"

It was a convenient lie. And honestly, Ms. Gagnon had no reason to suspect me. "Yes, I was curious if you had ever visited the house?"

"Only a couple of times. My uncle suggested the cousins take piano lessons together, but it didn't end up working out. Too far for anyone to visit regularly." She shifted in place. "I didn't really like it and didn't have much talent anyway."

Where was I supposed to go with that? Was I supposed to ask if anyone had ever been killed? If anything strange had ever happened there? Clearly she didn't believe in the experience her dad had as a child. "Did you know my mom? You may have been around the same age when she used to spend her summers here. Grace Odlin?"

Her shoulders relaxed. "I did, actually. Your mom came to drop some things off for my dad once. There were some old photographs in the house that he wanted, and she came into town more often than they did."

She didn't specify who "they" were, though I imagined it was Uncle Peter and Aunt Dione. "Do you know when that was?"

"I think it was a couple of years before she left. She came over with her little friends. They were sweet, all of them—they're still around town too except for the boy, Jordan. Katie and Helga are both lovely women." She shook her head. "I never believed all the sensationalism. Our newspapers are more gossip rings than anything."

"Sensationalism?"

"Over the goat."

I blinked. Had they done a newspaper article about our goat being killed? No. Ms. Gagnon was talking about this like it had happened a while ago. "The goat?"

Her eyes widened. "Oh, did you not know about that? I guess I just assumed . . . but of course Grace probably wouldn't want to talk about that. Don't worry about it." She stood up and brushed nothing off her skirt. "I'm sorry, guys, I have to get washed up and get dinner going. It was nice to meet you, and good luck with your assignment." She pointed to King. "Tell your mom I'll be coming soon to cash in that two-for-one coupon."

"We're gonna get our palms read," Mackenzie said with a smile.

"I'll let her know." King smiled back, easy, big but restrained. The adult smile.

"Good fortunes only," Ms. Gagnon said over her shoulder as she went into the kitchen.

He called back, "Of course."

Mackenzie turned to us after her mom had gone. "I hope that helped out."

"It was great. Thanks." King gave Mackenzie an indulgent smile that she shone under. That was the one for peers and students in the hallways.

Back in the now-freezing truck, I turned to King. "Does this place have a library?"

He rolled his eyes. "Obviously. It's not Siberia."

"Maybe Siberia also has a library, and you just offended them as much as I, apparently, offended you."

King didn't say any more, just kicked the truck into drive and pulled away.

CHAPTER TWENTY-EIGHT

The Timmins library was easily nicer than any Toronto branch I had ever lived near, to the point where I understood why King was offended that I didn't even think they had one. The building was massive. I spotted it on one street, we turned down another, and it kept going.

It had huge windows set into it and one space in particular where they went from floor to ceiling, tinted a tasteful light blue. We parked and made our way inside. Wooden beams stretched up from the floor and split like the branches of a tree as they reached to the towering ceiling, which was almost double the height of those in the mansion.

The seating in the space actually looked comfortable. There were armchairs and couches with thick cushions colored in the same light-blue hue as the windows and accents in the library.

And it was deserted.

When we walked in, there was a moment where I wasn't sure if we were the only people there. I guess that Tuesday afternoon wasn't exactly a peak time.

There were no dead, either.

I swallowed. How far could the house call? How far was it stretching to grasp the living, catching the dead in the same web?

"Okay," I said, turning to King and shaking off the unease. "Where do they keep the old newspaper files?"

"I don't know. I never come here." He pointed at a desk over by the second entrance. "Ask the librarian."

"Fine."

I had to sign up for a library card to get access to the online records. Once I got mine, I made my way over to the computers with King and sat down.

My phone buzzed, and I checked the screen. I had sent Mom a message to say I would be back later than usual, and she hadn't responded until now:

Just leaving the police station. Everything is fine. See you at home.

Something in the middle of my back unwound. It was like there had been a pressure pushing down and digging in that was gone now.

"Everything good?" King asked.

I nodded. "Yeah."

In the search box, I put in "goat" and scrolled back through to the years when Mom would have spent her summers in Timmins.

The headline jumped out: TEENAGE CULT SACRIFICES GOAT.

"Shit," King muttered.

"Yeah." I couldn't think of anything else to say.

The article detailed the events in which, allegedly, the farmhand at Helga's parents' place had seen the teens sneaking in and out of the farm. One of them, who he affectionately called "the Black girl," had a cooler bag filled with "God knows what." When he went into the barn, he found the goat gutted on the ground. He also said that they drew a cross in blood, but the reporter stipulated that they couldn't find any supporting evidence.

"They killed a goat together and maybe took something from it—that's the gist of this, right?" King said, leaning his chin against his elbow.

I tried to remember if anything had been missing from the goat at the house but couldn't. I hadn't exactly been concerned about examining the body. The only thing I did know was that it had been cut open by a person, not an animal. In the back of my mind, I had thought that one of his aunts had gone behind King's back to try and scare us, even though there wasn't any evidence of that. It was better than imagining a complete stranger sneaking onto our property to murder the goat. I was dealing with enough without bringing that unknown into my brain.

Helga and Joe did leave us all the pieces after they butchered it. I was busy packing the meat into the freezer. Technically, Mom could have set aside a piece of it. But why?

"Why was this being called a cult thing? 'Cause of the cross?" I asked.

King shrugged. "I think most people assume ritual animal sacrifice is a cult thing."

"Why a goat, though?"

"No idea. There was that one movie with like that evil goat. And it was Satan. Maybe that's why?"

I gave him a skeptical look. "Aren't you the occult guy?"

"Uh, no," he said, crossing his arms. "We tell fortunes and do the occasional cleansing. Not Satan worship stuff."

I rested my head on the desk and sighed. What had Mom been doing?

Jerking up, I looked at the date of the article. I ran the numbers through my head, and when I finished, sagged back in my chair.

"What?" King asked.

"She was pregnant with me when she did this." I swallowed. I twisted my hands in my lap. I didn't really know how to feel about that extra tidbit of information.

"Fuck," he breathed. I agreed.

"Is there any more to the story with your great-aunt? Maybe there's a detail in there that you missed."

He raised his own skeptical eyebrow.

"You never know!"

"I've told you *everything*. My family's powers exist to bring the house back into balance with whatever bullshit supernatural eco-system it exists in. The cleansing is the only thing my aunt figured out to deal with it. It never got this bad for her, so she didn't need more."

"She doesn't have a spell book or something?"

He threw me a deadpan look. "We're psychics, not witches."

"You know what I mean!"

"No. She was the only one in the family with any type of clair-voyance. What she found, she managed through a lot of time and research. And unfortunately, time is not a thing on our side, and I have no idea where to even start with figuring out what to do."

I sighed and tried to get the facts in order.

Ivy said the house was an animal. It was supposed to eat the dead but sometimes changed that behavior and started chowing down on the living. That's when it needed to be reeled in to its "natural" state, and when King's family had their ability activated. Usually, they did a cleansing and that fixed things, but it was too late now. "What usually happens after the cleansing? It just stops?"

King nods. "Yeah, and the knowing goes away. It only appears when needed, like when it first developed in my aunt. And if the house acts up again, the knowing ability reappears in my family, always a new person. Only one at a time. When *your* mom used to live here, *my* mom was the one who knew. Peter wouldn't let her do the cleansing, but she kept asking. And after a couple of years, the knowing just went away. Like it expired or something. And the house was fine." He shrugged again. "Right up until Peter died. Then I got it."

"Why did it suddenly stop and then start again?"

"No idea."

What was different between the time when King's mom got their family's ability and when he got it? No one had died during her time. Meanwhile, King's knowing appeared with Peter's death. Did that mean that the house actually killed him? The same way it potentially killed that girl? Either way, the ability was triggered by the mansion's behavior. "If the knowing appears when the house starts eating people . . . it would only randomly go away if the house stopped eating, right?"

King's jaw dropped. "Wait, wait, hold up. Who is the house eating?"

I was about to ask King why he didn't know what Ivy had told me, then realized me and Ivy were blocked from King's knowing, and besides that, we had had that conversation inside the house—which was also blocked. I quickly caught him up on everything she'd said. I also got him up to speed on what happened with his aunt.

"Shit," he said, leaning back in his chair. "It's going to keep going—you know that, right? Its 'stomach' will keep growing, and it'll eat and kill endlessly unless we find a way to make it stop."

I swallowed. We could try and shut down the Airbnb, but if the house could call people to it, it wouldn't matter. If we destroyed it . . . I stopped myself before I went on that train of thought. No. I couldn't. We needed this house. This was *our* house. *My* freedom.

Maybe if I were a better person, I would care more about the people dying. About the potentially catastrophic level of damage the house could cause. But it felt too big. Too far away. More than anything, I cared about what I had been working for my whole life. Something I would never get if things went completely sideways. "Why are you doing this?" I asked King. "Why are you so devoted to helping? Sure, okay, you're worried about me and whatever scary thing is in my future, but there must be more."

"Do I need more of a reason than wanting to stop a supernatural house from drawing in and killing potentially hundreds of thousands of people? Everyone in my hometown at a minimum."

"Yes. Sure, let's stop people from dying. But that can't be everything."

King slipped on a smile. Not the one for peers or adults. The one for me. "I'm doing this for the same reason you are: stopping this house means being free."

He knew what this house meant to me. The escape.

Of course he knew.

But what he wanted was to *not know*. If the house never stopped feeding, his ability might never go away.

It wasn't like back when his mom had the power. There was no mysterious thing making the mansion work the way it was supposed to again.

Now it had enough power to go on seemingly forever.

King wouldn't get his freedom.

For all intents, we were both laid bare now. Our intentions set out. Both of us aligned on this singular goal.

Researching was supposed to help me fix things. To improve the situation, not make it more complicated.

Uncle Peter was liked except when he was hated. Aunt Dione seemed to not even exist. Mom was running around killing goats with me in her belly and might or might not have killed another one.

And we had no idea how to stop the house.

I needed to get to the heart of the mansion, and I only knew one person who claimed they could communicate with it.

I needed to talk to Ivy.

And this time, she was going to give me answers.

My phone rang, and when I looked down, I saw Dad's name.

Clearly, I wasn't the only person seeking answers from someone.

He must have heard about the death. I wouldn't put it past him to be stalking Timmins news sites. He was obsessed with the idea of something going wrong at the house, and now something had. There was no other reason for a call during a weekday.

"I have to take this," I said to King, quickly making my way out of the library. I answered, "Yeah?"

"Daisy, please, for the love of God, go stay with your grandma. I know you don't like her, but I can't take you out of the province without your mom's permission, and I know she won't give it."

I froze. It hadn't ever occurred to me that Dad didn't offer his place because he wasn't legally allowed.

I hadn't replied yet, but he kept going. "I know that I'm not the dad you want. I just . . . fuck, I don't know what I'm doing. My parents used to dump me on my grandparents every summer. I had to call my dad 'sir.' I spent most of my childhood being friends with teenage girls, and somehow it hasn't helped with having one for a daughter. It's fine if you never like me, just please, please, leave that house."

"Why? How many times do I have to ask before you tell me?"

His breathing increased, getting rougher. "She wanted you to be the way you are. That's why . . . That's why she brought me into the house. She wanted you to see those things."

The cold air flooded my throat and swallowed me whole. I would have gasped if I felt like I had any breath in me.

"You would talk to the air." Dad stumbled through his words. "I couldn't . . . I couldn't go through it again. She left me in that room! She left me! She said she didn't, but I know she did! She never cared about any of us!" I heard a thump, and Dad suddenly sounded far away. Like he dropped the phone and ran.

She wanted you to see those things.

You would talk to the air.

I knew Dad was scared of Mom. I had always known.

Now I knew he was afraid of me, too.

"Dad . . . What do you mean that Mom wanted me to be the way that I am?"

There was silence. So much silence. I waited. It felt like more than seconds were passing. I was stuck in an eternity of frigid cold.

"Children conceived in that house are different. *You* are different."

My lip trembled. "I don't believe you." No. She wouldn't. That couldn't be it. What was he even suggesting? That Mom made some sort of pact with the house for a daughter who could see ghosts? It didn't even make sense.

But part of me whispered that maybe it did.

I squashed it.

"Daisy! You have to leave the house! You have to—"

I hung up and blocked him.

CHAPTER TWENTY-NINE

There was no alarm today. Saturday. Though I still had a ringing in my ear. I lay in bed staring at the ceiling, knowing I had slept in but still not feeling rested. The blind over the window was up, and I had stopped bothering to put it down anymore. The sunlight was full and bright, though I knew it would be cold outside. From this vantage point, I could see the tiniest bit of myself in the vanity mirror. If I strained up, probably I could see myself fully. Not that I wanted to.

Even after solidifying my alliance with King and wanting to do something, I hadn't actually done anything yet. There were police officers filing in and out of the house on a regular basis, and Mom was supervising just as frequently. Though she continued to avoid going in.

Almost an entire week was wasted.

But today they would finally be gone.

And I would get to start another day with the full weight of everything that I had yet to accomplish.

Dad's words kept circling in my mind.

He probably tried to call again. I didn't know. I still had him blocked.

I didn't want to move.

But I did.

I got out of bed. Brushed my teeth. Peed. Washed my hands, obviously, before making my way to Mom's room.

I gave her the courtesy of a knock before I let myself in. She was bundled up in blankets with only her head poking out. It could have been funny, but mostly it was sad. I leaned against the doorjamb and let the wood press into my skin.

"What's up?" My voice was casual. Maybe that was appreciated. Maybe it wasn't.

Mom flicked her eyes to me. "The police are done inside." I knew that already. Had overheard the conversation. "There will be new people coming tomorrow morning. I need you—"

"You can't be fucking serious." I sagged against the doorway.

"Language."

"Someone just died in there!" I shook my head and pushed away from the door. My body felt flooded with energy. I needed to move.

"The woman had a brain aneurysm. It's a medical anomaly." She sat up fully in bed, her hair disheveled and coming out of its twists. "We are running a business, Daisy. We need to have money coming in to cover costs." She let out a huff. "And if we stop booking people, it'll look suspicious."

A brain aneurysm. Not murdered. A medical anomaly . . . and yet, it was the same way Uncle Peter had died. The death that had potentially triggered King's knowing. No way that was a coincidence.

Still, I wasn't willing to share with Mom what I had learned. I couldn't imagine myself telling her. I knew what she would say.

What is wrong with you?

I swallowed. "How will it look if the next guests die too?"

Her eyes got sharp, and she stared straight into mine. "No one was supposed to die in the first place."

I shrank back and hated myself for it. None of this was my fault. "Something is wrong with the house." I had to get this across to her somehow. That she needed to stop letting people into it. All we were doing was making feeding easier. "I . . . I heard moaning." I technically had. Maybe this would be unsettling enough to make her pay attention.

If I knew Mom, she would confirm nothing. But if it gave her pause, that was enough.

Her eyes got sharp. "You heard that inside the house?"

"I heard it from outside, but yes, the sound was inside. Moaning, like someone in pain."

"A man's voice? Or a woman's?"

"Does it matter?!"

"Yes." Mom was perfectly still, staring at me.

I thought back to that day, to the way the groans sounded as I ran out of the mansion. "A man . . . definitely a man."

A smile slid onto her face. I only saw it for a moment before she pressed her hands against it, hiding it from me. And yet, at the same time, the beginning of tears leapt to her eyes. "It's probably nothing," she choked out from between her fingers. "A squatter maybe. I'll let the cleaning staff know to be on the lookout."

"You haven't heard anything?"

"No," she said. "Let me know if you notice it again." Neatly brushing me off. But she couldn't. There was no way she was going to pull this shit with me. To pretend it wasn't anything. I saw that fucking smile. What was there to smile about?

"Mom. Something is wrong with the house."

"Enough!" she shouted suddenly, hands dropped, the smile gone from her face. "You cannot fall apart like this. Not again! This isn't hard. I've barely asked you to do anything." Her shoulders slumped, and the beginning of tears that sat in her eyes spilled out. "I am doing my best. I have *always* done my best. For you! Why can't you just meet me halfway?"

It was so unbelievably difficult to be me, and she would never understand that. It was torture living like this. Seeing what I could see.

"I wanted you to just be able to be a teenager and not worry about any of this shit. I really wanted that for you. But you insist on making everything a challenge." She sucked in a breath of air and shook her head. "I just can't. I can't."

She cried then. Great heaving sobs. Eventually she leaned forward until her face was pressed into the pillows and cried more.

It was like this before, too. In that school hallway. Where she shook me by the shoulders, and I tried to tell her why I had done what I had done. That I was sure that girl was dead. That she was going to hurt me like the others had. That I had to protect myself.

And all she had said was, "What is wrong with you?"

Now I stared at her shaking shoulders and listened to her sobs.

I cried a little too. But I stayed quiet. And by the time she looked up, I was long done. "I'm going to go water the plants," I said.

She slunk back underneath the covers, exhausted, and turned away from me.

I began to pull the door shut when she spoke behind me, "I'm a bad mom, aren't I?" Her voice was soft, but I could hear it.

"You aren't."

In some ways, she was. In others, she wasn't. I never went without food. I always had a roof over my head, even if we had to spend days touring apartments to get it. She never hit me. Sometimes it was fun to be around her. We could watch shows together, listen to music, go out to eat. Those were the best times.

But there was a distance. This physical divide that extended from her past and crawled its way to my present. It was the things she wouldn't say.

I didn't really know who Mom was. I had this person I had been living with my entire life, and I didn't have any idea who she was. And yet I was still marching to the beat of her drum. She made sure of that.

I closed the door behind me and tugged on my outdoor clothes before making my way to the greenhouse. The trellis was covered with a thin layer of frost. I wouldn't be able to even attempt to grow ivy through it until the spring, and who knew what the spring here would be like. None of it seemed to be growing on the mansion, though it was hard to tell if that was because the plant couldn't thrive there or if grounds staff were pulling it off so the place could continue to look brand-new.

When the glass doors came into view, I stopped.

Then I ran.

I rushed through the doors, shoving them open where they banged against the walls of the space. I sprinted through, checking the plants, the heat wafting over me, so humid that I had to shrug off my jacket.

I speed-walked through row after row before stopping still.

At least half of the plants in the greenhouse were dead or dying.

Sick yellowing leaves overtaking smooth green ones. Limp hanging pieces sagging, wrinkled, and withered. When I pressed my fingers to the soil, it was wet. Too wet. Half of the things were drowning in their pots as if someone overexcited and undereducated had tried to take care of them. They reminded me of how my plants looked the very first time I started caring for them.

I pressed the heels of my hands against my eyes and choked down a sob.

Everything that was mine. Just for me. My one thing, was destroyed.

I should have been checking on them every day after school. Only me. No one else should have been here to mess these up so royally. It's not like the guests were going to suddenly do some light gardening on their vacation. Even then, I should have been around often enough to catch them and put a stop to it. I kept trying to find the memories of what should have been daily visits. To remember walking into the space, and the calm that always settled over me when I cared for them.

But I couldn't find anything.

There were gnawing holes. Spaces where I should have remembered something but couldn't.

I began the slow process of tipping the pots over to help drain them. Shears clipped and cut into the ones with dying leaves. The dead were pulled from their graves, cradled, and deposited in the leftover yard bags.

When I was done, the space was again a haven of greenery, my fingernails had packs of soil stuck underneath them, and my neck felt stiff—the muscles were tense and corded.

I stalked out of the greenhouse and made my way back into the bunkie. The only bright spot was that the ones inside the bunkie were still okay. I remembered taking care of those. My monstera was alive. I gave myself a moment to touch its leaves, frowning at the slightly browned edges that shouldn't have been there.

I was slipping up.

More than that.

I had already fallen, and I was only now realizing—scrambling on the ground, grasping at the earth and snow and cracked leaves, desperately trying to get up.

Leaving the plant, I walked to Mom's room. I assumed she was inside because the crack under the door showed the lights were still off. I gently pushed the door open.

She lay covered in her blanket, soft snores floating out of it. I tiptoed to her dresser, opened it, and pulled out the house keys she stashed there. A glance at her confirmed that she hadn't noticed. I backed out and made my way to the mansion.

Ivy said it showed you more when you were alone.

Fine.

I was ready to see what it had to give.

CHAPTER THIRTY

I went in through the front door. The space was the same as it had been the first time. Sparkling grand chandelier, gold filigree-accented staircases, and impeccable and expensive-looking entryway furniture. No one would have been able to guess that someone had died in here on Monday.

But I knew.

I could see her dragging herself across the hallway. She looked exactly like the photo they flashed on the news. Only, her eyes were empty. Without direction or even awareness. The dead were like that when they were fresh.

And there were more. So many more than when I had been here last.

I ignored them and walked forward. I didn't give myself time to think before I thrust my hand into the woman's chest and locked my fingers around her heart.

I can't fix it. Do I even love him anymore? Too young. Maybe they were right. Such a beautiful home. Music. The most gorgeous piano I've ever seen. I can't play well. Who's that?

I stumbled away from her too hard and fast, landing on my ass on the floor. I gasped from the pain and tried to sort out the images in my head. It was so chaotic. My teeth chattered, and I tugged my arms around myself, trying to warm up. I was tempted to try again, but I was too cold.

Someone came into that room with her.

She wasn't alone.

I just didn't know who it was.

A moan from the top of the steps reached me. Louder than it was before.

I got to my feet and raced up the stairs. Ivy wasn't here to guide me, but it didn't matter. I reached the upper floor and began opening the doors to the rooms, one by one. Over and over. They were mostly the same, endless bedrooms with plush sheets and silver accents. Towels hanging from gilded hooks. Balconies with gauzy white-and-midnight-blue curtains that flapped in the breeze.

I was in the process of turning down another hall when I stopped. On the wall, there was a painting of a barren tree, enormous and spindly, its branches reaching out like long dark fingers and covered in white snow. The piece was taller than I was, stretching from my knees to above my head, and it was wider than my arms could reach. Across the very top was a detailed banner that proclaimed "Belanger."

Somehow I doubted that the family tree Mackenzie's grandpa so prized looked anywhere as grand and detailed as this one. I pressed close to it. It was like she'd described. It had small, detailed portraits of each of the family members.

I crouched down to find Aunt Dione and Peter. They were at the very bottom, clustered together. Underneath Peter's name it said "deceased."

I shot to my feet and stepped back from it. Who had updated that? When? And why? I couldn't see Mom tracking down the artist just to get that on it.

At the end of the hall, a door creaked open, and a long, agonized moan sounded from it.

My head snapped in its direction.

It was the same room. That door.

If King were here, he would say not to go in there. It would be obvious to him that it was the room to avoid.

The moan got louder, and the voice sounded clogged, the way you do after crying. But I still felt like my guess was right. It was a man.

I wouldn't learn anything if I shied away. There were secrets in this house. And one of them might tell me how to stop anyone else from dying. How to smother the house's voice. Besides, that smile . . . the way Mom reacted when I told her about the moaning . . .

I walked to the door.

Before I could make it there, it expelled what was inside. That was the only way I could describe it. A man slid out, twisted and contorted in a way that was difficult to comprehend, his skin translucent, barely discernible, and it was slick and pale green and yellow, like vomit. Like the room had thrown him up, disgusted. He was like a wisp. He moaned again and turned to me.

I had never seen anything like it. His face was mutated and inhuman-looking, the features out of proper order, but familiar somehow. I stumbled back and must have walked into a vase because it shattered behind me. I whipped around automatically to look at it, heart hammering in my chest, and when I turned back, the moaning man was gone.

My chest burned, and I realized that I wasn't breathing. I gasped and, legs shaking, dragged myself to the room he'd come out of.

When I stepped into it, it transformed. Changing from the standard mansion room into something more lived-in. There was still the massive bed, this one with thin curtains draped around it, like a princess's sleeping quarters. In a corner, I spied a cluster of photos tucked into the vanity mirror. Even from this far away, I could recognize Mom in miniature form. I was relieved to focus on her instead of the dead man I had seen.

There was Mom at all different ages. In some photos, she was little, maybe ten or eleven, and in others she was older, closer to my age. I ran my fingers over the prints. There were more people too, not just her.

A girl at a piano whose short black hair and warm brown skin marked her as Ms. Kuru. A Black boy lay on the grass, springy twists on his head, and a smile on his face. Dad. Another girl, with a round face and a crown of daffodils in her white-blond hair, laughing at the camera. Helga. There was one of all four of them too. It wasn't on this property—maybe Helga's family's cottage? They were grinning at the camera, except for Mom. But she didn't look unhappy. There was a calm contentedness to her expression.

I tugged the photo from the vanity and cradled it in my hands.

The Mom I knew didn't have friends. She had work acquaintances and the occasional neighborhood person she would share small talk with. Otherwise, she had just Grandma and me. And I didn't think she considered Grandma to be great company.

The door slammed shut.

I almost dropped the photo.

I turned to rush at the door, but I couldn't move my legs.

The room dimmed. It was like watching the world on fast-forward. Outside, darkness fell in seconds instead of hours.

Only when it was completely dark did the door open.

And Mom walked in.

She was younger. Maybe thirteen or fourteen. Her face was tight. She closed the door behind her and pressed her back to it. Mom's hair was in braids that brushed the tops of her shoulders, and she wore jeans and a black hoodie. For as long as I had known my mom, she'd dressed up. Form-fitting dresses, heels, jeans accompanied with a tight top, and meticulously done makeup. Unless she was having a day when she couldn't get out of bed at all.

She moved away from the door and went to the bathroom, where the sounds of teeth brushing filtered over to me. I still couldn't move.

Finally, she changed into pajamas and crawled into bed.

She didn't lie down to sleep. She sat there. Upright, staring at the door.

Time passed.

It was slow. Crawling by. She didn't read a book or play games or anything like that. All she did was stare at the door.

As if willed by her, it creaked open, and she stiffened. "Grace?" A head peeked into view along with the feminine voice. A Black woman. Her dark hair was straight and fell around her face in short, soft waves, stopping around chin length.

I had only ever seen Aunt Dione in photos. It was otherworldly to see her in person.

Mom's shoulders uncoiled, and slowly the stillness in her body unwound. "Yes?"

"Sorry, did I wake you?"

"Yeah, it's okay, though," Mom lied smoothly.

If Aunt Dione thought it was strange that the sheets were perfect instead of rumpled and slept in, she didn't feel the need to mention it. "You know that conference at work? They ended up needing me to go after all, so I'll be gone for the weekend—"

"No! Don't go!" Mom sprang from the bed so fast she almost fell on the floor.

Aunt Dione sighed. "Grace, please."

"I don't want to be here alone."

"You won't be alone. Peter will be home, don't worry."

Mom didn't seem comforted. "Why do you have to go?"

"They need at least one of us to get that training, and my coworker's kid is sick." She crossed her arms. "Besides, I almost always get to work from home, and my other coworker is a single mom, and she can't leave her daughter alone or get a sitter this short notice. I don't have any kids, so I need to go. It's only fair."

"I'm a kid. I'm *your* kid. Isn't that what you said?"

Aunt Dione shifted in place, and her eyes softened. "I know. You are. But you're also fourteen. Old enough to go running through the bush on your own with your friends."

Mom's eyes welled with tears. "I want you to be here."

"This isn't a conversation, Grace. I'm going, and you'll be fine." She reached out for her sister, maybe to touch her or hug her, and Mom stumbled back. Aunt Dione's face crumpled for a moment. Mom didn't see. She had already turned around and tucked herself under the covers.

All the way under.

It was familiar in a way that made my gut ache.

Aunt Dione left the room, and Mom lay there and cried. Sobbing punctuated by choking out that she didn't want to be alone.

The door creaked open again.

Mom fell silent.

When I looked away from her to the door, it was light again. The transition was so sharp that I had to press my hands over my eyes because it hurt. Once I got them open again, Ivy was standing in the doorway.

Her face was eerily still. It reminded me of Mom in a way that made goose pimples bloom on the back of my neck. "Sometimes the house can show you memories," she said. "They're usually other people who have lived here. I've seen this one a couple of times."

"Cool." My voice trembled the slightest bit.

How did the room stop without me giving anything up? Wasn't that the rule? Maybe it was different for memories. Or maybe this was a benefit of the house liking me like Ivy claimed it did.

"Do you know who that was?" Ivy's voice lacked the aloof, dreamy quality that I had come to expect. It was tight, strained, like someone had their hand up against her throat. It made me think of lying in a bed with the word "stop" on my lips that went unsaid.

"Who?" I asked.

"The girl." Ivy's eyes bugged out, wide and urgent. "I've seen her in lots of the house's memories. It likes her, too."

I froze.

To me, it was obvious that it was Mom. It should be evident to most people. She didn't look that different, after all.

But that was the thing about the dead. They were stuck in time. It was hard for them to understand the passage of it. To recognize people who changed as it went on.

I gritted my teeth.

When I'd first met Ivy, way back when, King was right next to her. Talking to her. His family mentioned her. But corporeals could make themselves seen when they wanted to. I had gone back and forth this entire time wondering if she was real.

She was creepy as fuck, but that wasn't good enough criteria for being dead. I'd thought the other girl was creepy too, standing alone by herself on the playground. I had never seen her before. Then she looked at me, paid attention to me, tried to be my friend, and that's when I was sure she was *wrong*.

But she hadn't been. Mom had slept through her alarm, and she hadn't dropped me off at school until lunchtime. I had missed them introducing the new girl in the morning. She was alone because she hadn't made any friends yet. I was alone because I hadn't learned not to talk to the ghosts I saw fast enough. Kids thought I was weird.

I sucked in a long breath.

I just didn't want it to happen again, what had happened before. When I had noticed too late that someone was dead. But after that, I was terrified to confirm corporeals. I didn't want to be crazy Daisy again. I refused.

Maybe I was wrong about Ivy, but this time, I didn't think I was. I gripped my hands into fists at my sides.

"Who was she?" Ivy pushed.

"I don't want to talk about it."

Ivy's mouth twisted into a snarl that made me step back. I knocked into the vanity and turned back to adjust it. The photos that had been there were gone. I searched for the one in my pocket, but it was gone too.

I licked my lips. "You want to know something that I know, and I want to know something that you know."

"The girl who died."

"The girl who was murdered," I corrected. Official cause of death might have been a brain aneurysm, but coincidences seemed unlikely to exist in this house. I didn't think either of them died by chance. Not her, and not Peter, either.

Ivy turned away from me and walked out the door. "Come on."

Walking alongside Ivy felt as though I were spending time with a friend I had known for years. There was no expectation. Not from her for me, and not the other way around, either. But that didn't mean I trusted her. Especially now when I was sure that I was right. Had been right all along.

She wasn't like me. She didn't see the dead because she had my ability.

She saw the dead because she was one of them.

We made our way back down the stairs and into a room on the ground floor tucked along the entryway with heavy drapes covering the windows. In the center was a grand piano. It was much larger than the one in Mackenzie's house and had a distinct expensive sheen to it.

Ivy stopped in the doorway.

I waited to see if she might go inside, but she didn't. She stayed at the threshold of the room. I stepped into it and made my way toward the piano. And only then did she come inside.

"This is where she died." My voice said it like a question, but it wasn't.

Ivy didn't answer anyway. She was busy walking next to the windows.

"We were here, weren't we?" I pinned my eyes to Ivy.

Everything in the room was familiar. I had never been here, but then, I had. The hardwood underfoot made a sound that I remembered. I could see in my mind the girl sitting here, putting her fingers to the piano keys.

"Where do you go at night?" is what Mom had asked me.

But it was the wrong question.

Where do *we* go at night?

That was the right one.

Because the instant the dead were corporeal, and you gave them your name, they had the opportunity to crawl inside you. To inhabit your body and make it their own. That's what the dead kids on the playground had tried to do at first. But they were sloppy. I could tell what was happening. It was the moment I finally realized they were dead, and it was too late. But I held on tight to my sense of self. Some basic part of me knew that was the right thing to do. They were shut out easily. That's when they decided maybe it would be better if *I* were dead. And once a ghost was corporeal, they could kill the same way anyone else could. Those children were blunt and obvious in the end.

But not Ivy.

Ivy had snuck into my life with the deftness of a splinter sliding under the skin. You didn't notice it was there until the pain started.

Now it was becoming clearer.

It was her precious butcherbirds. That's how she got into me. That perfect moment of fear and disorientation. Mom and King hadn't seen the birds. But I had. And they looked real. They *felt* real. They weren't just dead. They were corporeal. And somehow Ivy could get inside them, too. Could make them do what she wanted.

Ivy was not like the kids on the playground.

She was much worse.

"Are you going to answer my question now?" Ivy asked.

"You didn't answer mine."

"You go first."

Never give the dead what they ask for.

"No," I said, my voice quiet but even.

The door slammed shut behind us, and her expression darkened. "Then I guess we don't have a deal."

CHAPTER THIRTY-ONE

For a room that was supposed to be filled with music, it was suffocatingly quiet now. Ivy stood against the cream-colored wall with the drapes shut innocently beside her. No one could see us, and no one knew I was here. I kept circling my eyes around the room, following the many windows to the door that I was too far away from. Probably it wouldn't open if I tried. The room had a hint of Pine-Sol that at the moment smelled nauseating—I took quick, short breaths to stop from being overwhelmed by it.

I made myself stand still and clenched my muscles so they wouldn't tremble. Only a couple of feet from Ivy, I didn't have a lot of options of where I could go and didn't trust myself to be fast enough. There was nothing else to do but stand my ground.

"You make this so hard," Ivy groaned. Her voice was clipped but somehow desperate. "Haven't I done enough for you? All I want is to know who that girl is." Her sunglasses were abandoned on the sill of one of the windows. Without them, she actually looked her age. Not that that mattered now that I knew she was dead. She could be a lot older than fifteen.

She was dangerous.

"You told me you were real," I said.

Ivy narrowed her eyes. "I am real."

"You're dead."

"I don't sleep. I don't eat." She curled her lip. "But I can walk, I can touch things, I can talk. I can make people see me if I want, when I want. Except for you, apparently. I really was trying not to be noticed by anyone but King that day at his house. I had shown myself to his family earlier, and they were bitchy about it. Figured it was better to lie low."

"They were probably upset because you're not supposed to be here." Assuming they knew she was dead. They must have. King too.

Sometimes I know things and shouldn't say them.

Ivy snapped, "At least I have dreams and ambitions. Which is more than you can say."

"You're dead."

"I *know*!" she screeched. I stepped back despite myself, and she advanced forward.

Dazy.

Dazy.

Dazy.

I shook my head to keep myself present. I couldn't go back to that playground where those grubby fingers held me down. The chanting of my name. The dirt in my throat.

I wasn't a little girl making friends with dead things anymore.

Ivy stopped and laughed. "You don't care about anything, but you're the one who's alive? How is that fair?"

A fine tremble began in my fingers. "It isn't fair."

"Shut up," she said. "You're pathetic. Your life is so useless and empty that you don't even notice when you can't remember half of it." She continued stalking toward me. "I'm smarter than you. I actually give a shit about the world. I should be the one who gets to be in it. It should have saved me, too! Like it saved her! I only let you see so you could help!"

Let me see? What did that mean? I thought the house showed me that memory, but now Ivy was acting like she was the one who made it happen.

She stopped in front of me. We were almost chest-to-chest. If she leaned forward the slightest bit, we would be touching. I stared into the brown of her eyes, both consuming and comforting.

Ivy's face relaxed; her voice became the even calm that I was used to. "Just let me take over. I'll do a better job. I've already gotten us better grades. We can go to a great university. I can help you."

"You've been doing things with my body at night."

Ivy had been inside me for at least a month. Almost the entire time I had been in Timmins.

She sighed. "The house doesn't like when I leave it. And we have school during the day. So I have to come back in here at night."

I thought back to every time I was in the truck with King. That sense of anxiety that would strike me as we drove away, every single day. Was that because of Ivy? Because the house was pulling at her? If I went far enough, would she be forced out, or would I be forced to stop?

"Why were we here when that girl died?" I asked her, trying to stay on track.

Ivy pushed out a breath that blew hot on my face. "Who was the girl in the room?"

"You killed a fucking goat!" I knew that now. The bleating in my dream. It was so loud. It was because I was hearing it. Because *we* had taken the knife out of the kitchen drawer. Now that I was trying to remember, I had a hazy recollection of it. Of its warm fur grasped under my fingers, gushing blood running over them.

"She was going to kill it anyway." Ivy crossed her arms over her chest. "I thought if I got there first, maybe she wouldn't be able to use it."

"She?"

"Your mother," she ground out.

What the hell was going on with this goat? Ivy somehow knew that Mom wanted the animal and had tried to kill it before Mom got a chance to. But all the pieces had been there when Helga and Joe butchered it. It didn't even make sense.

"Who is the girl?" she screamed.

I flinched back despite myself. "I can't tell you."

Ivy whipped away from me and screamed, "I cannot believe you! I thought we were friends." She turned toward me. Her eyes shone, glassy.

"Friends don't possess friends."

"Fuck you," she snarled. "Fine. You don't want to be friends? I don't need any. I've made it my whole life with just one." A smile slid onto her face. "You want to know who it is?"

I didn't.

My eyes flicked to the door.

"Pay attention to me!" she roared.

"Who is it?"

"The house, of course." Even as she said the words, there was an air to her voice like she wasn't quite convinced. She'd just admitted that her only friend was an object, and yet she was unsure about it.

In the bedroom, she said that the house liked the girl, Mom. And that it saved her but not Ivy, whatever that meant. Was that it? She wanted to know who her competition for best friend of the house was?

It was pathetic.

And it must have shown on my face because Ivy's expression soured. "It's getting stronger—can't you feel it? There are so many more people listening to it now, not just the dead. So many of them coming in. Feeding it. It's gorging." She grinned. "I guess you're too delicious to resist after all. It's going to save you for dessert."

"I thought animals didn't eat dessert."

"I'm sure it can make an exception."

I swallowed. I thought maybe I wasn't being lured in like King's aunt because of some strange occult reason. But what if it was as simple as Ivy said? Being saved for later. Like a special meal. "You need to tell me what happened when we were in the room with the girl. Did the house kill her? How?" If Ivy knew what went down, maybe she would also know how to stop it.

"Tell me who the girl in the bedroom is, and I'll tell you about your girl."

Never give the dead what they ask for.

I shook my head. "No."

She dropped her chin to her chest. "There's something in your hair," she whispered, just loud enough for me to hear.

My hand went up automatically and ruffled the soft curls on it. Something fell off and onto the ground. I stared at a tiny white maggot, curling and twisting on the ground. I stumbled back, and my gut gurgled.

Bile surged from my stomach as the memories of the worm invaded my senses. My throat filled and I threw up on the floor. The sick was thick, pus yellow, and filled with squirming, crawling maggots.

They were still in my mouth. Wiggling on my tongue and caught in the gaps between my teeth. I cried out and tried scraping them off with my nails. I caught sight of the skin on my arms, moving and curling as the outlines of the tiny bugs squirmed underneath.

They were *inside* me.

I screamed and more came tumbling out of my mouth. I couldn't stop screaming. I ran to the door, banging on it and trying to work the knob, to no avail. I ran to the window, yanking aside the curtain and thumping on the glass.

An arm pulled me and I ripped myself away, screaming even louder.

"Daisy, calm down!" Mom shouted in my face, but even seeing her couldn't calm me.

They were inside me.

They were inside me.

They were *inside* me.

And the chanting was back.

Dazy.

Dazy.

Dazy!

Their lips were so close to my ears, whispering so loud, spittle flying against my face. And I spun. Around and around and around. They kept turning me on the merry-go-round and slapping my face. Pulling me off only to press my head into the ground.

I couldn't breathe.

I was suffocating.

Dying.

I would be one of them.

Mom shoved me onto my back and crawled on top of me. The angle wouldn't let me spit out the maggots in my mouth. They were crawling from my throat. Sticking to the sides and trying to get out of my body.

I smacked at Mom, trying to get her off me so I could spit them out, so I wouldn't drown in them.

She pressed me down harder, shoving her hand against my cheek to get my head to turn. She lifted her other hand, holding a pair of tweezers, and there, wiggling in the metal prongs, was a thick maggot the size and length of an index finger, white as untouched snow.

I screamed louder. Fought harder. Twisting my hips to try to buck her off me and slapping at her more fiercely. But her grip was iron. Even when my fingernails scratched lines across her face, she kept shoving me down and lowering the maggot to my ear.

It was singing. I could see a little mouth opening and closing.

Dazy.

Dazy.

Dazy.

"No!" I screamed. "Please don't! Mommy, please don't!" Tears flooded from my eyes, and I screamed more as I felt a maggot trying to push out with them, ripping my tear ducts open with the force of it.

Mom said nothing, just shoved me down harder until I could feel the maggot pushing its way through my ear, burrowing, crawling forward.

My world narrowed to the feel of it making its way through and my screams—shrill and constant. Over and over and over.

Until it ended.

Abruptly.

Everything.

No one calling my name. No maggots. No screaming.

Silence.

CHAPTER THIRTY-TWO

I heaved deep breaths and stared at Mom. She was still sitting on top of my chest. Her face was red with scratches and blood, and under her right eye it was starting to turn purple.

We were the only ones in the room. Ivy was gone.

"Mom," I whimpered.

Her eyes filled with tears. "I told you not to come into this house without me! What part of 'as necessary' are you having trouble understanding?!" She shook her head. "I had *one* rule. *One rule!* To protect you. Everything I do is to protect you."

"How was I supposed to help without coming inside?" I cried.

"You weren't! You were never the solution. You were the insurance!"

"You don't under—"

"Yes, I do," she snapped. "You can see fucking ghosts! Does that make your ears not work? Your brain not work? Why can't you follow simple instructions?"

I bit my lip, tucking the entire bottom one under the top. Trying to hide the way it trembled. Of course she wanted to talk about it now. It was off-limits every other time. Forbidden. She forgot that I followed that rule very well.

Between Mom and me, the dead were not to be discussed. Just like the study sessions.

Mom sighed and brushed away some of the tears on my face, her expression softening. "Why don't you ever listen to me? Haven't I done enough to show you that I know what I'm talking about? Have I ever steered you wrong?"

When I was six, I went over to a classmate's house for a birthday party. Her mom was a yoga teacher and also practiced meditation. On my way to the bathroom, I saw her, sitting alone in a room with her eyes closed. Mom never did anything like that. I went over and asked what she was doing.

I thought it was so cool, meditating. When I got home, I told Mom all about it. How I wanted to sit and clear my mind.

She forbade it. "You can't leave yourself unprotected like that. You need to be on guard." She leaned into my face, sandwiched my cheeks between her hands, and tugged me close until we were nose-to-nose. "You can *never* clear your mind."

"Why?" My voice was a whisper.

"Because you might let something else in."

She held that stare with me until my eyes watered. Only then did she let me go.

It wasn't as simple as just never meditating. I had to constantly pay attention to any attempts on my mind. I needed to be vigilant.

It stuck with me. Penetrated my kid brain. So when those dead children tried to get inside my head the next year, I understood what I needed to do to protect myself. And instinct helped me figure out how to follow her instructions.

I thought possession attacks would always be like that. Obvious. I couldn't have predicted Ivy.

Mom clambered off me, and I sat up. I let go of my bottom lip, and it popped out of my mouth with a wet plop. "Do you know who Ivy is?"

"The dead girl possessing you, apparently."

My jaw dropped. "You *knew*?!"

"Not right away. Your nighttime activity started to clue me in, so I kept an eye on you. Which clearly made her paranoid. It's not exactly your normal behavior to slaughter goats. She probably wanted to make sure I didn't have a way to help you. A lot of people think the goat has to be fresh, but apparently, it doesn't matter. Not so long as you get to it before it spoils." Mom tilted her head to the side. "Don't know how she knew what I was going to use it for, though."

"Why wouldn't you tell me that I was possessed?" My voice cracked as I spoke.

Mom shrugged. Like it was nothing. "You can't tell possessed people that they're possessed or the spirit may lash out. You know that. Have you forgotten absolutely everything?"

That was probably why King hadn't told me either. When we got out from school, he was trying to hint at it. Trying to tell me without telling me. There had been that moment when we first went into the house too. When I'd asked him about using his ability on Ivy, and he had been confused and started to say something, then stopped. He was probably about to tell me that it didn't work on dead people, but if he knew then that I was possessed, even telling me that much might have set her off. So he'd kept his mouth shut. And I'd stayed ignorant of the fact that we were hanging out with a girl who was joyriding in my body.

No wonder Mom thought I didn't know anything.

What had I really done here? Read a couple of dead people to barely learn anything? Let myself be jerked around by a corporeal girl? Everything I tried to do on my own to help with this house, I had fucked up somehow.

Like always.

"Did you know her before, Ivy? Like when you were here?" I could barely croak it out. I was choking on my own mediocrity.

"No. I told you no."

"Mom," I said, balking at her. "Now is not the time to be hiding things."

She let out a breath and looked at me. "I don't know who Ivy is. But if she could possess you, then she's corporeal, yes?"

"Yeah."

Mom hissed through her teeth. "She must have killed that girl. This is her fault."

"*The house* killed that girl." At least I thought it had. I mean, I'd accused Ivy too, but thinking about it more, what was the motive? From what I had seen so far, she just watched the house do terrible things—she didn't do them herself.

Mom's eyes narrowed. "The house doesn't kill people. It has *never* killed people."

"It's killing them now! You *knew* something was wrong with it! You say I never listen to you? You never listen to me!"

Mom stared me down. "I don't listen to you because you can't keep a handle on yourself. You panic and freak out, just like you did with that girl at school. And then I have to come save you, *again*."

I had nothing to say to that. She was right. She had to save me from the dead kids too. No one really came to that crappy park behind our building because there was a new one down the street. The kids hadn't even bothered to make themselves invisible. Sometimes I thought about what would have happened if they had. If Mom hadn't come outside to check on me and seen what was happening. If she had come out too late and discovered my lifeless corpse. I would be a ghost too, only able to watch her. Trapped with the children who'd killed me.

But she had come.

When she ran over, the kids finally made themselves invisible, but it didn't matter. They were corporeal. They could be touched.

Mom kicked, punched, and slapped children she couldn't even see anymore, and pulled me to my feet.

They were deadly to me, but she was an adult, and in the end, they were just children. They had been kids I'd thought were my friends who, in reality, hated me for being alive. And now, here, she had saved me again.

I owed her. It was the tether that kept me latched to her. How could I leave when she hadn't left me? I couldn't. She needed me in every other way, but for this, this was the only thing I needed her for.

This house would settle the score.

She hadn't said what I would be doing. Only that I would be needed. And if she was happy with how things went, I wouldn't be needed anymore. Classic Mom. Vague as fuck. But if everything with the house was successful, she would fund anything I wanted to do. I wouldn't be limited to Mom's savings that I could only use for a college that I didn't want to go to. I could do or be anything. And the only way we got that money would be through this house.

Except it had been the opposite since we arrived.

Mom gave me no tasks. Nothing to prove myself. And yet everything was under threat from the start.

She shook her head and stood up. Her limbs were straight and steady. They didn't tremble like mine did when I tried to stand. "This is all wrong. This was supposed to be easy. Years of work, years!" She covered her face with her hands and shouted, "Fuck!" into her fingers. It echoed off the high ceilings.

Mom pulled her hands away from her face and tore out of the

room, yanking me by the wrist behind her.

"The house . . . It's calling people with whispering and rustling sounds," I said.

She scoffed. "I don't care about whispers or 'rustling.'" She made an air quote with her free hand and rolled her eyes.

"But you care about the moaning," I shot back. I remembered her face. That smile. "I saw him again, the moaning man. He's dead, but something's wrong with him."

Mom froze with one hand on the front doorknob, and the other locked around my wrist.

"I've never seen one twisted up like that."

"What did he look like? Where was he?"

He looked familiar, were the words that came to mind. I couldn't place him still, but it felt like I knew him from somewhere. "I think he was in your room."

Mom's fingers tightened around my wrist to the point of pain. She only stopped squeezing when I gasped aloud. "Sorry," she said. Then she opened the door and dragged me outside.

The wind hit me and cooled off my face. I was covered in sweat and only now noticing. I wiped the salty liquid off as the shrikes chirped above us.

The fresh air seemed to have shocked Mom out of it. She let my arm drop finally. We both made our way inside the bunkie, where on the kitchen island there was a bleeding gray mass with at least four fat maggots wiggling inside of it. I slapped my hands to my mouth and stumbled away.

"Is that . . . Is that from the goat?!" I cried.

"It's okay," Mom said, pressing a hand against my shoulder. "These are the good ones."

"You put that in my ear!"

"To protect you. You had one in already, which you've had since you were seven, by the way. I put it in shortly after the playground incident. You used to be a deeper sleeper. Got it in while you napped. I had to go through a very uncomfortable request with a farmer who now thinks goat stomach is a Caribbean delicacy to get it." She shook her head at me. "Once you went in the mansion—which you weren't supposed to do for that reason—I'm sure the house did whatever it could to get you to take it out."

"Why didn't you just tell me you'd put it there?!"

"Because I wanted you to have a chance to be a normal teenager!"

"Are you fucking kidding me? I can *see ghosts*! I was never going to be normal!" If we were going to talk about it, then we were going to talk about it. "You can't both ask me to use my ability to deal with this house and expect me to be your average everyday teenager!"

"Language!" Mom slammed her hands down on the island countertop. "And yes, your ability was *insurance*. Like I said. As necessary, only. In case we have a problem, which I can see now that we do."

"We had a dead body in the house! It should have been necessary the instant that happened! If this fails—"

"It's not going to! I know what I'm doing, Daisy. And I know a lot more than you."

I wanted to interject that as someone who'd lived my life day after day, I disagreed. But I kept my mouth shut. It would be a waste of time to argue about it.

She continued, "Do you know how lucky you are that summers in that house let me recognize what you could do? If you'd had any other mother, you would be in an institution right now diagnosed with something you don't have that they would have *never* been able to help you with. Some people need that. Do better with that. But not you. No one else can help you but me. You'll get what you want after we figure this shit out. No one should be dying on this property."

I had been shoving it down ever since Dad said it, but now doubt rose in me. "Did you know that I would be born like this?"

"Meaning?" Her expression was neutral, maybe still a bit irritated. But I couldn't tell if it was left over from the situation or from this question.

I didn't want to keep going. Didn't want to know. But I had to. "Were you purposely trying to have a kid who could see the dead? Did you make me like this on purpose?"

"Let me tell you something about your dad," she said, her voice smooth and airy. "He's always been afraid of you. I thought he would outgrow it, but he hasn't. And now he's filling your head with bullshit. You don't even need to tell me that he was the one who said that to you. That's how predictable he is."

Mom had never talked about Dad like this. This wasn't business. It wasn't past tense. And that felt important.

I nodded, feeling the tension in my shoulders loosen. Still, she was right. Hadn't I realized that too? That he was scared?

That house tortured people, and it seemed like Dad had had an experience. And unlike most people, he hadn't forgotten. Clearly, whatever he saw messed with his head.

It couldn't be true.

She wouldn't do this to me on purpose. Wouldn't have cursed me like this, for what? To have a house? No. She wasn't that bad. *She wasn't.*

"We need to fix this Ivy issue," Mom said.

"The dead are not the problem," I said. "The house is the problem."

Mom rolled her eyes. "No, it's not. The house is not as independent as you make it seem. Why do you think it went from being completely dormant to suddenly killing people? Your uncle Peter lived here for years without that ever being an issue. The house needs *help*.

It eats the dead. The only way it can consume the living is if they're given. Sacrificed. By a person." She crossed her arms. "I thought that person had to be living, but apparently not. That girl, she's the reason it's acting like this. She's making the sacrifices, and the house is just eating what it's given. Without her, it'll go right back to a dead-only diet. Get rid of her, and you get rid of our problem."

My instinct was to argue back, but I ground my teeth and attempted to see things her way. For one, even if she refused to share with me, she did know more about the house than she was letting on, the same way she knew things about my ability. I didn't think she was pulling this sacrifice thing out of her ass.

And she was right. Even King said that back when Mom was here and his mom had the knowing ability, the house suddenly stopped being a threat anymore even though no ritual was done. When Mary and Ted were being tortured, Ivy was there. When that girl died, Ivy was there. She made me kill a goat. She communicated with the house, and more than that, she was desperate to impress it. To be friends with it. Ivy's entire "relationship" with the house was ridiculous. It wasn't out of the realm of possibility that she'd helped the house kill Peter and kicked this whole thing off.

But then that also raised the question of why no one else had died in the two years after Peter. The cleaning staff would have presented more than enough victims. And also, why did King's mom gain the knowing at all? "Wait, but then who made a sacrifice back when you were here?"

Mom frowned. "What are you talking about? The house didn't eat people when I was here. Forget that. About Ivy, you remember how to make her pass on, don't you?"

I fought a flinch and nodded. That was something that I couldn't forget even if I wanted to. "Is that why you killed the goat? When you were my age? To stop someone else from being possessed?"

Mom froze. "How—I . . . It wasn't for possession. The house seems complicated, but it's very simple: either you are a predator, prey, or below notice. Most people are the latter. But if you're either of the former, you need to protect yourself. The house didn't seem to care about my friend, but I didn't want to take chances." She sighed and shook her head. "She didn't take well to it anyway. Thought I was crazy, and then we weren't even friends anymore."

"Which one am I? Predator, prey, or below notice?"

"I didn't want to wait to find out. Like I said, better to put one in just in case than to be too late."

"How do you know all of this? About the mansion? The dead? Everything." It wasn't the first time I had asked her, but she'd never answered.

The muscles in her face twitched. Normally, in this moment, the conversation would end.

I didn't know if it was the fact that she had moments before held me down and stuck a maggot in my ear. Or if it was because we were finally talking openly about what we had been skirting around since we got here. Or even if it was because I'd caught her in a fit of nostalgia.

But for once, Mom said the truth. "The house told me."

CHAPTER THIRTY-THREE

BRITTNEY

Jayden and I are about to have a problem.

We're staying at the Senator Hotel while in Timmins. The logo is, seemingly randomly, Greek-inspired with a blue-and-gold color scheme. It also boasts a conference center that, if the amount of flyers in the lobby are to be believed, has a healthy amount of events. The room is also nicer than I thought it would be. We have a view of the whole city from the window, two big queen beds, and a clean shower. The latter being where my cohost is at the moment. I, meanwhile, sit on my bed with my laptop opened.

I gnaw on my lip.

Ever since our interview with Katie yesterday, Jayden's been acting weird. Getting lost in intense typing sessions at his laptop where he's so concentrated that it takes him a minute to realize I'm talking to him. Between then and now, he's also had several phone calls that he walks out of the room to take. I'm used to Jayden having conversations without a care for my presence. He doesn't even *like* talking on the phone.

It's like when I went to Mom's first big book event. In the car on the way over, she said, "I know you're not pretty, but smile like you are. And keep it on until this is over." I was eleven.

She sat me right in the front row next to her publicist. The crowd was so loud when she came out. They loved her. She did a reading of the first time Robert hit me with a belt instead of his usual open-palmed smack. It was just regular corporal punishment in enough households. Didn't all us Black kids joke about that? Hearing that belt snap and running away? Honestly, it's fucked-up how universal that experience is in the first place. And in my case, I was being punished for accidentally dropping a cookie on the ground.

A cookie I didn't need to be eating anyway, according to him. Because when you're fat, people love to police every single thing you put in your mouth.

Everyone in the audience alternated between throwing horrified looks at Mom and then at me. At the end, she cried and embraced me. I knew that if I didn't hug her back, there would be hell to pay, so I did.

Just like that, she was the hero.

Like a switch flipping.

I never expected my best friend to have this second part of himself that I had never seen. It brings everything into question. Our friendship. Our partnership. The season that we're filming right now.

The sound of the shower running cuts off and propels me back into the present. I'm downloading everything Bertrand "Bert" McClaine agreed to send in a file. It's mostly pictures and a Google doc where he gives a quick rundown of the events in the house. He refused to speak to us on-camera, even with an offer of money to sweeten the deal. I don't blame him.

"Bert's stuff came in!" I shout to Jayden, who's shuffling around in the bathroom. I want to be normal. Maybe if I give him a few days, he'll get over whatever is happening.

Another part of me whispers that maybe he won't. I've spent this entire time trusting him, but now I realize how fragile that hold was.

"Cool! Be out in a bit!" Jayden shouts back from the bathroom.

I flick through my phone where, as predicted, an email had come through from Grace barely an hour after we spoke with Katie to discuss setting up a conversation. This is what I need to be concentrating on. The phrase "I don't know what she's telling you" was brought up twice in the exchange. She also refused to use Dione's name in any capacity, simply saying "her" and "she."

The same day, I had taken a careful screenshot of the part of the message that showed it coming from Grace's personal email address, along with the bit at the bottom where she asks to set up an interview. It had already been almost a full day with no response from Dione.

I need to get both of them in one room. No one else has ever managed that. Not even Tower. We could finally have an answer for what really went on in that house. And thanks to the contact, we know there's even more between those two to be discovered.

After checking my email, I hold my phone in my hand and stare at it. There haven't been any new voicemails. I don't truly believe that Mom would give up just like that.

It's wild. I don't want her in my life. But I want those apologies. And at the same time, I know they're bullshit. And now here I am, waiting for her.

Jayden walks out of the bathroom looking fresh-faced with a plain black button-down and pajama pants. His hair is its natural shade today, though curled enough that he must've put some sort of product through it.

I raise an eyebrow at him.

Be normal.

"We're not going anywhere today," he says. "Why bother getting dressed up?"

"You'll still be on-camera."

"Yeah, but no one will see my pants." He double-checks the cameras that we've set up in front of the bed. We'd planned to read through Bert's stuff and then do a recording of us discussing what he sent. Jayden collapses onto the bed next to me. "Anything from Dione?"

"Nope."

He groans. "She makes everything so hard."

"If this doesn't work, I honestly don't know what else will make her talk. Grace is supposed to be our secret weapon."

"At least we'll have Grace?"

I scowl. "She won't talk to us if she realizes we don't actually have her sister. And I wouldn't trust Grace even if I was the most gullible person on the planet."

Jayden starts to open his mouth.

"I'm not being biased! I don't disbelieve everything she says, but I also don't trust her." I shake my head. "She's making a mint off a place where the fact that people have died in it is part of the sales pitch."

"I don't think anyone online thinks she was some sort of innocent victim. She's complicated. That's what's juicy about it."

"Exactly! How can you trust a person like that?"

"You can't about everything, but you can on some things. For example, Toronto is expensive as hell. This is a free house. Paid for with a built-in way to earn money. Her wanting to do that is natural. And she's not the only one profiting off sordid history. That's basically our sales pitch too."

I scowl. "Please don't compare us to her."

Jayden gets up and pops a pod into the Keurig. "I'm not saying she's innocent, but that doesn't mean she's not a victim."

"No, but it also doesn't exclude her from being a predator. Which she is."

He makes a sound in the back of his throat.

We're never going to align on Grace. I think that much is obvious.

He thinks of Grace Odlin as someone in a gray area. A victim of the horrors of that house but also someone who did what she needed to do to survive, as if continuing to book guests in a mansion with a body count to make a living is on the line instead of way over it.

I, on the other hand, think Grace is a master manipulator. Maybe at one point she was a victim of the house, but there were too many people caught in her orbit, too many pieces that she was slotting together. That didn't happen by chance.

And maybe I would think differently if I'd had Jayden's upbringing. If I'd had parents who loved and took care of me. Who went through some hard times but always looked out for me despite it.

Sometimes I think that to Jayden, it's impossible to imagine a parent like that. Someone manipulative who would put themselves before their child. But I can. I grew up with one of those. Grace feels like a more palatable version of my mom. I know I'm not supposed to compare them, but I can't stop.

Jayden pulls his mug from under the machine. "Whatever she is, Grace is compelling." He swallows and pauses for a moment, like he wants to say something more but holds it back.

He's never held anything back before.

Jayden is the sort of guy who, with me, always says what's on his mind.

That's why we're best friends.

At least, it was.

"Should I just move the one lav back and forth? Boom style?" Jayden asks, holding up the tiny lavalier microphone. "Or do you want to get mic'd up properly?"

"The one lav is fine."

"Cool. Just raise your hand or something before you talk so I know to move the mic." He turns on the camera before sitting down next to me with his drink and pointing at the computer. "Let's pull up Bert's stuff."

Bert lives in Thunder Bay and had enjoyed a fairly unremarkable existence until his wife, Liza, died of a brain aneurysm in the mansion ten years ago. They were a young married couple too. Exactly my age when it happened. Which, honestly, is horrific enough. You couldn't pay me to be married right now. But the detail to look at was the fact that Liza's death would just be a tragic twist of fate if it didn't happen to be the exact way that Peter Belanger had died.

I shake my head at Bert's account. "Who goes from a small town to an even smaller one for a getaway?"

"He seems cheap. Besides, this was an ultimatum, remember?"

Right. The official Timmins Police accounts said that Bert and Liza's relationship had been rocky lately because of how much he was working at his new job. Liza's friends said she'd threatened to get a divorce if he didn't make time for her. She had booked their Airbnb on his credit card without telling him.

"This account isn't much different from what he reported to police," Jayden says. "He woke up later than usual, around one p.m. Lay in bed and played on his phone for an hour or so. Noted that Liza had forgotten her phone in the room, but he assumed she was doing her own thing. He got dressed and went to the kitchen to make them a late lunch. When he went to grab her for the meal, he found her dead in the piano room. He immediately called the police—that was around three thirty p.m.—but it took them a while to get to the property. Daisy arrived shortly after police."

Liza had actually died sometime during the night before. Bert had admitted that he slept heavy and that she could have left the bed in the middle of the night without him realizing. There were a few news videos in circulation where they'd gotten to Bert before he decided he didn't much like doing interviews. His face looked agonized in every single one. It was lucky for him that it was deemed a medical accident. Anything else and he probably would have been charged with murder.

To call that house "the Miracle Mansion" is a fucking joke.

"Hold on," I say, scrolling to the end where Bert's written a little add-on. I read, "'Almost forgot, and maybe this isn't important, but you asked about Grace and Daisy. Daisy seemed mad at Grace when she saw us with the police. I didn't understand why. But you know teenagers, they get angry about things out of nowhere. I figured it was something like that, and she couldn't turn it off. I didn't really care, honestly. Hope that helps.'"

Jayden raises an eyebrow at me. "Okay . . . and?"

"He said Daisy was mad at Grace. Why would she be upset if she didn't think her mom had some responsibility for what happened?"

"She could have been upset because someone died on their property, and her mom didn't say anything to her. Police documents state that when Daisy arrived on the scene, she didn't know what had happened. Wouldn't you be annoyed if your mom didn't text you about that?"

My mom would have texted just to share the gory details. To turn someone's death into gossip. And if I'd called her out on it, she would have found some way to punish me for "sass."

My phone rings, and I rush to grab it. But the number on the screen declares "Kevin," so it's not Dione calling to agree to an interview. Or my mom. "Hi, Kevin!" I say, all chipper Brittney voice.

I open up the folder with the pictures that Bert sent and turn the screen toward Jayden. He gets up with the laptop and props it on the TV stand to scroll through them, apparently tired of sitting.

"Hello!" Kevin says, just as chipper. "I wanted to check in. Are you still good for Ottawa on Monday?"

I swallow. It's Thursday now; we don't have a lot more time. "Yup, we're just wrapping up." We promised a week of interviews per episode in order to get six episodes out of six weeks of the company paying our way.

"Happy to hear that you're on time."

"It's the will of the road, though. If we need a bit of extra time here, I'll let you know. It's the first episode of the season, so we're trying to get it airtight."

He makes a sound in the back of his throat. "The budget . . ."

". . . has room for a bit of extra time. We asked the stakeholders about that, remember?"

"I just want to help keep you on task is all. But you're in luck: the Airbnb sponsorship came through. You only need to stay at an Airbnb property on every episode and mention that it's Airbnb."

That's the downside of success—we suddenly have stakeholders who give a shit about what we're doing and sponsorships to uphold. "Okay, sure thing."

"They would love it if you stayed in the mansion."

"We already planned to tour it." This guy was in charge of our project, and he couldn't even remember what was in our proposal.

"No, no. They want you to stay overnight."

My eyebrows go all the way up. "In Grace's mansion?"

"Yes! It's one hundred percent safe now, isn't it? Miracle Mansion and all that. They want you two to comment on your experience. You know, if you feel changed."

It takes everything I have not to scream into the phone. "That's not really the *Haunted* brand."

Kevin makes a sound that is almost definitely a huff. "You don't have to do night vision or anything. But you need to push the envelope more. This will be a good way to dip your toes in and build up to bigger scares later in the season. The stakeholders have research to back that the audience likes that sort of thing. Start saying no now, and we may not have any budget next summer. I've already been able to negotiate a room with Grace, and we had to pay the people who had the space a good chunk of money to give it up for us. You're booked for tomorrow night with a Saturday morning checkout. That gives you an extra day to get any last bits of footage you need."

Kevin's much less of a wimp over the phone. It's annoying. He's presenting this as a choice, but it's clearly not. I grind my teeth. "We'll be there."

"Good. One last thing: We were able to book Grace's interview for you. She said you were in contact with her already? She just sent in the signed contract."

Breath rushes out of me. "Contract?"

"Yes, to get her to agree to the interview. I'll email you a copy of it. But, in short, she'll talk to you, but you can't slander her or Daisy in any way. Don't make them look bad."

"Excuse me? We're supposed to be finding the truth here."

"Documentaries are biased by nature. I'm sure you'll work something out." Kevin rushes out a goodbye and hangs up before I can keep him going.

I sag back into my seat. The sound on my phone was jacked up high enough that I know Jayden heard everything. I can't bring myself to look at him. "Was this you?" I say to him.

"What?"

I turn to face him. "Was this you? You running around with all your secret phone calls. You pushing the whole 'Grace is a victim too' and 'give her a fair shot' bullshit. So you went behind my back to Kevin? Now that *Haunted* is getting some real attention, you're ready to steal it from me?"

Jayden stares at me with his mouth half-open.

"You don't have anything to say?!" I snap, voice louder, standing up.

"You're acting like you don't even know me," he says, speaking barely above a whisper.

I grab my phone and rush across the hotel room, pulling my shoes on. I yank open the door and say, "Maybe I don't."

All of this, chasing down the truth so everything could finally be out in the open. To show people what's really going on. To get justice for a dead Black girl. It was for nothing.

I rush out of the Senator. Outside, I'm hit with a lash of humidity. Thick, hot air pressing against me in one giant wave. Ducking behind a pillar with some shade, I try to catch my breath.

Am I the unreasonable one?

Am I the one ruining this?

Is Jayden actually turning against me, or am I just so fucked-up that I'm destroying the only positive relationship I've ever had?

My phone vibrates, and after a brief moment of hesitation when I see who's calling, I pick it up.

"How you doing, honey?" Mom's voice sounds sweet on the other end in a way that makes me think she's in public. Somewhere people can hear her, and she can say, *Oh, I'm just talking to my daughter.*

I swallow down the sob in my throat, but she's already heard it.

She starts that "tutting" sound she makes when I cry. It takes me right back to being a child on the living room carpet, trying to suck them in so Robert wouldn't get annoyed again. If he did, I would get hit for crying too much.

Mom says, "You can't handle this life, I told you that. You're not cut out for media stuff. No one wants to hear from you. And that's not on you, Brittney. You just don't have a compelling story. Most people don't."

I can't do anything but keep crying. I should hang up. I know that. But I can't do that, either.

"It's time to come home. No more of this film school and apartment thing," Mom continues. "I'm tired of this. You not answering my messages. Wasting time. Your company contacted me—did you know that? Talking about your show. They want me to chat about my experiences."

"Someone called you?" I choke out. Who the fuck would call her? Without saying anything to me? I suddenly think of Jayden sneaking out for his calls. He wouldn't, would he? "Who?"

"You know what?" she says, her voice lengthening into a drawl. "I think it was that boy you film with? What's his name?"

"Jayden."

"*Jayden*," she coos. "That's him. I'm happy to be on your show, hon, as long as we tell the truth."

My limbs feel weak. Like my legs could drop out from under me, and I could collapse.

The truth.

She means *her* truth.

To go on my show, with her, and talk about how the house changed her life. How we get along so well now. That she's a different woman.

Mom breathes, and I swear that I can feel her smile through the phone. "Or you can forget this whole show business and come home. But if you're gonna keep on with it, and I'm cosigning your loans and leases, then the least you can do is have me on it proper."

I can't trust Jayden.

I can't get the truth from Grace.

And now I can't even film my show without Mom twisting it to suit her narrative.

"Brittney?" Mom asks. "What are you going to do?"

I let out a long, pained sigh that shakes my entire body.

I'm sorry, Daisy.

CHAPTER THIRTY-FOUR

DAISY

The next day, I took the boat out to the launch by myself and picked up the new guests. It was honestly shocking that Mom had bothered to teach me to drive it, but it was supposed to be for emergencies only. Which, apparently, included ferrying guests when she had better things to do.

These days, the dock was pretty abandoned. The summer sun had left and taken the flock of cottagers and campers with it, and in its wake was emptiness. Just a huge swath of grass and a boat launch without any boats but our own. The dead were gone too. I wondered if they'd all made their way to the mansion. Drawn by the whispers and rustling that Mom didn't seem to care about.

I gave the guests the widest smile that I could manage as I welcomed them onto the boat. Another nondescript older couple. They graciously accepted the blankets while I stumbled through small talk. We docked at the house, and I led them inside and handed them their welcome basket. Mom had neglected to grab the guests' grocery order, and the house only had the basics—tea and coffee, some sugar and leftover milk. I promised I would get their stuff right away. Meaning I now had to waste an hour going into town because Mom couldn't get her shit together.

I walked into the bunkie with my coat and hat still on. Mom was bundled up on the couch though it wasn't cold inside, with her laptop on her legs, typing furiously.

"You forgot their grocery order," I said.

She looked up and blinked. "Sorry, I'll text you the details. Just pull the money out of the joint account."

She didn't seem concerned about how I would get to the grocery store. Of course she wouldn't be. Now I would have to trek over to the Okekes' and bug King for a ride.

I squinted at her screen. "What are you doing?"

"Making bookings," she muttered, back to being engrossed in the screen.

Reservations remained steady. Unaffected by the death in the house. Mom acted like it was her marketing skills. I suspected that we both knew what was really drawing them in. Calling to them, like the shrikes did to one another.

I stood there for a moment. The conversation about the dead was firmly cut off. Mom had gone to bed shortly after her declaration that the house spoke to her, and when she woke up, she was back to normal. She refused to talk about anything we had discussed. All she wanted to say was, "Could you please go pick up the guests because I'm busy?"

She talked to the house. Just like Ivy. Ivy knew it too, in a way. She knew that little girl spoke to it. She just didn't know that girl was Mom.

And if the house told Mom about the goat and maggots, that must have been how Ivy learned about it too.

Despite myself, I thought of Dad's phone call again. Was it far-fetched to wonder if the house had told Mom that if she and dad were "together" in the house, that their baby would see the dead? An ability that was apparently needed. Because a corporeal could clearly exert power over it. Like Ivy was.

I was necessary.

But was I part of a plan? Was I a checkmark on Mom's list of things to do to get this house? To make this business work?

I shook it off.

No.

That was . . . ridiculous. Who planned something like that when they were sixteen? Fuck, who followed through on that seventeen years later?

No way. Even if Dad was right. Even if I was like this because they made me in the house, it would have been by chance.

I didn't need to be thinking about that. Mom and I had the same goal. We wanted this house to work.

We could both still get what we wanted.

I just needed to find Ivy.

She'd disappeared after the incident in the house and hadn't reappeared since. At least now she couldn't get into my head. Mom's maggot was my protection against her.

"Do you want anything from the grocery store while I'm there?" I asked Mom.

She bobbed her head in a nod. "All Dressed chips and more hot chocolate. And a pizza bun. Maybe two."

"Okay." I grabbed a handful of reusable bags and stuffed them into one before putting my shoes back on and heading out.

The bush was quiet. The shrikes in the trees didn't chirp. All they did was stare. No Ivy, either, poking around anywhere. My curls were squished underneath the neon orange hat.

I shoved my hands deeper into my coat pockets and walked faster.

When I reached the Okekes' house, I knocked on the back door.

There was a shout of "Go get that!" and an accompanying shuffling toward the door.

It opened, and King appeared in a TH&VS sweatshirt, his hair undefined for once, looking more like a tall afro, though his lips shone with moisture.

"Hey," I said.

"Hey," he said back. He jerked his head toward the house. "How is it?"

"What do you remember knowing? I'll fill in the gaps."

He rubbed the back of his head. "Everything you and your mom talked about in the bunkie. What happened in the house is missing as usual. Though I can speculate. Ivy?"

"Ivy," I sighed.

"I'm sorry. I couldn't tell you. When we first met, I couldn't know about you, so I didn't realize that you could see the dead. Otherwise, I would have just said what she was. And after . . . well, when the birds got you, it was already too late to warn you about her. Then I worried that even outright saying that Ivy was dead would make her freak out. I'm pretty sure she's what's been blocking me from you. Her being inside your body. Though that doesn't explain what was stopping me before or right now."

"I think she's probably not the only block."

He raised an eyebrow.

"It's the maggot. That's what was blocking you originally before Ivy got in, and it's what's blocking you now that she's out."

"Maggot?" He balked.

Talking it through with King confirmed that the worms from the goat were a complete black hole to him. He didn't know they existed at all. He knew from my conversation with Mom in the bunkie that she had put something in my ear, but not what it was. I also filled him in on everything that went down in the mansion.

He gave me a look heavy with meaning. The meaning was, I guess, *Didn't I tell you not to go in there without me?*

"Yeah, yeah," I said, looking at the ground. "I fucked up. I always fuck up."

He could have pushed on it. Latched on. Dug in.

He didn't.

"You wanted to go to the grocery store, didn't you?"

"Wow, what an interesting detail to use your powers to discover."

He pointed to the reusable bags in my hand. "Yeah. My powers of deduction."

I scowled and left him, walking to the truck. With a chuckle, he followed. "I can't believe you just let me be possessed," I grumbled.

"I can't believe that you're a medium who doesn't even know when she's being possessed." He didn't turn to look at me, just shook his head as he got into the truck.

"I'm not a medium," I muttered.

"Then what would you call a person who's the bridge between our world and the next?"

I got in and slunk into my seat. "Fuck off."

I wished he just wanted to sleep with me. That would be normal. Predictable. Safe. I almost missed the time when Noah was the only thing occupying my mind. Before my memories started to shift and twist. I didn't even know what to think of him anymore.

He used to be on the very small list of things in my life that I controlled.

But the more I thought about it, the more that seemed a lie.

What I had to fight for now was freedom.

King and I were more alike than I ever thought we could be. And he wanted to fix this house. Even though Mom and I had the same goal, it felt like we were working against each other. King was the only person who seemed to actually be on my team.

I turned to him. "Let's do it. Stop Ivy and stop the house. Be free."

"I thought we were already doing that?" he said with a smile.

"Obviously. I mean, we need to really go for it. Go back inside. Together this time. Find her."

He swallowed. "You're going to make her pass on, aren't you?"

"Yes."

"Okay." His voice was resolute, but there was a crease between his eyebrows that made me wonder exactly how much he knew. What he was holding back so he didn't make it come true. "You have to be committed when you do it."

"I will be."

"Like, no matter what, you can't back down."

"I *know*," I said, getting irritated.

"Okay," he said again. Then one more time, "Okay." He put the truck into drive, and we were off.

This time, there was no anxiety.

It made me wonder exactly how far Ivy could go before the house pulled her back into its embrace.

We reached the familiar grocery store plaza for the Metro, which shared space with a constantly populated Tim Hortons, Value Village, Goodlife gym, and Fabricland. The parking lot was packed, of course, because it was Sunday.

King and I got out of the truck. We had to park way back from the entrance to get a spot. We were almost to the front door, me with my reusable bags swinging at my side, when I spotted Ms. Kuru with a full garbage bag by the outdoor Value Village drop-off box.

"You go ahead," I said to King. "I'll be back."

He sighed. "You do know that I didn't actually need to come here, right?"

I ignored him and made my way over to Ms. Kuru. She lugged the bag over her shoulder and shoved it into the drop-off box. She was wearing an oversized tan coat and a hat that looked hand-knit.

"Fall cleaning?" I offered by way of opening, and immediately hated myself for it.

She spun around and smiled. "Daisy! Nice to see you." She waved a hand at the bag. "I figured it would be good to get some cleaning done before guests come for Christmas. I'm hosting this year."

It was only October. I couldn't fathom that level of advance planning. It would be Christmas Day and Mom would look around the apartment and ask, "Should we have gotten a tree?" It was one of those things that felt too sad to organize on my own.

"Did my mom ever give you a call?" I asked. "For the dinner?"

Ms. Kuru grimaced. "No . . . I'm sure she's busy with the Airbnb. Especially now . . ."

In a town of roughly 41,000, it wasn't surprising that people already knew about the girl who'd died in the house, even if it had happened an hour away at Kenogamissi. "If you want, I'm happy to pass on a message."

"Oh." She rubbed at her arms like she wasn't wearing a jacket that protected her from the chill. "No, no, that's okay. I didn't have anything specific to say anyway. I just wanted to chat."

"Right . . ." I could walk away now, but then I couldn't. I had to dig. There weren't enough people who knew Mom that I could lean on. And I couldn't stop wanting to know more about her. "Why did you help her, with the goat?"

"Oh God," she moaned. She looked around the parking lot as if expecting someone in the plaza to run over and save her. "It was just . . . Grace, I mean, I'm not blaming her." She let out a huge breath. "You know what happened to her. I . . . It happened to me, too, in that house. I felt like maybe I was helping support her. My parents were very good about it. I told them the summer that Grace left for good, and they pulled me right out of lessons. I never went back to the mansion." She shook her head. "I know Grace didn't have that sort of family support. Didn't get along with her mom and had a falling-out with her sister. So I really don't blame her for the goat thing."

What happened to Mom? What did that even mean? Had the house done something to her and Ms. Kuru in its rooms? Did Ms. Kuru somehow remember her experience like Dad did? Or did she mean that the house talked to her like it, apparently, did to Mom? Whatever it was, she had told her parents about it. "They believed you?" I asked, trying not to sound incredulous.

Ms. Kuru's face filled with pity. "I think it was a hard pill for them to swallow, but yes, they did."

"Did you tell anyone else?"

"No. I . . . No, I didn't want to tell anyone else except my wife and therapist."

Therapist? I mean, I guess if you saw a ghost, you might talk to them about it, but I would think she would want to keep that to herself. Now I wasn't even sure we were on the same page. Fuck vague details. "Can you tell me? Exactly what happened?" I needed to have a solid answer. Ms. Kuru was different than Mom was. Stable somehow, while Mom was walking on ever-shaking ground. Maybe they hadn't actually had the same experience. But I needed to know.

My biology teacher's face went slack for a moment, wiped of emotion. "Oh my God, you don't know." She pressed her fist against her mouth.

I shifted from foot to foot. "You can't just tell me? To confirm."

"I . . . No, I really can't. I honestly think it's better if you speak to your mom about it." She shook her head. "I'm sorry. I thought you knew. I shouldn't even have mentioned it."

There it was. The dead end. "My mom doesn't really like to talk about what being in the house was like."

"I don't blame her," she said. "Neither do I." Ms. Kuru gestured to her car. "I need to get going, but it was nice chatting with you." She started to back away before I even responded.

"Bye." There was no point chasing her down or trying to make her stay. Whatever shared experience she and Mom had, I wasn't going to learn about it from Ms. Kuru.

I thought of what the house showed me, of Mom sitting in that bed, terrified, of how much she didn't want Aunt Dione to leave.

I paused on my way into the grocery store. Aunt Dione lived in that house too. I couldn't ask Uncle Peter, obviously, but she was still an option. At the very least she could say why Mom hated her so much.

There were more pressing things to deal with. There was Ivy. But I couldn't help but latch onto this scrap of Mom's past.

I dug out my phone and dialed a number that I had never bothered to call before.

"Hello?" came through the line, crystal clear.

"Hi, Grandma, it's me, Daisy."

CHAPTER THIRTY-FIVE

Before I even asked, I knew how far would be too far. Toronto, eight hours, definitely too far. North Bay, four hours, getting better, but still too far. New Liskeard, the other new girl's hometown, around two hours—it might take some convincing, but doable.

In the end, it turned out Aunt Dione didn't live in any of the places I thought she might. She had settled in Iroquois Falls. An even smaller town than Timmins with a remarkable 4,500-person population that was only an hour away.

The Airbnb guests would have to wait a little longer for their groceries.

The information was worth the excruciating conversation with Grandma, which I had to deal with while I walked around in the grocery store. I hadn't posted any photos online, but somehow she knew I'd cut my hair, and she was happy to chirp that I was now "bald-headed" and was going to be single until it grew out, yet simultaneously had time to berate me for dating at my age. She threw in a comment about my chicken legs and "little peckers" to sweeten the deal. Likening my body to birds was, apparently, the theme of the phone call.

Now King and I were cruising toward Iroquois Falls. He had one hand on the wheel and the other on the armrest, which in the truck was actually high enough to be comfortable.

"Thanks," I pushed out. "For taking me."

He shrugged. His music was playing through the stereo, that same odd mash-up of genres that he enjoyed. "That's what friends are for."

I shifted in my seat. Friends. I guess, in a way, we were. At least until we stopped the house.

After, I didn't know. I wasn't very good at being a friend. I still couldn't understand why Megan stuck around.

I hunched over in my seat. "Aren't you off to university next year anyway? How long will we actually know each other?"

King said, "No, I like staying in town. Maybe I'll go to Northern."

Northern College was local and, to be honest, I didn't know much about it. But mostly I didn't want to talk about the whole "being friends with King" thing. "What would you do there?"

"I don't know."

"You don't want to be a psychic, but you don't know what else you want to be?"

King leveled a stare at me. "For someone who hates to talk about her own future, you sure are nosy about mine."

I crossed my arms over my chest and turned away from him to the window.

"I like it here. My family is here. My friends, too. I like going in the bush, growing my vegetables, fishing, all that shit. When I was younger, I thought about leaving. Just to try it. But I don't think I would stay. This is my home, you know?"

I guess I understood that. For me, even being here, home was still Toronto. It was hard to shift that feeling.

"Besides," he added, "the house is here. Stopping it now isn't a guarantee forever. If, for any reason, the knowing came back and cycled through to me again, I would rather be in Timmins. It's more manageable than in a city."

"Is it really that bad? Knowing?" I asked.

I would swap abilities with King in a heartbeat. It was better to walk through the world unseeing. I couldn't stand it. The dead were everywhere. Here was an exception, and I suspected it was because of the house. Normally, it was crowded. Shivers made things unbearable for hours. I wanted the ignorance that everyone else had. Out of the two of us, he had the better deal, from where I was standing.

He licked his lips. "Imagine meeting someone for the first time, and knowing everything about them. And you have to ignore it and go through the motions of getting to know someone as if you aren't already keyed into their business."

"I think it would be nice," I said with a shrug. "No surprises."

King glanced over at me. "I know your asshole ex used to do things in private that you didn't like, but you couldn't say so. I know your mom put this ghost-monitoring-and-controlling shit on you despite the fact that it terrifies you. I know that sometimes you have no idea if anything is real and wonder if everyone around you is dead, and you just don't know it yet. I know you wanted to take Ivy up on her offer to let her take over because you think she would do a better job. I know that in a few days from now you'll have a fight with your mom and need to be careful about what you decide to say to her. I know—"

"Stop!" My body shook so much that I clasped onto the armrest to ground myself in something. "I get it. I fucking get it."

"I know all of that. And I only got to know you for an instant. Other people, I get reminded of everything whenever I look at them." He tapped his fingers on the wheel. "And then I have to just interact with you, knowing it. Knowing things from the future, too, and not being able to tell you." King licked his already-moist lips again. "I know you. Better than most people, I would guess. No matter how you think of me in your mind, in mine, we're closer than that. We're friends. Which is why, given the circumstances, I have no problem taking four hours out of my day to drive you back and forth to see your aunt."

"Would a friend say all that crap to me?"

"Yes," he said. "Because friends call you out on your shit. Sorry I couldn't make it prettier. But making personal fortune seem better than it is is something I charge for."

I wondered if King knew exactly what Noah did "in private" that I didn't like. He probably did. He knew about the fingers around my throat. Now he was the only one, besides me and Noah, who did. And he was making it a big deal, which it wasn't.

"Noah's not an asshole," I muttered. It felt natural to defend him, even if I could barely get my heart into it.

"Isn't he?"

"Lots of people like that stuff," I countered, but my voice was soft.

"But you didn't. I won't pretend to be a sex expert, but if one of you is crying during, isn't that something that should be addressed? Only an asshole would be cool with doing it over and over again without asking if you actually liked it when it was obvious that you didn't."

It was one tear, once. Maybe he didn't notice. And I never said no. He wasn't a mind reader. It was fine. It wasn't a big deal.

But then . . . it felt significant. And King thought it was important enough to mention.

I didn't want to talk about it anymore. "I didn't think you would know things like feelings," I said, blatantly changing the subject.

"Yeah, neither did I before it started happening." He let out a long breath. "The feelings are what make it a lot to deal with."

It took a minute for things to sink in. "That's why everyone likes you," I said. "Because you know how people think and feel."

"It's not like I go out of my way. But yeah, if I know someone hates the way they look and that compliments make them feel worse, I don't compliment them. And so they naturally like me more than people who do." He tapped his fingers on the steering wheel again. "I didn't even realize I was doing it until one day I turned around and I was popular."

I thought of our drive and its destination. "You know what's going to happen at my aunt's house."

"Yeah."

"But you won't tell me?"

"No."

"Because if you do, it'll happen for sure. Which means, I'm guessing, that it doesn't go well."

His fingers flexed on the steering wheel.

"There's something worse, too, isn't there? That's why you're helping me with the house?"

"I told you. The house blocks things out. I only know what most likely happens *after* being in the house."

"But you *do* know, don't you?"

"Yeah."

I leaned back in the seat and let him drive without saying anything for a few minutes.

King looked over at me. "Just remember that's what I'm trying to do. Help you."

Right. Which is probably why he'd brought up the upcoming fight with Mom. He'd purposely avoided what I said to her, only that I needed to be careful about what it was. I had the power to change things. I just needed to accept the help that I asked for.

I could do that. Couldn't I?

We got to Aunt Dione's place earlier than expected because Google Maps assumed you drove the speed limit, and King went over the whole time.

My aunt's house was a small, plain single-level with cream-colored vinyl siding. The front porch was painted a fading white and housed a lonely clay pot with soil and the remnants of a dead plant.

"I'll wait here," King said, already scrolling through his phone.

"No warnings? You know, some ominous crap that helps me avoid falling flat on my face?"

He bit his lip. "I don't know how to make this go well."

Well, that was positive.

I hopped out of the truck and made my way to the front door. Instead of a doorbell, she had a touch screen, lightly dusted with snow, that had a bell icon on it and the word "ring." It was weirdly high-tech for a house that seemed anything but new. I pushed the icon, and a chime sounded throughout the house.

The camera above my head whizzed to life.

A second later, a woman appeared on the screen. I recognized her from the photos at Grandma's place. But she didn't seem to know me.

"Can I help you?" Her voice was the same as it had been when the house showed me that memory. Even her face didn't look much different. Smooth brown skin, a narrow face, relaxed hair cut short.

"Hi, um, I'm Grace's daughter, and I wanted to—"

Her face twisted, and her image disappeared from the screen.

"Hello? Aunt Dione?"

Nothing came back through.

"Hello? I just wanted to talk with you for a minute. Hello?"

"Please go away!" The voice came quick and shrill through the touch screen without an accompanying image.

I tried again. And again. And again. For at least five minutes, I shouted down her house. And besides that initial plea to leave, she never said anything.

I stood there for a moment. Quiet.

Tears welled in my eyes.

I was so fucking tired of not being able to do anything right. I couldn't even get my own aunt to talk to me. It was already pathetic that I was here. That I needed someone else to tell me about my own mom.

Maybe I was destined to be a fuck-up.

It was like the children chanting again. I felt unstable. My life shattering to pieces underneath me. Why had I ever thought I could be more than a scared and trembling Dazy on a merry-go-round?

This was why it was useless to want anything.

Because before you even started, everything was already determined. King was living proof of that. Except I had been trying to change it. This whole time, I was trying.

And I was failing.

I brushed the tears off with rough swipes at my eyes.

"I didn't believe her," came a whispered voice through the touch screen.

"What?" I choked out.

The voice came back again. "She tried to tell me what was going on in the house, and I didn't believe her. And I'm sorry."

I was so over tiptoeing around things. "About the ghosts? You didn't believe her about the dead? Or the house talking to her and torturing people? Or . . . ?"

Aunt Dione's face flashed back on the screen. "What are you talking about?"

I blinked at her, tears falling down my face. "What are *you* talking about?"

"I'm talking about what Peter did to her."

The complete and utter confusion must have shown on my face because Aunt Dione started to look just as confused.

"Did she not tell you?" she asked.

"Tell me what?"

"I . . . You just need to ask her. I . . . I need to go. Please leave." The touch screen shut off again, and I didn't think it was going to go back on.

I wiped the tears from my eyes and stumbled back to the truck. Inside, I searched King's face. "Do you know what she was talking about?"

He pressed his lips into a line. "I know because you find out. In this case, it's better to stay the course." He paused for a moment and gripped the steering wheel. "And I don't want to be the one to tell you. It's . . . the sort of thing that feels wrong to share on someone's behalf." King examined my face. I was sure my eyes were red. "Are you okay?"

"Fine," I ground out, buckling my seat belt. "Let's go."

We pulled away from the house, and I curled into my seat.

For the first time, I wondered how many people I talked to about the house, like Aunt Dione, weren't talking about the mansion. Who were actually talking about Peter.

About my uncle and whatever it was that he did to Mom.

CHAPTER THIRTY-SIX

When I got out of the truck for the final time that day, the sky was dark and the air felt dry. It was only something like five thirty p.m., but the evenings were already getting shorter, bringing on this sort of constant afternoon fatigue that wasn't easy to beat. Frost clung to the grass. We still hadn't had a full snowfall yet, though apparently, Halloween was a popular day for it—meaning we could expect snow in a few weeks. King had mentioned that his costumes as a kid were pulled on top of puffy jackets and boots.

"I can walk with you," King said. He stood beside the truck with his hands tucked into the pockets of his significantly-warmer-than-mine jacket.

I grabbed the bags of groceries and shook my head. "I'm fine." I paused and added, "Thanks."

"You're polite now?"

"Fuck off," I muttered, and made my way onto the path toward home.

"Is it because now you know that we're friends?"

I raised my middle finger at him and continued on.

I couldn't say that I wasn't afraid of the bush. The feel of the butcherbirds as their tiny beaks broke skin was still a memory I couldn't forget. But I didn't want King to come either.

If I asked him, it was different. I was the one in control.

If he offered, and I caved, that was another thing altogether.

I took care of me.

I had done it for so long. Constantly. The only time I hadn't was with Noah. I let him decide where to go, who to hang out with, what to do. He chose it all. And here I thought he was something in my life that I was controlling. Maybe I subconsciously craved leadership and guidance. A born sheep who thought she was a wolf.

Sticks and leaves crunched and snapped under my feet in the otherwise silent air. I almost missed the sounds of summer, predatory as they were. The silence felt worse. Eerie. I found myself looking over my shoulder, expecting something to jump out from behind the birchbark trees.

Noah kept looping in my mind. I had done so well for so long keeping him out. I could always find something to remind me of him, but I didn't get stuck. I didn't obsess. But now I couldn't stop.

I was picturing Mom lying on a bed with fingers pressed around her throat and her not liking it, but it kept happening. And when I followed the arm up to a face, it was that old photo of Uncle Peter with his blondish-brown hair parted neatly, panting on top of her.

And when I thought of it like that, that mantra of "It's all right, I didn't mind" fell apart and just seemed so fucked. But I couldn't put myself back in the picture. Because if I put myself back, and put Noah back, it made my throat so dry and parched that I wanted to choke from it.

I forced my feet through the bush faster and faster, until I was nearly running, sprinting. The trees whipping past me too fast to pay attention to. Too swift to look at until I broke out of them into the property.

Only when I stopped to catch my breath did I realize that I was heaving. My breaths short and staccato. It was like I was gasping. Gagging.

Ivy was leaning against the side of the house, watching me, a shrike perched on her finger.

I needed to deal with her, but not right now.

I dropped off the groceries for the guests inside the door of the mansion and texted to let them know, using the number Mom had given me. Keeping what I had bought for me and Mom, I left and made my way inside the bunkie.

Mom was curled up on the couch. When she turned to me, I held up the bags of groceries in lieu of a greeting.

She cheered. "Put the chips in a bowl, please."

I found the biggest mixing dish we had and dumped the All Dressed chips in before shrugging off my jacket.

I made my way over to the couch with them, setting the bowl on the coffee table and tucking myself under the blanket with Mom. She plucked out a single chip and chewed on it. She ate everything one at a time, no matter what it was. Soon it would be pomegranate season. Mom would sit there and pick off each pearlescent ruby seed and eat them individually.

Her body was warm from sitting under the blanket, and I pressed myself closer to her, laying my head on her shoulder. The show she was watching went on in the background. One of the reality ones where they followed around plastic surgeons and their clients. The man on-screen had some sort of botched nose job that they were going to fix.

Mom's body rose and fell the slightest bit with each breath. When we were like this, it was easy to forget everything else. It was simple to imagine that we were an ordinary mother and daughter. There was none of the dark history of the occult between us. None of the looming force of this house and its legacy. There were no expectations of a daughter in university or a mother with a successful business.

It was just me and my mom.

"I was dating a boy in Toronto," I mumbled. "Before we left. He broke up with me."

Mom turned to me, and her mouth fell into a slight frown. "Did I know him? A boy from school?"

"No. To both."

She pulled in a deep breath and let it out. "You know, I always thought I would be a cool mom. The sort where you would just tell me that kind of stuff while it was happening, and we would gossip over it." She gazed back at the TV. "But I guess it's always going to be an awkward thing you don't want to talk about with your parents."

I didn't really know what to say to that.

"His loss," she said with a little smile.

It was so normal. That was what she thought this was. And I didn't want to ruin it for her. But it kept looping in my head, and my eyes stung with it, and my throat ached with it, and if I didn't say it now, I didn't know that I ever would. "He would . . . choke me, when we . . . you know . . . in bed."

Mom's face became still. Her eyes were concentrated on the TV, but she no longer seemed to be watching it. Even her shoulder where I rested had gone hard. Slowly she turned to face me. "Were you okay with that?"

"I let him." I shrugged. But it wasn't quite right. My own shoulder was laden with the burden of pretending everything was lighter, easier, unimportant. And it couldn't quite pull it off. It just jerked up without falling right.

Mom hissed through her teeth. Surgical. Like the delicate prick of a needle, stealing breath from me like sucking blood through a thin tube into an empty vial. "Some men are good at taking things from you and making you think that you gave them up." She stared deep into my eyes. "I didn't ask you if you let him. I asked if you were okay with it."

The word was in my mouth, but I couldn't move it. It trembled on my tongue for fear of speaking it into the world.

I could only think of King's words: *I know your asshole ex used to do things in private that you didn't like, but you couldn't say so.*

I hadn't understood why he'd phrased it like that. *Couldn't say so.* Like something had inhibited me. But now with that simple two-letter word sticking in my throat, I could only agree.

No.

I could have never said it to Noah.

Because I was never sure that he *would* stop if I asked. And it would be worse. It would have always been worse if I had said no and it kept happening. Because then I would know that I never could have controlled it, or changed it, or stopped it. Just like everything else in my life.

I couldn't answer Mom's question, so I said something else. "What did Peter Belanger do to you?"

Even as I asked, I still expected the shutdown. For her not to say anything. To brush it off.

I took a stiff inhale. "Ms. Kuru said what happened to you in the house happened to her. Ms. Gagnon, his own cousin, hated him. Aunt Dione said that he did something to you."

"When did you even talk to these people?" she muttered. "You don't even know *her.*"

"I called Grandma."

Mom pressed her lips into a line.

"We are staying on his property, and he gave us this house. You said he was like a father to you, but . . ." But not all fathers were good fathers. "What did he do to you?" I whispered. Though I already knew.

She exhaled and turned away from me back toward the TV, staring at the surgeons opening up the man's nose. Blood poured along his incisions, and the sickly vibrant yellow of the fat under his skin was bloated and run through with blue veins.

I was about to ask her again when she spoke. "The very first summer I came here wasn't the first time I met him. They dated for years before. Met in Toronto when he was at the conservatory. He would come over for family dinners. I had been alone with him so many times and it was fine. When he would visit, he always brought all these foods and gifts. She loved him. Mom loved him. I loved him." She smiled. "I was even the flower girl at the wedding. Though I was nine, a little too old, but they let me anyway. He really was like a father to me. They were going to adopt me, you know? So I could be away from Mom. They were sure they could take Mom to court and get custody. I was so excited about having a dad. A real dad."

I remembered the wedding picture at Grandma's house. Mom with her hair done up in two plaits, braided around her head like a crown, with flowers weaved in. I wrapped my arms around my knees and crushed tighter to Mom's side.

She continued, "When Peter's dad died, they moved into the mansion. I was ten and had sprouted these mosquito boobs that, of course, meant Mom got the signal to start criticizing my body. She—you know who, anyway—she knew how hard that was, so she invited me to spend the summers at the mansion. To escape. And to practice. See what it was like to be a real family together." Mom laughed, still staring at the screen. "It seems ridiculous now. I kept coming back because somehow, everything altogether, was still better than being with Mom nonstop."

Once, Grandma told me I was so skinny that I looked like a full-on rectangle. It wasn't funny or even particularly cruel. But I couldn't stop thinking about it. Every time I passed a mirror, I stared and wondered if anyone else noticed. But Mom always got the brunt of it. She was beautiful by anyone's standards, but Grandma could always find a way to call her ugly.

Mom shifted her weight from left to right. I could tell she was getting uncomfortable with how close I was to her, so I stopped pressing against her so hard. Her shoulders dropped a bit. "That first summer, I was there for almost the whole three months without anything happening. Katie would have her lessons. I wanted to join in—why not? But he didn't like that. 'Katie's family is paying for private lessons, so unfortunately you can't join.' That's how he would say it. And make this face like he was so sorry about it. And I believed it because why wouldn't I believe it?" She turned to me finally, as if I had the answers for why or why not she should or shouldn't have believed it.

I didn't.

She licked her lips. "Katie's family was going on their annual camping trip for the end of the summer. She was so happy about it. Ecstatic. I had been camping with Peter and you know who, and sure it was fun, but Katie looked like she might cry, she was so happy to go." Mom flicked her gaze away from me. Not at the TV, just sort of down. "I understood why later. It's interesting how things looked so different after. There were these details I hadn't noticed or seen, and after, they were so obvious. So completely obvious that I hated everyone else for not noticing. And I hated myself for not noticing too."

I realized that she would say Peter's name but not Aunt Dione's name. I didn't mention it. I didn't want to interrupt her and end the spell that kept her going. I bit down on my lip.

Mom said, "I went and got ready for bed like I always did. Brushed my teeth and changed into pajamas and got under the sheets, and she would come check on me and say goodnight. I always waited up for her so we could do that." Her voice was fast now. Rapid. Some words blending together as if she couldn't wait to get it out of her mouth. "And that first time, he came inside, and he kind of sat on the bed. And we just talked. And he told me about something in his lessons that had upset him, parents complaining, but could I please not tell my sister about this because it would worry her, and this was just between us."

She stopped. Cut off completely. The room filled only with the sounds from the television, the man waking up from his surgery.

Then she started again. Not fast anymore. Slow. Careful. "I thought that was okay. Maybe that was just a thing dads and daughters did. I didn't know. It was just talking. The summer break ended, and I went home like nothing. The next summer, it didn't seem weird that it continued. Not at first. He did that at least once a week, came in and talked. And it just escalated, so slowly. That first week we talked and he left. The next week he talked and gave me a hug before he left. And then the next week he kissed me on the cheek. And the next on my lips. And then the next he pulled up my shirt to kiss there. And the time after that, my pajama pants had to come off, and I hadn't wanted to, but I had let everything else happen, so when was I supposed to say no? And how? Now it had gone so far, and he said she would be sad, and I knew she would be. It just felt too late for everything."

I curled my hands into fists to stop them from shaking. But they shook anyway. I knew exactly what she meant even though I didn't know. But I did. I knew what she meant when she said that it felt too late. When she said that she had let it happen before, so how could she say no later? But then it felt so wrong because she hadn't let anything happen. It had happened *to her*. Like it had happened *to me*. It had happened *to us*.

Her gaze was firmly on the blanket we were both under. "And then I just kind of learned to lie there. Very still and quiet. And he stopped bothering to talk before, after the first few times. When Katie was around, it didn't happen as often. Maybe once every couple of weeks instead of weekly. But she knew. Because you just know once it's happened to you."

Mom became still again. Like the little girl she was describing. And I understood now what it was. This forced stillness that she adopted, where she became stonelike, like a figure carved and left to the pigeons. It was a response to fear. A response that he created.

She looked at me for a moment, then away again. "Peter isn't your father, by the way. Your expression . . . You seem like you're wondering."

I swallowed. I was. I felt sorry suddenly that it was so clear on my face.

Mom chuckled. It was humorless and dry. "He was proud of that. Proud of holding back. 'I'm not a monster,' I'm sure he thought. I think he wanted me to be grateful that he left that tiny bit alone for me. That he never went that far." She paused and licked her lips. "The worst part is that I am. Grateful. I don't know if I could have survived more. I was barely making it through as it was."

"You never told anyone?" I whispered despite myself. Even though I knew that sort of silence. Knew the quiet of Noah squeezing his hands around my throat, pressing, and pressing, and keeping everything in.

Mom laughed again. "I did." I expected a whisper, but Mom's voice was the same even tone as if she were speaking about something ordinary. "I told *her*. The summer I turned fourteen. Because that was the summer when I started having to touch him back. That was the summer when I finally asked Mom if I could stay home, and she said no because she was enjoying the summers off. That was her vacation, me being gone. And everything seemed like the worst it was ever going to be. I couldn't imagine anything worse than that."

The words hung in the air between us, floating, idling, searching for somewhere to land.

Mom let it crash to the ground. "She didn't believe me."

Without asking, I knew Mom had never told anyone else after that. Her face was so compact. Held tightly. Gripping. Never moving. I knew now why she held everything in her life so close to her chest. Because when you told a truth so intimate and had it thrown back at you, why bother sharing anything ever again?

"I believe you," I said.

Mom's head jerked up. Her eyes were wide as she stared into mine. She looked at me as if she had only just realized I was in the room with her. Then her face crumpled. It compressed and broke. Because it wasn't marble. It was paper painted to look like it. Something fragile pretending to be unbreakable because that was the only defense it had.

She tugged me close and cried into my shoulder. And I cried too.

I cried for that little girl waiting in her bedroom.

I cried for the other girls out there, the ones like Ms. Kuru, and maybe Ms. Gagnon, whose pain could only be seen by people who had experienced it.

I cried for myself, for the me pressed into sheets, voice choked into silence.

I cried for the mom that I could have had, that I would never know, because of the people who had left scars that I couldn't see and couldn't fix, even though I kept trying to.

And I cried because now I knew that what Mom feared the most about the house was never the mansion itself. It was the memory of the person who came into her bedroom at night. The man who could torture a girl worse than any room in a haunted house ever could.

"The moaning man," Mom said suddenly. "I know you said he was distorted. But think hard. Who did he look like?"

I felt disoriented for a moment. Caught off guard by the change in subject, until I realized it wasn't a change in subject at all. I gripped my hands into fists on top of the blanket. I had recognized him, but I was so thrown off by the way he looked in the house that I hadn't realized who he was.

And he was in her bedroom.

Every. Single. Time.

He was in *her* bedroom.

"Peter . . . ," I whispered. "It's Peter." He died in the house and never left. Couldn't leave without the mansion's intervention. Just like every other ghost in there.

Mom licked her lips. "Did he seem like he was in pain?"

"Yes," I breathed.

She smiled. "Good."

CHAPTER THIRTY-SEVEN

They came the next day on the boat with four video cameras, huge enough that they needed to be carried on broad shoulders; six tripods; a seemingly endless parade of lighting; and puffy Canada Goose coats—though it wasn't cold enough for that. It was Monday morning, and Mom had been rushing around the bunkie since at least six a.m. When I rolled out of bed closer to seven thirty and padded into the living room, she was gone.

Only when I snuck over to one of the bunkie windows and pulled back the curtains did I see them. All of their camera equipment had the same logo stamped on it. It was a silhouette of the CN Tower with TOWER written in uppercase letters inside the shape. How Mom had managed to get people from a multimillion-dollar company with just as many YouTube followers was anyone's guess. I didn't think the house was specifically calling to people based on platform size.

Though it wasn't hard to figure that something as juicy as someone dying in a giant mansion hidden in the bush in northern Ontario wouldn't have a certain kind of draw.

Mom was animated, at her peak entertaining mood. She wore her own Canada Goose in a mossy forest green. I didn't know why she'd bought that. The thing cost almost an entire rent payment, but she brushed it off. They all looked like they were out of an ad for thousand-dollar coats, Mom with her hair in a short, straight bob— one of her more expensive wigs—and the rest of the Tower crew. I recognized one of the girls; she was white and had a short blond pixie cut with tattoos up the side of her neck.

I knew her videos, too. She would go to remote or unique Airbnb locations, stay there for a night or so, and catalog the whole experience. Interview the hosts, explore the town or city, and do a generally in-depth review. If she liked your place, you got a shit ton of bookings. And if she hated it, you still got a shit ton of bookings. Unless you said something messed-up—sexist, homophobic, and/ or racist—you were pretty much guaranteed success as soon as she showed interest.

Now I *really* didn't know how Mom had swung this.

She was fluffed up. Her chest high and proud, and her mouth moving constantly. Words floated in from outside, far away and faint. All that I caught was something about the mansion and breakfast.

I didn't know when she'd managed to grab groceries because she hadn't gotten any last night, as far as I knew. We had cried, she'd claimed exhaustion and crawled into bed, and I'd showered, standing under the faucet with hot water stinging my face, feeling like I had been peeled back. Layer upon layer of skin painfully torn from my body and pushed out into the cold without the protection of a dermis. Just exposed yellow fat and muscle like the nose-job guy on the TV.

I hadn't been able to get the image of dead Peter out of my mind.

Why was he like that? If the house spoke to Mom, if it liked her, was it doing that *for* her? To what end? It was hard to believe that a house that fed on people would be sentimental. But it was torturing him and doing it without making him pass on.

I thought of the times when Mom had caressed the side of the house. Every time she'd said the house wasn't the problem. Was that the truth? Or was that because it was doing this for her?

And worse . . . What was she doing for it in exchange?

I let the curtains fall closed as Mom led the camera crew inside the house. A quick check in our fridge confirmed my suspicions. She had collected a bunch of the groceries I'd bought for us yesterday to fill their order. I speed-walked to my room so I could see them make their way into the mansion.

Mom's foot hovered for a moment on the threshold as the crew walked past her, but she did it—she went in.

I guess it shouldn't have been so shocking. She had already gone inside to save me. Besides, she had her maggot protection, and the house liked her. The only thing keeping her out was her memories. These people were high-class guests. Their words could make or break the business. If there were ever a time to push herself, this was it.

The image of Ivy hovering near the mansion came back to me.

She was the danger. She was the one we needed to stop.

Ivy said the house liked me, so why had it done those things in its rooms to me? But then, it hadn't made me give anything up either. When Ivy was there, that's when I pulled the worm from my head, that's when I was tortured with the hallucination of them in my body, that's when I saw the memory of the girl who Ivy wanted to know. Every time, Ivy was the one who benefitted.

Even if I didn't 100 percent trust Mom's motives anymore, it stood to reason that the house didn't do those things to me of its own will. Ivy had power over it somehow.

It was like Mom said: the house wasn't as independent as it seemed.

I thought of the Ivy who'd dragged me out of bed that night to go to the room where the girl died. Who was likely the *reason* that girl died. Who pressed her ear against the door to listen to that couple tormented by bees.

That was not someone I could convince to stop.

I had to make her pass on. It was the only way.

Mom burst through the bunkie door so suddenly that I jumped. "I need you to keep an eye on them during their stay. Ivy needs to be controlled." She paused and gritted her teeth. "And I can't be with you. If you get caught by them, I can spin a story. If I get caught, it'll ruin everything. Just keep out of the rooms so Ivy won't be able to lock you in again."

There it was. Finally. My permission to go into the house. My chance to prove myself. To earn my freedom.

And no more of this pretending to be a normal teenager, since I was going to have to skip school.

"Okay," I said. I had planned on watching over them anyway, but it felt better to know Mom was finally on board. "How long are they here?"

"Two nights." She took a deep breath in and out. "If things get bad . . . listen to the house. It'll help you. Trust me, it doesn't want Ivy pulling its strings either."

I froze. "Listen to the house that's torturing people?"

She sighed. "It's like a plant. It's in its nature to survive. Sometimes it feeds from the dead and sometimes from people. It doesn't kill them, and they don't remember. But it needs help. It needs *gardeners*. Some, like Ivy, let it grow wild and out of control. Not like us. We're the good ones, Daisy. We keep it pruned and manageable. The house is not bad. The house is a function of its gardener. It helped me, you know? When he was . . . it was the only thing I had. The only one who I could tell everything to. And it wants me to help it. It wants *you* to help it. So let's take care of the corporeal and move on with our lives."

A chill settled over my shoulders as if one of the dead were pressed against my body, pulling me to its chest, trapping me in its arms. I didn't like the way she talked about the house. It felt like reverence. Like she was in church, praying at its altar. This thing that fed on fear and pain.

Ivy called it an animal, and Mom called it a plant.

The house is a function of its gardener.

I swallowed but nodded. First, Ivy needed to be stopped. We could figure out where to go after that. "Okay. When do I go inside? Now?"

"No, I need to go finish giving them a tour, and then I need to go get the Jeep. Actually, you can drive me out to the launch to pick it up and then bring back the boat after. Just sit tight until then."

As she made her way to the house, I followed her out and veered off into the greenhouse. It didn't take long to look after the plants, and by the time I finished, Mom would be done with her grand tour.

The garden was doing better. Some plants were still struggling from the overzealous caretaker that I could only assume had been Ivy in my body, going through the charade of being me so as to not be suspicious. I watered the ones with drying soil and dusted the leaves of some of the larger palms with a damp cloth.

"More and more. There are so many people coming in and out." Ivy didn't even try to go through the door properly. There wasn't much point now in pretending to be something she wasn't. She simply walked through the glass.

"Why did you even bother watering the plants?" I asked. "Why not just come in here and walk around if you wanted to pretend to be me?"

Ivy gave me a sweet smile—dark red lipstick and dark sunglasses. "I want to know who the girl in the room is."

It was sad, really. The barriers between the dead and the living were sometimes so fluid and other times so stark.

I said, "Stop making the house torture the guests and kill people, and maybe I'll tell you."

She scowled at me. "It's in the house's nature to feed."

"But not to eat *people* and not to kill, right? It needs help, doesn't it? And that's you."

Ivy's lips pinched tight. "Tell me who the girl is."

I shook my head. "I already made you an offer." Part of me thought about trying to make her pass on now, but she was too on guard. It wouldn't work if her hackles were up.

"Fuck your 'maybe,'" she snarled. "'Maybe' is an excuse for a lie that you know you're telling. You can say 'maybe' forever, and I have forever, and it's too long."

The door opened, and I turned my head toward Mom. "Let's go," she said.

When I turned back to Ivy, she had disappeared.

The boat ride was quiet until Mom looked over at me, wind whipping through her hair, cheeks pale from the cold. "You can do this, right?"

"I'll figure something out," I muttered.

"No, you will not 'figure something out.' You are going to use the things you learned in the study sessions you seem to have conveniently forgotten."

I hadn't 'conveniently forgotten.' I *purposely* tried not to think of them.

"As a reminder, those sessions were to help you. You know

how to deal with aggressive spirits, so deal with her."

I chewed on the inside of my cheek and said nothing.

It was different to practice things in safe settings with Mom versus coming here and dealing with something real. And it's not like Mom had given me any idea of what to expect. She hadn't even wanted me involved until now. But I had read the dead to get information. I'd held on to that much. But then I'd wasted so much time not being sure if Ivy was or wasn't a ghost and then got fucking possessed.

Enough. I would end this.

I would make Ivy pass on.

Forcibly.

I had done it enough times before.

I cleared my throat and bundled tighter in my jacket. "I'll deal with her."

When I was nine, for one of our study sessions, Mom took me to an abandoned warehouse in the West End of Toronto, almost in Mississauga, it was so far west. It was this old discount shoe place. The signs in front proclaimed it was private property, but they didn't have any cameras or security. Mom and I just walked in.

It must have been something like eleven at night. The whole place was dark, and Mom wouldn't use the flashlight on her phone. That July was already hot and humid, but inside the warehouse it was somehow more so, like soaking in a hot tub. The whole place was this giant empty box with dirty floors littered with beer bottles and trash.

"Just like the other times, there's someone in there who needs help passing on." Mom pressed her hand on top of my head and gripped it. It was a gesture that was partially affectionate and partially for control and focus. I used to like it. "But it's going to be a bit different. I need you to stay strong, okay?"

I tried to push down the fear that rushed through me at the idea of what was new about this session. But I wasn't very good at it back then, and I trembled even as I sweat.

I searched the space for the person we were looking for. Eyes bouncing off the once-vibrant shoe-sale signs and empty shelves.

When I found him, I stopped.

A little boy was curled up in a corner, his knees pulled to his chest with his chin resting on them.

And I knew him.

That same boy had held my face against the ground while I choked on dirt.

I cried out and turned to run, but Mom wouldn't let me. She settled her hands on my shoulders and turned me around. "Daisy," she said, tone sharp. "You are not the same age as him anymore. You're a big girl now. You cannot spend your entire life afraid. Mommy worked *very* hard to find this boy for you. It was not easy. But lucky for us, he's still as much of a bully as he was before. He's been scaring kids in the area. Look, even I can see him. He's not even trying to hide. Now you'll take care of him."

There was an intensity to her voice that scared me, and her grip was too firm to break out of. I twisted in her arms, whimpering.

He was going to hurt me.

I was going to die.

I needed to run.

I could hear them again.

Dazy.

Dazy.

Dazy.

"Daisy!" Mom snapped. "Didn't I save you last time? I'm right here. Nothing bad will happen."

That stopped me.

I stared into her face, pinched with irritation, and I knew she was right. Mom had saved me from those kids.

But still . . . Every other ghost I had faced in a session up until that point had been, at most, semi-opaque. They didn't have the ability to hurt me. But a corporeal . . . That was different.

Mom must have sensed my hesitation because she squatted beside me and pointed at the boy. "Look at him. He hasn't even noticed we're here. He's alone and has wandered so far from the playground he was in. It isn't like it was before. You'll see. After you do this, you'll feel so much better." Her expression was so earnest. She smiled, and it was full of hope. I knew that she felt this was the answer. That this would help me stop being so scared.

I swallowed and nodded. "Okay."

"Good girl." Mom stood and gave me a little push forward.

At the time, it felt encouraging.

The boy looked exactly the way he did when I was six. He was white and wore faded blue-denim shorts and a washed-out red T-shirt. His sneakers were a pair of dirty white Nikes. The dead were a snapshot of who they used to be beyond the sadness or violence of their deaths. I shouldn't have been surprised that he hadn't changed, but I was.

"The words," Mom prompted.

I swallowed again and shuffled forward until I was in front of the boy, only a couple of feet of space between us.

Mom was right. He was so small now compared to me. When I was six, he had been a giant. "How can I help you pass on?" I squeaked. Mom had put beads at the end of my braids, and they clinked together as I trembled.

Any moment now, he would come to life and attack me.

I stiffened my muscles, braced for it.

I remembered his name from when we had played together. Before he hated me.

Jonathan. We called him Johnny.

He looked up, and I jumped back. But he didn't do anything. Just squinted and said, "Who are you?"

He didn't remember me.

The fact hit me hard and fast. I thought about him all the time, about them all. About what they did to me.

And he had no idea who I was.

"Prompt him again," Mom said, using her impatient voice.

"How can I help you pass on?" I asked again, louder this time, the way Mom taught me.

Johnny ignored me and looked at her instead. "Who is she?"

Mom sighed. "Next steps. We already know he's been around too long."

If they didn't answer the question, then they didn't want to pass on. Which meant he wouldn't go away over time. Which was obvious because he had been around for at least three years now. That made things harder. Because now I would have to force him.

My legs shook as I made myself step forward. I needed to do this. I needed to keep going. Because however terrified I was of him, somehow the idea of disappointing Mom was worse.

I reached out my hand for him, and before I could touch him, he slapped it away.

That had never happened before. Usually, the dead didn't understand what I was doing. They would watch passively, and by that time, it was too late. Besides, the other ones hadn't been corporeal. They physically couldn't make contact with me like that.

But Johnny was a boy who sneered at you from the top of the slide as he pushed you down. And apparently, he didn't want to be touched.

For a moment, all I did was stare at my hand, feeling the sting of pain lace through it. Like I was confused about what was happening.

Then I screamed.

It was going to happen again.

He was going to try to kill me.

"Daisy!" Mom shouted. "You're stronger than him. Just push him down!"

I didn't want to do that. I wanted to run away. I wanted to not be there. But Mom kept shouting, and Johnny was standing up now, coming toward me. He looked annoyed.

"It's you or him, Daisy! You or him!"

Later, I wondered what had driven me forward. If it was my own desire to overcome my fear or if it was my desperate need to avoid disappointing Mom.

I wanted it to be the former.

But I couldn't ever say so with confidence.

I remember screaming. I remember pushing Johnny in the chest with all my strength. Being shocked by how easily he went down. He hit his head and started crying.

I was so scared.

I pulled him up by the collar of his cheap shirt and slammed him back down on the ground. Again, and again.

I was so scared.

He was dazed, his eyes rolling in his head. And there was blood and tears. I didn't know that ghosts could have blood and tears just because they were corporeal.

I was so scared.

I thrust my hand into his chest, and it went through. Smooth. Like he was a translucent. Just like I had with so many others by then, I wrapped my fingers around the place where his heart should have been. Where it *was*. I could feel it, beating frantically, like he was a living person.

Cold ran down my arm like a shock.

I had done this before. It was how I read the dead. Touching their hearts.

But this time, I squeezed.

The chill disappeared, and I was flooded with warmth.

Johnny's eyes shot open, and he screamed. And screamed. And screamed.

I was on the merry-go-round again, and his screams were blending with mine. And was I screaming right now too? Were we both screaming?

His body dimmed. His transparency increased, more and more until even I couldn't see him, but I knew he was there because I was still holding his heart.

I saw people he had loved and lost. People he hurt. Times he was happy. Times he was sad. Everything in flashes too fast and disorienting to comprehend.

His screams faded too, until they were so small and faint that I wasn't sure if I was hearing them or just listening to an echo playing in my mind.

Then, my hand snapped into a fist. The thing I was holding on to was gone.

Gone forever.

Everything I had seen faded with him, but the effects remained. I trembled. I was bundled in a heat that burned.

And I was terrified.

I hunched over on myself and wrapped my arms around my body.

Who had that been? That girl slamming Johnny's head into the ground?

That wasn't me.

I was the girl whose head he was pressing into the ground.

Choking on earth.

Dying.

I was supposed to feel better, but I was more scared than ever. And now Johnny and the kids weren't the only thing that scared me.

Now *I* scared me.

"Done?" Mom asked.

"Done," I whispered, tears streaming down my face.

She tugged me up under my armpits and got me into standing position. "See? You faced your monster, and you won. You were stronger." Mom had the biggest grin I had ever seen on her face. She was beaming. Overjoyed.

Proud.

Proud of *me*.

We went to Dairy Queen right after. Mom got me an Oreo Mocha Fudge Blizzard and let me choose the size. I got a large. It was too much for me to ever finish, but I ate whatever I could. The whole time she smiled at me and ran her hand along my head.

And I knew that I would always do anything she wanted if I could feel like that again.

Even if making the dead pass on felt like I was dying too.

CHAPTER THIRTY-EIGHT

King met me at the back door of the mansion. I'm sure Mom didn't imagine he was part of the plan to look after the group, but I'd told him that we were going to do this together, and I'd meant it. He was wearing all black like this was some sort of spy movie, and I rolled my eyes at him.

We went inside the mansion through the back door and found a place in the hallway of the upper floor to watch the group from afar without being spotted. Their setup was mostly in the kitchen off to the side of the entrance, which consisted of the usual kitchen essentials: fridge, oven, et cetera, and a long dining table. Conveniently for us, we could get a pretty good look inside from the right-most set of stairs while staying hidden. Or at least, when any of them came out of the room, we could duck into the hallway to hide.

King and I communicated by texting even though we were beside each other. Both of us were unwilling to talk and get caught. Mom, at least, was expecting me to be here, but the Tower folks were not.

After a moment of hesitation, I texted: I talked with my mom last night about Peter.

I know, he responded.

Yeah . . . I just wonder, you said your mom had your ability when my mom was living here.

I thought about adding more but didn't know how to ask what I wanted without seeming like an asshole.

King let out a breath beside me before he texted, I asked my mom about it once I knew that you and your mom would have that conversation. I figured my mom would be sensitive. It's not like I was just spreading Grace's business around.

I get it.

Everything with Peter happened in the house, so she couldn't see it. But she knew your mom was afraid of Peter. That's why she kept inviting her over for tea, so she could learn more. But Grace refused to come by. Without someone willing to come forward, she wouldn't have gotten far throwing out an accusation. When I told her, she was really upset. She wished that she could have done something back then.

At least she tried. I didn't know what else to say. I couldn't blame Mom for not wanting to confide in a complete stranger.

The media team didn't do anything particularly interesting. Mom took the Jeep into town to replenish our groceries and to get the team a few pizzas from a local place we hadn't been to yet. The group did some editing of their existing footage and, while they ate, chatted about what they would film tomorrow. They had plans to go into town, where they had mine tours scheduled and a visit to some sort of hotel that, apparently, had caribou on the property, a spa, and crème brûlée.

It was boring, to be honest.

Ivy didn't appear, and the house seemed calm without her. They had only been in their rooms quickly to drop off their bags and otherwise spent most of their time out exploring the bush around us or inside the living and kitchen area.

When they finally went to bed, King and I decided to take sleeping shifts. Him texting me that he apparently "slept hard" and would really need to be shoved to wake up. He was supposed to take the first shift, and me the second, but I couldn't get to sleep, so we both stayed awake.

I waited for any telltale screams, once even standing outside of their rooms while King was lookout. But it was only soft snores. With the exception of one room, which was filled with heavy moans and breathing. I guessed quickly that at least two of the team members were more well acquainted than the others.

King wiggled his eyebrows at me over it, and I texted him to go fuck himself.

But it brought me some comfort. The house should be feeding the first chance it got, shouldn't it? The fact that it wasn't now and that Ivy was missing confirmed that she was the one pulling the strings. And the next time I saw her, I would end this.

Eventually, I fell asleep tucked up with a blanket in an alcove on the upper-floor hallway, and King continued his watch.

The next day, the group was gone on their tours. In the morning, I learned that King was telling the truth about "sleeping hard," and I had to kick him to get him up. While Tower was gone, King left and got us both some sandwiches from his house. His mom and aunts being invested in stopping the mansion's control was the only reason they were letting him miss school. Otherwise, we passed the time playing games on our respective phones. I also texted Megan, who was deep into her early exam prep and longing for someone to complain to.

The whole group came back in the evening chattering about

something called Cozy Corner, which was, apparently, a Chinese food place in town. They slammed down a box of beer on the countertop, which they drank while they edited their footage.

When they made their way to bed, I let King go to sleep first. He refused and insisted on staying up, telling me to wake him if he fell asleep. But I guess he hadn't slept well the night before and passed out anyway. After an hour or so, I padded back down the hallway to linger near their rooms. I wasn't exactly jazzed to listen to snoring and enthusiastic sex again, but at least it would be over after tonight.

Except when I turned the corner, Ivy was there, squatting down with her ear pressed to the door.

I turned and ran as quickly and quietly as I could back to where King was. I kicked him in the side, but he just let out a grunt without moving. I rolled my eyes. I couldn't waste time trying to get him up, even if that's what he wanted.

I went back to the hallway and approached Ivy. "Don't," I said. "Whatever you're doing, cut it out."

She scowled at me. "Tell me who the girl is and maybe I'll ask the house nicely to stop." She grinned at me. "Don't tell me, and maybe I'll ask it to do more. More, and more, and more."

I couldn't tell if she was serious or bluffing. It could be either.

"Like the girl in the piano room?" I asked.

Her face faltered for a moment before it hardened. "Yeah," she said, though she stumbled over the single word. "He's better off anyway. Her husband."

"Why did you do that to her?" I said, shaking my head.

Ivy wrapped her arms around herself. "She was going to leave him, did you know that? She was talking about it on the phone during the day. About how it wasn't working, and the vacation hadn't helped. She was going to wait until he was asleep the next night and just leave."

I swallowed. "You don't know the whole story. Maybe he was abusive, and she needed to escape."

"He wasn't," she insisted. "I watched them. He was nice to her. He was happy. And she didn't say anything. She was just going to disappear!" Ivy's voice shook. She forced it into something calm. "Now she's gone. Or . . . kind of."

I knew what she meant. The dead girl was still in the house. Stuck.

Ivy too. Being in my body got her farther, but even corporeal, she couldn't go for good.

"You can't leave this house, can you? Even in my body?"

She frowned but didn't dispute it.

It didn't matter. Nothing changed what I would have to do.

I waited until she turned back to the door, and I knelt down beside her. She didn't act any differently. Why would she? That was the thing about doing this. Most of the dead didn't know any better. Johnny was an exception. And even then, he hadn't understood—he was just reacting.

In this case, I wouldn't risk asking Ivy if she wanted to pass beforehand. Besides, I knew that she didn't.

Ivy didn't move until I thrust my hand into her chest and squeezed her heart.

Her scream was shrill and panicked. She thrashed underneath my hand. Her arms, solid and corporeal, slapped at my face hard enough to bring tears to my eyes, but I forced myself to keep my grip steady.

Images flashed through my brain. *The house. The halls. A room. A cold box. Dancing around in that room. Alone. Always alone.* Everything too fast. It hurt me, too, but I held on.

I needed to do this. She was the danger. And she had basically admitted to murdering that girl.

Ivy started to cry. "Please stop, Daisy, please stop. It hurts, it hurts, you're hurting me. Why are you doing this? I'm sorry that I'm bad, I'm sorry, I'm sorry, Daisy, please stop." Tears streamed down her face as she lost color and started to fade. Her hits no longer hurt because they went straight through me.

But it felt like the blows were still coming. It was like there was someone grasping my heart in turn. She looked so young. So afraid.

This wasn't like the man in the burned-down gym, or that woman in the old apartment, or anyone else I had ever done this to.

I *knew* Ivy. And not like I had known Johnny. He was wrapped up in a terrible memory that I still struggled to shake.

But Ivy was different.

She could have done anything with my body, but instead she was in school studying, for God's sake. Why would she do that unless she never got the chance when she was alive? Ivy was cruel, but she was also sad and young.

She was competing with a memory of my mom to be the house's best friend, and meanwhile, according to Mom, the house wanted her gone too. It was tragic.

"Please stop, please stop," she cried, shaking. Her voice was small, but her words still cut deep. "Why do you hate me?"

The words crawled into my body and burrowed there. How many times had I had that thought when I was younger? When I looked at Mom as she shoved me toward the dead. As she rejected my attempts to get to know her, to form the sort of relationship other girls had with their moms.

My fingers lost their grip. Just for a moment, they slipped away from Ivy's heart.

And it was enough.

She flashed straight to corporeal and kicked me in the stomach. *Hard.*

I cried out and doubled over.

Ivy jumped to her feet and threw open the door to the room. The girl inside, with her short pixie blond hair and tattooed neck, shouted in surprise.

I scrambled to my feet. "Don't!"

Ivy turned to the empty fireplace next to the bed, lifted out a heavy iron poker, and swung it at the blond girl's head just as I ran through the doorway.

The girl's scream pierced as sharp as the poker. It sliced through her face like it was nothing. The skin peeled back from her flesh as blood splattered across the bedsheets and floor. The crimson of muscle shone through the wound as it gushed. The hooked tip of the poker had latched onto her nose, and white bone, cracked and splintered, stuck out from her face.

The poker clattered to the ground.

Ivy grinned at me from across the room.

I stood frozen in the doorway as the girl screamed and clutched her face.

Because she couldn't see Ivy.

All she knew was that she had been attacked.

And I was the one standing in the doorway with a bloody poker at my feet.

CHAPTER THIRTY-NINE

I decided to eat a Pizza Pop for breakfast. It was something like nine a.m., and I was out in the living room because I was tired of being in my bedroom with the mansion outside my window, butcherbirds staring with their beady eyes. Sunlight that my plants were soaking up poured in through the living room window facing the dock. My plants were doing great. A lot better than me. My monstera had even sprouted a new leaf for the month. I balanced my plate on my lap and shoved the too-hot cheese, pepperoni, and bread combo into my mouth while a talk show played on TV.

My first thought after everything went down was, *I guess I should have woken King up.* He must have known what would happen. He couldn't see things inside the mansion, but he must have seen this aftermath. *Commit*, he had said. *No matter what, you can't back down.* He'd wanted to be awake so he could remind me to keep holding on. To not let my fingers slip. And just like everyone else he'd tried to help, I didn't listen.

Mom wouldn't look at me. Wouldn't speak to me. Wouldn't leave her room. The single exception had been to go to the lawyer, Mr. Helms, who, apparently, also did criminal law, and even then I suspect Mom only went to avoid looking worse in the public eye. I stared at her bedroom door. Closed. As it had been since yesterday when she got back and in the week since everything happened.

My face was still sore. Across my cheekbone was a black, purple, and yellow bruise. It was like I was a rare succulent, blooming in more colors than expected, and left alone to fend for myself because, of course, I could handle it.

Jeremiah, one of the girl's camera guys, had seen me standing in the hallway while she screamed—a girl I'd learned was named Hayden, though everyone now called her "the victim." When he'd seen me there, with her hurt, he gave me a punch to the face so strong that it knocked me out and shattered my cheekbone.

Apparently, that's when King woke up and came barreling around the corner. Managed to stop Jeremiah from beating up on my prone body.

Legally, it was undue force, especially considering that I wasn't attacking Hayden when he punched me. He would be charged criminally, though we wouldn't be suing him. Mr. Helms advised that he didn't think it was the best use of our resources to go after him for little things like Mom's missed work to take care of my injury.

Hayden, however, *was* suing us for lost wages from missing work, personal injury, and mental distress. Mr. Helms said Mom had already agreed to pay, though he noted that Hayden didn't seem satisfied with that even though the outcome was in her favor.

Technically, Hayden and I were *both* victims. Though most people weren't on my side, unsurprisingly.

I was messy when I woke up in the hospital. Mr. Helms was the only person in my room and had just enough time to snap at me to say nothing before the police came in. I didn't need to be told that. I was Black. I was very aware of all my rights when it came to law enforcement. In the end, all I did was cry. Mom wasn't there in the hospital. Later, Mr. Helms drove me to the boat launch, where King picked me up, and we had one of our usual silent drives home. Though I could tell he wanted to say something.

Mr. Helms said he was confident this wouldn't go to trial and that he could reach a settlement with the Crown that worked for everyone. Jail time was unlikely—stays in a facility were for more frequent offenders in situations where they were likely to reoffend. Though my history of violence wasn't exactly helpful for showing that I wasn't going to do anything bad again. That would be the hard part for Mr. Helms. Either way, it would be months before it was sorted out.

I didn't go to school anymore. I might have been suspended, but mostly I just decided not to, and Mom wasn't exactly present to stop me.

King was at school.

Mom wouldn't speak to me.

Suddenly, despite everything, I wished for Ivy. For that little terror. It was better than the constant silence that stretched over the bunkie.

But I wasn't going to seek her out.

I had no plan, so there wasn't any point.

In the end, I went to the garden because that was where I went when things were bad. I spent my day patting soft soils, caressing leaves, muttering to them whatever came into my head. I went back to the bunkie maybe twice for snacks.

In the afternoon, King knocked at the glass door.

I shrugged at him. "Come in if you're coming in."

He entered with a grim set to his thick lips and a downturn to his eyebrows. Most people would shuffle over with bad news. Not King. I guess because he already knew it was coming. "I think you need to see this."

"Why does this not make me feel rosy inside?"

"It'll be worse if you find it on your own." He sat down on the edge of a planter and waved me over. "Just watch."

I came over and sat next to him, closer than I wanted to, but I needed to see the tiny screen of his phone. Our legs were pressed together. Mine so much smaller than his, weaker. It was almost a wonder that Jeremiah hadn't caved in more of my face with that hit.

The title of the video was "I Was Attacked at This Airbnb."

Every muscle in my body clenched and compressed at once.

King hit play.

It started off as a positive video. It would have been a great review. They chatted with Mom on the boat about how she had inherited the property she'd spent her summers in and decided to share it with the world. Mom played it up. Said she spent the best times of her life here and that she had been struggling in Toronto as a single mom. Half-truths. Maybe times with Dad and her friends had been good, but considering everything it probably wasn't the best time of her life. And yeah, maybe sometimes she struggled as a single mom, but we were never homeless or anything. Her greatest trial had been me and my connection to the dead. But maybe that was enough.

The whole crew loved the boat ride. When they got to the house, it was even better. Mom gave them a full tour. Opening the doors to rooms and pointing them out without stepping inside. There was a basement that I didn't even know about with this huge walk-in freezer that, according to Mom, was apparently sealed shut, and a hangout nook with a bed, a couch, books, and a small TV. A special servants' quarters probably. Mom said she would eventually reno-vate it to be a gym or spa area.

Mom drove them into town the next day. She turned it into this whole off-roading adventure in the Jeep, which they also loved. They went to that hotel with the caribou that was apparently called Cedar Meadows. Inside, they had luxurious spa appointments and that aforementioned crème brûlée. Apparently, Mom cut a deal with certain vendors so that people staying at the Airbnb would get discounts at places in town they visited.

At the end of the day, after dinner, they met Mom by the boat launch, and she drove them back onto the property.

Everything was great.

Hayden talked about how she was from Timmins originally. She was a Belanger, a twist of fate that made me want to cry. She hadn't known Peter or his father well—she was some sort of removed cousin—but she knew the property was in the family and had been too young to get to go before Peter had moved in permanently.

Mom had done her research and found her. That was how she got this prolific Tower producer out here.

The video went black for a second. Words appeared, warning of blood and violence. I tensed so hard that my neck cramped.

The video resumed, but this time instead of the scenic wide shots, it was a vertical video clearly taken on a phone, with Hayden crying and pressing a blood-soaked towel to her face, asking, "Why would she do that?" while one of her crewmates was telling her everything would be okay.

They ran to the bunkie and pounded on the door, and Mom came out, beautiful and fresh-faced from her lack of makeup and heavy night moisturizer, though bleary-eyed. Her eyes opened good and wide when she saw Hayden.

Jeremiah appeared in the frame, screaming at her, bearing down on her, and she shrank away from him, almost shriveled. Confused and terrified.

When I saw him on-screen, he was a giant against my mom. He must have been 6'5". Thinking that he was the one who'd punched me in the face, I was shocked that I was alive.

Hayden was still filming on her phone and crying. Mom ran into the bunkie to grab her jacket and keys and drove them straight to the hospital.

The final clip was of Hayden explaining that she had been attacked and would be suing us, and that she was advised by her lawyer to avoid sharing any more details. She was recovering, and the wonderful folks at Tower would be footing the bill for any necessary cosmetic surgery that insurance didn't handle. Her face was wrapped in so much gauze that her voice was muffled. They had to put subtitles at the bottom so you could understand her. She implored Airbnb as a company to do more thorough background checks on its hosts and their families to avoid these situations in the future.

King tried to pull his phone away when it ended. I grabbed it from him. He made a small noise of protest but didn't snatch it back.

The comments were worse. People had looked into the Airbnb listing. They found out who I was and added it to the narrative. There were former classmates happy to share details of what I had done to that girl in elementary school. Others already knew that a person had died in the house, and there was speculation that either Mom or I or both of us had been responsible for that, too. There were people accusing us of murdering Peter to get the house, for fuck's sake.

Tower was a liberal media company, so maybe the outright racist comments got deleted, but there was still plenty of "those sorts of people" and "people like them" language that made it clear enough how they felt.

And at the top with over a hundred likes on it was a comment that even without all the thumbs-ups would have stood out. I recognized the username immediately, BeingNoah147. He thought it was funny to name himself like a lifestyle channel, then add on something ridiculous like a series of numbers. Mocking vloggers who weren't unique but thought they were. The likes on his comment kept going up.

"Daisy," King said, voice soft and tentative.

The comment read:

I knew the girl who led this attack. I used to think she was a smart young woman with a lot of potential and did my best to help her through the mentorship program where I met her. However, she developed a crush on me and took it to another level. She would stalk me and my friends. Insisted we were dating when we weren't. And then she had the nerve to stalk my new partner and confront me at my apartment about it. I think that deep down, she's a nice girl, but she's also very unstable. It's sad that this happened, and I really feel for Hayden being the victim here. I hope that this girl gets the mental health support that she needs and that people understand the importance of early intervention.

Girl. He kept saying that. *Girl.*

The commenters were rallying to support Noah. They were saying what an amazing human being he was for taking the time to mentor troubled youth. They were telling him that he needed to acknowledge that he was a victim too and should sue me as well. They were unspecific on what grounds that would be, but were very specific in calling me a crazy, desperate, jealous bitch who didn't deserve to be alive.

Dazy.

Dazy.

Dazy.

My face crumpled, and a sob tore from my throat. I struggled to breathe. I cried like I had never let myself cry before. I hunched forward, tucked my head against my knees, and bawled.

I didn't know anything anymore. Had I ever dated Noah? Was he right? But I had these memories of us meeting his friends and hanging out at his apartment. Times where we held hands and laughed while walking through the park interspersed with memories of him holding me down on a bed by my throat. Those were my memories. But what were my memories worth anyway? Ivy had messed with them easily enough. Who was to say that it hadn't happened before?

King rubbed his hand on my back. "Don't let him get in your head."

"Maybe he's right," I blubbered, and King's hand paused. "Maybe I made everything up, and my head is fucked."

"He's not."

"But—"

"You do know that I'm psychic, right?"

Despite myself, I let out a small laugh.

The door to the greenhouse creaked open, and I jerked my head up. Mom was standing there in the doorway with bloodshot eyes, no jacket, just her housecoat and winter boots.

She was going to ask me to fix it. Again, and again, and again. I would spend my entire life trying to fix her fucked-up one.

No.

Not anymore.

I rose from the planter even as King stiffened beside me and said, "Daisy, remember what I told you."

I know that in a few days from now you'll have a fight with your mom and need to be careful about what you decide to say to her.

I should listen to him. How many things had I messed up by just doing whatever I wanted?

But I was tired.

I was so fucking tired of doing what everyone else wanted.

"This is your fault!" I screamed at Mom, tears coursing down my face. "You ruined me! You ruined my childhood, forced me to do those things to the dead even when they cried out. I would have dreams about them all the time. About feeling them die while you stood there and made me keep going."

Mom opened her mouth to say something, and I shook my head.

"No! I'm talking now. I have spent my entire life trying to help you. If you hated your job and wanted a new one, I supported you. I helped you find listings and made suggestions. If you hated our apartment and wanted a new one, I helped you look and helped move everything over while you fucked off to do whatever else. When you said you wanted this house and that I needed to use my ability to help you in whatever vague way that was, I dedicated my entire life to doing it. Because for once, there was going to be something for *me* in it. I have done everything for you! I don't have any dreams. I don't have anything I want to do. There's not even a fucking point because I have always just existed to help you! And *for what*?!"

Mom didn't say anything, just kept her mouth closed, lips pressed so tightly together that they wrinkled in the middle.

And finally, I said the thing I had refused to believe was true. "You *knew*. You knew that if you made me in that house, I would have this ability. It's too perfect. It's too convenient that the one person you had to have, the gardener for your precious house, fell into your lap like this. No way. Not you and the mansion. 'Cause you're best friends, right? You said that it told you all this stuff you know about the dead and what I can do. Why would it do that if it didn't expect you to have a child like me? To have me here for your perfect revenge. *You knew.*"

Mom's bottom lip trembled, and she bit onto it to stop the shaking. Finally, she spoke. "I was sixteen. I didn't know what it would mean for you to have this power. The house needed someone like you... and I wanted to help it. It didn't tell me how bad it would be to see ghosts. And I thought that maybe if Jordan and I . . . if it happened in the same place, that maybe it would erase everything else that happened there. But I wasn't ready. I was a mess after, and Jordan tried to help, but I just wanted him to forget everything, and it said it would make him, but then he remembered it all. It *lied*. How could I forget that sometimes it lies? It did so much good for me otherwise." She shook her head, hugging her arms around herself. "But nothing is working like it said it would. Everything is going wrong."

I thought she was better than that, but she wasn't.

Hadn't she shown me that, time and time again?

I wasn't her daughter. I was a tool. A part of a plan. Hell, even Dad was part of it. And she had acted like he was the problem.

And if that was a lie, why wouldn't everything else be?

Maybe she was never going to finance my escape.

I would never get away from her. I would never get to figure out who I was, what I wanted. I would be stuck with her forever. Bound. Unable to tear myself away, no matter how objectively possible it should have been.

Freedom was not for me.

"I hate you!" I screeched. "I hate you! I hate you! *I hate you!*" The last scream took so much that my voice cracked and shattered. My body let loose a torrent of sobs that I couldn't control. I crumpled back onto the ledge of a planter and buried my head in my arms again.

Mom's voice filtered through the noise anyway. "I'm sorry," she said. "I just . . . I really thought that I could make it up to you. Give you time to be a normal teenager. Only get you involved if you absolutely needed to be. I thought that I could control this. I'll talk to it, okay? I'll see what we can do for you. I'm sorry. I'm so sorry."

I wasn't in the mood to hear "sorry" or any of the other disjointed mumbling she had to share. It was still her fault. I didn't want her apologies. Not now. And she didn't say anything after that.

She just tugged her housecoat on tighter and left.

I didn't know how long I stayed there. It didn't feel like much time at all. When I looked up, King was staring at me, his expression carefully arranged. Like he was forcing himself to hold it together.

"What?" I croaked, my voice hoarse and sore. "Sorry, you can't control me either. Not anymore."

He shook his head. "I wasn't trying to. I was trying to *help* you." He ran his hands through his hair. "I'm sorry, Daisy. I'm sorry that you're so used to people jerking you around that you don't know what sincerity looks like. But until you do, I can't do anything for you. And believe it or not, being psychic doesn't mean I'm not human. That I can't get fucking tired of watching you make the same mistakes over and over."

King waited for a moment, maybe for me to say something.

But I didn't have anything else to say.

He left then. Turned around and walked out of the greenhouse.

Done with me, I guess.

After a while, I got up too and headed to the bunkie. I stepped inside and paused. Mom's winter boots were missing. I walked to her room and threw open the door. Empty.

I ran out and looked at the dock, where the boat was covered and tied. I rushed to the entrance of the bush where Mom had started parking, but the Jeep sat unoccupied.

I sprinted into the bush and called out for her. "Mom!" I screamed. "Mom!"

What was it she was saying in the greenhouse? That she would talk to it . . .

The house told me.

Shit.

I turned around, and the mansion towered over me. Every

butcherbird on their perch—on ledges, rafters, eavestroughs—turned their heads to look at me in unison. Silent. I watched a mouse twitch, impaled on a thorn. Blood-soaked fur.

If I wanted to be free, to be my own person, to never have to fix anything ever again, I could stay right where I was.

I won't pretend that I didn't think about it.

That I didn't stand there one moment longer to imagine what that life could be like.

And then I ran straight for the house.

CHAPTER FORTY

don't text King to let him know what I'm doing. He made his stance clear. So much for being friends.

But he was right. He'd told me to be careful about what I said to Mom. He had probably come to show me the video specifically so he could help me avoid exploding on her. Instead of letting me find it on my own and screaming at her. Which I did anyway.

And now Mom had run into danger because of what I'd said.

I pushed open the front door of the mansion and froze. The dead. They were looking at me. Just like the butcherbirds, their gazes homed in on my body in a way they hadn't before. A fine tremble rolled across me like a wave—from the back of my neck to the balls of my feet.

"Stop it," I whispered. Then louder, "Stop it!"

But they wouldn't.

They kept staring.

I was exposed under their gazes.

They couldn't speak, but together they mouthed one word:
"Dazy."

They weren't corporeal. They couldn't hurt me. But it didn't matter. I couldn't stop shaking.

Mom.

I needed to find her.

I forced my legs to move and made a beeline straight for the bedroom where I had seen the vision, desperately trying to ignore the penetrating stares that followed me. I kept a lookout for Ivy even as I searched for Mom.

Ivy wasn't predictable anymore, if she ever was, and now she knew what I could do to her. She could evade it, run away, fight back if I ever got near her. And she could be vengeful. Ivy could shove Mom into a room and let it torture her until she was the next person found dead.

I couldn't let that happen. Even after everything.

My life was this mismatch of events that felt like they were orbiting around me. Circling without ever touching. Mom was like the sun of that solar system, and I couldn't help but follow her around, even though it burned.

I was like my plants that way. I needed her, but she could just as easily destroy me.

Without her, what would I be? I wanted to escape but not like this.

I stopped short at Mom's bedroom door. Cries and moans sounded from within. Masculine. Peter. The agony was palpable, like something I could taste on my tongue, viscous and bitter.

"I know who you're looking for," Ivy whispered into my ear.

I jumped away from her and pressed myself against the wall. "Where's my mom?"

"Did you like my trick? With the dead?" She let her arms fall to her sides and stared at me through the darkness of her sunglasses, mouthing, "Dazy."

How the fuck had she done that with them? She was . . . *controlling* them. Like she had with the butcherbirds. With the house. With *me*.

Was she possessing them? It was the only thing that made sense, even if I had never seen it done. I didn't know about any dead who could do this. Control multiple hosts, the dead and the living—animals, even.

Ivy wasn't the house's gardener. She wasn't letting it grow out of control like Mom said. She was possessing it. Moving it like a puppet.

And yet she still couldn't defy the rule that trapped her inside it.

"Tell me who the girl is," Ivy said. "And maybe I'll tell you where your mom is."

Her obsession was all-encompassing. And even her being in my head for more than a month couldn't overcome the fact that the passing of time was an impossibility for her to properly understand. She was talking about Mom and still had no idea that the girl was her.

And she would never understand unless someone told her.

That someone wasn't going to be me.

"Where is my mom?" I hissed. Forcing myself to seem more confident, more assured, than I actually was. Ivy was too much of an outlier. She could possess, apparently, anything she wanted. She'd made the house torture and kill. She had resisted being suppressed.

She was both a teen girl and a monster.

Ivy shook her head. "I'm not telling you where she is until you tell me something I want to know."

"Why do you care so much about that girl?" I cried, throwing up my arms. "It doesn't matter. So what? The house liked her better. She's not even around anymore."

Ivy said nothing. Her expression was difficult to read with her sunglasses on. "Your mom is in the piano room, whispering to the house. Even took out the worm from her head to do it. It won't let me hear what she's saying." Her lips, painted with deep umber, spread into a smile. "But it's okay if we torture her, it says. The house doesn't need her anymore. Can you hear it? It's plenty loud on its own now. It wants her to give something up. I've been holding it back."

I swallowed. What the hell was Mom doing? Trying to get the house to *help* me? How deluded was she? "Why would you do that? Why would you hold the house back?"

"Leverage."

"Right," I muttered.

She smiled wide. "Tell me who, and I'll let her leave untouched."

"Or I could tell you, and you'd torture her anyway."

"Maybe . . . or maybe not. It's your decision."

"Tell me why? Why are you so obsessed with this girl?" My voice had a begging tone to it that I didn't like.

Ivy curled her lip. She wasn't getting anywhere with the threat alone. Maybe it was fine. Maybe she just had questions for Mom the way I did. Ivy looked and acted fifteen, said she was fifteen, but she could have been in this house a lot longer. I wouldn't put it past Mom to have known her as a child and pretend otherwise to my face.

But I needed to know so that I could be prepared for what came next.

Ivy pointed to Mom's bedroom door. "Go inside and I'll show you."

"Or you'll torture me."

She rolled her eyes. "What would be the point? I need you, unfortunately. Everything happened inside that room. Go and you'll see."

My options were few. Either I told Ivy that the girl was Mom now and risked whatever her reaction would be, or I refused to go into the room or tell her the truth and then Mom would be tortured, possibly to death. And a third in-between option where I learned why Ivy was so stuck on this in the first place, and it somehow turned out to be something beneficial?

At the very least, maybe it would waste enough time that Mom would leave before Ivy had a chance to get to her.

I opened the door to the room, and Peter tumbled out. I turned away from his twisted and gelatinous form.

Ivy didn't. "Go away," she hissed at him.

And he obeyed.

He immediately melted into the floor, disappearing into the boards, going God knows where.

Everything in this house, Ivy could control. And it was like part of her knew it and part of her didn't. She still acted like the house was the ultimate authority when in reality she was the one pulling the strings.

And I could never let her know that. She was bad enough now. What would she do if she realized she had more power than she thought?

Ivy waved me forward. I swallowed and stepped into the room, and she followed behind me. It was the same as before. She needed me to be first for some reason. The room shifted to the now-familiar sight of Mom's bedroom. When Mom came inside, she seemed to be the same age as when I saw her in the last vision, but she felt different.

Defeated. That was the word.

She quietly went about her bedtime routine before sitting in bed and staring at the door.

Only now I knew what she was waiting for.

Who she was waiting for.

Probably she couldn't sleep without knowing whether he would be paying a visit for the night. Ivy and I were only watching for a few minutes when Mom's face crumpled and she buried her head in her hands.

"I just want it to stop," she said. "Make it stop. I would do anything for it to be over."

She kept repeating some variation of the same plea over and over again.

Mom was in the middle of speaking when suddenly her voice cut off.

I looked to Ivy, who glanced at me. "You can't hear it, can you? The house? Not with that thing in your ear."

She was right, I couldn't.

But Mom could. She stayed in bed for a moment before slowly climbing off it to walk over to the wall and press her ear against it. She slid down lower and lower until she was sitting on the floor with the whole of her body pressed up against the wall.

"It picks people," Ivy said. "Special people who it decides to talk to."

I didn't know what made Mom and Ivy the sorts of conversationalists the house enjoyed, and Ivy didn't offer any reasons up.

"Would that make it stop?" Mom asked the wall. Of course, I didn't hear what it said. I looked to Ivy with raised eyebrows, but she didn't seem interested in translating.

Mom was enraptured by the voice of the house. Her tears had run dry. "What will happen when I bring him to the room? Will he die?" Whatever the house said back wasn't pleasing, because a frown formed on her face.

"How the hell am I supposed to understand this if I can't hear the house?" I snapped at Ivy.

She glared at me. "And if I told you what it was saying, would you believe me?"

I scowled. She had a point.

Mom kept nodding before finally she declared, "Okay, I'll do it. And you'll help me?" I didn't hear what the house said back, but whatever the reply was, it made a grin break out onto Mom's face.

Ivy went over to the door and wrenched it open. She threw out an arm to stop me from leaving. We left the door ajar and looked out into the hallway, but it was different. No, it was the same. But the feeling, that vision sensation that came over my body in the room, it hadn't gone away because we were still technically inside it.

Mom and Peter walked down the hall together.

"I saw it in there," Mom said, her eyes downcast and her finger pointing at a room across the hall. "I didn't want to touch it."

Peter had his blond hair parted carefully and walked casually with his hands in his pockets. As if he weren't strolling beside a child he'd abused night after night. "The cleaning staff take care of these things, you know. I have no idea how a dead bird got inside, but it's really not something we need to deal with ourselves."

"It's not dead, that's why I need you to help it." Mom stopped in front of the door and pulled it open, waving Peter inside.

He stepped over the threshold and turned back with a frown. "I don't see a bird."

Mom pushed the door closed.

I thought of when I'd first met Ivy. When she'd explained how butcherbirds hunted. Swiftly. They needed the speed and surprise because their talons weren't strong enough for a head-to-head confrontation. That they could even take down prey bigger than they were.

Peter was wrong. There was a bird.

It just wasn't the one he was expecting.

CHAPTER FORTY-ONE

Peter's fists banged on the other side of the door, the knob twisting and turning. He was crying Mom's name. Yelling at her to open it. And then he was shouting.

Then screaming.

Mom sunk to the floor, where she clapped her hands over her ears to block out the agonized shrieks coming from inside the room. She was muttering something, but I couldn't hear. I strained until I could finally make out her whispers.

"Work, work, work, please work, please let this work." The words tumbled from her mouth, repeated over and over like a mantra.

The screaming stopped, and the door opened. Peter walked out and blinked at Mom sprawled on the floor. "There's no bird in there."

"Oh" was all she said.

He looked dazed and tired standing in the hallway. Peter shook his head and glanced at the watch on his wrist. "I think I'm going to call Katie in for an extra lesson. She's been struggling with our latest piece." He gave Mom a longer look. "Don't bother me again about this stuff. Let the cleaning staff deal with it."

"Okay," Mom mumbled.

Peter walked away, and she shuffled closer to the wall. Mom pressed against it and shoved her fist against her mouth to quiet her sobs. Through her lips she muttered, "Thank you."

I stumbled back against the bedroom wall.

Mom hadn't put Peter in the room to torture him just for the fun of it. Mom thanked the house. *Thanked* it. And when Peter had come out, he'd left her alone. He was going to Katie now. To do to her what he'd maybe planned to do to Mom. Ivy said that the house took things, payment to stop the torture. Maybe it took away Peter's will to abuse Mom for the day.

The house got a meal out of a monster. And Mom got to avoid another day of torture.

She said the house saved her. Now I knew that it did more than offer some company in a dark time.

"You haven't seen it all yet." Ivy pulled me back toward the hallway.

Time sped by. I didn't know how many days had passed, but I watched Mom come in through the front door with a boy who looked about her age. I watched from the balcony as she led him into the piano room. It didn't take long for his screams to reach us.

Time passed faster. Mom aged. She brought five more people. They would go into a room, and they would scream and scream.

She acted like Ivy was the one making the sacrifices, but it was her all along. She was feeding it then and she was still feeding it now. She said the house hadn't eaten people when she was here, but that was another lie.

Dad appeared, and I knew that he must be sixteen years old. He and Mom came into the room. Headed for the bed. "Can we skip this part?" I asked Ivy. I didn't want to see my own conception.

"How do you know what happens?" she asked, eyes narrowed.

"Skip it!"

Time ran faster, and when I turned back, Mom was crying and Dad was trying to say something to her as he dressed, words soft and comforting even as they were confused. She ran out of the room, and the door closed. Ran away from an experience she'd thought would erase everything that happened in this room but hadn't.

The bedroom got dark.

I couldn't see what Dad was seeing, but I heard his screams. Heard him calling out for Mom. Watched tears run down his face. Stood beside him as his fists pounded on the door until his knuckles split and blood spilled between his fingers.

She'd sacrificed him, too. Why would she even do that? Strangers were one thing, but she was supposed to be in love with Dad. But then . . . I think back to what she was muttering in the greenhouse. That the house told her it could make him forget. That was why. Because people forgot what happened in the rooms after they were tortured. That was why she let him be a sacrifice.

But when the door opened and Dad stumbled out, he was shaking and gagging. He hadn't forgotten anything. Not even the part he was supposed to forget.

Ivy said only special people got to remember. But that wasn't it. Only people the house *wanted to* got to remember. Mom needed the mansion, but it needed her, too. It needed her to bring it victims. To have a baby like me who could protect it from corporeals. And what it didn't need was a boy who could have loved her and maybe given her a reason to give up on revenge and leave this house behind forever. It made him remember, and so he was afraid. He was afraid of Mom . . . and of me.

I wondered what the house made him give up. What part he left behind. Was it the bit that could have made him a good enough dad for a girl who saw the dead? The one thing that could have stopped me from coming here with Mom? Or was he always going to be the way he was?

There was no way for me to know.

But what I did know was that Mom was its gardener. And sure, maybe Ivy did kill that girl, but she wasn't behind everything. I got the impression that Ivy thought the house just decided to eat people. It didn't tell her everything that it told Mom.

But then Mom left, and the house was starved again. No more gardener. The threat dissolved, and the knowing that King's mom had went away.

Until Peter died.

Until Mom came back.

I stumbled out of the bedroom and cut off the vision, desperate for it to be over.

"You see?" Ivy said. "Why did it help her? Why did it let her leave? It needed her, so why? Why her? Why not—" Her voice cut off abruptly.

Why not me?

I didn't have the headspace to care about whatever it was that Ivy was going through. I dragged my feet down through the hall and slunk down the grand staircase. Mom, the version I knew in this time, walked out of the piano room with fresh tear tracks on her face.

"You've been feeding it," I said to her, stopping on the steps. "The sacrifices, it was you. It was *always* you."

Mom had taken care of this house with the same tender loving care that I gave to my plants. That's what she said it was, after all. A plant, existing and doing anything to survive, soaking up souls like sunlight.

Her mouth fell open. "Daisy? What are you—"

"You've been feeding the house!" I cried, my voice weak and cracking. "This wasn't about a fresh start. This wasn't about our future."

New tears sprang to Mom's eyes. "I didn't want you to misunderstand. It was bad for a moment, but then they would forget and be okay."

"But Dad didn't forget."

She winced. "Things went wrong with him. I know that was my mistake."

"They're not okay after. They're forced to give something up. They lose something to the house."

"It's things they don't even need. Just stuff the house wants. They always seemed fine after. They never seem to be missing anything."

"You don't know that!" I shook my head.

She crossed her arms over her chest. "It was starving. And it helped me. I wanted to help it too. I owed it that much."

Starving? What was she talking about? The house had a constant food source that it was ignoring—the proof was all around us. Not that Mom could see. "What are you talking about? The house can eat the dead anytime it wants."

"It doesn't get anything from doing that. That's why it wanted someone like you in the first place, to get rid of them the way that it can't. There's no way to help that they're drawn to the mansion. But it can't be satiated by them the way it can with living people."

I held my jaw still to keep it from dropping. She was delusional. Everything that Mom learned about the supernatural, she was told by the house. Clearly, it had spun a lie around its true nature to trick her into thinking it was starving and suffering without a food source. And that it desperately needed someone like me, someone she had to supply. I could deal with the corporeals, sure, but if the house made the dead pass on the instant they appeared, they wouldn't have a

chance to get that bad in the first place. It only needed me because it didn't want to do what it was supposed to.

Mom's expression showed complete belief in everything she was saying. She trusted the house. Even now. I didn't know where to begin with unpacking the lies. Instead, I said, "I understand why you did this back then, but why keep making sacrifices now? What are you even getting out of it? You can't possibly still feel like you owe it to the house."

She swallowed. "I'm helping it and in exchange . . . it helps me. Like I said, it doesn't get anything from doing to the dead what it does to the living. But it's doing it for me as long as I feed it. And when I'm done . . . I'll just stop. It's fine."

Peter. Of course. That fucked-up shape. If the house ate the dead, they would pass on. Instead, it was torturing Peter without actually consuming him in exchange for a better meal.

And Mom thought she could stop whenever. Like she did when she was younger. But if Ivy was to be believed, the house was too powerful now. Our first few weeks of guests had already surpassed the amount of people Mom had brought it when she was younger. The house didn't need her to sacrifice to it now. It could eat whoever and whenever it wanted. And with its voice, it didn't need her to bring it people either. "You don't realize what you've done," I whispered. "It doesn't need you anymore."

"It has *always* needed me."

The taste of vomit slipped into the back of my throat. "How was this worth it?!" I stumbled down the steps toward her. "How the fuck was this worth it?!"

"I couldn't just let him get away with it!" Her body shook with the force of her voice. "Hate me if you want." Her voice cracked. "I always knew you would one day."

Maybe this was the point where I lied and told Mom that I didn't

hate her after all. But I couldn't get the words out of my mouth. Not now.

"I couldn't let him get off easy," Mom cried. "I had to come back here. When I left, I tried. I really tried to move on, but there he was. Alive. Trying to friend me on fucking Facebook. And then I knew that I needed to do it. When the house first offered, it felt like too much. I left instead. But I never forgot that offer: feed it, and in exchange, when he was dead, I could make him pay . . . for as long as I wanted."

That was why Mom wanted this house. That was why she needed my help. Everything leading up to this revenge plot where she put people's lives on the line so she could torture her abuser. It was like when she brought me to that warehouse to force Johnny to pass on. She thought this would fix everything. But when I had done it, it had only made me more afraid.

"It was you, wasn't it?" I asked. "You had the house kill him. That's why this all started again."

She scowled. "I didn't."

"Don't lie!"

"I'm not!" she snapped. "I . . . I was going to. But someone beat me to it."

The longing in her voice was the only reason I knew she was telling the truth. She *wished* she had done it.

I couldn't help it.

I laughed.

Huge, great loud guffaws.

My entire life was a joke. I had no dreams. No ambitions. I lived my entire life for what I thought would be me and Mom making something new so that I could finally be free of her. That I was helping her so she wouldn't need me anymore. We would work this out. She wouldn't need a fixer. I could finally decide what it was that I wanted. I could be free so long as I helped secure her financial future, and mine, too, in the process.

I had run into this house still trying to help fix her. Meanwhile, all she ever wanted to do was make Peter pay for her ruined childhood.

And she had destroyed mine in the process.

"I can still fix it, Daisy," she said. "We just need to get rid of that Ivy girl. You can do it. I know you can."

"No, I can't."

It was over. The house was too powerful. It didn't need Mom, and she still didn't get it.

I looked at Mom, her face earnest. She really believed that Ivy was the problem. That she could still control the house. It was her savior, and she was devoted to it. She couldn't see the truth of the situation. In the greenhouse, it had felt like she was realizing that things had gone wrong, but now she had doubled down on her original plan.

"I hope Peter was worth it," I muttered.

"Peter?" Ivy's voice was light and small. I almost missed it.

Slowly I turned around to see her behind me, staring at Mom.

Staring at the woman who I had just in my anger revealed was the little girl. Because of course that's how Ivy would know Peter. The context of our conversation would be enough. The dead confused time, but from Ivy's face, she had finally figured it out.

I couldn't read her expression to tell if she was happy, or sad, or furious with the reveal.

"Now I guess you know who the girl is," I said. "Happy?"

She grinned. "She came back. She didn't stay gone. She still belongs to it. And I know she's not the favorite anymore."

Ivy was right. The house got what it wanted from Mom.

But I would never get what I wanted from her.

I was bad at it. Living. I had always been.

And I was so fucking tired.

This time, for once, I was going to rest.

I said to Mom, "Leave while you still can."

Her eyes narrowed even as tears continued to streak down her face.

When I spoke to Ivy next, my voice was empty, weary, done. "You can have it. I don't want it anymore. It's yours."

In the back of my mind, Mom was trying to get my attention. She couldn't see Ivy, after all. But I wasn't interested in giving her the time of day anymore.

"Can have what?" Ivy replied, taking off her sunglasses to squint at me.

I gave a weak shrug. "Everything."

And then I did something I wasn't supposed to do. Something that even a worm in my head couldn't stop, because this time, I wanted it to happen.

I emptied my mind and let Ivy in.

CHAPTER FORTY-TWO

Being possessed by Ivy was different the second time around. She wasn't trying to hide what was happening anymore, so I didn't have gaps in my memory. I saw everything. It was as if our roles had fully reversed, and now I was the one leaning my weight against her back with my chin on her shoulder, watching her life go by.

And she was better at it.

The fat maggot that was in her head shriveled and leaked out of her ear in a thick sludge of pus. Inside, I wanted to gag. To squeeze my eyes shut and pretend it wasn't happening. Ivy simply dug the rest out with her pinkie nail and washed it down the sink with a slight twist of her mouth.

Now the rustling was back. Though the quality of it had changed to a sort of whooshing sound. I liked to close my eyes and pretend it was the lake. Though sometimes it sounded like wings, which I didn't like nearly as much.

Ivy had no idea what to do with my hair but tugged a hat on, applied a fresh face of makeup, and made it work. Sunglasses were now a regular accessory. I only had one pair, and she made do by shamelessly stealing pairs from Mom.

Mom.

She would watch Ivy go about her business without saying anything to her and otherwise stay in her room for prolonged periods of time. She didn't leave like I'd told her to. The Airbnb functioned around her as usual—the house's voice was, apparently, strong enough to work against the negative press from Tower. Though I had a feeling that didn't mean Hayden had given up. Otherwise, the cleaners kept coming, and Mom had even hired someone to do the grocery orders.

Mom herself was vacant. Spacey and absent. She'd forgotten that her computer was open with its banking info. Finally, I saw the money that she'd hidden away all these years, pretending we had nothing.

She'd already had the financial stability I was supposed to be helping her with. And more than enough to pay my way too. Pretending she had nothing was just an excuse to cover what she really wanted. And a reason for me to stay with her and cooperate. To try to help her with this house and her plans.

Ivy didn't care either way.

I let myself fade into that feeling.

She had a singular focus on herself and her goals. I was listless, undirected, and when I finally had a trajectory, it followed whatever path Mom had laid out. Ivy was definitely not that.

At school, whispers followed her footsteps. King still drove her, but he said nothing during the trips. This did bother her in a way it hadn't bothered me. She didn't understand the comfort of silence. King didn't notice how much she hated it because on the outside, Ivy was unbothered as always.

The only time she did talk was to ask him to drive her farther. Much farther than she had ever gone. They got as far as the Best Buy, not even out of town, before she was screaming to turn back. There were flashes. Like when I'd tried to make Ivy pass on. I could feel her weakening under my skin. Like doing papier-mâché on a balloon and popping it once the piece was dry. My body stayed firm like the sheets of glue and paper, but within, Ivy was shriveling in on herself. It became clear that no matter how powerful she was, and even if she could get farther away than ever before in a living vessel, she couldn't go far enough.

She didn't try again.

The days of schoolwork missed were caught up on in a total of two nights of working nonstop. Ivy saved her grades and was regularly complimented by the teachers, even though some of them now seemed troubled by the act of praising a girl who had, allegedly, attacked another girl.

The first day back to school, at lunch, she'd turned to Mackenzie and her group, but the girls had quickly looked away. That was the thing that bothered Ivy the most. She obsessed over that moment on a regular basis. That instant kept swirling through my thoughts because they were so prevalent in hers. That single slight.

Most of the time, she kept what went on in her head locked down. But sometimes, those things leaked out.

Ivy sat alone during her lunches and studied. I slept. I wanted to sleep a lot. It felt like curling up against Ivy's back. Like she was giving me a piggyback ride. And I would just lie there asleep with my chin tucked against her neck and feel the gentle bumping of her moving.

Mom never gave me piggyback rides.

Ivy poked me out of those thoughts. She didn't like what she called "your sad shit." Because in the same way I could hear her loud thoughts, she could hear mine. I tried to keep those ones quiet and to myself. Just like the knowledge of how much control she really had over the house. I didn't want things to get worse than they already were. I shouldn't care so much. But I did.

On the third day, on the drive home from school, King gave Ivy a searching look, his fingers tightening on the wheel. "You doing okay?"

"Fine," Ivy ground out.

There were dark bags under her eyes when she woke up. I didn't have full-coverage foundation, only light, and minimal concealer. It made it difficult to hide them. The sunglasses helped. But Ivy was feeling the fatigue. I was too. I slept more and more. Which was fine with me. What I did didn't matter.

King's fingers gripped the steering wheel hard. "She's alive, you know that, right? You can't work her into the ground. You need to sleep and eat. What is even the point of this?"

I hadn't realized that she wasn't sleeping. But he was right. At night, she went into the house and studied there. I could still hear guests screaming in their rooms. So I would sleep and try to forget about them. During the day, Ivy didn't make any food. I didn't think she knew how.

"Why do you care?" she snarled.

"She's my friend."

Her body went warm at that. Or maybe it was just me, sleepy and comfortable. Because there was something about it that made Ivy feel the opposite. "I'll eat something and sleep," she said. "I just forgot."

King shook his head. "What's your plan? Really? What are you studying for? You can't even get as far as Northern in her body."

"I'm doing more to help than you ever could," she snapped.

King laughed. It was sharp and mocking. "Helping who? Her? Or you?"

Ivy's body shook from the effort of containing her rage. She hated King in that moment. Her thoughts spiraled through ways she could hurt him, but she couldn't do any of those anymore because her actions mattered. They would affect her in ways they wouldn't have before, now that she had a body.

She sat silent in the car, but she stayed mad in her mind. She kept thinking about that little girl who talked to the house, leaving to go to the city at the end of every summer and then coming back the next year. Leaving and coming back. Leaving and coming back.

Something Ivy could never do. Not the way she wanted.

It was ridiculous and sad. She was dead. Mom had been alive. It was obvious why she could leave when Ivy couldn't. But Ivy's thoughts circled on the word "unfair" repeated over and over, past the point when she was sick of it.

She said that she was over it now that she knew Mom wasn't the favorite anymore. That was a lie.

But I kept my thoughts quiet and to myself.

Ivy was working toward a future she couldn't have. As futile and useless as everyone else.

But everything I had worked toward wasn't even for me. I was a tool to help Mom. Like she was to help the house.

We would be swallowed up by it eventually. Lost to the rustling. Drowning in a chorus of flapping shrike wings.

As King continued to drive us home, I decided to go to sleep. Before I closed my eyes, I saw him staring out of the corner of his, and the way he looked made my throat dry and sore.

When Ivy walked through the door of the bunkie, there were cooking smells in the air. They roused me awake. Sizzling onions and spices wafted through the room, and Mom was standing with her back to her, pushing them around in a pan.

The last time Mom cooked for me, I was thirteen. She made this big show of putting a roast with potatoes and carrots into the oven. But she had undercooked them. Got impatient and pulled the whole thing out after an hour. Some of the meat was raw, and the vegetables were hard. I ate it anyway. But after a couple of bites she threw down her cutlery and said she was done with it.

I thought she'd meant the meal. But she'd meant the cooking. Or maybe it wasn't even that. Maybe it was that she was done with the whole act of it. The process of trying to be my mom. I couldn't tell.

I got Mom in bits and pieces of herself. It was like trying to identify an entire plant by scraps of its leaves that were delivered to you piece by piece on an irregular schedule. There was no way for me to make sense of it. And the odd time I thought I had a legitimate guess, it turned out to be wrong.

Ivy gave the pan of food a quick glance before going into her bedroom to study.

Mom came over a few minutes later and knocked on the door before opening it. "Come eat."

"I'm studying."

"Come eat before you kill my daughter with your negligence. How long do you honestly think you can use her body without eating or sleeping before she collapses? Get out here and eat."

Ivy got up and went.

The meal was a simple chicken stir-fry poured over rice. I tasted it through Ivy. It was good. Mom must have used an actual recipe. The sauce was sweet and tangy. It had a flavor like it was from a bottle, and I found myself turning Ivy's eyes to search it out until I saw it on the kitchen counter.

Ivy snapped her eyes back to the food, which she shoveled into her mouth like it was a chore. Which I guess it was for her.

"You're not the one causing it, are you? The feeding in the house."

Unlike before, Mom's voice wasn't strong when she said it. She was staring at her plate.

"The house eats. Doesn't need me to do that." She gave Mom a significant look. "It eats *everything*, by the way. The dead, too. It just doesn't like them as much." Ivy frowned and poked a piece of broccoli as if to demonstrate the distaste.

Mom seemed to be fighting something, opening and closing her mouth before finally settling on saying, "But it's supposed to need someone to help it eat the living. It's not supposed to be able to do it alone."

Ivy shrugged. "Not anymore." Mom made a sound in the back of her throat, and Ivy rolled her eyes. "Look, lady, think what you want about me, but torturing people 24-7 isn't my idea of fun. Besides, did you notice that your precious mansion still gorges all day while we're at school? How can I be making it do that when I'm gone?"

There was a long, drawn-out moment of silence.

Mom tightened her fingers around her cutlery. "She was right. It lied to me. Of course it did." She dropped her fork and pressed her fist to her mouth. "I told it to stop. It won't even talk to me anymore."

I knew Ivy was smug about that. About being the new favorite. But Mom said the house would help me get rid of Ivy. It didn't want her around either.

Ivy didn't like that thought at all.

I let it wither and pulled back.

Mom shoved her plate aside and put her head down. Her shoulders shook, and her sobs were the only other sound besides Ivy eating.

"Don't worry," Ivy said, shoving another forkful of food into her mouth. "Daisy likes it this way, you know. You ruined her. She's happier to just ride along. She says that I'm better at being her than she is."

Mom raised her head and curled her lip. "Get my daughter's name out of your mouth."

"Why do you want to be a good mom now? Or do you?" Ivy's lips pulled into a wicked grin. "This is what you wanted, isn't it? The house is plenty powerful now, definitely enough to keep torturing him forever. I agree with it. He's a stain on this world and the next."

Mom sat perfectly still in her chair. "Did you kill him?"

I found myself wondering too, then remembered that it didn't matter what I was curious about. Not anymore.

"Does it matter?" Ivy popped a piece of chicken into her mouth. "Sometimes, I leave him alone in a room for days and days, as long as I can keep it going. After a few, even the house gets tired. That's why he's all twisted like that."

Mom's swallow was audible.

"Isn't it nice? You worked so hard for this, and now you have it." She shrugged. "And even better, Daisy was needy. She wanted things from you that you didn't want to do." Ivy finished what was on her plate. "I never had a mom, and I don't want one either. You never wanted to be one, I bet. Now you're free."

Ivy, I decided, was infinitely better at being me than I ever was. Because never in my life had I said the truths about Mom that floated in my head as well and directly as she had.

She continued, "And if you're very nice to me, maybe I'll make it so you can die inside. Then you'll still have eternity to watch him suffer. Just take out your new worm when you're ready. I know you can." She stood up from the table and smiled. "Although I think that when the house is strong enough, not even that maggot will protect you." She left the table and went into her room, and Mom didn't say anything more.

I thought about the two of them. Mom and Ivy. Both chosen

by the house in some way. It made the decision to speak to them, and they listened. They were hungry in a way that I wasn't. They wanted things desperately. There were dark parts inside of them that it fed. Maybe that was what it needed. People who needed it back.

The weekend passed quickly. I slept. Ivy studied.

On Monday morning, lunch was made and ready for her. There was a sticky note on top of it. She rolled it into a ball and threw it in the garbage, but I had read it.

> *Have a good day at school. I miss you, and love you,*
> *and I'm sorry. Please come back.*
> *—Mom*

I made Ivy take it out of the garbage and put it in her pocket. She didn't like it, but she did it.

I couldn't remember the last time Mom had said she'd loved me in words, paper or otherwise. Though when she'd pressed a kiss to my forehead, I'd thought that was pretty close.

King was waiting in the truck when we came. The drive was quiet as usual. Nothing much for me to do but look out the window at snow-dusted trees or watch Ivy somehow manage to study on her phone.

Until he decided to speak. "I'm going to keep trying to help you after all."

"What?" Ivy barked.

King looked over from the driver's seat. "I've never liked what I saw in store for your future. And to be honest, you're the most frustrating person I've ever advised. But we said we would do this together. We're friends. I mean that. I'm going to keep helping."

When we got to school, instead of leaving me right away, King lingered. "You should come sit with us at lunch." He let out a breath. "I always wanted to ask you that, but I knew you would say no, so I didn't see the point. I guess you could have technically changed the outcome, but I was afraid that you wouldn't. I know so many things, and yet I'm scared all the time. I only do safe stuff. It was safer to not talk to you, and not know you, but I got wrapped up anyway." He turned his head up to the sky and laughed. "I even went into a haunted house with you, so you have to come back or I'll look really tragic."

I laughed, and it came out of Ivy's mouth.

King smiled, the open one, not any of the templates for other people, and Ivy clapped her hands over her lips. She walked away from him without saying a word. She didn't go sit with King and his friends at lunch, but she watched, and I knew she wanted to. Because her whole self was screaming that she wanted to go, to be with people and have friends for once, but she knew he hadn't meant her. He hadn't meant, *Ivy, come sit with us.*

He'd meant me.

And it would have hurt more than anything to go over knowing that.

The next few days were similar. Mom would pack lunch and leave a note in the morning, and I would force Ivy to save it.

Have a good day at school. I used to love my classes because then I could get away from him, but I didn't know how to be normal, and I liked my friends in Kenogamissi better. I know you hate it, and I've always pushed it on you anyway. I'm sorry, and I love you, and I miss you. Please come back.

—Mom

*I stopped talking to Helga and Katie and Jordan when
I left because I knew I was pretending to be something
I wasn't. They didn't know how horrible I could be.
Jordan thought he did, but I was worse than even that.
I didn't want them to hate me. I didn't want you to hate
me either, but I messed it up anyway. I'm sorry, and I
love you, and I miss you. Please come back.*
    —Mom

*I hate cooking. I'm bad at it. It's embarrassing. My
mom never made lunches for me either. Not because
she didn't have the time, but because she didn't want
to. I forgot how much that hurt. To feel like she didn't
care. I've always cared. I'm sorry, and I love you, and
I miss you. Please come back.*
    —Mom

When Ivy got into the car with King every weekday, he would talk. Almost nonstop about anything. I learned more about him in those few days than I had in the entire time I had known him.

"I don't think I actually like any sort of music—I just like to have something playing. It distracts me from thinking about the things that I know." He tilted his head to the window. "I always wanted to ask how often you see the dead. I've only ever seen Ivy because she shows herself to me. I hate talking psychic shit, but I wanted to know more about what you did. But I didn't know if you hated it the way I hate knowing. And that's why I said nothing."

I didn't hate the dead themselves, I wanted to say. I hated having to interact with them. Being hurt by them and having to hurt them back. I wished that we could leave each other alone.

"I do actually like being nice to people," King said on another day.

"Which maybe is kind of boring, but I do. I feel better that way. You would probably make fun of me for that. I wish you would, honestly."

I would have. He was such a do-gooder.

On a different day, King tapped on the steering wheel. "I know what I know, but I still like to ask people. I like to hear people talk about themselves the way they know it. I wish that I had asked you more questions. You could tell me about your last school, or your friends, or whatever you want. I want to hear it."

Noah didn't like to listen—he liked to talk. I was the listener. I listened to everyone. Right then, I wanted to talk. I wanted to hear whatever questions King came up with. I wanted to participate the way I did with Megan.

On Friday morning, Ivy grabbed lunch, and the note wasn't there. She tried to walk out the door, but I kept her rooted to the spot. Staring. Waiting.

"Have a good day at school," Mom said.

I spun Ivy around and faced her.

Mom's eyes were shining when she looked at me. "I was afraid to touch people because I worried that something would go wrong. Maybe that I would be reminded of what happened. Or that I wouldn't know how to do it right. I didn't let them put you on my chest when you were first born, and I regretted it. I just kept going on not touching you when I could help it. Or I did that head-grabbing thing. I couldn't get it right. And one day, I got up the courage to press that kiss to your forehead, and then I remembered that Dione used to do that to me, and I cried. But you liked it so much. You were so happy about it. So I kept on with it." She choked back a sob. "But then I hated myself because I realized that I had ruined you already, and I didn't know how to fix it, and I was afraid to try, and all I did was make it worse." She let out a gasping cry. "I don't care if he never gets tortured in that house again. I don't care if we don't live here. I don't care about any of that. I thought I did. But I don't. Not as much as I care about you. So *please*, Daisy, *come back*."

And then she did something that I'd never seen her do. She spread out her arms to me.

I ran forward into them. I pressed my face into my mom's chest and squeezed her, and she squeezed me back.

And I left Ivy behind.

CHAPTER FORTY-THREE

BRITTNEY

'm right back where we started in Timmins. Dragging my luggage through the tiny Victor M. Power Airport and trying to ignore the families and groups around me. It's a Thursday evening, but there's still a fair amount of people sitting on the black faux-leather waiting room chairs, scrolling through their phones, listening to music, or talking.

I'd booked my own flight. I don't want to deal with Kevin and whatever panic he would cause over me leaving. The company likely wouldn't pay for the return trip anyway. Not with this short notice.

Jayden shouldn't know that I'm here either.

After my call with Mom, I went back into the room, packed my stuff, and said that I would be staying somewhere else for the night. Which I guess he understood, considering our fight. Jayden is like that. Understanding.

I thought so, at least.

He still went behind my back with all of his shit. That's the thing about companies like Torte and Tower—everyone is in it for themselves. No matter how much they try to shove company values like teamwork and togetherness down your throat. Group work is the sort of thing people do when it's convenient. But in this industry, everyone knows that you have to step on a few people to get to the top.

I've been stepped on my entire life.

Maybe that's just the way things are supposed to be for me.

I would rather go back to Mom. At least I know what I'm getting instead of deluding myself into thinking that I have a real friend or a chance at a dream. I wanted to expose the truth, and this is it. This is my reality.

I booked the first flight available, but it wouldn't be taking off until ten p.m. I look at my phone. Still only seven.

Following the lit-up RESTAURANT/BAR sign, I head into the café that's off to the side of the waiting area. The woman at the counter looks like she's in the process of closing up. The entire kitchen area behind her is sparse, and she gives me the sort of look that says, *I really hope you're not coming here.*

Sorry, lady.

The sign says they're open until seven thirty, and I haven't eaten dinner.

I roll up to the front and put in an order for a BLT and a cup of coffee. Not that I need it. I'm too wired to sleep.

"Britt." I turn in the direction of Jayden's voice, and there he is, standing in the restaurant holding his bags and all our equipment.

"What?" I snap, the rage and hurt from earlier bubbling up. "Did Kevin shut the whole thing down because I'm gone? That's not like him. The stakeholders will be pissed."

"I had a messed-up feeling that you would be here. What are you doing?"

My shoulders hunch. I can't believe he figured it out. "I'm going home," I say finally.

"Why? Because you think I went behind your back on this Grace thing? Do you know how ridiculous that is?"

"Then what were your secret phone calls about?"

Jayden sets his bags down on the floor, and the woman behind the counter keeps sneaking looks at us like this is the most entertainment she's had all week. "Can we sit down?" He sits in one of the booths, and reluctantly I slide into the spot across from him.

He takes a deep breath. "I was calling around because, from the start, I wanted to do a documentary project about Grace."

I open my mouth to call him out, and he raises a hand.

"Can I finish?"

"Fine."

"Even before we decided on 'Houses That Kill,' I was curious about her. It's a big reason why I wanted to do this story, on top of being interested in the whole case and Daisy." He shrugs. "I wish I could have more noble reasons like you. Like wanting to avenge a dead girl. And I care about it, and you know I love spooky shit. But I've always been more compelled by Grace's story. I thought that if everything in this season went well, I could persuade her to do an independent project with me to submit for senior year. It would be my first step into serious filmmaking."

I'm not as altruistic as he thinks. Of course I want to expose what really happened. But there's still that part of me that wants to do it to bring down the Miracle Mansion. To debunk everything that my mom has built. And that's for me, not a forgotten Black girl.

I play with my fingers—cracking them to give me something to do. I'm not sure how this is supposed to be explaining things. If anything, it seems to support why he would go behind my back with Kevin. But I don't interrupt.

Jayden continues, "But we couldn't even manage to land Grace for an interview, so I gave up and moved on. Except when the contact pulled through and we booked her, it changed everything. I could actually meet her, and having done a previous project together would build more credibility for a proposal. I started calling around to some upperclassmen and TAs for tips on putting together pitches and to get eyes on what I had already, along with asking who to contact for meetings, that sort of thing. I know that you don't like Grace . . . so I didn't want to tell you about it. Or have you think that I was biased. I'm still committed to giving a true account of her. You know that's my thing. I'm here to show reality, not fiction."

Suddenly my body feels too cramped in the booth.

He's right. If I'd known that he wanted to do a doc with Grace, I would have brought it up as a bias issue on every shoot.

It's messed-up. I know Jayden. He wants to show the truth in the world, no matter what. His style of filmmaking is hyperfocused on accuracy.

Jayden says, "I was as shocked as you were when Kevin brought up that contract with Grace. I didn't know anything like that was happening. I definitely wouldn't have said anything to him about a side project. He would just want me to produce it for Torte instead."

"But what about the stuff with my mom?" I push. "Why did you get involved with her?"

Jayden's eyes slide away from me.

Guilty.

Of course he is.

Even if he didn't do that shit with Kevin to protect Grace, he still went behind my back with my mom.

"I'm sorry I didn't tell you about that," Jayden says, looking back at me. "I just . . . Kevin brought up interviewing her. He had already called her, even, without telling you. And I know what her book says, and what the media says, but whenever you speak about her . . . you seem . . . scared, to be honest. So I told him that we weren't going to talk to her. To not even bring it up with you because you already seemed like you were having a hard time. I even made a light HR threat to be sure he wouldn't try to go behind our backs on it like he had already." Jayden lets out a deep breath and runs his hands through his hair. "When did he even tell you about that? Not on the phone call I heard."

My jaw drops, and the woman at the counter calls me for my order.

She calls me one more time, but I ignore her, and she gives up and leaves the sandwich and mug of coffee on the countertop.

Jayden looks over at it. "I can grab it." He leaves the booth, and I stay exactly where I am.

Mom said that Jayden was the one who called to try to book her.

But Jayden is saying that Kevin tried, and Jayden turned her down and then kept it from me so I wouldn't get upset.

They're statements in complete opposition of each other.

And I fell for it.

Why would a notorious liar and manipulator like my mom ever tell the truth? Especially when using a lie that could get me to come home to her. To be under her influence again. I wonder if that's why she started leaving all those voicemails in the first place, because she knew that Jayden had protected me.

When he gets back to the table, I'm crying.

The woman at the counter mutters something about men being trash and goes back to her business.

"Britt . . . ," he says, and rests his hand on my shoulder.

He knew that at the first major sign of distress, I would try to get a flight out of here. Because he knows me. Because we're best friends.

"I'm going to ask you one more time," he says. "What's going on with you?"

"I'm sorry," I choke out, wiping my eyes. "I'm so fucked-up. She's just messing with my head. Doing this whole thing with that house, *her* house, the house she says made her this reformed person, but she never once became the sort of mom she pretends to be. She just got better at hiding it."

And she found ways to use me. To make it so that I would always need her. That without her money, I wouldn't be able to make it on my own, much less get into this industry.

Jayden gnaws on his lip and pulls his hand back. "Your mom . . . Is she like Grace?"

I laugh. "She's much worse."

To his credit, he takes it in stride. I guess because he's always suspected. "Look, I know that Kevin has this whole thing signed with Grace, but we can still find out the truth. Even if we don't put it in the final cut, we can ask the questions. Dione doesn't know that her sister has this set up with us, and Grace probably doesn't want her to know. She can't dodge the questions or Dione will get cagey too. And I get the feeling that Grace wants to see her sister spill as much as we do."

"You're right . . ."

And he is. I'd never even thought of it because I was so preoccupied with my own mom. She's been torturing me this entire time. Punishing me, *us*, for turning her down on this project. Because that's all she's ever wanted. The fame and the attention. To be seen as something better than she is.

Jayden points to his luggage. "If you really want to go and give up on *Haunted*, on all of this, I'll go with you. We're a team. This is our project. I won't do it without you. But if you want to go to the mansion, I'll follow. It's your choice."

"You can't get a ticket this late."

He pulls a piece of paper out of his pocket and slides it across the table. It's from Timmins to Toronto for the same flight I'm on. "Can't I?"

I blink at him. "You're serious."

"It's your choice. I'm the one who pushed this project when I knew you had troubles with your mom, even if I didn't know the specifics, because I wanted to investigate Grace. Now you decide what we do next."

I pick up my foil-wrapped BLT and my mug of coffee, then turn to the woman at the counter. "Can I get a to-go cup, please?"

I won't let Mom pull and push me around like a pawn. Before, I used to think that if this season went well, I could escape her. Now it *has* to go well, because I'm not going back.

Both Jayden's and my phone vibrate at the same time. We immediately raise our eyebrows at each other.

It's from our joint email account. The personal one separate from our Torte accounts.

And it's from the contact.

I look forward to meeting you after your interview.

The next day, we make our way to the mansion. We aren't exactly ordinary guests, but Grace lays out the experience like we are. Our Airbnb information came through the app, which let us know the address and provided a link to the mansion website for our check-in information. It was . . . comprehensive, to say the least. It had an "About" page that explained the history of the home's construction and the Belanger family, as well as openly stating the series of "supernatural" events that took place there. And of course, there was a huge portion dedicated to the "Miracle Mansion" label with a convenient affiliate link to my mom's book.

Grace also created a special login once you booked that let you go onto the website for detailed check-in information like scheduling airport pickups and drop-offs, whether you wanted to get to the property via boat (summer, spring, and fall only, scenic lake views) or Jeep (available year-round for a fun bushwhacking experience), and even a grocery-order system.

Jayden called the whole process "the most bougie shit" he had ever seen, and I agreed. She's definitely putting her web design experience to work.

Now we wait at the boat launch with our equipment. Grace still does the pickups and drop-off to the property personally, though she now has driving staff for the airport transfer that we'll be taking after our visit.

"Only two more days left in Timmins." Jayden hums as we watch the boats come in. It's still cottage season, so the launch is busy with families chatting at their campsites and swimming in the water.

I curl my hand tighter around the camera I carry. "Yup."

Not much time left to put together what happened and get answers that no one else had. To stop another Black girl from being forgotten. After everything last night, I'm more committed than ever.

"You made a call late after we got back to the hotel," Jayden says. "Was it to Kevin?"

My body stiffens, and I force it to relax. "No, just a bills thing."

"You're a bad liar."

"She didn't even pick up."

I hate myself. Not even a little bit. A lot. I fell into yet another trap. She was the one who called me first, I assumed to ask when I was getting in. I called her back twice to say I wasn't coming, and she hadn't answered either time. Probably planning to let me crawl back home on my own.

I'm the one who got caught in her game. I let this Grace-and-

Daisy bullshit get into my head and now here I was, under her thumb again after I had just gotten out.

"Don't let her get to you," Jayden says, his voice low as Grace pulls the boat in.

"Yeah," I mutter, keeping my eyes on our host. I can't let her get to me either.

Grace looks about the same as she does on media outlets and her socials. In her forties, but looking much younger. Her hair done up in passion twists that fall to her midback with the odd bit of gold jewelry woven into the strands. High-waisted jean shorts paired with a plain white T-shirt with THE MANSION written on it, along with an illustrated image of the house. It's cheesy to us, but I bet most people eat it up.

It's unnerving to see her in person after all this time spent researching her. All these theories and opinions developed about a woman I had never seen in real life until now. It's what I imagine going to Disneyland is like. I'm looking at her, knowing that underneath the outside layer, she's just a regular person. But I've built up so much around the costume. Around the image. Created my own version of her. And now the mascot head is off and I'm staring at a woman; I'm too confused about what's happening to respond properly.

So we walk over to the boat, where Grace greets us with a smile. "There you are!" She holds out her hands and shakes both of ours in turn. And I do it, mechanically and from somewhere further than my present mind.

"Jayden and Brittney, nice to meet you." Her eyes are warm behind the round wire-framed glasses she wears.

"Likewise," I say as we begin to load our equipment into the boat.

Grace ignores the elephant in the room as she shifts the boat into gear. She confirms our booking details, which suite we'll be staying in, our grocery order—which has already been dropped off at the house—and explains what activities are available on the property and in town.

"Summer is a great time because we have kayaks and canoes. I recently got in some Sea-Doos. You have to sign a release and do a quick course with me to use them, but it's pretty straightforward." Grace steers with comfortable ease even as she shouts info at us over her shoulder.

I nod woodenly, and she turns back.

Jayden squeezes my shoulder for a second and says, "You got this." Loud enough for me to hear, but low enough to be inaudible for Grace over the sound of the boat. I meet his eyes, and he grins. "It's just Grace."

I laugh without meaning to and smother it before our host hears. Right.

It's just Grace. Whether it's the version in my head. Or Jayden's version. Or Daisy's. Or Grace's herself. None of that changes what I've come here to do. What *we've* come here to do.

"Are the Okekes in today?" I shout to her, ignoring the cottaging activity suggestions. Getting back to business.

Grace doesn't miss a beat. "King won't talk to anyone."

"That's what you used to say." I lick my lips. "And I know he won't. I was wondering about his family."

She laughs. It's joyous and big. She even throws her head back a bit. It's both delightfully charming and overwhelmingly fake. "They're out of town. Once people started chatting about you two coming in, they split. Tower did a number on people here with their aggressive interviews. I'm surprised you got anyone to talk to you."

I had given up on hoping we would get to chat with Kingsley Okeke. He was somehow the hardest person to pin down. Even the contact couldn't get him for us. Whenever we called somewhere, he had conveniently just left. The guy was always two steps ahead. The most we could get was to book it over to Mackenzie Gagnon's place this morning. She didn't have much, though. She didn't want to discuss Peter and had little to say about King. Just said that she'd shared some information about the Belangers with King and Daisy once. She hadn't been surprised that King was helping Daisy, though. "He was nice to everyone" were her exact words.

But his insistence on not talking was what made me think he had more to say than everyone thought he did. I'd hoped we could grab his family, at least. Even a palm reading or something from them would have been awesome content. It's too bad.

We dock and exit the boat.

Grace walks us up the steep set of concrete stairs to a gravel path that leads to the mansion. It looks even bigger in person. People always say that in their reviews, but it's true. I wasn't prepared for the height of the place.

Jayden is immediately on it, doing several angles of establishing shots with the camera. Grace watches him with a faint smile on her face.

She turns to me. "Did your manager give you the details of the contract?"

"Yup, it's all sorted out." I want to wipe the smug smile off her face.

"Wonderful!" She beams. "Let's do a tour of the house, shall we?"

I don't bother talking during the tour, except for the odd comment on something looking nice. I let Jayden take over and walk behind him and Grace, gathering footage while we explore the rooms. Our host has some sort of "fun" detail for every space we go into and doesn't shy away from sharing the tragedies and miracles of each, more the latter than the former. In the piano room, she boils down Liza McClaine's death to "Unfortunately, a guest did pass away here, random medical accident," before launching into a long discussion about the piano with a casual drop of its $25,000 price tag.

I think of Bert's interview with that one news station, his shining red eyes as he talked about how much his wife loved exploring the house. About their last-ditch effort to save their marriage. The photos he sent of them both posing in front of the grand chandelier in the entryway.

Grace does not, however, make any mention of the room where her daughter hit Hayden Doukas across the face with a fireplace poker or the resulting fallout from the Tower video published. A brief mention of their smear campaign afterward is the only acknowledgment she gives them. I guess there are lines even she won't cross.

My mom would have.

She wouldn't have thought twice about spinning a tragedy about me for clout. That's what her entire career is built off of.

Grace and my mom are different.

That's the truth of it, and that's what I need to hold on to. I can't keep comparing my and Daisy's relationships with our moms because they aren't the same.

It only takes a short amount of time through the tour to realize that we aren't the only guests. The rooms, according to Airbnb, are constantly booked. There are at least twenty other people staying at any one time. The house now has seven additional kitchens set up in various rooms to accommodate the volume, two on each floor—one communal and one that's private as part of a deluxe suite.

We see some of the guests in the hall who are walking around the space and taking photos, or on their way to the kitchen, or out the door. They wave and smile at Grace, who has successfully charmed them as she seems prone to doing.

The woman can bounce back from anything.

The tour ends at our room, where Grace mentions that we'll find a complimentary gift basket inside and highlights some of the local items in it.

Finally, I speak to her. "My mom stayed here once. When you first opened."

"I know," she says with a smile. "I've read her book."

"Oh? What did you think of it?"

She tilts her head to the side as if thinking. "She kind of reminds me of my mom." Grace stares into my eyes. "What do you think of it?"

I lick my lips. It's not a question anyone has ever had the gall to ask me. The standard lie is on the tip of my tongue, but suddenly I don't want to tell it. "I think she's full of shit."

And then Grace does something I don't expect.

She grins.

All teeth.

She says, "People think the miracles here are from what the house gives you. I think it's from what you leave behind. I've always wondered what your mom left in this house. But I also think that it doesn't matter that much. People only care about the end result."

I can't decide what to say back to her, so I say nothing. What did my mom leave in this house? I would probably never know. But Grace is right. It doesn't matter to me. My mom didn't get better. Her miracle was just for her.

"Too bad you don't like the book much," she says as if it's no big deal. "I hope you enjoy your stay here. Let me know if you need any-thing."

And then she's gone.

We walk into the room, and I balk at the size of it. There's a living area with a giant TV and two couches along with a bathroom, and the new addition of a small kitchen. The bedroom is in its own separate space and features a comfy king-size bed. The deluxe suite. I don't want to know how much money Torte spent to kick out whoever had booked it so that we could stay instead.

I flop onto the bed. Meanwhile, Jayden carries over the gift basket that was lovingly placed on a side table. I make room for him, and he sets it between us. "I'm proud of you."

"Yeah, yeah, whatever," I mutter, though I'm a little proud too. I've never told anyone what I really think of Mom and her book. And here I chose Grace Odlin of all people to spill the secret to.

"That was weird, though. She totally loved that you hated it. Even though she gets so much traffic to the mansion because of it." He tears off the plastic wrapping on the basket and pulls out a box of chocolate-covered almonds. "Apparently, she doesn't speak to her mom."

"I feel like she just inducted me into the toxic-mothers-and-sad-daughters club. I'm never having kids."

Jayden laughs and pops a chocolate almond into his mouth. "I respect that."

I wake covered in sweat with my phone buzzing. There's a scuffle as I rush to pick it up, expecting to see Mom's familiar number on the screen. Instead it's some unknown call from Los Angeles. Junk. I hit ignore and flop back down on the mattress.

Jayden sleeps soundly on his side of the bed, dead to the world as he usually is. The room is dark, the blackout curtains more than doing their job.

I inch myself up in bed with my phone in my hand. Now that I'm awake, I'm restless, twitchy. Horror movie rules dictate that it would be a very bad idea for me to go explore the halls at night in a house that is potentially haunted. Jayden would say definitely haunted. I prefer my skepticism.

Kevin and the stakeholders would love it if I brought the

camera along with me to film anything dangerous or creepy that does happen.

I leave the room with my phone and nothing else.

The hallway that I expected to be abandoned at two a.m. is not. There are three guests walking in the opposite direction, arms clutched around each other, using their phones as flashlights.

Thrill seekers, apparently.

I'm about to move forward when a whisper reaches my ears. It's strange. Like someone's calling my name, but not quite. I look back at our bedroom door, wondering if Jayden did wake up after all. But when I step closer, the sound doesn't seem to be coming from our room but from just beside it. Another room, maybe? I lean forward to press my ear against the wall.

"Not nearly as haunted as advertised, right?" a girl says behind me.

I turn to face her.

What was I doing?

Right, exploring.

It's too dark to see her properly, and unlike the other guests, she hasn't bothered with a cell phone light. Her hair is long, in braids that go down to her feet, and— "Are you wearing sunglasses?" Clearly, this girl has no sense.

She grins. "They're those night-vision ones. Thought they would be good for walking around."

Figures. "Fun." I lift my cell phone. "I've just got this."

"It's better if you don't use anything." She takes off her sunglasses and tucks them into her jeans pocket before walking forward. "Want to see something cool?"

Though they sound like famous last words, I follow her.

The halls are different at night, but somehow not actually scary. The mirrors cast shadows, of course, and there is the odd statue that's kind of creepy, but otherwise it's okay.

I follow the girl to the hallway opposite ours in the other wing of the mansion. She looks comfortable exploring even without her night-vision sunglasses on.

"Do you like scary things?" I ask her. "Horror movies and stuff?"

"I like teen movies. The ones where they go to prom and kiss." She turns down another hall.

She doesn't really look like the rom-com type. Though I guess Carrie technically has a prom scene.

"It's here."

I follow the girl into a room that's circular and surrounded on all sides with windows. Moonlight beams through the glass and illuminates the space. It's colder out here too.

She looks back at me, and I nod. "It's pretty cool."

"Told you," she says.

My phone buzzes again and I dig it out of my pocket. Just some Twitter notification. I flick on my Do Not Disturb, tired of being so damn jumpy.

"Expecting a call?" The girl leans against one of the windows and points at my phone.

I shrug. "I thought my mom might." I don't know why I bother telling her. I guess it's nice to mention it to someone who knows nothing about it. Likely, this girl is visiting with her family, enjoying a nice vacation. The sort of shit I would have given anything to do when I was a kid.

The girl takes the sunglasses out of her pocket and twirls them between her fingers. "My mom gave me these. I like collecting them."

"Did you come here with her?"

She laughs, though it wasn't a funny question. "No . . . She doesn't like to keep in touch with me."

The room seems to get colder. "Oh."

"Sometimes, I think of all the things I would say to her if I could." She stares at me. "Do you think that would matter? That she would care?"

If I were a better person, a nicer person, one with a functional relationship with my mom, maybe I would say yes. Instead, I say, "If she hasn't reached out, then she probably doesn't want to hear it." Her face falls, gaze to the ground. My fists clench, and I take a breath. "But if it makes you feel better to do it, you should. Even if you're worried that when you reach out, she won't reach back. It's not really about her. It's about you. So if it'll help you, do it. And if it won't, don't."

She looks up at me with a small, sad smile. "You're not a bullshitter, eh?"

"No. I'm not."

"I'm gonna go to bed," she says. "See you." With a little wave, she exits the room and leaves me alone.

Another member for the toxic-mothers-and-sad-daughters club.

I stand there for a few moments before opening my phone and making a call.

She doesn't answer as usual.

But this time, I leave a voicemail.

CHAPTER FORTY-FOUR

DAISY

When I looked back at Ivy over my shoulder, she seemed to be shrinking and fading. Her face was a picture of perfect fury—lips twisted in a snarl, an anger so exquisite that even her nose wrinkled from the force of it. My legs sagged, and Mom had to keep me upright, stumbling backward onto the couch where we both collapsed over the arm of it. When I looked up again, Ivy was gone.

The possession had felt like being a tendril of delicate roots under soil, and this past week I had been stretching myself further and further while Ivy grew mostly unaware on the surface. Separating was like being tugged up and out of the cocoon of earth, and I was left shivering and exposed, but Ivy was worse for wear, hanging limp.

I could grow into something new, my roots salvaged and replanted, but hers were already dead.

There were no more wind sounds reminiscent of the lake anymore. It was something worse. The blaring in both my ears felt like when I was in the thornbush. Butcherbirds descending on me. Furious flapping wings.

I slapped my hands against my ears, wincing. "Do you hear that?"

Mom sat up and gently rearranged us. "No, I have my maggot."

It seemed impossible that it could have gotten this bad just in the time that Ivy was in control. That it was this strong now.

Ivy.

She would have gone to the house. Especially feeling as vulnerable as I'm sure she did. It was already bad, but she could make it worse.

"We need to leave," Mom said.

"What?"

"It's time to cut our losses with this house. If I were a better mom, I would have done this a long time ago. We'll grab some bags. As long as we're in the bunkie, we'll be fine."

"Mom," I said, my voice insistent. "This won't stop if we leave. The house is too powerful."

She stared at me for a long moment, and I watched the way her eyes watered. I knew that she understood now how bad things were. I wondered if the tears were because she felt helpless to stop it or because she was reliving the betrayal of a house that once saved her. Maybe it was both.

Finally, she nodded. "Okay, okay. We'll fix it—no, *I'll* fix it. We just need to get away for a bit. Not far. I'll make some calls. We may be able to stay with Helga. It'll be far enough to be safe for a little while." She waved her hand me. "Now go pack a bag."

I waited for a few seconds, staring at her, trying to gauge her sincerity.

"Daisy," she said. "Please."

And so I went and packed a bag.

I dumped out the notebooks and textbooks from my backpack and shoved in a few clothing items and some toiletries. When I came out to meet Mom, she had a whole-ass suitcase.

"Really?" I said with a sigh.

"I'm sorry we can't all be minimalists." She grabbed a plastic bag from our stash under the sink and threw something from inside the fridge into it.

The maggots, probably.

She caught me looking. "We'll put yours in at Helga's place. We just need to go, now."

I blurted out, "I'm sorry for what I said. I don't hate you." I couldn't tell if it was a lie or not.

I didn't think it was.

"I could say sorry every day and never make up for how I've been. You of all people don't need to say it to me." She nodded toward the door. "Let's go."

As soon as I stepped outside, I was hit by a gust of wind with hail pellets hidden inside like sharp concealed blades, slicing at my face and cheeks. My foot knocked into something beside the door, and when I looked down, I saw a pumpkin lying on its side.

"I was trying to be festive," Mom said, sounding sheepish. "For the guests."

I remembered now. It was only a few days before Halloween.

The snow had come early.

Flurries of it blurred my vision and coated the mansion in a haze of white. I pushed forward and Mom followed after me, and once we were close enough, we could finally see the house.

It had grown wild. Over the doors, windows, and even some of the path, thorns twisted and writhed across surfaces where they had never existed before. Butcherbirds hopped from branch to branch, delighted to be in their element.

Someone had learned how to possess plants now. Wonderful.

Mom grabbed my hand. "Let's go. *Now.*"

We took off at a sprint toward the Jeep that was parked by the entrance to the bush. One moment, we were running, my bag bumping hard against my back, and Mom's suitcase squeaking against the force of the movement.

And the next, the front door to the mansion flew open.

It happened at a speed that was as fast as a snap of fingers and yet as slow as sap dripping down a tree trunk.

Branches full of thorns shot from inside the house and wrapped themselves around Mom's body. She only had enough time to shoot me a panicked look before she was ripped from the ground and tugged inside the house.

The door slammed shut with a bang.

A group of birds flew from the house toward me, and I ducked out of the way with a shriek.

But they didn't want me.

They descended on the bag that had dropped from Mom's hands.

The birds dug through the plastic and seized the maggots.

"Wait! No!" I dived to save them, but it was too late.

The butcherbirds flew back to the house. The one above the front door took a squirming maggot and impaled it on a thorn. Pale white fluid poured out of it, and the bird ripped into its flesh as snow fell on them both.

Mom. I needed to get Mom.

I abandoned my backpack and rushed to the front door, trying to grasp the knob through the thorns. I was rewarded with slices across my fingers and palms. I kicked at it and screamed until my voice cracked while the violent flapping sound assaulted my ears. I was dizzy with it. The panic. The blood. The fucking noise.

The thorns were growing thicker, covering more and more, as if they planned to overtake the entire building until there was nothing else.

"Stand back," King's voice suddenly boomed.

I turned around, and he stood there in his warmer-than-mine jacket with a neon orange hat pulled over his curls and a shotgun in his hands. I blinked at him. "What are you doing here?"

He smiled. The one that I thought was specifically for me. "Had a feeling that you needed help."

"Of course," I said with a laugh. I moved out of the way, and he heaved the gun onto his shoulder and pointed it at the door.

He fired twice, and the pellets ripped through not only the door but the thorn branches. My chest leapt at the sight of it, but only a few seconds later, more branches came to replace the old ones and covered the opening.

King's face fell.

"What now?" I asked.

He set his mouth in a grim line and reloaded. "I don't know, I'm thinking."

There was no way the hole in the door was going to be open long enough for both of us to get through. By the time King put down the shotgun to rush inside, it would already be covered again. I couldn't leave Mom in there for that long.

I pointed at the door. "You shoot and I'll jump in right away."

King shook his head. "You can't go alone."

"We don't exactly have a lot of options."

He dropped the gun from his shoulder, and it hung limp in his fingers. "Don't go." There was a thickness to his voice, a strain and a shudder.

My lips quirked into a humorless smile. "I guess you know what happens, don't you? You have for a while. That future you saw for me. The one that made you decide to help." I swallowed. "Do I save my mom if I go?"

He shoulders sagged. "You know that I can't tell you."

"But wouldn't it be a good thing? If you told me, it would definitely happen."

"Yes. And not everything that would happen because of it would be good."

My throat went dry. He couldn't tell me, but clearly it wasn't the sort of ending that he wanted for me. He had said as much to Ivy when she was in my body.

His eyes started to water. "I'm trying to help you change it," he said. "But every choice just keeps being one that leads to it."

"Me making the same mistakes over and over again?"

"You making the best choices that you can in the moment."

My fingers shook. Nothing good was waiting for me in that house. But I didn't know what was waiting for Mom, either. "I guess now you get it, why people never listen when you try to help."

"Please don't go," he choked out.

Standing there, I wished there was more time. That this moment wasn't so urgent. That it could be stretched out and savored. "If I come back, I can make fun of you for being a do-gooder. I'll even sit at lunch with you and your friends."

He laughed, watery and loud, and wiped his eyes. "You're going, aren't you?"

"I'm sorry. I'm not listening to you again."

"Please just hear me out on this. Your life matters—you know that, right? It's not worth nothing just because you don't know what you want to do with it yet."

"I know." I didn't really, but I said it for him anyway. I flicked my eyes to the door with its splintered wood and thick thorns. "Now shoot."

King didn't hesitate to raise the shotgun to his shoulder and fire off two rounds. And I didn't hesitate to jump through the opening, landing hard on the tile inside with a cry.

I turned back and watched his face as the thorns grew over the top of the door.

He kept a smile on, even as tears rolled down his cheeks.

I think we could have been friends for a lot longer, me and King, if we'd had enough time.

But we didn't.

CHAPTER FORTY-FIVE

The moment I was inside, the sound cut off abruptly.

No more flapping wings. No rustling. *Nothing.*

It made sense. The house used its voice to draw people in. And now I was here.

Inside, the mansion looked the same as always, minus the blackout of light from the thorns draped over the windows and the eerie fall of silence.

The dead were still here.

Packed inside.

Even they looked uncomfortable with it. Dozens and dozens of them stuffed into the space like sardines, none of them moving, crowded among opulent furniture and gold-filigree banisters.

And they stared.

But this time, I stared back.

The house's voice might be loud, but this wasn't its domain anymore. It was Ivy's.

"Where's my mom?" I asked them.

The one nearest me raised a translucent hand and pointed up the stairs. Slowly others in the room followed, each of them pointing.

I raced up, taking the steps two at a time.

We had guests staying with us right now, but not one of them had come out to investigate the literal gunshot sounds. I could hear the murmur of voices in their rooms and even saw a couple of doorknobs turn, but the doors stayed closed. I suspected that Ivy had something to do with that, too. She likely wouldn't want any interference in whatever it was that she had planned.

There were more dead waiting at the top, and they pointed me down a hall. More and more of them showing me the way.

Ivy, leading me.

But I had already realized exactly where I was going.

My boots squeaked on the floor. I sprinted with everything that I had in my body until I skidded to a stop in the hallway in front of Mom's old room.

There Mom stood bound in a swath of thorns that covered every inch of skin but her eyes and nose. A torn-off piece of her jacket was stuffed in her mouth and held in place by the branches. Blood dripped from tiny cuts all over her body. Beside her, Ivy stood, braids long and shades on, with a grin on her face. "Record time," she chirped. "I thought it would take you longer."

There were no sounds of guest activity in this hallway. I couldn't tell if it was because Mom hadn't booked anyone into these rooms or if Ivy had done something to them.

"Let her go, please," I said. "What is it that you even want?"

"I thought we had an understanding, Daisy? You sit in the back-seat, and I get shotgun." Ivy turned toward Mom. "But you let her ruin it. And him, too. King." She spat his name as if it were a bad taste in her mouth. Mom was screaming something against her gag, but Ivy wasn't listening. "Oh right, can't forget the details."

A branch naked of thorns pulled away from the rest and plunged back toward the side of Mom's head, straight into her ear. She screamed, and her eyes rolled into the back of her head.

"Stop it!" I cried. "What are you doing?"

"Relax," Ivy drawled. "She's fine."

The branch came away from Mom's body, and she sagged forward, eyes flickering back open. It threw something to the ground, and I spotted a wriggling white body before Ivy crushed it with her foot. Blood spurted from the maggot, and it shuddered before lying still.

Ivy smiled at me. "There we go, no more interference."

"What do you want? Seriously?" I pleaded, words hollowed out and dry. "My body? You can't even do the things you want with it. The house won't let you go."

She heaved a heavy sigh and shook her head. "I have been trying to help you."

"By possessing me?!"

"Yes! Because you can't seem to get your shit together on your own. You can't help but get under her thumb at every turn." Ivy stabbed a finger at Mom. "Run away with her? You think anything will get better? She's manipulated you your entire life. She led people here to be tortured. I'm helping you get rid of her."

I shook my head and swallowed. "And you're better? You think this house is your friend? It's not! And you killed that girl, for what? To impress it?!"

"I tried to save her!" Ivy yelled.

What? I attempted to put the pieces back together, but all I could remember from that night was Ivy coming inside the house, using my body.

She scrubbed her hand over her face. "I got mad that she was going to leave her husband. Sometimes the house reacts when I get mad, but I didn't mean to!" Ivy's chin dipped toward her chest. "I did my best to stop it. But I just remembered why I was pissed off all over again, and it got worse and . . ."

Ivy gave the girl as a sacrifice to the house when she got upset. And when she tried to possess it again to stop it, she accidentally made it worse. Maybe I shouldn't have, but I believed her. The way her voice strained and her eyes got wide. She was, at least mentally, only a few years younger than me. And I was sure that she had no real idea what she was doing.

The plants. I thought they were like that because she wanted to pretend to be me. But that wasn't it. "You tried to take care of the garden too, didn't you?"

Ivy bit down on her lip. "I didn't know how."

"And what about what happened to Hayden?"

She at least had the decency to look ashamed.

"I can't," I said. "I can't let you take over again. Especially not now." I needed to save Mom, and I definitely needed a way to stop the house. If we left, eventually the mansion would call us back. We had no maggots, and I doubted we had time to grow a new batch. We wouldn't get far, not when the voice was this loud.

"You're going to let her control your life forever!" Ivy snapped. "So I'll make the choice easy for you. Either you let me take over and I can make better decisions for you, or I'll torture Mommy to death in one of the rooms. It's what the house wants the most now that it doesn't need her. It would be so simple for me to help it do it. I *am* going to be the favorite." Ivy slid her sunglasses off her face and met my gaze head-on. "One way or another, I'm going to save you from her." Her voice went quiet when she added, "Because no one wanted to save me."

I didn't know what she meant. She kept saying that. No one saved her. And I couldn't form a thought to try to understand with Mom screaming through her gag. She was saying something, but I couldn't make it out.

"Please don't do this, Ivy," I begged.

She clenched her jaw. "I'm doing this for you."

Mom screamed louder against her gag, and finally Ivy turned to her. "What?!" She must have made herself visible to Mom if they could address each other directly.

The thorns pulled away from Mom's mouth, and she spat out the gag to speak. "Leave her alone! This is my fault. I'm the one you want." She looked at me. "Just let her punish me. You go and live your life. I'll find some way to deal with the house."

Ivy frowned and spat at Mom, "Stop trying to control everything. This is Daisy's choice."

Mom laughed. "I think once you hear what I have to say, you'll prefer the option where you torture me and let Daisy go."

"What are you doing?" I pushed, stepping closer to Mom.

"I couldn't see her before, so I didn't know. I couldn't tell. But I can see her now," Mom said as she stared at Ivy.

The entire time I had known her, Ivy had shown herself to a small pool of people. King, his family, and me. And even then, that first time she hadn't wanted to be seen by me, but I saw all the dead. This was truly the first time Mom was allowed to see and hear her.

Because this time, she wanted Mom to watch me condemn her or sacrifice my life for her. Ivy could say this was for me, but I knew there was at least a part of her relishing this intimate torture of the little girl who was able to escape the mansion in a way she never could.

Tears welled in Mom's eyes. "I didn't realize I would hurt so many people when I decided to help the house. I just wanted him to stop. To leave me alone." She bit her lip. "But it never wanted to make him stop completely, because then I would stop feeding it." Mom gave me a long look. "It said that I should have a baby. That babies born in this house were special. They could see the dead. And that we needed one to protect the house from corporeals that could create problems."

Shivers crawled over my arms. I hated that this was the origin of my life.

"But I . . . I didn't want to be at the mansion anymore. I realized that if I had a baby, Mom wouldn't let me come back for the summers. I could escape."

Mom stopped coming to the house when she was sixteen. Grandma wanted Mom out of the way before that, but the idea of people talking behind her back about not being able to control her now-pregnant child would be worse. She cared the most about what other people thought of her. It was, like Mom said, the greatest dream and the perfect escape, but to hear it said so plainly, to know that I was a means to an end, stung.

I was a tool in two ways: the house trying to get another gardener, and Mom trying to get away.

"It shared so many things with me. How we could torture Peter forever if I wanted. How, when you were older, you could help. How to train you to make the dead pass on, because the house couldn't do anything about them—something that I know now was a lie. There were so many plans . . . but *my plan* was still to leave." Mom's lip trembled. "I felt bad. I had called Mom when I was outside the house. Told her I was pregnant. She was going to come get me. But the house had *saved* me. So I told it what I was going to do."

I got the impression that Mom sharing the truth with the house hadn't gone well. And from the way she cringed, I knew I was right.

"It was so mad at me. It begged me to stay. It would have no gardener. And it said that it would stop helping me." She swallowed. "Mom wasn't coming until the end of the summer. I still had a month. It wanted me to give it something to take my place. And it wanted proof that I would follow through. So when Peter and Dione said they could adopt my baby so that I wouldn't have to put my life on hold . . . it heard. And that's what it wanted."

Ivy narrowed her eyes. "Does this story have a point?"

"Yes," Mom said, voice firm. She looked at me. "I wasn't going to let them have you. I couldn't. Not *him*. Not *her*. You were the size of a fucking grape, but I already loved you."

She had saved me because she loved me. It was so simple, but I couldn't make it stick. Because if she loved me so much, why had she put me through all this? She was probably just pregnant and hormonal.

Tears spilled down Mom's cheeks. Her voice croaked as she continued, "I thought . . . I could just suffer through it until my mom came. But after just one night . . ." She sucked in a breath and sobbed.

It was too much. She couldn't do it. Which meant she'd found a way to appease the house. But how?

"I told it that I would give it another baby. A new gardener. One who would have the same powers you would, Daisy. So I crushed these antibiotics and put them in Dione's food so that it would mess up her birth control. I knew she was still . . . with him, even after everything I'd told her. I promised the house her baby instead of mine. And she got pregnant." Mom let out a dry laugh. "I was off the hook. And on that drive home with your grandma, on the highway, I saw a patch of blueberries and that one daisy. It was so fast. But I didn't miss it. And I named you right then. It was the greatest dream that I've ever had because it was real."

My name wasn't an outright lie after all. It was a white lie. Sanitized to hide the hurt and pain beyond that car ride.

Mom traded another life for mine. One that wasn't even in the world yet. I didn't understand how that connected to Ivy until Mom turned to her with watery eyes. "You look just like her," she said. "I'm so sorry. I stopped talking with Dione. I assumed she'd had the child, and I thought maybe things were okay. But then my mom never mentioned the kid. I thought she'd miscarried." Mom sucked in a sob. "So you see, it's my fault that you were born to them. My fault that this house sunk its claws into you. I wasn't smart enough to avoid it, but you shouldn't have had to make that choice. Punish me, but leave Daisy alone."

Ivy wasn't just some random soul called by the house and stuck inside like the rest. This was *her* home. She was Peter's child. And somehow she had died here. She existed because Mom promised her to the mansion before she was even born, knowing that she was giving a child to not one but two monsters. To save me.

But no one had saved Ivy.

Ivy's face was slack and impassive. She didn't move, didn't speak for a long moment, then turned and looked at me. "I'm sorry, Daisy. I have to be selfish this time and make the choice for you. You're better off without her."

"No, Ivy, please!" I yelled.

It was too late.

With a flick of her wrist, the door to Mom's old room opened, and the thorns tugged her inside.

"Mom!" I rushed to the door, and it slammed shut in front of me.

Her screams rung out from the other side. I turned around to Ivy. "Stop this! I'll do it! I'll give you my body!"

Ivy glared at me. "You need to learn to value your life. Yours! Not your mom's." Her fingers shook. "I am dead. *Dead.* There are so many things that I wanted to do and never can. And even when I was alive . . . being in this house was a nightmare. I never had a chance, right from the start. But you do. You can be anything and go anywhere. Maybe once you have to give something up, you'll understand. I'm sorry, but it's for your own good."

The door to the right of me opened, and a swath of thorns broke free from the window and pulled me inside.

I didn't even have time to scream.

CHAPTER FORTY-SIX

Several ideas of what I expected to find in the room came to mind. The first was, keeping in theme, more maggots, and I clenched my muscles and swallowed my last bit of wiggling-body-free saliva. Or maybe it would be the kids from the playground, come to make another attempt at killing me. Or it would be Noah looming over me, spreading his fingers over my throat and pushing down until I stopped breathing.

What I did not expect was Mom sitting on the bed.

Her hair was in its usual twists, and the gold edge of her round glasses glittered in the small bits of light that managed to peek through the thorns twisting around the window. She looked comfortable on the cream-and-midnight-blue sheets. Natural. As if she weren't actually over in the next room experiencing whatever horror lay inside under Ivy's will.

I turned around and tried to open the door, though it wouldn't budge. I didn't think it would, but I had to try.

"Let me out!" I screamed, hoping that the house would finally speak to me, but it remained silent. Of course it would. It got power from torturing me, and I wasn't about to bring it sacrifices like Mom had. And it didn't even need her anymore.

"I thought you were like me," Mom said behind me.

I turned, though I knew I shouldn't.

She smiled, calm, serene. "I used to think you were strong and capable. Ambitious. You were like that when you were little. When you grew those plants after the first one died. But then there were so many ways you weren't like me. Scared and sensitive. You couldn't even take the most casual jibe from my mom. I was listening to much worse at your age."

Hearing her made my stomach churn as if there were maggots swimming around in there after all. At least that was straightforward. This was something entirely different.

"You cried over ghosts. It was ridiculous. They were already dead. You couldn't take even the slightest push in school. And yet you always acted like you were *my* caretaker. Like I would fall apart if you weren't there to help." She propped up her chin on her hand, and her grin grew wider. "I just needed to give you something to be good at."

"What does that even mean?"

"Sometimes I would crash and burn so you could fix things. Give you a bit of self-esteem." She shook her head. "I shouldn't have. It just made you slack everywhere else. You never got better at school, and you certainly never became a better medium."

I opened my mouth to dispute what she said, then shut it again. Because I didn't really know. Mom was full of so many secrets and lies. Would it even be shocking if it were true?

I crossed my arms and jerked my head from side to side. "This is the house talking. Why tell me all of this if not to just mess me up and distract me from saving Mom?" I turned around and went back to trying to kick down the door.

"Oh, honey," Mom laughed. "I'm telling you this because it's your biggest fear. Don't you know? You're scared of the truth."

I froze with my fingers on the knob.

"You always were. You let dead kids bully you, and realizing they weren't alive nearly destroyed you. So much so that you almost killed a little girl over it. You don't like learning the truth. It's why I never bothered telling you." I turned back toward her, and she shrugged at me. "For example, you're just not smart enough to go to university. But you tell yourself that it's because you don't try. Or you don't care."

I gnawed on the inside of my cheek to keep from saying anything. From shouting out denials or caving to what she was saying. I couldn't tell what the truth was anymore. My own thoughts kept getting looped together with what was being said.

I was on the merry-go-round again, turning, and turning, and turning.

Dazy.

Dazy.

Dazy.

Suddenly their heads were pushing themselves out of the wall. Tiny childlike limbs, arms, and legs, and smushed faces. They were like Ivy. Furious at me for wasting the lives that they couldn't have.

I stumbled away from them to the door, but they were inside those walls too, calling to me.

Dazy.

Dazy.

Dazy.

"You know I don't love you," Mom said with a sweet smile. "You're a tool. You got me away from this house. Your ability to communicate with the dead made you useful even though you messed that up too. Even your body was a tool to keep Ivy preoccupied so she wouldn't interfere with the guests. The torture is necessary, but the deaths make everything so messy." She played with the end of one of her twists. "And now you're a means to save me. And you'll do it. Because you want me to love you so much. You'll do anything. Not that it matters. You'll always be a tool to me."

I lurched back against the door, and Johnny's distorted face screamed, "Dazy!" in my ear. I scrambled away from the walls, which only brought me closer to Mom.

"Give up loving me. What's the point? Everything will be better if you do. Give it up, and you can go free." She grinned. "Freer than you've ever been in your life. Don't love me. You know I don't love you."

No. She was my mom. Of course she loved me. Of course she did. But even as that went through my mind, I thought of every time Mom had thrown me under the bus. Of every secret revealed where I was being used and manipulated to help her. Us being in this house was one huge manipulation after another, and for what? Revenge on a man who was already dead.

I understood how much she was hurting from it. I could understand why she wanted his suffering so badly. But that didn't change the fact that she used me, her own child, more than once.

It would be easier if I didn't love her. Everything would be.

She was right. She didn't love me.

But then . . . "Why didn't you give me to the house when I was a baby?"

Mom frowned. She opened her mouth and closed it. Finally she said, "Sometimes mothers can be sentimental. Even me. It doesn't change anything."

My lips quirked the slightest bit. It was the same thought I'd had when Mom shared that tidbit with me and Ivy. Because every time there was evidence of her love for me, I found something to dispute it. Some reason why I was wrong.

And it always felt right in my mind, but hearing it said back to me gave it a different caliber. It seemed like shitty reasoning.

"This is the truth," I said firmly. "The truth is that it's impossible to understand the sort of mom that I have. The truth is that it's painful to put together the fact that she loves me with the things she does that hurt me. The truth is that I don't have a good mom, but she's mine, and I love her anyway. And maybe that makes me look weak and desperate, but I don't really care. Maybe I'll regret saving her. Maybe she'll just hurt me again. Maybe I would be better off walking away. But I can't. And that's *my* choice. No one else gets to decide that for me. She's trying, so I won't leave her, not forever. I want to give her a chance." I press my lips into something like a smile. "You, on the other hand, I have no problem leaving behind."

"But can you?" Mom's voice morphed, changing, deepening. Her nose swelled until it split open with a crunch of bone and spurt of blood. It dripped down her face as a small black beak poked through.

I stepped back toward the door without touching it, mindful of the various child-body parts writhing in it, still chanting, "Dazy, Dazy, Dazy." Mom laughed as her face tore open more, and the bird wriggled its way out, its black, gray, and white feathers covered with a thin layer of glistening blood. Finally, it popped free of her face, and more followed.

Butcherbirds.

One after the other shoving themselves out from her bloody face to the symphony of her cackling, and the snaps of broken bone and cartilage. Each bird simply hopped out and they all surrounded her. Some standing on the bed, or her body, or the floor. More and more of them.

When they were finished, her face was split so severely that the bone white of her skull was visible, and her eyes dangled from their sockets, the familiar brown I had grown up with. Her lips were a ripped and bloody ruin with pus-colored fat peeking out from her lipstick. She said, "No Mommy to save you this time."

And all at once, the shrikes took flight.

These ones did not peck with tiny sharp pinches. There was something different about them. The first took a nip out of my arm, and with it pulled off a chunk the size of a quarter, so deep that I saw the shine of bone underneath the slick coating of my blood.

I screamed.

One tore at my eye, and I felt it come away with a rough tug on the stringy nerves that held it in its socket. Whole tufts of my hair and scalp were cleaved away at once. A small group of them started pecking at my skull, doing their best to get at the soft insides of my brain.

And she was right. Mom wasn't going to save me this time. King wouldn't either.

I was going to die here.

And they would find my body, not in pieces devoured by shrikes, but whole, lying prone, and chalked up as a brain aneurysm.

Mom would be dead too.

I couldn't let it happen.

I wouldn't.

All I had to do was give something up.

Give it up. Give up on loving her and this can stop. GIVE UP!

I forced the voice from my head. No. I wouldn't give it that. That was mine.

I knew this house now. This was a house that told an abused girl that it would help her, then threatened to take it away. This was a house that told a girl who just wanted to be loved that she could be its favorite when it really wanted to be rid of her. This was a house that told you that you needed to give it what it wanted, when the rule was simply that you give it *something*.

This was a house that found the prey of bigger predators and fed on their fears.

It wasn't Mom's innocent plant, simply a function of its gardener, and it wasn't Ivy's animal, unable to help its nature. If it was anything, it was human. It chose to lie and manipulate to get what it wanted, and it dined on the dark monstrous bits of the people it used, growing stronger only through the combination of their wills. Mom and Ivy were right about that much. In the end, it still needed us to become what it was now.

I would not be another girl devoured by whispering walls and false promises.

I forced the sensation of my flesh ripping and tearing out of my mind. And I pushed my thoughts somewhere new. I thought of the moment in the bunkie, only a few minutes before now, where I was wrapped in Mom's arms and for the first time in years felt wholly that she loved me.

I languished in the thought, in the sensation, in the complete sense of acceptance.

And I gave up the part of me that said it was a lie.

When I opened my eyes next, the shrikes were gone, and there was only Mom sitting on the bed, whole and untouched. "She'll always disappoint you. You know that, right?"

I didn't answer. Instead, I turned the knob and pushed the door open.

CHAPTER FORTY-SEVEN

vy's lip trembled as she watched me come out of the room. She took a step back and shook her head. I had only a moment to rush forward and shove her into the first open door that I saw. She fell hard on her back, and the momentum had me stumbling into the room behind her.

The door shut with a crash.

"Shit," I muttered. This wasn't how I wanted this to go. But all that mattered was I got her into the room first.

Because Ivy didn't realize how much control she had of this house.

And from the way she treated it every other time, the visions belonged to the first person who entered. And this time, it wasn't me.

Around us, the space transformed. The walls became a plain slate gray, and though it was the same size as the bedroom, it felt smaller, cramped. There was a single bed in the corner along with a small TV set surrounded by instructional dancing and romantic comedy DVDs, textbooks and study aids littered on the ground, and a standing rack filled with the offensively bright clothing I associated with Ivy. On the opposite side of the room was the door, and beside it a much larger white door covered in small icicles that had a thick silver latch.

"No, no, no, no," Ivy was muttering on the ground. She was shrinking, not in size but in how she held herself. The sunglasses fell from her face, and the confidence she usually had withered and died.

Steps echoed in the room, coming closer and closer. Ivy crawled to her bed, curling up and trembling, terrified. The blanket pulled over her head and tight around her body so only her face peeked out from the covers. I recognized the room now from the Tower video with the Airbnb tour. It was the basement space that I had assumed was an old servants' quarters.

The door opened, and Peter stepped in. He walked calmly into the room. "You interrupted my lesson."

"I'm sorry," Ivy mumbled from under the sheets. "You were rushing since you were late and forgot to lock the door. I wanted to listen to the music."

Peter frowned. "Take that off your head. Look at me when I'm speaking to you, please." His voice was even and polite. He wasn't shouting or speaking harshly.

Ivy pulled the blanket off and let it pool in her lap as she looked at her father.

"What did you see?"

"Nothing!"

Peter's frown deepened. "Really? Nothing?"

Ivy nodded, frantically, desperately.

Silence stretched between them, longer and longer. The more it went on, the more Ivy seemed to crack under the pressure until she finally started to quietly cry.

"Innocent people don't cry," Peter said. He strolled over to the giant freezer door, unlatched the lock, and pulled it open with a tug. Inside were frozen cuts of meat, zip sealed, a couple of pizzas, and some fries. "Go on."

"Please," Ivy cried. "I didn't see anything. I won't say anything. Who would I even talk to? I'm always down here by myself!"

"Ivy."

"I'm sorry. I'm *sorry*."

"Ivy!" he finally snapped.

She flinched from his voice and rose from the bed, her blanket wrapped around her, and made her way to the walk-in freezer. Before she went in, Peter tugged the blanket away and threw it on the ground. She stared at it sadly before going inside.

He shut the door and locked the latch in place. "I'll be back in an hour. See if you've learned your lesson."

The only indication I had that time was passing were the flickers on the TV.

And then the dead came.

They started piling into the room. More and more of them.

No.

Ivy was like me. She could feel the cold of them, and she was already in a freezing room.

Why were there so many? The house should have been eating them. King didn't get his knowing until after Peter was dead. Meaning that the house should be functioning as normal, consuming them. It shouldn't have any other food source.

Muffled screams thudded against the freezer door, and I stumbled back. The latch jerked as Ivy tried to open it from the inside. But it wasn't working.

My eyes darted to the door. *Peter.* He must be hearing this. Why wasn't he coming? What the fuck was he doing? No . . . He said he would be back in an hour. If he left the house, he wouldn't be able to hear.

An hour in a freezer, Ivy would live through. But not with the dead piling in like that. They would make it so much colder.

"Help!" Ivy screamed from inside. "Please, help! I'm sorry I didn't listen! I didn't want to hurt people! But I'll help! I'll help!"

The house.

The mansion could unlock the door. It could free her.

But the latch remained shut.

I pressed my ear against the freezer door. "Ivy?"

She didn't answer, just kept screaming for help.

When I gripped the latch and pulled, it wouldn't move. The house was holding it in place.

"Ivy!" I shouted. "You can make it stop. You can make the house stop. You don't have to relive this." She was corporeal. It couldn't make her pass on by eating her. That was why it wanted someone like me who could see the dead in the first place. But it was torturing her anyway.

Except Ivy didn't know that. She also didn't realize how much power she had over the house. She could make this stop.

"You can open this door!" I screamed.

I kept watching the handle jiggle to no avail.

"You can stop this!" I had to keep trying. I couldn't leave her like this.

"Help me! Please, help me!"

The mansion wasn't going to save her. It *hadn't* saved her. For whatever reason, it had let her die.

But I wouldn't.

I didn't care that this had already happened.

For her, this was real.

The house was trying to stop me from interfering, but Ivy could control this if she wanted. I couldn't convince her. But maybe I could do something else. Ivy wanted someone to save her. No one had come back then.

"Ivy!" I shouted. "I'm here. I'm going to help you. I can unlock it. Okay?"

There was a fresh sob on the other side. "Okay."

If she knew I was here, knew someone was going to help, and desperately wanted to be saved, she could imagine it happening. She could *make* it happen.

Once again, I put my hand on the latch, and pulled.

The door swung open and the room dissolved, leaving us sitting in an empty space.

Ivy was curled on the floor, shaking. She looked into my eyes. "You could have let her die, your mom. You would be free. She hurts people. She'll just keep hurting you. Like he hurt me."

Part of me couldn't believe that Ivy saw any similarity between Mom and Peter. I had never in my life been abused like that. But to her, she saw what she saw. She saw a mom who used me. Who put me in danger.

I'm trying to help you.

I pressed my palms against my eyes to stop any tears. Ivy possessed me to help me do better in school. And to help me keep going when I wanted to give up. She helped me when I wanted to go into the house. Even now, she thought killing Mom would help me escape her.

"Why?" I choked out. "Why are you so desperate to help me?"

Ivy's eyes watered. "Isn't that what friends do? I've never had one. I thought maybe if I did, things would have been different."

Friends.

I swallowed, and it hurt my throat going down.

Everything came down to that.

Ivy didn't want to take over my life.

She wanted to be my friend.

Ivy's mouth twisted into a grimace. "I didn't listen to the house before. The things it whispered scared me. But after I died, it said that if I got stronger, I could punish him one day for what he did to me. Only I didn't want to wait that long. I was so mad when I saw him. So mad, Daisy. My whole life in that box in the basement. And I got so strong so fast. I pushed him into a room, and the house helped me. We did it together." She looked at me, her expression open and sincere. "We could do the same for you."

If it were anyone but Ivy, it would have been unbelievable. To become a corporeal that fast. To instinctively possess the house and use its power to kill her abusive father. All within an hour of dying. It felt impossible, but she had done it. Then again, Ivy was special.

And hers was the first sacrifice. That was why King got his knowing before me and Mom even arrived. And why it was too late to do the cleansing once Mom made her guest sacrifice. The first sign that the house had gone wrong was Peter, but the house hadn't belonged to anyone yet. No homeowner to give the Okekes permission to perform the cleansing.

"It helped me," Ivy said, a smile on her face. "And I'm going to be its favorite now."

"But it didn't save you."

The smile slid from her lips.

"Ivy . . . The house did that on purpose. It was supposed to be eating the dead, but there were so many. It was starving itself so that the next time Peter left you in that freezer, you would die. You said you didn't listen to it. You didn't help it the way it wanted. That's why it didn't open the door. It could have saved you, but it didn't want to. It wanted you dead, and then it used you to kill Peter."

The house would have known that even dead, Ivy could still give it permission to kill. And with Peter and his heir out of the way, the house would be inherited by Mom. By the gardener who *had* helped it. And she would bring me with her, and I would force Ivy to pass on.

It felt like a gamble, but it wasn't. The house *knew* Mom. And it knew that with Peter dead, its offer to torture him forever would be a temptation she couldn't resist.

"No," Ivy breathed. "It wouldn't . . . it wouldn't do that to me." But even as she said it, her shoulders hunched and tears gathered in her eyes, and I knew she understood the truth of it. Because hadn't she been wondering all this time? Hadn't she kept asking?

Why didn't it save her?

And now she knew.

I got down on my knees and took her hands in mine. She stared at me. Snot dribbled down her nose, and she wiped it away messily with her hand. "You're stronger than this house, Ivy. You have the power to make it do whatever you want. Just like when you were inside me, and the butcherbirds, and the thorn branches. You can get inside the house. You can make the rules. You can make it stop eating."

"I can?"

"Yes."

"But then . . . when the house stops, you'll leave, won't you? You'll go far away. And I'll be alone again."

She was right. She knew it, and I knew it too.

There was only one way to assure her that I wouldn't.

Sorry, King.

"I'll stay with you. If I die here, I won't be able to leave. I'll always be your friend."

Ivy's eyes got wider with every proclamation I made.

"And in exchange, you'll let my mom go, and you'll help me stop the house from feeding." We couldn't quiet the mansion with a ritual, but we could starve it. Stop it from feeding even if it called people to the house.

And Ivy was the only one who could do that.

In exchange, I would give her this guarantee that I would never leave her. Death was permanent. She couldn't call my promise a lie.

"But the house has more power than me," she mumbled.

"Trust me, you're stronger than you think." I squeezed her hands in mine. "We'll work together."

Mom had said she would find a way to stop the house, but what if she didn't? What if she'd just run from it? We would have left Ivy behind.

The little girl my mom sacrificed to save me.

My cousin.

I wasn't going to leave her.

This time, Ivy would be the one to be saved.

"We'll fix it," I said to her with a smile. "I'm good at fixing things."

The thorns on the front door parted, and King was sitting there, legs crossed, with the shotgun on his lap. The tears on his face had long dried, but his eyes got glassy again when he saw me. Ivy stood next to me with her sunglasses perched on her nose. Looking unruffled, as if what happened in the house hadn't occurred at all.

The snowstorm outside had calmed too. The wind brushed lightly against my face, and flakes drifted in with it. Everything felt quiet in a way it hadn't for weeks.

"Can you come get my mom, please?" I asked King.

King nodded without a word and came into the house and retrieved Mom from the floor of her bedroom. She hadn't been tortured. Ivy admitted that after we solidified our deal. Mom's initial screams must have been fear of what she'd expected to happen. But Ivy wouldn't subject anyone to her father, and definitely not like that.

No matter how badly the house wanted to feed on its gardener. But she had fully intended to suffocate Mom with the thorns, she'd told me a little sheepishly.

We made our way back to the front of the house. I looked at Mom, her head lolling on King's chest, and said to him, "Go out and find a place where people will see you. Text me when you get there."

"It's not your job to right her wrongs," he said, voice strained.

But it was. It had been my job for so long that I didn't know how to do anything else. Maybe it wasn't right for me to do it. Probably it wasn't. "But you know why, don't you? Why I'm doing it?"

King looked down at the ground. "You don't like listening to me, do you?"

"Nope."

I loved Mom, and she loved me. I wanted to give her a chance to do better, but what if that version of her in the room was right? What if she never stopped hurting me, and I never stopped fixing her messes, and she never stopped making them?

I didn't know how to escape that.

But I knew how to fix things.

I knew how to tend to a garden.

And I thought I knew how to take care of Ivy and protect people from the house.

This wasn't the sort of future anyone wanted for me. But it was the only one that seemed to fit.

King looked past me to Ivy. "You could change your mind," he said. "Help out of the goodness of your heart."

She scowled. "I'm not you."

"Maybe you are. I'm selfish too. I want you to save Daisy, even if it means you being alone. Even though out of everyone, you deserve that the least." He shrugged. "I guess it doesn't matter. It was always going to be Daisy's choice in the end." He looked at me again, but I was sure he knew that I wasn't changing my mind.

Ivy turned her back on him, her arms crossed. He looked at her for one last moment before moving to go.

"Hey," I said to him.

He turned toward me.

"I was happy to be your friend."

He smiled. The one that was just for me. "Me too." He left then.

Ivy and I waited in the entryway until his text came in that they were in position.

She turned to me. "How would you like to die?"

"Why don't I just hang out with you?" I said, looking back with a smile that I couldn't make work all the way.

CHAPTER FORTY-EIGHT

BRITTNEY

Grace sent a text directing us to meet them in the main dining room. Jayden and I got up early to scout the space on the second floor. It turned out to be the same room where I went with that girl last night. Huge and open, with a skylight and each wall paneled with glass. The newly renovated kitchen is empty of any guests. They were probably told it would be in use today.

The dining table could easily fit twenty people and is overkill for our soon-to-be party of four, but it would work.

I let Jayden make himself an Earl Grey latte with the espresso machine while I set up the cameras at the end of the table closest to the windows to take advantage of the natural light. I don't tell him about my walk with the girl during the night. I will eventually. But right now it feels too surreal to mention. And knowing him, he would try and convince me she was a ghost.

"Knock, knock." Grace's voice floats in from the doorway.

I turn around and beam at her and Dione, who is standing about a foot away at the exact other end of the doorway. Neither of them is looking at the other.

This is going to be wonderful.

We get them mic'd up and seat them so that Jayden and Dione sit on one side, and Grace and I on the other. I want to force them to stare at each other. Face-to-face.

And this time, I'm starting.

"Thank you so much for joining us, Grace and Dione. It hasn't been easy to get you two in a room." I swallow and curse myself for already freaking out. I need to be calm. "I would say you two don't need an introduction, but if you can do one for the camera and mention your connection to Daisy, that would be great." Jayden and I decided that this interview would be in present tense.

Grace launches in without further prompt, "I'm Grace Odlin, Daisy's mother. I am the owner of the mansion, which I run as an Airbnb serving up to twenty-six guests at any one time."

I gesture to Dione, who wiggles into a straight position and looks at the camera. "I'm Dione Odlin, previously Dione Belanger. I'm Daisy's aunt and Grace's sister. I run a private bookkeeping business out of Iroquois Falls."

So far, so good. "How long has it been since you last saw each other?"

"When the police called us in to identify the body." Grace laces her fingers together. "I was walking one way down the hall while she walked the other way, and I looked at her, and she pretended not to see me."

Jayden and I share a quick look. "Is that true, Dione?"

"I didn't *pretend* not to see her. I didn't see her," Dione says. She's straining to keep her voice level.

Grace rolls her eyes but doesn't push it further.

Abruptly, I can't take it. I can't take the fact that I've brought these two together to discuss a dead girl, and it's already started with this squabbling. I can't do the interview the way we've done the rest. I can't do it the way I've done *any* interview.

"Can we cut the bullshit?" I say, looking between the two of them. Jayden's eyebrows go way up into his hairline, and he gives me a look like *What the fuck?*

"Excuse me?" Dione says.

Grace can't even form words.

"You don't like each other. I get that. Maybe that's always been a you thing. Maybe it's because of something that happened. But I came here to discuss the fact that a girl died on this property. The property that you lived on with your ex-husband, Dione. The property that you now own, Grace. So why don't we put your shit out on the table right now so we can move on to what we actually care about." I let out a breath after I finish, eyeing them. Jayden looks like he's struggling to think of a way to smooth that over, but not even he can find the phrase.

Grace laughs. It's abrupt and loud.

Jayden smiles at her. "Care to let us in on the joke?"

"I just realized," she says, wiping a stray mirthful tear from her eye, "that I don't know why Dione doesn't like me. I'm actually interested to hear it. Why don't you like me?"

Dione sits up straighter in her seat but says nothing. It doesn't matter, though. Grace is talking enough for both of them.

"Is it because I ruined your fairy tale? Because I showed you that you could make a bad decision too? Because he gave me the house that you screamed up and down that you didn't want? Because Mom hung you out to dry more than she ever did me, even though I was the one who kept fucking up? What? What is it?"

My lips are dry, and my ChapStick is in my pocket, but I'm too afraid to reach for it and break the moment.

"I never hated you," Dione whispers.

"Bullshit!" Grace hisses. "You don't avoid talking to someone for more than half their life when you like them."

"You didn't want me to talk to you."

"You don't know what I wanted!" Grace snaps. Everyone goes perfectly still. She shakes her head, passion twists flying. "This is why I didn't want to do this. I knew you would just make me go off. I knew you would. But I never expected a bold-faced lie like that."

"I'm not lying!" Dione slams her hand on the table. She looks at it for a moment, shocked that it moved that way. "I never hated you. Not once." She takes a deep shuddering breath. "I hated myself . . . and I was ashamed. How could I . . . How could I ever come back from what I had done? How could I ever be better in your eyes? I didn't want to face you . . ."

Grace's face goes slack. Her mouth even drops open a bit.

"What were you ashamed about?" I ask Dione. There were things I felt she should be ashamed of, like whatever her role was in this girl's death, but now I wanted to know what *she* felt she should be ashamed of.

Dione steals a glance at Grace. "It's not my place to say."

"It's not your place to say what you're ashamed of?" Jayden says, then blinks, shocked at his own interjection. Each of us is losing our damn mind in this interview.

Silence stretches the moment. Dione looks away at the window, and Grace stares down at the table.

Finally, Grace opens her mouth. "I thought a lot about when I would finally say this out loud. For a long time, I thought I never would. But if there were ever a time, I guess it's now." She looks at Dione. "Besides, when else am I going to get a chance to show people who you really are."

Is this the secret that the contact told us about? Finally coming out this early in the interview?

Grace says, "Her husband . . . Peter . . . sexually abused me for years." She plays with her fingers.

It isn't what I was expecting, but it's not a complete surprise either. Not after what Katie said. What Helga said. Hell, even the way his family seemed to want to distance themselves. Though I don't know how much they know.

"The summer when I was fourteen, things got worse, and I told her what was happening." She stares down at the table as she speaks and flicks her hand at Dione. "And she told me it was a dangerous lie to tell. That she thought I was better than that."

Well, fuck.

My head slowly turns to Dione, and it takes everything inside me to keep the judgment off my face. "Is that true?"

Dione's eyes fill with tears. "He taught piano to so many little girls. He had at least three students a day, three days a week. Grace had been spending summers with us since she was ten. We were planning to adopt her, for God's sake." She sucks in a breath. "I didn't want to believe it. But then . . . I would try to do things so that it would just be me and Grace, but after that . . . she didn't want to spend the time with me. After she left, I did too. Went to set up a practice in Iroquois Falls to avoid him. I wanted to call Grace and apologize. But I would pick up the phone and just see her staring at me, telling me what she had, needing my help, and I would hear myself saying back to her that she was a liar. And it seemed unfair. It seemed selfish to try to put myself back in her life after that."

Maybe this would be the bit that Grace would object to having in the final cut. It's the only piece that I would willingly exclude for her. But if she didn't . . . how many more people would come forward? And how many would be silent but finally feel some semblance of justice, seeing their abuser outed? How many people had Peter Belanger hurt?

"I'm sorry," Dione cries, tears spilling down her cheeks. "I'm sorry that I didn't believe you. I'm sorry that I stayed with him so long. That I tried to pretend nothing was happening. I'm sorry that—" She cuts herself off by physically slapping her hands over her mouth.

I turn to Grace, who sits there, staring at her sister, with no expression whatsoever.

This isn't something she should have even had to reveal to us. This is intimate. Private. Painful.

Grace Odlin is a survivor.

It excuses nothing, but it casts so many other things in a different light, and now I have to backtrack and look at it all again in this new view. Even though a large part of me had been prepared for this to be true.

I turn back to Grace. "Why would you take this house? With those sorts of memories . . . why would you stay? Especially with people dying? Especially with Dais—"

"I wasn't going to let him scare me out of having it. I always knew he would give it to me. He liked playing mind games like that. It's why it took me so long to even say anything to my sister in the first place. I wanted this house, and I was going to have it. He *owed it* to me."

"Even while your daughter was having a mental breakdown?" I ask. Grace was a victim. But so was Daisy. And I couldn't forget that.

Grace pushes her lips together.

I look between Grace and Dione. "There were two girls found in the freezer that day. One was dead, and one was barely alive. I know you both know Daisy. But there was another girl in there, and I think you both know who she was too. Even if your police statements sing a different tune." I clasp my fingers together and squeeze. "When they pulled Daisy out of that freezer, she kept apologizing over and over to a girl named Ivy. Then she had a moment to be alone with you, Grace, and suddenly she had no recollection of the girl." I lick my lips. "The two of you lost an entire relationship because one of you told the truth and the other thought it was a lie. Now is a perfect time to be honest. Don't you think?"

Neither woman says anything. Jayden reaches into his pocket and produces a tissue for Dione, which she gratefully accepts.

"True or false?" I say. "Peter Belanger sexually abused Grace Odlin."

Both women say, "True."

Grace blinks at her sister as if surprised that Dione agreed.

"True or false?" I say. "Daisy knew who the dead girl in the freezer was."

"True," Grace whispers.

"True or false? The dead girl's name was Ivy."

"True," both women say. Grace's eyes widen at her sister's agreement. *There.* She didn't know that Dione knew who the girl was. Or maybe she just didn't expect her to own up to it. The contact said they were hiding something, but they never said they were hiding the *same* thing.

"Both of you pretended not to know her. You let her be a Jane Doe. Forgotten." I made sure both of them were looking at me. "People have implied all sorts of things about her over the years. That she was a runaway who snuck in and accidentally got locked inside. That she was on drugs, trying to rob the house. Every single thing they could say to act like looking into what happened to her, using resources to find her family, or putting her on the news would be a waste of time. Just some dead Black girl."

Both of their eyes drop away from mine, but I continue, "We know that our faces are not the ones they want to put on the news, asking for sympathy and help. But this girl didn't even get a chance. That's all we want to do for her: give her a chance to be known. Now I'm going to ask you once, who was Ivy?"

Dione dabs at her face with the tissue, and says, voice weary and hollowed out, "She was my daughter."

I fight to keep my expression level, and Jayden hides a gasp as a cough. I can't make myself speak, stunned into silence.

Grace, however, does not look surprised at all.

"Would you please elaborate on that?" Jayden says, clearing his throat.

"It was shortly before Grace left. I was trying to pretend like things were normal between us all."

Meaning she still had the stomach to be with a man who her sister said was hurting her. Again, I have to fight to keep the judgment off my face.

"Something went wrong with my birth control, I don't know. I realized I was pregnant. Peter wanted the baby, but I didn't want him to have it. Especially not after we knew she would be a girl . . . I spent most of the pregnancy away. I only came back because we had arranged the adoption through an agency in Timmins. Iroquois Falls didn't have one. Then I left right after."

I ask, "How did Peter get your baby, then? And moreover, how did you know she was yours when you saw the body?"

Dione swallows, her lip trembling.

Grace mutters, "Can't believe you had the gall to look at your own daughter and say you didn't know her."

Dione puts her head down on the table and sobs. Cries tear from her throat and shake against the hardwood.

"And you had the gall to keep your daughter in a house you knew was damaging her mental health to prove a point to a dead man," I say to Grace. "She almost died."

Now it's Grace's turn to look ashamed. Something I didn't actually think she was capable of.

"I'm saying both of you aren't innocent. Nor are you the only victims." I stare between the two of them. "Luckily for her, Daisy has been fine for a long time. She did a year's voluntary stay at a mental health facility, which, by her own admission, was incredibly helpful and certainly a great negotiation in lieu of jail time for assault." I look over to Jayden, who gives me an encouraging nod. "Everyone loves this story. They love the creepy coincidental brain-aneurysm deaths. They love the warring sisters. Everyone loves to hear about the mysterious and scary things that went down in this house. People pay a premium to stay in this allegedly haunted mansion. They say that they can hear the dead girl wandering the halls. That she whispers thoughts of violence and suicide into their ears like she supposedly did to Daisy."

I shake my head. "But more than anything, they love to gloss over the pain that happened here. People call this the 'Miracle Mansion' like only good comes out of it. All of the hurt that happened here is buried and hidden or made light of. We do a show called *Haunted*, sure. We love spooky. But that's not why we came here. We came because there is a girl with no grave and no name, and she's not like that because she doesn't have a name. She's like that because you, the two of you, refuse to say it into the world. You would rather that she be forgotten. And I think that it's time for people to know who she was."

Silence settles across the table. Dione raises her head, and Grace looks at a point past my ear, apparently unwilling to even make eye contact.

Dione croaks out, "I didn't know her until she was eight. Like I said, I thought she had been adopted. I hadn't set foot in the mansion that entire time. I only came back because I had found someone new, and we wanted to get married, and I hadn't finalized my divorce to Peter yet. He said I could come get my personal things from the house before we signed in town with the lawyer the next day."

I give her what I hope is an encouraging look so she can continue.

"And he had her in the basement. It was like a pageant, him revealing her to me when I arrived. She came out with her hair . . . It was a mess, he didn't know how to do it. This big uncombed afro pulled in a ponytail, and she did this dance in a ballet tutu and named all the provinces and territories in Canada and their capitals. And Peter did these big hands, like 'ta-da' with her at the end." Dione shakes out her hands to demonstrate the gesture. "And I asked who she was because I hoped it wasn't her . . . and she got this sad look on her face and looked at him, she was so confused. And he got mad. She stayed in her room, and we went outside to talk. He explained that it was our daughter, and he paid some people off to work everything out. He wasn't supposed to have her, so she was in the basement to make sure people didn't know she was living there. I didn't ask for more details. But it was illegal, and he said that we would both get jail time if I talked. That no one would believe that I didn't know about her, and he would push back at me with the divorce and drive it into the courts for years, and all this stuff."

Jesus fucking Christ. The more I hear about him in this interview, the more I'm convinced that people really don't understand just how much of a monster Peter Belanger was. Dione's no angel, but even without saying it, it's clear that she felt he held power over her.

Dione takes a breath and wipes at her nose with the tissue. "I went into her room after. And I said I was sorry for not knowing her, and she was fine with that. I braided her hair nicely, properly. I didn't have anything for her, so I just gave her the sunglasses off my head and said it was a special gift. She was so happy."

She pauses for a moment, as if remembering that little girl's expression as she handed her a pair of shades. Sunglasses of all things as a present for an eight-year-old. "I asked her if Peter had ever touched her on her privates or made her touch his, because she had been his secret for so long, and I was scared that he had done that to her, too." Dione's lower lip trembles. "She said no. And I kept asking. And she kept saying no. And I kept asking and asking. But she didn't even understand what I was talking about. So I felt confident it wasn't happening." She stops speaking and sits there with her hands over her face.

"But you didn't know for sure that it would never happen."

"No . . ."

"And what did you do after that?" I ask, even though I know the answer.

"I left," Dione croaks. "Signed the papers the next day and pretended that I never saw her. When Peter died, I kept thinking they would mention a girl, but they never did. So I thought maybe she had run away or he had given her up for adoption properly, or . . . I don't know."

I can't help it. Part of me hates her. I hate that she couldn't do the right thing. Not for her sister. Not for her child. Not until right now when Ivy is already dead.

I say, "The autopsy reported that the girl had wounds on her body. Old ones, consistent with injuries from frozen extremities. The popular theory is that she was homeless and therefore spent a lot of time outside. Was looking for food, and that's how she got trapped in the freezer. But it's interesting, because if Peter was keeping a secret daughter in his basement, wouldn't he keep that door locked so she couldn't go outside and reveal herself?"

Dione just stares at me, not understanding.

Jayden cuts in. "Meaning she didn't actually get to go outside. The only cold environment she would have had access to was that freezer.

And what child would hang out in one for fun? She must have been kept inside of it, against her will. Seemingly multiple times." And yet somehow the theories about Peter killing the girl never caught on. As far as everyone knew, he was squeaky clean. No history. No priors. "And the last time she was in that freezer, Peter died of a brain aneurysm."

I add, "And because no one knew she was there, she died."

Finally, everything registers on Dione's face. She can't seem to form a response to what I'm saying to her. She's just staring endlessly.

This is what the contact meant.

Dione knew that girl was there, and if she'd told someone, *any-one*, they could have saved her before it was too late. Before she became another victim of Peter Belanger.

I look at Grace, whose eyes are watering. "How long had you known about Ivy?"

"I only knew when Daisy found out," she mumbles.

"How did she know?"

She shakes her head. "I don't know."

"Why didn't you say anything? When they asked you to identify the body, both of you said nothing. Why?"

I know why. Of course I do, but I want to hear them say it.

"I was ashamed," Dione whispers. "And I never forgot what Peter said. What little of a life I had, I didn't want to ruin it. And she was already dead. I wasn't." She looks over at Grace.

Her sister sighs. "It looked bad. I already had a dead body on my watch. Daisy had just . . . She had tried to kill herself, and she attacked that girl from Tower . . . It was just one more thing. I didn't think it would matter."

But it did matter. Ivy mattered. And now everyone else would know too.

Only thirty minutes after the interview, we have our stuff packed and are about to head out of the house. Ever the gracious host, Grace sees us off at the door.

I pause and look at her. "You know," I say. "You could tell your own story from the very beginning, if you wanted to."

She just sort of looks at me, not sure what to say.

I nudge Jayden on the shoulder. "I know someone who has a great pitch for you."

His eyes go wide, and he gives me a look that clearly asks what I think I'm doing.

Grace turns to him. "You would want to do a project like that?"

"Uh yeah, yes. Yes."

I leave them alone to talk while I walk a little ways down the property, staring around at the grounds. I try to picture Mom walking into this house with whatever terrible boyfriend of the week she wrangled up and meeting Grace, just like we did. She thought she came out of the house better than before, but I *know* I have.

I hate to say it, but maybe I did have my own miracle after all.

Just like Grace said, I left something behind in the mansion.

I left the forgotten Black girl inside of me. The one who desperately wanted those phone calls from my mom. The one who thought she could never amount to anything. Could never really be loved by anyone. Who thought she would always be her mother's daughter.

Today that girl saved another one like her. And that means something.

I take that part of her with me, and I leave behind the bits that my mom created.

When I walk away from the mansion, I'm a better version of myself. For real. Not a lie like Mom.

Jayden comes over to me with a grin on his face. "She's going to look over it and check with her legal team and manager."

I smile back at him.

He pauses for a moment. "Thank you."

"You're the only person I trust to do a Grace Odlin doc. I hope it works out."

"Me too."

Our phones buzz, and Jayden and I stop to look at them. "Contact is down by the boat!" he says with a grin. "Ready to have this mystery solved?"

"About time," I grumble.

We make our way down the steps to the boat launch, and after only a few, I stop dead. Spotting the person waiting for us by the boat. "No fucking way," I breathe.

Jayden straight up cackles.

Daisy Odlin is waiting at the bottom of the steps in a pair of green shorts and a white tank top. I would recognize her anywhere, even if she weren't plastered on dozens of home magazines for her elaborate interior and exterior garden designs. Out there charging hundreds an hour to arrange plants nicely. Rich people are a trip. She smiles and waves.

She's supposed to be our next interview. Neither of us thought much about it. She's one of the few people involved who does speak to press. But she always gives the exact same story, no matter what. I didn't expect her to share anything different, so it wasn't as exciting as the new juicy pieces we could get from people who hadn't been interviewed before.

But this whole time, she knew the missing pieces. And I guess she was done with telling the same tired tale.

She gets into the boat behind the steering wheel. Like this, she really does look like Grace, but she's such a different person.

Tears prick behind my eyes. Now that I know the things that I do about her, I'm in awe of the person she's become.

Jayden and I load our bags and equipment onto the boat with Daisy's help. Both of us collapse into our seats as she starts the engine.

"You, the whole time," I breathe.

She laughs, and it's free and open. "Back then, I'd wanted to get on with my life, so me and my mom wrote up a script, and I followed it for ten years. Gave interviews that were boring as hell so people would lose interest in me. Much more exciting to get secondhand reports from other people."

"Not anymore."

"No," Daisy says. "Not anymore. I figured you two would tell the story right. All I needed to do was help steer you toward the right people. Even if not everyone's opinion of me is the best." She shrugs. "It's not only about me, after all. I figured if you knew it was me from the start, it would seem biased. Better to stay secret for a while."

Daisy's not wrong. It would have definitely made it seem like we were being led to a narrative if we knew she was the contact.

She pulls us into the open water, slow and rocky. "How was your sleep?"

Jayden and I look at each other and laugh. Out of all the questions she could ask us after that interview.

"Good!" Jayden says. "The bed was unreal. I'm feeling fresh."

"No supernatural activity? No miracles?" Daisy raises her brow.

"It was a miracle we got through that interview," he says with a sigh. "I think I'm too heavy of a sleeper for ghosts."

"The interview was definitely the tiring bit," I add, handing Jayden a camera to hoist onto his shoulder and get a last shot of the house disappearing as we ride away on the boat.

Daisy smirks. "I'm sure it was. Mom and Aunt Dione aren't the most forthcoming sort of people."

"You could be," I throw in. "The *real* story. Not the scripted one. We do have an interview scheduled."

"Do we?" she asks. "I think I double booked. But you've got enough, don't you?"

Fair enough. I guess some things in that house will always be a mystery, but we've uncovered the most important part: a girl that will get to be known.

Daisy looks over her shoulder from the driver's seat. "So when can I see 'Forgotten Black Girls'?"

"It's 'Houses That Kill' now," Jayden says with a shrug. "Our company nixed the Black girls thing."

"No," I say, and Jayden blinks. "We have the only interview with Grace and Dione Odlin. I think we can do better than that."

Jayden's eyes light up, and he grins at me. "Me too. Way better."

"Though it would really help if we knew a certain someone who could get her mom to reconsider a certain contract that doesn't allow us to 'slander' her?" I say to Daisy.

Her gaze meets mine, and she nods. "I might know someone like that."

I grin and stare out at the house. "Do you come back here every summer?"

She smiles, even and serene. "Every summer."

"Why? Why do you bother with her still, your mom? After everything."

I expect her to look offended, but she doesn't. "She's never been perfect. For a long time, she wasn't even good. But she's trying. Actually trying this time. It doesn't feel like a manipulation, and I don't think it is. I've had enough practice by now. That's the real difference." Daisy stares off at the house. "I think of those summers she spent there. Painful ones with small happy bits in them. And I can't help but want to make them better. A lifetime of better summers." She looks back at me. "That's the thing, right? You can spend years messing up, but just ahead of you, you have an entire lifetime to make it better. Or to try, at least. And if it doesn't work out, then it doesn't. But she hasn't disappointed me again since. She told you the truth, didn't she? Or some version of it, anyway."

"Some version of it?"

"The version for people who don't believe in ghosts."

Jayden perks right up, head jerking between the two of us.

Daisy and I stare at each other for a long moment. Not saying anything.

No one ever found out how Daisy learned who Ivy was. There were no documents in the house or any evidence she could have gotten to learn the girl's identity. It was also a mystery why, out of all places in the house, she would go down into that room, in that freezer.

A freezer that was sealed shut. Enough that firefighters had to take jackhammers to it. And excusing how she even got inside, why wouldn't she have left when she saw a dead body in there? Why lock herself in with it?

Slowly, deliberately, Daisy tugs a pair of sunglasses out of her pocket and hands them to me. Even before they're in my fingers, I recognize them from the girl in the house. "She said you could have these. That she was over the whole sunglasses look. There isn't actual night vision, though. She likes to lie sometimes."

I didn't have anything for her, so I just gave her the sunglasses off my head and said it was a special gift.

I swallow, and the spit hurts going down.

Jayden looks between the two of us, clearly trying to understand what's happening. I can't figure out how to even start explaining this to him. But once I do, he's going to lose his damn mind.

My phone rings, and the screen lights up. It's my mom.

Daisy points at it. "You going to answer that?"

I stare at the screen for a moment. In the next few seconds, I block the number. I smile up at Daisy. "Nah."

CHAPTER FORTY-NINE

DAISY

In the end, I didn't die.

King told me his side of the story after.

He said that he knew I would be in that freezer alongside Ivy's dead body, and I was dead too, frozen. That he only knew because they pulled both our bodies out of it like that. Zipped us up in matching body bags on the gravel out front while the butcherbirds watched.

He had pulled into a gas station with Mom still asleep in the passenger seat. Already he had texted me, and I had only responded "thanks." He was about to go inside and point back at my mom, saying some bullshit about how he'd picked her up and she'd dozed off on him. Something so the attendant would remember them both. Their alibi so they wouldn't be blamed.

King was out of the car, standing there, ready to walk in, when he decided that he didn't want to.

He wasn't ready to give up trying to save me after all.

He got back inside the car and woke Mom up, and she screamed at him, of course, but they both made their way to the house, calling emergency services to meet them there. The thorns had calmed down by the time they'd arrived because Ivy was happy to be getting an eternal best friend.

Mom and King ran straight to the basement. The place he knew they found my dead body.

The freezer was sealed shut. Ivy had kept it that way since she died, not wanting to confront what happened to her. She'd opened it only so I could get inside. Neither King nor Mom could get it open. Not even the firefighters who came could, the thundering sound of their machines rattling in our heads.

Ivy's hold was an iron grip.

That was when my side of the story kicked in.

I heard Mom and King pleading and begging.

Before we'd gotten in there, I had gone to the bunkie and mixed up a cocktail of whatever pills we had lying around and chased it down with a half-empty bottle of vodka that someone had left in the communal fridge.

When the door lock clicked shut, there was something like regret. A lot like regret. *Exactly* like it. But it was too late.

I thought so anyway.

Until I heard them on the other side.

Ivy bit her lip. "They came to save you."

"I have to stay here with you."

I had made a promise, and it needed to happen. There was no other way to stop the house without her help.

She leaned her head against my shoulder, her breath misting over my neck. "If you tell me to, I'll open it. But only if you want it. It's like King said: it's your choice in the end."

"But—"

"I'll still do it. I'll still keep my promise."

I looked over at her, my eyes filling with tears, because I knew what I wanted to do.

She closed hers, her expression pained.

"I don't want to die," I whispered. "I want a chance."

I thought that we both knew what I meant. I wanted a chance to live my life differently than I had been.

The door unlocked and swung open. The firefighters took credit for it.

That day, when I was ready to give up my life, four people I loved chose to save me.

It was a welcome surprise that one of them was me.

And it mattered because I was the only one who could change my future.

And despite me not keeping mine, Ivy did keep her promise. She stopped the house from feeding on the living. Its voice quieted shortly thereafter, and it started consuming the dead as it was meant to.

The house wanted a gardener, and it got one, but instead of helping it bloom unrestrained, Ivy was there to clip its branches and make sure it never got too tall.

Now nothing but grass flattens under my feet as I make my way through the bush. The shrikes overhead chirp at me. I don't mind them so much anymore. Though sometimes looking at them makes my skin itch.

It's summer in the north. Sometimes it seems like this place will never have one, and yet every year it comes back. I step into the clearing and sigh.

This spot is perfect. The trees close in overhead, letting in the barest hint of sunlight, and the shrikes like to roost here. Though the latter is likely *because* of what's here.

King is already inside the small structure. His ratty T-shirt is tight over his back as he bends over to adjust the flower beds.

They're lacquered cedar on the outside, painted with a white wash that purposely shows the odd crack or knot, and the inside is lined with a thin layer of marble with drainage holes carefully cut into the bottom.

Maybe it's excessive, but I also think she's earned a bit of opulence.

King straightens, and I pull myself taut. Suddenly I'm self-conscious about everything. About the faded blue overalls I wear that I had found in a vintage shop and cut into shorts, and the crop top that I have underneath that exposes the sides of my stomach wherever the overalls don't cover. About my hair that reaches my shoulders in hundreds of little curls that I can now manage to get as juicy-looking as his own. I even straighten my hair sometimes. But only because I want to. Not because I think it's what someone else would prefer on me.

King makes his way out of the building. It's small. About the size of a storage shed. The whole thing is glass, perfectly transparent, with only thin lines where the walls meet to mark the seams, but tall enough that even King can stand straight in it.

He throws me a big smile. "Is that local celebrity Daisy Odlin?"

I laugh and roll my eyes. "Excuse you, I'm a *national* celebrity."

And it's that easy. We're back to being friends. That awkwardness I felt at not having seen him in person since last summer falls away.

We walk toward each other until we stand face-to-face. "Are you too cool to hug childhood friends now?" he asks.

"No," I say, and throw my arms around him. He returns it. Though it's embarrassing to say, I've become a hugger. I want to hug absolutely everyone. And every time I do, I'm reminded of that moment with Mom. That perfect single instant where I felt more love than I ever had in my life. Megan and I hug every time we see each other and say goodbye. I even hug people I've just met with a sort of wild glee.

"How was your dad's place?" he asks.

"Good. Got him to eat some spicy noodles, and he almost died. He's a big wimp," I say, and the affection is real.

When I was in the hospital, recovering from the freezer experience, Dad showed up. He was sweaty and hassled and looked terrified to see Mom, but he was there. I guess almost having his child die was more than enough motivation to confront whatever lingering fears he had about me and his role in my life. I got a long lecture about going into the mansion and then an equally long hug as he clung to me and cried. We had a talk after that. The three of us.

The mental health facility I stayed in happened to be in Vancouver, and I saw more of my dad than ever before. We got to know each other properly. He finally learned my favorite color and what music I listened to the most, and I learned that he had been trying for years to enjoy spicy foods.

I gave him that chance to connect with me because he finally showed that he wanted it.

"It's kind of weird to see you outside of a screen." King steps back and tucks his hands into his pockets. "Glad you're doing well."

"Thank you, and since I can't just 'know' things, how are you?"

He rolls his eyes. He can't know things either anymore. That power is long gone and, thankfully, hasn't passed to anyone else in his family.

"Good," he says. "On that daily grind shit."

King, as he always wanted, got out of the psychic business. And he discovered what he wanted to do, which was life coaching. I made fun of him mercilessly for finding a way to make being nice into a career. Though he insists that he isn't always. Now he's in the business of helping people who actually want to make changes in their lives and do it. It's a perfect fit. He turns around and waves at the structure. "And I even got this up for you, didn't I?"

"You did."

I've texted or video chatted with King almost every day since I left, twelve years ago now. The only time we haven't is during the summer, when I'm back here.

Somehow I figured out what I wanted. I went back to the one thing that I knew I loved: plants. I started with friends. I went to Megan's house and arranged her family's garden along with the plants inside, took photos, and posted them on Instagram. I finally got that blocker off. I was pretty sure I wasn't going to look up Noah anymore. People would send me messages asking what I charged, and I would make it up on the spot, go and do it, then post more photos.

Over and over again until I was arranging plants in penthouse condos in Toronto, Los Angeles, and New York. Until I was being commissioned by private companies and governments to do arrangements. Until I was being brought in on Home and Garden TV to consult on their projects.

And now I'm doing the most important arrangement of my life, for a special friend.

"Have you seen the show yet?" King asks, sitting on the bench outside the greenhouse.

I shake my head and sit beside him. There's more room, but somehow I end up close enough that our thighs press together. I have also become "touchy-feely," which is equally embarrassing. Mom spent so much of her life keeping people out. I did it too, back then. Now I'm the opposite. It's like I'm constantly trying to pull everyone closer.

King especially. He has a special place in my heart and always will. We're like vines, sometimes snaking together, and sometimes moving apart. I can't predict how we'll land in the end, but we'll always be something to each other that we aren't to anyone else.

He opens up the app on his phone, and I smile at the banner that appears right at the top. There's a photo of both Brittney and Jayden, and in the background, the only photo of Ivy that has ever existed. One that Aunt Dione took to remember a child she left behind.

She's in a ballet tutu with a pair of sunglasses on her face, her hair in a dozen thick braids. She stares up at the camera and grins.

Ivy's chin rests on my shoulder, and a smile works its way to my lips. I tilt my head to where she is behind me, looking at the screen. Her braids are still as long as ever, though she's permanently ditched the sunglasses.

Every year, I ask if she's ready to pass on, and every year she says no.

Peter is still around too. No longer distorted from torture. Ivy and I put a stop to that. But still, I can't bring myself to help him move on.

I'm not ready either.

But someday, both of us will be—Ivy and I.

We'll have to be.

Mom always told me that the dead pass on eventually by themselves, but I had never seen it. The house lies—we know that now. If ghosts would leave on their own at some point, why did I have the ability to make even the translucent ones go? Why did the house exist? It didn't make sense for us to perform a function that nature did on its own. It's like King's mom theorized. We're all part of this supernatural ecosystem. Me and the mansion, we were both necessary. And if that's true, then there must be more around the world. More places like the mansion and more people like me.

I guess I wouldn't know unless I searched for the answer. But I think it's better to leave the ghost hunting to the professionals. Just living with them is already enough for me. I've gotten better with them. I still avoid their attention, but I've settled into the knowledge that this ability is never going to go away, and I have to be okay with that.

It helps that I'm doing a lot better these days. After all, they don't care for happiness.

And for the hard times, when I don't have enough joy to keep them away on my own, there's always Kidz Bop.

And sometimes, when I'm feeling up to it, I find one who looks lost, and I ask if they want help passing on. Unlike with Mom's method, I only do it if they agree. In hindsight, because Mom couldn't see the dead, she was only ever able to find troublemakers who, of course, weren't ready to pass on. It goes a lot better when they *are* ready. No screaming. No hurt. Just memories and a life moving on as their hearts disappear and my fingers grasp onto air.

"Is he going to play it or what?" Ivy says.

I reach over and tap the play button on the screen.

Brittney and Jayden pulled out from Torte and pitched a new show to a streaming service. Torte retained the rights to their footage, but the streaming company was able to make an agreement so that it could be used in the show with credit to Torte. After all, Brittney and Jayden made *Haunted* what it was. Better to get guaranteed money selling rights to what they shot than to risk failure trying to launch their show without them.

The new show evolved beyond what *Haunted* was. It was what they wanted, but it was also more. It wasn't just spooky stories. It was also about true crime and social justice. Jayden even pitched a miniseries to Mom to tell her story, but she turned it down.

When I asked about it, she said, "I think people have heard enough of my side of the story. How about yours?"

I hadn't planned on saying yes, but Jayden was so excited about it. He's been making his own name in documentary shorts since graduating, so I agreed to be in one.

I look down at the title on the screen.

Not *Haunted*. Or "Houses That Kill." Not "Forgotten Girls." It's "Forgotten *Black* Girls." The way it was always supposed to be.

Finally people knew who Ivy was and what had happened to her in that house. They also knew what had happened to Mom and other girls. Ms. Kuru had come forward to share her story, and Ms. Gagnon had submitted her own anonymously—something she took the time to share with me, Mom, Ms. Kuru, and Mackenzie. I understand that. Keeping silence where you need it. I haven't talked about what Noah did to me with anyone but Mom, Megan, King, and my therapist. I don't want to speak about it with anyone else. Not now. Maybe not ever. But also, maybe someday.

Now people knew the stories of the girls who survived. And the girl whose life was taken. They knew that the real monster in the house wasn't a ghost at all. It was a man who took advantage of young girls, and the hurt he created that kept spreading pain through at least one more generation. We were all survivors of him, either directly or indirectly.

They couldn't forget us anymore.

I breathe out and steal a glance at King. He catches me doing it but only smiles.

My smile.

I grin back.

When I was seventeen, standing outside of that house, I'd wished I could have more time.

Now, because of King, because of my mom, because of Ivy, because of *me*, I do.

I have all the time in the world.

There's a rumor about a mansion that sits along Kenogamissi Lake. It's passed from local lips in stuttered whispers and traded between cottages like campfire s'mores. It says that deep within the bush, past the imposing manor that houses giggling tourists and a dark history, and beyond the fields where electric lines hum, there is a spot. Never if you search for it. But somehow always there. A glass house with a girl inside, with hair long enough to reach her feet. The white of her bones glistens in the summer sunshine and sparkles amid the winter snow. And she is surrounded by daises and wild blueberries, growing abundant in the flower beds beside her. In the trees above, butcherbirds make their nests. All across the glass, ivy vines grow and wind around it.

And on a metal plaque, attached to the front of it, always kept clean and visible, even on days when there are blizzards, it reads:

HERE LIES IVY ODLIN.
SHE WILL NEVER BE FORGOTTEN AGAIN.

ACKNOWLEDGMENTS

First and foremost, I would like to thank my mom, who this book is dedicated to. When I was eighteen, I remember realizing that was when she'd had me, and I was unable to imagine caring for a child at that age, much less raising one with the amount of love that I was given. I knew that I wanted to tell a story that could capture the intimacy of a close mother-daughter relationship, of how complicated they can be, and the power of what gets passed down. I'm thankful to my mom for my creative spirit and for the peace of mind in knowing she would be proud of me no matter how my life turned out.

Another thank-you to my amazing literary agent, Kristy Hunter, who very much took things in stride when I suddenly let her know that I was writing a horror novel and brought such amazing passion to the project. Thank you to my editor, Sarah McCabe, who embraced *Delicious Monsters* with so much enthusiasm and excitement and, as usual, gave fantastic notes that changed it for the better. A huge thank-you to the whole Simon & Schuster and Margaret K. McElderry team, from sales to marketing, publicity, copyediting, and more—all the work you've put into this book has been so appreciated. Thank you as well to Carlos Fama for the gorgeous cover illustration and to Greg Stadnyk for the wonderful cover design.

I would also like to thank my constant beta reader, Cassie Spires, for once again providing amazing feedback, and also for all the much-needed emotional support. Thank you as well to the wonderful Lindsay Puckett and Jess Creaden for reading an early version of the manuscript and giving such helpful advice. I would also like to give a huge thank-you to Nancy Cooper, who helped with an insightful, thorough, and invaluable authenticity read of the novel.

Thank you to my partner for supporting me throughout this process, sharing in my excitement, and listening to my plot rants that I suspect made no sense to you. Also, thank you to my little coworker beagle, Beau, who has witnessed more of my writing ups and downs than anyone else and is a constant source of comfort and companionship.

Finally, thank you to Stephen Chbosky for *The Perks of Being a Wallflower*. It was the book that I didn't even know I needed, and I'm so grateful for it.